Claudia Carroll was born in Dublin, where she still lives. She has worked extensively as an actress on the Irish stage, but is probably best known for her role as TV's nasty Nicola Prendergast in the long-running Irish soap opera *Fair City*, a character she describes as 'the horrible old cow everyone loves to hate.'

Claudia is single, and this book's title comes from a phrase she finds herself using quite a bit, particularly after a really bad date.

Also by Claudia Carroll

He loves me not . . . he loves me
The Last of the Great Romantics

Remind Me Again Why I Need a Man

Claudia Carroll

BANTAM PRESS

LONDON · TORONTO · SYDNEY · AUCKLAND · JOHANNESBURG

TRANSWORLD PUBLISHERS
61–63 Uxbridge Road, London W5 5SA
a division of The Random House Group Ltd

RANDOM HOUSE AUSTRALIA (PTY) LTD
20 Alfred Street, Milsons Point, Sydney,
New South Wales 2061, Australia

RANDOM HOUSE NEW ZEALAND LTD
18 Poland Road, Glenfield, Auckland 10, New Zealand

RANDOM HOUSE SOUTH AFRICA (PTY) LTD
Isle of Houghton, Corner of Boundary Road & Carse O'Gowrie,
Houghton 2198, South Africa

Published 2006 by Bantam Press
a division of Transworld Publishers

A catalogue record for this book is available from the British Library.
ISBN 9780593055397 (from Jan 07)
ISBN 059305539X

Typeset in 12½/15pt Bembo by
Kestrel Data, Exeter, Devon.

Printed and bound in Great Britain by
Clays Ltd, St Ives plc.

3 5 7 9 10 8 6 4 2

Papers used by Transworld Publishers are natural, recyclable products made
from wood grown in sustainable forests. The manufacturing processes
conform to the environmental regulations of the country of origin.

To my great friend Marion O'Dwyer, who,
as we walked down Dawson Street in Dublin
one sunny summers evening,
gave this book its title.

Acknowledgements

Thank you so much, Marianne Gunn O'Connor, my wonderful agent, for everything you've done for me in the last year. In October, this amazing woman rang me from the Frankfurt Book Fair with the overwhelming news that she had sold the US rights of this book to HarperCollins, New York. So a huge thank you to Claire Wachtel, Sean Griffin and everyone who works at that fabulous office on East 53rd Street. I loved meeting you all last November and can't wait to work with you.

Thank you, Pat Lynch, for your calm patience and humour. You've become such a good friend.

Thanks to the divine Francesca Liversidge, for all your encouragement and for generally making my job so easy. I'll keep on nagging you until we have another night on the town in Dublin! And thanks to everyone at Transworld Publishers in London, especially Nicky Jeanes, who really put in overtime helping me to get this book just right. Thanks also to the lovely Laura Sherlock for everything she's done: your next trip to Dublin won't come round soon enough! Thanks also to Vivien Garrett for all your kind words, which I really appreciate.

Thanks to Declan Heeney, and Gill and Simon Hess, who do so much hard work here. I couldn't feel happier, luckier or more grateful to have you guys in my life.

Thank you, Vicky Satlow, for the unbelievable job you've done selling this book around Europe. To see my book translated into languages I can't even speak is such a thrill.

Thanks to all my family for their much-needed support, especially Mom and Dad (who once made a trip to a well-known Dublin bookshop and took photos of a window display the store had kindly given me – I'm not joking). Thanks to Paddy and Sam, Richard, Lilla, Ellen and all my family in Scotland, Mai, Ted, Sequoia, Warwick and Ellie.

Thank you so much to Clelia and Miss Clara Belle Murphy for coming with me on book signings and generally being angels, the pair of them. If it's the last thing we do, the three of us are going on another holiday, and this time I will *not* take no for an answer.

Special thanks to all my fantastic friends, especially Pat Kinevane, Karen Nolan, Larry Finnegan, Susan McHugh, Sean Murphy, Marion O'Dwyer, Alison McKenna, Fiona Lalor, Sharon Hogan, Ailsa Prenter, Karen Hastings, Kevin Reynolds, Kevin Murnane and, of course, the Gunn family. I really don't know what I'd do without you.

Thanks to Anita Notaro, great friend, great neighbour and a constant inspiration.

Thanks to all the wonderful people who have come into my life since I started writing, especially Patricia Scanlan, Kate Thompson, Sarah Webb and Marisa Mackle.

Thanks to Derick Mulvey; I'm really looking forward to working with you and only hope I don't let you down!

Finally, after fourteen happy years, I've made the incredibly hard decision to leave *Fair City*, so I can devote more time to writing. I want to thank everyone on the team for being so good to me over the years, especially Niall Matthews (who very kindly said he would leave the door open for Nicola to return), Kevin McHugh, Mary Halpin, Karen Nolan, Elaine Walsh, Ferdia McAnna, Ann Myler, Johnny Cullen, Tony Tormey, Jim Bartley, Tom Hopkins, Una Crawford O'Brien and, of course, the one and only Joan O'Hara. You have no idea how much I'll miss all of you, but please remember, I'm only ever a stone's throw away . . .

Prologue

FATE IS LATE!

Right from the off, the first line grabbed my attention.

THIS IS YOUR YEAR!

. . . ran the banner headline on the office noticeboard. But it was the next bit that made me not so much blush as hot flush.

YOUR YEAR TO GET MARRIED!!!

I tried my best to act all cool and unconcerned and pretended to be utterly absorbed in a load of ads for second-hand Fiat Puntos and neutered cats for sale.

THIS COURSE WILL CHANGE YOUR LIFE FOR EVER! SIMPLY APPLY THE PRINCIPLES TAUGHT AT HARVARD MARKETING SCHOOL TO YOUR LOVE LIFE AND YOU'LL

BE EXCHANGING 'I DO'S' BEFORE THE YEAR IS OUT!

I read on. Well, wouldn't you?

BY REVISITING ALL OF YOUR PAST RELATIONSHIPS, WE'LL SHOW YOU WHERE YOU WENT WRONG, SO YOU CAN EMBRACE THE FUTURE AND MOVE FORWARD CONFIDENTLY WITH THE PARTNER OF YOUR DREAMS! FOR ANY WOMAN OVER THIRTY-FIVE WHO'S READY TO VAULT TO THE ALTAR THE SOLUTION IS SIMPLE. COME TO MY EVENING CLASS, GET ON MY TWELVE-STEP PROGRAM AND YOU'LL HAVE ONE FOOT IN THAT VERA WANG GOWN BEFORE THE YEAR IS OUT!

And that's pretty much where my story starts . . .

Chapter One

The Lovely Girls Club

I work as a deputy producer on a television soap opera and often think that if this job came with a catchphrase, it would be, quite simply: '*I HATE ACTORS!*' Well . . . I should more correctly say all actors except my darling friend (and honorary 'Lovely Girl') Jamie French, whom I'm meeting later on tonight.

At the moment, while resting between acting jobs, Jamie's working as a waiter in Nosh, a hip, protein-only celebrity restaurant in the heart of Dublin's Temple Bar. Although, according to him, they only call it a celebrity restaurant because Enya once had a coffee there. There was also a rumour that Bono went in once looking for directions, but it turned out to be just a lookalike. Anyway, it's Nosh's first birthday party tonight and me and the other 'Lovely Girls' are all going along. Now, I use the term 'Girls' in the loosest sense, as we're all well into our late thirties, but none of us is quite ready to graduate and start classifying herself as 'a proper grown-up woman'. At least, not just yet.

OK. Lovely Girl number one is Caroline, who is easily and effortlessly the loveliest one of the lot of us. (Although, admittedly, there's not much contest there.) Caroline is stunning; she's amazing; she's just fab. When I grow up, I want to be her. She's my oldest and closest pal, ever since we first met at primary school, when we were both cast as angels in the school nativity play. One hundred per cent pure typecasting in her case.

Two things about Caroline: (*a*) she's led little short of a charmed life and (*b*) in the thirty-odd years I've known her, she has never, not once, ever been in a bad mood. Gorgeous-looking (the image of the blonde one in Abba) as well as smart, she modelled professionally for a bit after college and then did what we're all supposed to do. Got married to her steady, lovely boyfriend Mike (six feet four, a dentist, a rugby player and general all-round lovely guy) and became the ultimate yummy mummy with her two perfect, straight-out-of-a-Mothercare-catalogue babies. They're very rich, outrageously happy and you couldn't even hold it against them. They're both just too *nice*.

And then, drum roll, da–da–daaaaaaaaaa, there's Rachel. Or Joan Collins as we've nicknamed her. The reason being that, although the same age as the rest of us, Rachel has already had two husbands. I'm not kidding. Number one was Parisian, a very cool-looking architect who she met way back when we were all in college together. They led an über-so-phisticated life in a loft apartment on the West Bank, with Rachel point-blank refusing to marry him on the grounds that living together annoyed her mother more.

Now this is where it gets complicated. There's something I need to tell you about our Rachel, a kind of running gag amongst us, which I should explain. We call it the lethal Rachel pheromone. It's almost like a chemical she exudes from her pores which says, 'I'm not looking for a man; I don't particularly want a man; come any nearer and I'll slit your throat.' But the more she gives this off, the more guys chase after her like a Benny Hill movie speeded up. The irony is, here I am dying for a fella I can call my own and they run a mile from me, whereas all Rachel has to do is snarl at a guy and he immediately turns into her slobbering lapdog. I often wonder, is my desperation and her lack of it something that single men can smell?

So anyway. Back to Paris and husband number one. After years of trying to persuade her that annoying her mother was a really lame excuse for *not* getting married, he handed her an ultimatum. Either we break up, or we get hitched.

I know, I know, normally it's the other way round, women are the ones who are supposed to give men the shit-or-get-off-the-pot-type ultimatum, but this is Rachel's world, not mine. She didn't particularly want to break up, so, while on holiday in Las Vegas, she impulsively married him Britney Spears-style, at the end of an all-night drinking session, with two cleaners for witnesses. And then the unthinkable happened.

She came back to Dublin for a flying visit to break the news to all of us, but ended up having a vicious row with her mother, who nearly hit the ceiling when she realized that now she'd never get a Jimmy-Choo-clad foot into a mother-of-the-bride rig-out. So, unexpectedly, Rachel decided to hop on the first flight she could get back home to Paris to surprise her brand-new husband.

Big mistake.

Rachel says to this day she can vividly remember racing up all fifteen flights of stairs and breathlessly flinging the door open — to find him in bed with a close, mutual friend of theirs. Stunned, she somehow made her way back to Charles de Gaulle airport only to realize that she had absolutely no money. Nothing. Not even enough to make a phone call. So she did what we'd all do in similar circumstances. Sat on her suitcase in the middle of the concourse, cigarette in hand, bawling.

Second big mistake.

It just so happened that there had been a big match on that weekend, and the airport bar was packed to overflowing with fans on their way home. So, one of them spots this gorgeous damsel in distress (Rachel looks a bit like a 1920s silent movie star: you know, snow-white skin and dark bobbed hair, kind of like Louise Brooks, except with muscles) and he goes to help. He was a big, beefy New Zealander, who seemed like the answer to her prayers; i.e., he bought her drinks, paid for her flight home and offered to rip number one's head off on her behalf. As far as Rachel was concerned, he came along in such a haze of romance, he may as well have been riding on a white charger. Who could resist? Within a year, she had divorced number one, married number two and then divorced *him* only a few months later.

Could you make this up?

'In the space of eighteen short months,' she often says, 'I managed to get married to the two most useless men in both the Northern and Southern hemispheres. For God's sake, my first husband's idea of fidelity was to bed only one woman at a time, and my second husband's idea of foreplay was to brush his teeth. So, as far as romance is concerned, that's it, that's my lot, I've had my chips. Love and passion are only for teenagers. I'm standing on the edge of the Grand Canyon, staring into the romantic abyss that is single life after thirty-five and you know something else? *I don't care.*'

Now she owns and manages one of the swishiest and most expensive boutiques in Dublin, dresses like a dream, drinks like a dowager, has a mouth like a sewer and is easily the funniest person I know.

I often think that being friends with her is the closest I'll ever come to living in 1920s New York and hanging around the Algonquin hotel with Dorothy Parker all the time.

The 'Lovely Girls' club (christened by Rachel) has been on the go for over twenty years now, when the four of us became inseparable back in college. They are my best friends/soulmates/urban family/shoulders to cry on and I would unhesitatingly do anything for any one of them. Well, anything except be on time.

'LATE!' they chant as I finally spot them and make my way through the throng.

'Sorry, sorry, sorry,' I pant breathlessly, 'actor disaster in work.'

'Don't tell me, Rob Richards got drunk at lunchtime and made a move on you,' says Jamie who, although he's meant to be working, is perched very companionably between the other Lovely Girls.

'Eughhhhh!' the rest of us chant in unison.

Rob Richards, I should explain, is a long-serving cast member on the TV soap opera *Celtic Tigers*, which I've only just started to work on. He's been in the show since the very first episode, all of ten years ago, when he was actually quite attractive. 'At the risk of sounding like a primmer version of one of those spinstery type parts that Maggie Smith always plays,' I say, 'may I just point out that I only ever kissed him *once* at the studio wrap party and, in my defence, it was Christmas, I was lonely, I had knocked back four glasses of Pinot Noir on an empty stomach and, well, you know what I always say?'

'"Christmas is not for single people,"' they all chorus, impersonating me very accurately. Well, I can't really give out; it is yet *another* one of my catchphrases . . .

'Laugh all you like, girlies, but it's only the truth. Any

festival that makes you think it's a good idea to snog the face off a man you'd ordinarily cross the street to avoid, just because there happens to be a mangy bit of plastic mistletoe hanging from a glitter ball with John Lennon singing "Merry Christmas (War is Over)", can't exactly be good for you, can it?'

'She didn't know what she was doing, your honour,' says Rachel theatrically.

'She could have been kissing Bin Laden for all she knew. Or cared,' says Jamie.

'Pay no attention,' says Caroline sweetly, playing with a strand of her long, golden hair. (Natural, natural, natural. Honestly. The only time Caroline ever goes near a salon is when she needs to get chewing gum cut out of one of her children's hair.) 'Anyway, isn't it a kind of rite of passage for working on *Celtic Tigers*? You're not officially part of the show until you've had a squeeze with Rob Richards.'

'Just because he's Mr Big Shot Household Name doesn't entitle him to some kind of medieval droit de seigneur,' says Rachel crisply. 'Men like that have absolutely no difficulty in releasing their inner PUA.'

'Their what?' I ask.

'Pick-up artist.'

'It's a rare occurrence, I know, but don't you just hate it when Rachel is right?' Jamie says.

OK, time for me to get off this highly embarrassing subject . . . 'So, anyway, we're filming his big wedding to Glenda tomorrow and the final run-through this evening was a disaster. Neither of them has a clue of their lines. I had to spend the last two hours scribbling them down on three-foot-high idiot boards because everyone else in the office had gone home. I swear, humble and all as a deputy producer's job is, I really don't get paid enough.'

'OH MY GOWWWWD, Rob Richards marries GLENDA?' Caroline, a stay-at-home mom, is the only one of the Lovely Girls who actually watches the show. 'I never in a million years thought they'd actually go through with it. I mean, not after he had a one-night stand with Shantania on his stag night and then confessed it to Glenda the next day. And he's not been out of the coma all that long either.'

'Honey, you have *got* to get out more,' said Rachel, shoving an uneaten bowl of tapas away from her. 'Why is it that everything in here tastes like regurgitated bat vomit?'

'It's protein only,' Caroline explains helpfully.

'This is protein? I thought it was house insulant.' Then she picks up an empty champagne flute and waves it threateningly under Jamie's nose. 'Excuse me, lounge boy? Refills badly needed, please.'

'Oh, you are so sweet!' Jamie replies, delighted. 'You really think I could pass for a lounge boy? Because they're only, like, sixteen. God bless Crème de la Mer, that's all I can say. Oh, stay cool, my lovelies, cute guy alert. You know that divine manager I told you about? Here he comes, so just act natural, everyone.'

This has precisely the opposite effect as we all do 180-degree neck swivels to see who he's talking about.

'Too butch-looking for you, darling,' says Rachel.

'Whaddya mean, too butch?'

'I mean, not your type. Not artistic-looking enough.'

'Oh, please, it's not like he just came in from branding cattle and smoking Marlboro.'

'Hey, I just don't want you to go out with someone and for people to think you met in a police line-up—'

'Don't bother finishing that sentence, Rachel,' says Jamie, a bit miffed. 'I'll just catch the rest of that gag on the *Antiques Roadshow*.'

It may sound like they're on the verge of a feud but, honestly, Jamie and Rachel really are best friends. This is just the way they spark off each other. However, I judge it a very opportune moment to change the subject. 'I have news.'

'So do I,' says Jamie.

'So do I, but let Amelia go first,' says Caroline with typical niceness. 'She never gets to go first.'

I take a deep breath, then whip the 'FATE IS LATE!' ad out of my handbag, carefully spreading it out in the middle of the table for them all to google at. 'So. What do we think?' I ask hopefully.

The silence alone should have alerted me.

'You have got to be taking the piss,' says Rachel, scrutinizing it. 'Are you seriously telling me that you're supposed to track down all your exes and then say – what? What was it about me drove you nuts when we were going out? Now *that's* ironic, Alanis Morissette.'

'Something like that, yes.'

'And this is going to help you find a soulmate?' Rachel's on her high horse now. 'Face it, sweetie. We're your soulmates. Whether you like it or not.'

OK, maybe not the reaction I'd hoped for, but I'll plough on . . . 'Thanks very much, two divorces. What do the rest of you think?'

'Oh, honey,' says Caroline, clocking the hurt look on my face, 'I know you've been single for a long time.'

'Yeah,' says Jamie, 'ever since you broke up with *He-whose-name-shall-forever-remain-unspoken.*'

The gang all make gestures of sticking their fingers down their throats and throwing up, at the mere hint of the name Jamie has just conjured up, which I gamely choose to ignore. Not the time, not the place.

'Apart from him, I've pretty much been single for most of

my thirties, bar a few horrific dates which we won't even bother going into.'

Rachel starts to chortle. 'Do you remember that guy you went on a blind date with who turned out to be in the IRA?'

'Well, that just shows that I've been a brave little foot soldier,' I reply, wincing a bit at the memory. 'And that I'm prepared to get out of my cosy comfort zone. I mean, if a girl can't find a husband among the non-paramilitaries—'

'If daytime television has taught me nothing,' Caroline gently interrupts, 'it's that the man of your dreams is out there somewhere for you, and that you'll meet him when the time is right. There has to be serendipity about it. I honestly think these things are bigger than us. I really do.'

'If I was married to a big ride like you are, I'd probably say the same thing,' says Jamie. 'Look, we all know you really want to be with someone, Amelia—'

'No, I've been with people. That's *not* what I want. I want to be married. Sorry if this sounds old-fashioned, but *I want my husband*. Look, just say I live to be eighty, then I've already lived almost half my life alone. I'd love someone to share the second half with, that's all. Yes, it's about having kids before it's too late and all of that, but it's the little things too. You know, just . . . someone to read the papers with in bed on a Sunday morning and, I dunno . . . someone who'll give me a hug at the end of a rough day. Girlies, I'm thirty-seven years of age and I've been dating since I was sixteen. I'm officially worn out. Where is he?'

'Not on some bloody night course anyway,' says Rachel. 'Unless he's teaching it. I'm sorry, darling, but face facts. If it hasn't happened by now, it's not going to. The secret of a happy life at our age is to gracefully accept that yes, men do like strong, independent women, once they're hot, sexy and under thirty-five. It's like that fabulous quote: "Being an old maid is a little bit like drowning. A really delightful sensation once you give up the struggle."'

Just then, an imposingly tall, good-looking, preppy guy, who looks and dresses like he has a proper job, approaches Rachel. 'Hiya,' he says confidently. 'Just wondered if I could buy you a drink?'

'Piss off,' she says, without even looking at him.

See what I mean about the lethal Rachel pheromone? The poor guy skulks off without even a backward glance in my direction and suddenly I get all defensive. It's OK for her, she's had two husbands; it's OK for Caroline, she has a perfect life; and it's OK for Jamie, he changes boyfriends the way the rest of us change shoes. I just have to work a bit harder at it, that's all.

There is no lethal Amelia pheromone.

Nor can I help feeling that this is my very, very, very last chance to do something about it.

'Well, I've tried everything else,' I reply. 'Internet dating, speed dating, blind dates; short of joining the Knock marriage bureau, you name it, I've given it a whirl. And all with zero per cent success. I must be doing something wrong, so why not try the business marketing approach? I mean, huge corporations spend millions on this sort of thing, so if it works in the world of commerce, why not dating?'

'But, Amelia,' says Caroline gently, 'you have such a fantastic life as it is. Try walking a few miles in my shoes and you'll appreciate just how great you have it. You get to stay in bed all weekend, if you feel like it. Your purse is full of disposable income.'

'Yes, we loveless loners are so lucky.'

They all roar laughing, but I wasn't trying to be funny.

'Come on, girlies. I don't know why it is, but finding a

partner is just so *easy* for some people, but to me it's like climbing Mount Everest.'

What I really mean is . . . I seem to have a hex on me. It's almost as if some wicked fairy came to my christening, just like in the Disney cartoon *Sleeping Beauty*, and said, 'OK, I got good news and bad news for you.' (In my imagination, the wicked fairy talks a bit like a mafia don.) 'The good news is, everything in your life will be great, but the bad news is, you're destined to live it out alone. Capeesh?'

I may not be able to break the curse, but one thing's for sure: I'll get there or die trying. This is the year.

I'll give it twelve months and if it still hasn't happened, then I'll gracefully give up and spend the rest of my life going on lesbian walking tours at weekends. I'll leave instructions in my will that my headstone is to be engraved with the immortal phrase: 'Here lies Amelia Lockwood, spinster of this parish. She may have died single, but at least she bloody well tried.'

'Well, I think it's a fabulous idea.' We all turn to look at Jamie, intrigued. I was fully expecting him, of all people, to make mincemeat of the whole thing. 'I mean, just look at you, Amelia. In every other respect, you're completely and utterly at the top of your game. You're so pretty; I always say behind your back that you're one of the undiscovered beauties of Ireland. You know, a bit like the Antrim coastline.'

'You're comparing her to scenery in Northern Ireland?' says Rachel.

'I am *trying* to be complimentary, girlies. Just look at her, she's an SHB.'

'A what?'

'Oh, please, do none of you watch MTV? A super-hot babe. If Amelia was played by a Hollywood actress, it would have to be . . . Meryl Streep.'

'She's fifty-something!' squeals Caroline.

'Can I finish? Meryl Streep twenty years ago, in *Sophie's Choice*. You know, when she was young and gorgeous and had the long, swishy hair and that ephemeral, dreamy thing going on. Devastating combination.'

'You only chose her because we both have big noses,' I say.

'Not true. Amelia, I'll only say this once, mainly because then it's time to talk about *me*, but you're successful, talented, you've got a fabulous penthouse apartment, a flashy car, your dream career and . . . well, put it this way, what did you spend last Saturday night doing? Watching *Parkinson*? Taking calls from telemarketers?'

'No, I was saving that for my birthday.'

Now Rachel is cackling. 'Oh, for God's sake, look! The teacher is called Ira Vandergelder. You seriously want to enrol on a course run by a woman called Ira Vandergelder? She sounds like the mother out of *Rhoda*.'

'Shut up, Rachel,' says Jamie. 'I think Amelia should go for it. It's been so long since she produced a boyfriend that people will start thinking she's GUPO.'

'What's that?' I ask innocently.

'Gay until proven otherwise.'

I turn to Caroline. 'I will give you one hundred euro if you change the subject right now.'

'No, it's my go!' says Jamie. 'Amelia's had her airtime and I haven't even *started* the bitch-fest about my little dalliance last weekend yet.'

'Can you all stop the sailor talk for a minute?' says Caroline, taking a deep breath and pausing for dramatic effect. 'I don't mean to sound prudish or anything, but there's an expectant mother in your midst.'

'AGHHH! You're up the duff again!' Rachel and I squeal, almost going ultrasonic as we smother her in hugs.

'This is it, though,' says Caroline, 'this is definitely the last one. As my mother always says, never have more children than you have windows in your car.'

'Shame on me, I should have guessed the minute you ordered a virgin bloody Mary,' says Jamie, sounding a bit choked. 'I am *soooo* happy for you, sweetheart, I feel like I'm in a musical. Does anyone else feel not just happy, but *Broadway* happy right now?'

Hours later, as I'm crawling into bed, I think about Caroline. And Mike. And their perfect life and their two perfect children, and now another one to come.

And how *lucky* they both are.

Right there and then I make up my mind. I have absolutely no idea what the coming year will bring, but I'm certain about one thing: I'm getting married.

Chapter Two

The Pity Party is Over

Next day in work is a battlefield. This is nothing unusual, it's just that by mid-afternoon I still haven't had either the chance or the privacy to pick up the phone and book myself a place on the 'find a husband' course.

At times like this, I really feel like calling up Jayne Lawler, my predecessor on *Celtic Tigers*, and offering her my entire annual wage packet, plus any vital organ of mine she may have a use for, if she'll just come back to work. Jayne, however, is younger than me, happily married to a gorgeous guy and now on extended maternity leave, which is why I was drafted over from the current affairs department to deputize for her in the first place.

Jealous? Me? Bitter? Moi?

Anyway, I'm up to my eyes casting for a major new character that's coming into the show in a few weeks' time. This may sound straightforward enough, but actually involves (*a*) contacting every actor's agent in Dublin to see who they have on their books who'd be suitable, (*b*) winnowing out the ones who can act from the ones who can't and, most difficult of all, (*c*) fielding calls from Jamie who's been pestering me all morning demanding that I cast him.

'I am so perfect for the part it's not true. There's nothing I can't play, you know. I'm an actor's actor.'

'Jamie, just listen for a moment—'

'Don't you think I'm TV pretty? You know, kind of like that gorgeous guy who plays Will in *Will and Grace*? A straight gay type, that's the look I'm going for.'

'You're wonderful-looking, as you very well know, but the problem is—'

'If I don't get a decent job soon, I will be *unable to shop*.'

'Jamie, you're not listening—'

'You have GOT to give me the gig. Otherwise what is the point of me hanging around with Miss Big Shot Deputy Producer anyway?'

'Sweetheart, you know me; ordinarily I'll cave in to emotional guilt, but in this case, you're wasting your time. You're completely wrong for the part.'

'Wrong, how?'

'Well, for starters you're not over six feet tall.'

'I can wear shoes with lifts, like Tom Cruise.'

'And you're not from Nigeria.'

'You've never heard of make-up?'

'Jamie, forget it. If we were to cast you, the make-up budget alone would bankrupt the show. I've told you a thousand times, I'm on the lookout for the right part for you, but trust me, this isn't it. Now go away, I have to work.'

He sighed. 'I suppose you're right, darling. You know me, completely NID.'

'NID?'

'Not into details.'

Then Rachel calls. 'Hey, sweetie, just wondered if you'd booked yourself on to the I'm-so-desperate-to-find-a-man-I'm-prepared-to-go-back-to-college course thingy.'

'Still haven't had a chance. Can I call you back?'

'I'm just trying to be the voice of reason here, before you do something you'll live to regret. Are you really sure this is what you want? To go back in time and live the rest of your life in a 1950s detergent commercial?'

'No, just a husband will do fine, thanks.'

'I just think that, at your age, you should be slowly eliminating the need for a man out of your life. Maybe think about going on a kill-a-spider course instead.'

'Rachel, call you back!'

Five minutes later, I'm outside in the TV studio car park, frantically trying to get through to the UCD admissions office from my mobile. I don't normally make phone calls from the car park, you understand, it's just that . . . well . . . in this life, there are some conversations you don't really want anyone to overhear and as anyone who works in an open-plan office will tell you, loose lips cost ships.

'And which evening class are you interested in booking?' asks a warm, friendly woman's voice.

I glance over my shoulder, just to double-check there's no one around. 'The one about how to find a husband . . .' I mutter under my breath.

'I'm really sorry, but you're breaking up on me. What did you say?'

'Over the age of thirty-five.'

'The signal must be terrible where you're calling from. I'm sorry, what was that again, please?'

Whether I like it or not, I'm forced to raise my voice, while hopping around the car park like a demented lunatic trying to see if the signal will improve.

'I said the one where you learn how to find a husband over the age of thirty-five.'

The administrations woman is shouting by now too. 'Hello? CAN YOU HEAR ME?'

'YES! I CAN HEAR YOU LOUD AND CLEAR. THE COURSE I WANT TO GO ON IS THE ONE WHERE YOU LEARN HOW TO FIND A HUSBAND OVER THE AGE OF THIRTY-FIVE.'

'Sounds very interesting.'

I turn around and there's Dave Bruton, easily our nicest and most gorgeous director. (Married, worse luck . . .) Anyway, he must have spotted me through the office window and followed me outside.

'I'm sorry about this, can you hold for a moment?' I say into the phone, trying to sound all businesslike and . . . well, you know . . . *normal*.

'Didn't mean to interrupt you,' he said apologetically, 'I just wanted to let you know we have another three actors at TV reception waiting for the auditions. I'm just going to have a quick chat with them about the scene I want them to read and then we'll be ready when you are, Miss de Mille.'

'Fantastic,' I laugh nervously. 'Just give me two secs and I'll be right with you.'

'Take your time,' he says. 'I'll let you get back to your call. Booking a night course then, are you?'

'Ehh, yes . . .' I stammer, frantically trying to think of something plausible when Rachel's words come back to me. 'It's a course for single women, in killing spiders and . . . emm . . . rodents and, well, you know, basic household pest control really.'

'For the over thirty-fives?'

'Yes . . . well, you know, whatever your age, it's never too late to learn the basics about . . . emm . . . rat poison.'

Dave smiles and moves off.

'I'm so sorry,' I say to the nice admissions woman who, miraculously, I can hear clear as a bell now, 'I just . . . well, I just didn't want anyone in work to know what I was up to.'

'Oh, don't you worry,' she laughs, 'just about everyone else who's enrolled for the course has said pretty much the same thing. First class is tonight at eight p.m. sharp.'

'Tonight? Oh, OK then. Thank you.'

'And bringing a paper bag to put over your head is entirely optional.'

I hang up, delighted. This really feels like a step in the right direction. You know, like I'm finally facing up to the problem and taking control, instead of doing what I normally do which is to (*a*) moan about being single and dumped, (*b*) read loads of happiness-and-romance-are-just-within-your-grasp type self-help books, realize none of them actually work and then (*c*) go out and get trolleyed drunk with my friends.

I once read a book about creative visualization, a self-help technique where you envisage yourself living your perfect life to help you through stressful times. Apparently they teach this to the astronauts at NASA, to help them cope with the claustrophobia of being cooped up inside the space shuttle and to stop them going completely mental and pressing all the wrong buttons, as I probably would if they were ever daft enough to send me on a mission to the moon. You take a deep breath and imagine yourself in a wide open space or on a sandy beach, miles away from Cape Canaveral and flight simulators and voices on headsets saying, 'Houston, we have a problem.'

In my case, the dream situation is a little different. I close my eyes for a second and try to drown out all the background noises.

My perfect life . . . OK. A couple of nice, deep, soothing breaths. Here we go.

I'm in a beautiful long silk wedding dress (off-white, Vera Wang, Empire line . . . What can I say? I've put a lot of thought into this) walking down the aisle, ring on the finger, bouquet in hand, blissfully happy with my lovely new husband by my side.

My headless husband, that is.

Well, how am I supposed to know what he looks like? And I don't want to superimpose any physical images of my ideal man on to him either. I'm thirty-seven years of age and should gladly and gratefully accept whatever the universe chooses to send me, even if he has two heads and I have to wheel him down the aisle holding up his saline drip. I repeat this a few times, almost like a mantra, inhaling and exhaling deeply.

I am doing the right thing.

And besides, anything that helps me get over *He-whose-name-shall-forever-remain-unspoken* can only be a good thing.

My friends have all been fantastic in helping me through the awful break-up; Caroline with her warmth and wisdom and belief that everything would work itself out; Rachel for telling me he was a worthless bastard and that I'm miles better off without him; and Jamie for showing me that there's nothing so tragic you can't find something to laugh at. But now it's time to take matters into my own hands.

Going back to my old Alma Mater, University College, Dublin, turns out to be a very weird experience. Still the same concrete jungle feel to the place; still the same smell of cheap perfume and testosterone. With one exception though. Although it's a Tuesday night, the campus seems deserted, except for a few swotty-looking stragglers all making their eager way up to the library.

Now, in my day, the bar alone would have been completely packed on any given night of the week. In fact, that's what college effectively meant to us: it was basically school, but with boys and bar extensions and minus the awful uniform. But this generation seems to be here to study, work hard and then get good jobs at the end of it all. Unheard of, back in the dim, distant eighties.

The hardest part is forcing myself to get out of the car. It's a bit like going to the gym on a cold winter's night; the worst bit is physically dragging myself out of my lovely toasty-warm apartment, through the freezing night air and into the health club. Once I'm on a treadmill, I'm grand. Same thing.

OK, here goes. I repeat my mantra ('I want to be happily married to the right guy, please, universe, if it's not too much trouble to ask'), stride purposefully out of the car park and make my way into the Arts building, which, thank God, at least I remember my way around.

I check the noticeboard and there it is.

HOW TO FIND A HUSBAND OVER THE AGE
OF THIRTY-FIVE.
TUTOR: IRA VANDERGELDER.
ROOM 201, SECOND FLOOR.

So far, so good. I make my way upstairs and find it easily enough. Taking a very deep breath, I resist the last-minute temptation to bolt for the hills and force myself to open the classroom door.

To my surprise, it's quite full. Of women, naturally enough. There's a free seat at the end of the second row, so I sneak in, trying really hard not to make eye contact with anyone and silently praying that there's no one here I know. No one is even chattering, which is unusual in a room full of women; as if we're all so silently mortified to be there in the first place that we can't even force ourselves to make small talk.

It's so deathly quiet; all you can hear is the buzzing of the fluorescent light overhead and the odd cough. *Oh God, I feel like such a saddo, will I just run for it? I mean, it's not as if I'll ever see any of these people again . . .*

No, I say to myself in my most assertive deputy producer voice, you've come this far, you are *not* chickening out now. Sitting here is not admitting that I'm a total failure when it comes to men, it's saying I'm prepared to do something about it. Besides, I remind myself, when is the last time I got a Valentine's Day card? Or flowers from either a straight man or an actor who didn't just want a job from me?

I shut my eyes and do a quick creative visualization.

Yes. There I am, in the Vera Wang, with my headless husband, Rachel and Caroline are my bridesmaids, Jamie is my bridesman, my dad's beaming with pride now that his only daughter has finally found someone and my mum has that glazed, shell-shocked, can-this-wondrous-miracle-really-be-happening look that lottery winners always seem to get . . .

Another deep, soothing breath.

Yes, I can *do* this.

I can do one class.

If it turns out to be rubbish, I'll just never come back again.

It's worth a try.

Bang on the dot of eight o'clock, the door is thrown open. 'So, I bet you're all sitting there with one question. Who stole my veil?'

We all look up as the woman herself makes her grand entrance.

Ira Vandergelder is probably sixtyish, absolutely tiny and immaculately dressed in a Chanel-type pillar-box-red suit, with platinum-blonde, Margaret-Thatcher-helmet hair and a big knuckleduster diamond on each perfectly manicured finger. She looks like Nancy Reagan and talks like Joan Rivers, the same great New York no-bullshit directness.

I like her immediately.

'Sure, you're probably all looking at each other, thinking: What am *I* doing here? I'm pretty, I'm gorgeous, I'm successful, I should be home with my husband. Well, I got news for you. This is your wake-up call, ladies. By the very act of sitting in my class, you have effectively dialled Marriage nine eleven.'

We all look at her, riveted. I swear you could hear a pin drop.

'You see, you all represent what I call my "Lost Cinderella" generation,' Ira went on, taking her place at the front of the classroom, barely pausing for breath. 'Sure, you broke the glass ceiling, but you also broke your glass slipper along with it. If you wanna moan and whinge about it, there's the door. But if you stay here and do exactly what I tell you, you will be married within a year.'

The woman beside me has, by now, actually started to take notes. She has short red hair, untrendy paperweight glasses and I find myself silently betting that she was a milk monitor when she was in school.

'Before we start, I got just one question for you ladies.' Ira is standing in front of the whiteboard now, hands on hips, a woman not to be messed with. 'Short of doing anything illegal or immoral, I want you to ask yourselves this. Am I prepared to do anything, and by that I mean *anything*, to find a husband this year? Because if your honest answer is no, the door is right there. The good people at UCD will refund you the class fee and no hard feelings.'

There's an awkward silence as we all shift uncomfortably in our seats. No one moves, although I have to resist the temptation to text Rachel to tell her what she's missing.

'Good. You all passed the first test,' says Ira, approvingly. 'OK, ladies, let me just set you all straight on a couple of things. One: I don't care why you're still single. Maybe you're looking to get married for the first time or the fourth time. Maybe you're constantly dating the wrong type of men – and, God knows, we've all been there. You know, the ones who can't get over their ex or the ones who'll live with you but won't commit to you, or, when they do, the whole thing gradually fizzles out over time. Maybe you've been badly hurt in the past and don't wanna get burned again. Or maybe you've devoted so much time and energy to your career that suddenly you wake up one morning and there you are. Single, over thirty-five and panicking.'

I look around. There's a lot of murmuring and heads nodding in agreement, my own included.

'Like I said, I DO NOT CARE why any of you lovely ladies are unmarried,' Ira continues. 'My question is: What are you gonna do about it? If you wanna follow my program, let me warn you right now, it's not gonna be easy. This is a huge commitment; there are rules and sacrifices involved. Over the next ten weeks you are going to learn how to see the problem of finding a husband through the eyes of a marketer. You are gonna change your entire mind set, you're gonna do exactly what I tell you and, within a year, I will personally dance at each and every one of your weddings. Now, are there any questions so far?'

There's a silence as we all try to digest what she's said.

Eventually, swotty note-taking girl beside me tentatively puts her hand up.

'Yes, the lady with the red hair, second row.'

'I've lived in this city all my life and my question is: What if there are just no single men in Dublin? All the ones I meet all seem to be either married or gay.'

Before Ira has a chance to answer, someone else who I can't see has piped up from the back row. 'Or with girl-friends? I've met loads of interesting men, but they all seem to be very happy with their long-term girlfriends.'

Someone else at the back says, 'Yeah, me too. And you know what they say, married men are easy, men with girlfriends are impossible.'

This is greeted with raucous laughter and by now, there're about a half-dozen hands enthusiastically waving in the air.

'I think we're geographically challenged, you know,' says swotty girl beside me to no one in particular. 'I read an article recently that said that you really have to go west of the Shannon to find a partner these days. The ratio of single men to women is three to one in Connaught.'

'Ladies, ladies, please,' says Ira, regaining control. 'Let me just debunk a few myths here. Sure, single women out-number single men the world over. Plus, you gotta face up to the hard, cold reality that many guys over thirty-five want younger women. And they're in a buyer's market. Accept that fact and then address it. This means no more narrow criteria about what kind of guy you're looking for. No more "Oh, my ideal man has to be a rich handsome doctor, who my mother will love, who plays sports, gives to charity and does meals on wheels at weekends." Your future husbands may have great qualities but they could also come in very different packages than you imagine. You're gonna learn how to cast your net wide. Your husband could be divorced, have kids from another relationship, be shorter than you or be completely different from any other guy you've dated in the past. Now. Any other questions before we start?'

Almost involuntarily, my hand shoots up and before I even know what I'm saying, the question is out. 'Can I ask you something?'

'Sure.' Ira peers over and I'm aware that all of room 201 is staring at me.

'It's just that . . . well, in your ad, you mentioned something about revisiting past relationships. Does this mean getting in touch with ex-boyfriends? Or, by any miracle, did I read the ad wrong?'

There's a few titters which Ira immediately quells. 'What's your name?'

'Sorry?'

'Your name, please.'

She's standing right beside me now and I'm beginning to feel like a seven-year-old about to be asked maths tables. 'Amelia Lockwood,' I mutter, hoping the entire class won't hear. What the hell, I can always run out of the door if she turns nasty on me. This is a university, not a women's prison.

'Amelia Lockwood,' Ira repeats, slowly. 'You're a very pretty lady, Amelia. So why are you still single?'

'I honestly don't know.'

'*You don't know?*'

'No,' I answer in a voice I hardly recognize as my own. Am I really saying this in front of a room full of total strangers? 'I don't have the first clue. I've been on so many dates I've lost count. You name it; I've done it: speed dating, internet chat rooms, blind dates, singles nights. I don't know why I'm still single. My parents don't know why I'm still single. My friends don't know why I'm still single. All I know is that I'm sick of it. I'm sick of going home to an empty, dark house with gone-off yoghurt in the fridge and nothing but the TV for company. And I'm especially sick of getting phone bills for five hundred euro a month because I'm so lonely I have to spend three hours a night talking to my friends or else I'll go off my head. I could be mistaken, but I can't help feeling this isn't how my life was supposed to turn out.'

Ira is eyeballing me now, and it's disconcerting. 'Well, Amelia, I got news for you. Clearly, you are doing something wrong.'

I'm dimly aware of swotty girl staring at me.

'I have absolutely no idea why any of your exes didn't want to pursue a relationship with you, but I can tell you one thing.'

'Yes?' I ask, figuring: What the hell? I can't be humiliated any more.

'You are going to track them down and you're gonna find out. Exactly like an exit interview. Sure, it's gonna be tough, you're gonna hear a lot of home truths about yourself, but how else can you learn from your mistakes of the past and move on? And it doesn't matter who broke up with who, what you want to learn is why these men were wrong for you to begin with. Remember the magic word: *feedback*. And that applies for all of you ladies,' she says, directing her attention back to the class. I'm relieved that the focus is off me, but the next thing she says sends a shiver down my spine. 'In fact that brings me neatly to your assignment for next week. I want you all to make a list of your ten most significant ex-boyfriends, starting with the first and ending with the most recent.'

For the first time this evening, swotty girl looks a bit flummoxed. 'But suppose you don't have ten exes?' she whispers to me.

10

Ira, it seems, is one of those people who can hear the grass grow in her sleep. 'If you can't think of ten ex-boyfriends, then ten guys who asked you out will do. Come on, ladies, you're all over thirty-five, you must have been on at least ten dates in your lives.'

There are loud mutterings in the class.

'That's the easy part of the assignment, let me tell you,' Ira goes on, undeterred. 'Before next week's class, you're gonna have made steps to contact your first serious boyfriend. And so on, one ex a week for the whole ten-week duration of this course.'

'Suppose they've left the country?' comes a panicky-sounding voice from the back row. 'Or suppose their wife answers the phone?'

'And even if I do get to speak to him,' says someone else in the middle of the class, 'what do I say?'

'I will tell you exactly what you say,' says Ira. 'I'll hand you the goddamn script. The question is: Are you ready to hear the truth?'

Driving home later that night, I have a flashback. An omen for what lies ahead . . .

THE TIME: *Mid-July 1984.*
THE PLACE: *Blinkers nightclub in the Leopardstown race course.*
THE OCCASION: *Nothing in particular, it's just free for girls on a Wednesday night.*

Bruce Springsteen is belting out 'Born in the USA' and the crowd are all singing along and stomping their feet as I make my way through the packed bar and spot where the Lovely Girls are all perched around a table.

'LATE!' they chant in unison.

'Sorry, sorry,' I reply breathlessly. 'Don't laugh, but I really wanted to watch the end of the Olympics.'

'Oh, how did Sebastian Coe do? He is so yummy . . .' says Caroline, ever the hopeless romantic.

'I'm sorry, but I'm politically opposed to watching,' says Jamie, who's wearing black eyeliner and looks like the really scary one from the Cure. 'Without the Soviets, it's like . . . oh I don't know . . .'

'Charles without Diana,' says Caroline, looking a bit like an early Diana herself, all blonde and bobbed in a sailor dress with pearls.

'You look good,' Rachel says, eyeing me up and down approvingly. She goes to loads of trouble with her own clothes and is always really interested in what everyone else is wearing. Tonight, she's all dressed in black, with a glittery crucifix hanging off her neck, backcombed hair, a long duster coat and really, really heavy eye make-up. 'Take it from me, the puffball skirt is here to stay. It's a design classic. And the white stilettos just complete the look.'

'You look amazing too,' I say, 'a bit like Madonna in the "Holiday" video.'

'Ughh, Madonna,' groans Jamie. 'If I hear that crappy song once more, I'll puke. What a one-hit wonder. Oh, oh, oh, cute girl alert.'

'Who?' All our heads turn as a tall girl in pink and yellow striped dungarees walks past us, nose in the air, completely oblivious to poor Jamie, who's busy adjusting his mullet haircut in a bid to catch her eye.

'Isn't she stunning?' he says, all full of puppy-dog adoration.

'Looks like a poor man's Molly Ringwald,' Rachel cuts across him.

'I'm sorry, there's a beautiful woman in the vicinity,' says Jamie, 'you're all just big blurry shapes to me now. What do you think, girlies, will I ask her up to dance?'

'Not to this, you're not allowed,' says Rachel bossily as the Special AKA come on singing 'Free Nelson Mandela'.

'Yeah, this song really gets me too,' I nod in agreement. 'Like they're ever going to release Mandela.'

'Anyone for a drink?' asks a passing cocktail waitress.

'Four orange juices please,' we all reply, trying our best to look innocent, as if we're four teetotallers on our way home from choir practice and that's genuinely our order.

'Did you bring it?' Jamie hisses at Rachel.

'Yup, but we have to go easy. If my mother smells booze off me when I get home, I'll be under curfew for a month.' She then fishes around in her pocket and produces a tiny club soda bottle, filled to the brim with neat, blue-label vodka.

'For God's sake, don't let the waitress see you topping up our drinks,' says Jamie. 'I'm already barred from the Berni Inn for getting caught doing that.'

'Amelia,' Caroline says slowly, 'don't look now, but I think you're being eyed up.'

'WHAT?' I nearly fall off my chair in shock. She and Rachel are always the ones who get chatted up and asked to dance whenever we're in Blinkers; it never seems to be my turn.

Ever.

'She's right,' says Jamie. 'Over there, by the Malibu promotion stand. Tall, rugger-bugger type. Bet he went to Blackrock College.'

This time, we all turn to look. It's considered the height of cool if you can nab a Blackrock boy: the ultimate arm decoration.

'Oh, he's lovely,' says Caroline dreamily, 'kind of like Richard Gere in *An Officer and a Gentleman*.'

There's no mistaking it. In fact, not only is he staring over at me, but, prompted by Rachel's demented waving, he smiles and makes his way over to our table.

'OK, just act natural, girls,' says Jamie. 'He might have mates. You know those Blackrock types, they hunt in packs.'

'Stay cool,' Caroline whispers to me as the waitress comes back with our drinks. 'Remember you're single and ready to mingle.'

I'm not in the slightest bit perplexed as I'm full sure he'll want to chat up either her or Rachel, which is usually the normal outcome. To my astonishment, he makes a beeline for me, takes me by the hand and asks me up to dance.

I'll never forget it.

Lionel Ritchie came on singing 'Hello' as he led me on to the dance floor. The gang looked on, giving me very unsubtle thumbs-up signs and generally making a show of me. But I didn't care. A gorgeous guy just asked me to dance.

Me.

The others could have mooned at us and I'd barely have noticed.

He was way over six feet tall, well built, with twinkly blue eyes and floppy light brown hair. Miles better looking than Richard Gere any day.

'I'm Greg Taylor,' he said, holding me so tight, my tummy did somersaults.

Three Malibu and Cokes, one more slow set and about fifteen snogs later, he had officially become my first proper boyfriend.

First guy I fancied who actually fancied me back.

First love.

First broken heart.

And now, after all these years, somehow I'd have to contact him again.

Chapter Three
Mr Wrong, the First

Brunch on the first Saturday of every month is something of a sacrosanct tradition for the Lovely Girls by now. In fact, nothing short of one of us being terminally ill and on life support would be considered an acceptable excuse for getting out of it. But then Jamie has always been a bit of a Houdini when it comes to wriggling out of long-standing commitments.

'I'm soooooo sorry to let you down,' he trills down my mobile phone as I scour the car park for a space, 'but my agent has set up a meeting for me with a theatre director who's so hot at the minute he's practically smoking. Every actor in town is sawing a limb off just to get to *meet* this guy, so you can just imagine how I feel.'

'How?'

'Like Santa Claus finally got my letter, sweetie. Remember that all-male production of *Romeo and Juliet* that won about twenty-five Olivier awards? Same guy. José Miguel Fernandez. From Catalonia. Very, very sexy. Hot to trot.'

'So he's gay, then?'

'Bent as the Soviet sickle, darling. If he was played by a

41

Hollywood actor it would have to be . . . Antonio Banderas. And you know how much I *adore* those Latino types. So you see my dilemma, baby.'

'Well, no actually, I don't,' I reply firmly, mobile clamped to my ear as I try to squeeze into a parking space the size of a fruit pastille. 'Jamie, you *hate* the theatre. You said it's a dying art form, and that the only reason you go at all is because occasionally you like to watch the corpse decompose.'

'I know, I know. Theatre's really just there so that the ugly actors have someplace to work. But this director is just soooo cute and it's been so long since I had sex that I'm starting to wonder if it's any different now.'

'You've barely been single for two weeks.'

'For a gay man, that's an eternity. We're a completely different species to you. Just think of us as a parallel universe.'

There's a slight pranging noise as I inadvertently tap off the bumper of the car in front.

'Are you parking, Miss Magoo?' (This is my nickname, as I'm both short-sighted and an atrocious driver to boot.)

'Yup. I have a brunch to go to. I would never dream of letting my friends down. Not even if Colin Farrell begged me to have naked brunch with him instead.'

'You're such a doll; I know you'll break it gently to the others why I can't be there. And I know that you'll cope with their devastation at not seeing me. I am, after all, the nucleus around which you all revolve. It's quite a responsibility.'

'And as modest as a postulant,' I sigh wearily. Jamie's made up his mind to cancel and that's all there is to it. 'OK then, you win. I'll do your dirty work for you and pass on the message that some cute guy is more important to you than the Lovely Girls. But God help you when you speak to them next.'

'You are an angel from on high. Men have gone to heaven for less.'

'And by the way, I hope you get a dose of the DDs for letting us down.'

'What's that?'

'Double diarrhoea.'

'Too late, I'm so nervous about meeting him, I already have. That's the theatre for you. Nature's laxative.'

We've arranged to meet in the Cobalt Café, a gorgeous bright sunny restaurant with colourful Cath Kidston table-cloths, a jazz quartet playing in the background and a wine list to die for.

'I adore brunch,' says Caroline, tucking into a plate of omelette and chips fit for a builder.

'I know,' Rachel replies, 'it's kind of like breakfast with booze.'

We've all expressed our disappointment at not seeing Jamie, tinged with friendly understanding that his career must come first, or, as Rachel dryly puts it, 'I will rip out his still-beating heart and wave it in front of his disloyal face the next time I see him, that's if he's lucky and I happen to be in a good mood. He chucked us over for a *theatre* audition? He told me he thought the theatre was a hideous bitch-goddess.'

'I know,' I say, 'I got that speech too.'

'And if he thinks I'm going to fork out to see some bloody show *if* he gets the part, he's got another think coming. Not after that Beckett play he made us sit through.'

This was a production of *Waiting for Godot* Jamie was in about a year ago, which the director, for reasons best known to himself, decided to set inside a German concentration camp.

'It's meant to challenge the audience,' Jamie had said at the time.

'And in a way, it has,' Rachel had muttered darkly. 'Certainly challenged me to go up to the box-office manager, thump him and demand my money back.'

'Did you have to remind me?' I groan. 'I'm just out of therapy to recover from seeing that particular show.'

We've also discussed Caroline's pregnancy; she's just at the twelve-week stage now, and looks like a glowing ad for it. I don't think she's ever experienced nausea once in her entire life. In fact, I've had worse symptoms and certainly a far more swollen tummy with a bad dose of PMS. She strenuously denies this, naturally, claiming that she's eaten so much, the control-top gusset on her tights is in shards.

And then the chat turns to me. As I knew it would.

I'm prepared though. For Rachel, anyway. Caroline would support any of her friends even if we decided to sell up and emigrate to Fallujah. But Rachel is another kettle of fish entirely. Don't get me wrong, I love her dearly, but she's so smart and so sharp and is permanently three steps ahead of me and she uses witty banter to put her point across and she's always at her funniest in front of an audience and she really doesn't want me tracking down all my exes and I know it's because she's looking out for me – but guess what?

I'm a big girl now. And I want a husband. So I've come fully prepared for Rachel.

'Well then, honey?' Caroline asks, gently patting my hand. 'How did you get on at the find-a-husband night class then? And if you could postpone your wedding till after the baby's born and I fit back into a size ten, I'd be very grateful.'

'Or have you faced up to the un-face-up-toable and accepted that *we* are your soulmates?' says Rachel and I know by the glint in her eyes that she's only warming up for a good old ding-dong.

'If you're my soulmate, then God help me. You call screen during *Desperate Housewives*.'

Told you I was ready for her.

'Me and half the Northern hemisphere. For God's sake, everyone call screens during *Desperate Housewives*. I just meant that if you were going to meet someone, you would have met them by now.'

'Rach, you can be very cruel when you're sober,' I reply, taking a deep breath and reminding myself that she's only saying these things because she cares about me. But . . . well . . . does she really have to be so *down* on the whole idea? This is a very tender subject, kind of my own personal Achilles heel. If Rachel wants to show off how funny she is, couldn't she just slag off my haircut instead?

'All I'm doing is pointing out the obvious, Amelia. If you're going to get all worked up about it, then go crush a pill and put it in your drink.'

'Girlies,' says Caroline, tactfully intervening, 'no way have I forked out ten euro an hour for a babysitter to listen to you pair squabbling. Rachel, call off the dogs.'

'Sorry,' she says, but I don't think she really means it.

'It's OK,' I answer, but I don't mean it either.

'So how did you get on?'

'Short answer or long answer?'

'Long, naturally.'

I take another sip from my glass of Sancerre and brace myself. 'Apparently, to find Mr Right, I have to revisit all of my past Mr Wrongs. Starting right at the very beginning and working from there.'

'OH MY GOWWWWD!' Caroline squeals, 'Greg Taylor? You have got to be kidding me! Don't tell me you have to get in contact with him again, after – what's it been?'

'Twenty years,' I answer calmly.

'And what'll you say?'

'I've a fair idea of what *he'll* say,' says Rachel. 'Any spare change?'

'I don't know yet,' I say, ignoring her. 'The tutor gave us all these questions you're supposed to ask, so I can figure out whatever it is I'm doing wrong, but I suppose I'll just cross that bridge when I come to it. And I can't put it off for much longer, either.'

'What would you say he's up to now?' Caroline asks excitedly.

'Mmm, let me just apply my mind to that question,' says Rachel, acidly. 'In prison? In rehab? Or maybe a mental home?'

'Don't change the subject,' says Caroline. 'I need to pee, but I'll be straight back. My life is so domesticated these days; I have to live vicariously through you.'

'OK,' says Rachel, getting up. 'I'll pop outside for a quick smirt.'

'A what?'

'You've never heard of a smirt? It's what the young ones in work call a smoke mixed with a flirt.'

No sooner have they both left the table than I have another memory flashback . . .

THE TIME: *13 July 1985.*
THE PLACE: *Old Wesley Rugby Club, Dublin.*
THE OCCASION: *Live Aid is on: it's the only reason I remember the date so clearly.*

Two massive video screens dominate the whole bar area, both relaying live feed from Wembley arena. Queen have just come on stage and stormed the show with a foot-stomping, mosh-pitting rendition of 'Bohemian Rhapsody'. Even the operatic bit in the middle sounded incredible. The crowd, those lucky enough to be in Wembley and here in Dublin, have, predictably, gone mental.

'You are watching the greatest show on earth!' Bob Geldof is now screaming into the cameras, 'so get up off your f**king arses and start donating more money! Now!'

Jamie and I are perched on bar stools, with a brilliant view of the screens. 'Wow,' we both say, overwhelmed by Queen's electrifying performance.

'Isn't Freddie Mercury unbelievable?' I say, blown away by his operatic muscularity.

'I heard a rumour he's gay, you know,' says Jamie, sounding like an aul' one gossiping in the hairdresser's.

'Yeah, right,' I say, sneeringly. 'Next thing you'll be telling me so's George Michael. Or else someone happily married like – oh, I dunno, like Elton John.'

'So where's Greg this evening?'

'Who's on next, Bruce Springsteen?'

'Unavailable.'

'The Boomtown Rats?'

'Unavoidable. Now stop trying to change the subject and tell me where your boyfriend is.'

I take a sip of my Ritz lager and twiddle nervously on my long, feathery earrings. I was dreading that question. The truth is, after almost a year of going out, I don't know where Greg is tonight. And it's a big night. Everyone's out tonight. Half of UCD is here and have been here all day, ever since the show started.

Except for Greg.

He hasn't called, or answered any of my messages: not in ages. I've been postponing telling the Lovely Girls for as long as I could, because I know how they'll react, but I honestly don't think I can put it off for much longer.

'Amelia? What is it?'

'I don't know where he is. He hasn't called me in . . . oh, I can't remember when.' I try my best to sound all blasé, but I'm a crap actress. Jamie sees through me straight away.

'Yes you can. When?'

'Two weeks, four days and oh . . . about thirteen hours.' By now Freddie Mercury is belting out 'Crazy Little Thing Called Love'. The irony is too much for me and I start getting teary. 'I don't know what to do, Jamie; I'm so knickers mad about him.'

'Oh, come on, babe,' he says, slipping an encouraging arm around me. 'He took you to his debs ball, and that was only a few weeks ago.'

'Yeah.' I try to sound convinced but am not really doing a very good job of it, mainly because Greg spent most of the night chatting up Sandra Sweetman, the pin-up girl of first-year Arts, UCD. Literally. She ran in the students' union election and not only was voted in by a landslide, but all her posters (in which she looks stunningly gorgeous, a bit like Lucy Ewing) were nicked and are now hanging in student bedsits the length and breadth of Rathmines. 'I was kind of hoping that the reason Greg hadn't called was because he was *so* mad about me that he couldn't bring himself to pick up the phone . . .' I trail off lamely seeing the look of disbelief mingled with pity on Jamie's face.

'Now, you know what I'll say to that,' he says, gently.

'Probably, but say it anyway.'

'That's a bit like saying, "Oh, I just love that song so much that I'm never going to listen to it ever, ever again." Or, "I love that movie so much I'll never watch it ever again, as long as I live." You know, a bit like the way I feel about *The Breakfast Club*.'

'I know, you're right.' I take another gulp of Ritz and try

really hard to keep the wobble out of my voice. Wesley's packed and I really don't want to be seen bawling in public.

'Hey, you know the real reason Jerry Hall wouldn't marry Bryan Ferry?' says Jamie, trying to lighten the mood, bless him.

'No, why?'

'Well, would you want to be known as Jerry Ferry?'

By then, Rachel and Caroline have made their way back from the loo, looking just like Krystle Carrington and Alexis Colby from *Dynasty*, all pencil skirts and shoulder pads. Their faces alone are a dead giveaway.

'You were ages,' says Jamie. 'I was nearly going to have to go in there after the pair of you. Any longer and you'd have missed your precious David Bowie.'

'I don't care,' says Rachel, sitting down opposite me and taking my hand.

This also raises the hackles of suspicion on the back of my neck, mainly because Rachel adores David Bowie; she's been waiting all day for him.

In fact, she and Jamie are always having great heated debates about the Thin White Duke, although Jamie's main grievance against him isn't musical. It's that he called his son Zowie Bowie. 'Anyone who'd wilfully do that to an innocent child,' he says, 'deserves nothing better than a long career in regional panto.'

Caroline cuts straight to the chase. 'Suppose we had just heard something really, really awful and we didn't know how to tell you?' she says to me, genuinely concerned.

'We *have* to tell her. We wouldn't be proper friends otherwise,' Rachel snaps.

'WHAT? Tell me *what*?'

'OK,' says Caroline. 'When we were in the loo, I met my neighbour Sarah Daly . . .'

'Yes? And?'

'And you know how her sister is going out with Peter Hughes?'

'Well, no, but I do now.'

'And you know how his brother plays rugby with Greg?'

'Please, just tell me whatever it was you heard, the suspense is wrecking my head.' I've got a nervous knot in my stomach and I don't know why. I'm also finding it really hard to keep the impatience out of my voice.

'OK,' says Rachel, taking up the baton. 'Well, Sarah was playing Trivial Pursuit the other night with the sister and Peter and a gang of his mates and one of them is on the Leinster team with Greg—'

'No, you're telling it wrong,' Caroline interrupts. 'Peter's brother Seamus is the one who's on the team with Greg. Remember? The guy who failed the Leaving Cert three times in a row? Oh, you know who I mean; high eyebrows, low IQ.'

I know they're both trying to be helpful and that they mean well, but by now I'm fit to be tied. 'Girls, it doesn't matter if Peter's brother plays in a fly-half position with Ronald Reagan, what did you hear about my boyfriend?'

They look at each other shiftily.

'He's going out with Sandra Sweetman,' Rachel eventually says. 'For definite.'

'*WHAT?!*' Try as I might, I can't stop the tears from welling. I feel like I've just been punched.

'Hang on, hang on,' says Jamie, taking my corner. 'So you heard this from your neighbour's sister's boyfriend's friend?'

'Ehh, yeah,' says Caroline.

'Oh well, that's practically CNN,' he says sarcastically.

'It can't be true,' I sob into my Ritz, 'Greg said he loved me.'

'What?' says Rachel. 'When?'

'The night of his debs in the back of his car.'

'He really said that?'

'Well, I told him I loved him and asked if he felt the same and he didn't deny it. But then he did go back inside and spent the rest of the night chatting her up.'

David Bowie is on stage now, singing 'Modern Love'.

'And this was our song,' I bawl, like a five-year-old.

The others have all put comforting arms around me and then the single worst moment of my seventeen-year-old life unfolds. I spot Greg. With Sandra Sweetman. The bar is packed and smoky, but it's definitely them. As if to confirm their couple status, he's wearing his *Miami Vice* pants and she's wearing the matching white jacket over her ra-ra skirt. She looks all blonde and tiny and is snuggled into him possessively as loads of her bloody student union pals at the bar call them over, offering to buy them drinks.

All I want to do is crawl under the table and pray really hard for an aneurism or a heart attack or any medical emergency that'll get me out of this, when Rachel takes over.

Looking like the Amazonian giant that she is, even scarier than one of those girls in the Robert Palmer video 'Addicted to Love', she picks up her pint of Fürstenberg and strides over to them.

Greg blanches a bit under his designer stubble as he sees her thunder towards him at her most intimidating. Even over the noise and David Bowie and all the screaming fans in Wembley, I can still hear her loud and clear.

'Amelia is too sweet a person ever to say this to your face,' she snarls down at him as the packed bar is eerily silenced, 'so I'll do it for her. You are a lying, cheating scumbag and if you *ever* come near her again, I'll do this to you.'

With that, she flings the pint of beer into his face, smashes the glass on the floor and strides back to where the rest of us are sitting, gobsmacked.

'Problem solved,' she says. 'Are you OK?'

I'm too dumbstruck to speak, so Jamie expresses what we're all feeling. 'Well, congratulations, Rachel. You just became my personal heroine.'

Chapter Four

Who Says Only Mafia Wives Wear Leather?

In my darkest moments of despair, when I'm seriously thinking that the universe has given up on ever finding me a life partner and wondering if I'm destined to live out the rest of my natural life alone, there's one bright, shining thought which never fails to fill me with renewed optimism and hope for what lies ahead.

Caroline and Mike and their perfect, soulmate marriage.

Caroline and Mike are one of those couples that you just look at in awe and marvel at. He's as lovely as she is; she adores him and he idolizes her. In fact, he's put her on a pedestal so high that if Catherine Zeta Jones left Michael Douglas for him, the chances of him even noticing would be slim to negligible. They're lucky, lucky people and you can't even begrudge them, not for a moment. If ever I find myself wondering whether I'm better off alone, Caroline and Mike come into my mind and I think: NO. It doesn't matter what anyone says, true love exists and marriage *does* work. Spectacularly well, in fact.

We're just finishing up brunch when Mike arrives to

collect Caroline, carrying a bunch of stargazer lilies, her favourites.

'Well? How are the champagne Sheilas?' he asks, pecking me and Rachel on the cheek, but only after giving his glowing wife a bear hug and presenting her with the bouquet, as if he hasn't seen her in weeks instead of only a couple of hours ago.

Did I mention that, in addition to being both husband and father of the year, filthy rich and great fun to boot, Mike is also incredibly handsome? He's very tall, broad-shouldered with classic, preppy good looks, bright blue eyes and alert good manners; the type of man who really *listens* to you and cares about what you're saying – and it isn't an act. He's not only the type of man Ralph Lauren would kill to have in one of his ads, but the yardstick by which I unconsciously measure all future boyfriends/life partners/lovers/quickies/husbands.

Even Jamie fancies him a bit.

'Actually, we're remarkably sober,' replies Rachel. 'For us.'

'So what'll you pair get up to for the rest of the afternoon?' Caroline asks as we all say our goodbyes. I mutter something about having some shopping to do, but before I can say my five favourite words in the English language, 'seasonal stock reduced to clear', Rachel has ordered another bottle of Sancerre.

'Feck it anyway,' she says to me as soon as the happy couple have gone. 'When you're out, you're out.'

'Rachel, can I ask you something?'

'As long as it's not my real age. As Oscar Wilde says, a woman who would tell you that would tell you anything.'

'Do you ever look at Caroline and Mike and envy what they have?'

She almost choked on the Sancerre. 'Are you mental? Have you been inhaling cleaning products?'

'I'm serious.'

'So am I. Why would I envy anyone, just because they're married? I have absolutely no desire to come home to lovey-dovey coupleland because I've been there and it's all complete crap. Look at *me*, Amelia. I used to be like you. Idealistic and romantic and believing in the happy-ever-after fairy tale. *This*' – she points threateningly at her own face – 'is what two husbands have done to me. I am now looking down the barrel at forty and I'm not prepared to compromise my life ever again for any melon-headed man. Sorry, but I happen to like getting drunk on a Saturday afternoon with my friends if I feel like it. I like smoking in bed. I like eating, or not eating, or living on take-outs entirely depending on how I feel. The sad single is a marketing notion pedalled to us by Hollywood and it doesn't exist and the sooner you realize that the better. Living on your own is cool, and you know it.'

'Come on, Rach, do you honestly want to end up alone and childless?'

'Fingers crossed, yeah.'

'Is that why you're so down on me doing this course?'

'No, I just don't want to see you getting hurt, that's all. I know you're still getting over the emotional car crash that was *He-whose-name-shall-forever-remain-unspoken*. And you're doing really well, and we're all so proud of you. So why go delving back into the past and opening up a whole new can of worms? Seems to me you have an awful lot to lose and bugger all to gain.'

I shudder, as I always do, at the mere mention of *He-whose-name-shall-forever-remain-unspoken*, but I should probably give a tiny bit of background. He's South African, and has now gone back to live in Johannesburg, permanently. Here is how each of the Lovely Girls feels about him, in no particular order.

Jamie: 'If you'd got married and he'd whisked you back to stab city with him, mark my words, you'd have ended up living in a mud hut, sending letters home saying, "Please, I beg you, for the love of God, send penicillin."'

Rachel: 'Or else you'd be writing, "Dear all, Guess who came to visit our village today? Bob Geldof! With any luck we should have running water by 2020. PS: My typhoid is clearing up nicely. Am returning the make-up you sent me as my husband says cosmetics are the work of Satan. If you could send some corrugated iron for the roof instead, I'd be very grateful."'

Caroline: '"Dear Lovely Girls, It's been fifteen years now, why have none of you come out to visit? Could it be because you have to squat over a hole in the ground to go to the loo?"'

Jamie (again): '"Dear all, Unfortunately, I have to return the beautiful Manolo Blahnik sandals you so kindly sent me for my birthday. It's such a shame, as the post took three and a half years to get them here. However, they have deeply offended the tribal elders in our village and anyway, my husband prefers me barefoot."'

Rachel brings me back to the present, still in full rant-mode. 'You have such Pollyanna ideas about marriage, Amelia, and it's all utter bollockology. I'm sorry, but you want to track down Greg lying, cheating Taylor? Who didn't so much break your heart as smash it into smithereens? Publicly too, the worst way possible.'

'I never thanked you, you know.'

'For what?'

'For dumping him for me. Wasn't life so much simpler back then?' I mused, topping up our glasses.

'How do you mean?'

'Well, if you fancied a guy, it was all so straightforward. One of us would just go up to him and say, "My friend fancies you, do you want to go out with her?"'

'Thereby completely eliminating any fear of rejection he might have.'

'Precisely. And then when dumping time came, which it inevitably did . . .'

'Usually after two weeks of sweaty slow sets in Wesley and a couple of snogs.'

'Your mates did it for you. Or else told you in the toilets that his friend had told them that it was finished. Simple.'

'It hurt like hell, but it certainly was effective.'

We both start snorting now as the Sancerre really begins to kick in.

'So what are you up to later?' Rachel asks.

I take another sip of wine. She's so dead-set against the whole idea of me doing this course that she'll probably fly off the handle if she hears what I have planned, but then I figure: What the hell. I'm a grown woman and I'm doing this with or without anyone's blessing.

'It's homework for the course.'

'*Homework?* What, do they make you take tests and then grade you?'

'If you're going to be like that, I'm not telling you.'

'Sorry, go on.'

'Well, Ira Vandergelder says that—'

'How can you even say that name with a straight face?'

'Do you want me to tell you or not? Anyway, one of the famous marketing principles they teach at Harvard, apparently, is called creating your best look. Packaging, basically. The product I'm selling is me, so I have to revamp my wardrobe a bit. You know, smarten up. Just like you would for any big job interview.'

She looks at me with that great bit of devilment she gets in her eyes and in a moment all our feuding is forgotten. 'Well, boy, are you out lunchtime boozing with the right person.'

Another bottle of wine later and not only have I abandoned my car but am standing in my bra and knickers (which, thank God, at least match) in the changing room of Urban Chic, the ultra-cool boutique which Rachel both owns and manages.

The shop is closed by the time we get there, but she opens up, almost sets the alarm off (we're that tipsy), orders me into a changing room and barks at me to strip off. 'Right. Let me just explain something,' she says, coming in with about five different changes of outfit draped over her arm (none of which I'd ever be caught dead in). 'There are two basic types of woman in the world. There's the bikini type and then there's the swimming togs type. Now, you're a classic example of a bikini body trapped inside a twenty-five-euro pair of swimming togs from Marks and Spencer with matching sarong. I always tell my customers that you've officially reached middle age when you find yourself wandering through the ladies' department of M and S and saying, "Oh, look at those slacks, they're really nice."'

'Rachel, you're drunk. This is one of those times when only doctors can understand you.'

'No, no, hear me out,' she slurs. 'Look at you. FAN-TASTIC figure. You have the body of a Romanian gymnast.'

'I'm waiting for the but.'

'But why do you insist on going around wearing old lady camouflage? There are women out there who would pay a top surgeon any amount of cash to end up with a figure like yours, and what do you go around in? Baggy jumpers and jeans that do absolutely nothing for you.'

She's right. I am a stylist's nightmare, and it's very unlikely you'd ever catch my name on a best-dressed list. Nicole Kidman, Cate Blanchett, Hilary Swank et al. needn't lose any sleep on my account.

'It's just because of work, you see,' I protest feebly. 'No one on a TV crew dresses up. The office is so casual that if I came in looking glam, they'd probably call security. And then with the early morning location shoots too, ninety per cent of the time it's so cold that I never really care what I look like. I just want to be warm. Comfort will always win out over fashion with me.'

'Amelia, listen to me. You know I think this course you're on is a load of horse manure.'

'I have a vague recollection of you mentioning something about that, yeah.'

'But there is one thing I can do for you. Protect you from your natural instinct, which is to dress like an Estonian air hostess.'

'Thanks very much, I'll just leave my self-esteem at the door on my way out.'

'Shut up and put this on,' she says, thrusting what I can only describe as a costume from the Moulin Rouge at me: a black, corsety-type thing with red-ribboned shoulder straps and a tight leather jacket. With, and I wish I was joking here, a matching black suede miniskirt. It flashes through my head that, in this clobber, I look like I should be fronting the TV makeover show *Pimp My Ride*.

'Are you kidding me?' I laugh incredulously, sticking my head over the saloon door of the changing room.

'What's wrong with it?'

'Let's see now, where will I start. Number one, I am not

Beyoncé Knowles and I am not performing in a live stage show in the Point Depot tonight. Number two, nor am I soliciting for business on street corners after hours. Number three, does the phrase "mutton dressed as lamb" mean anything to you?'

'Just try it on, that's all I'm asking,' Rachel cajoles, disappearing upstairs to the stock room. 'Shop's empty, no one can see you except me.' A minute later she reappears waving a bottle of Veuve Clicquot. 'And if you do, there's a glass of bubbly in it for you.'

'OK, OK,' I say reluctantly, 'but I'm only doing this cos you got me drunk. And if there's CCTV in here, you are so dead.'

Two minutes later, I emerge from the changing room, in a state of shock. Rachel's absolutely right, the outfit actually *works*. To my astonishment, I don't feel ridiculous or middle-aged or tarty. This feels sexy and funky and . . .

'WOW!' Rachel exclaims, circling around me. 'Oh my God, I am sooooo good at my job! I thought it would work well, but, baby, look at you!! Scarlett Johansson eat your heart out.'

'Oh Rach, I *love* it! I never thought I'd hear myself saying this, but you are going down as the woman who put me back into a mini for the first time in a decade. I don't care what it costs, I have to have it.'

She pours two very large glasses of champagne and hands me one. 'On the house.'

In her own way, it's almost as if she's atoning for giving me such a hard time about the course earlier. Rachel can be like that. One minute, you're a foil for all of her wisecracks and wittiness and you have to be on your toes like a bantam-weight boxer just to keep up with her; the next, she's being so overwhelmingly generous, you're left with tears in your eyes. Everyone should have a Rachel in their lives. Like I said, it's the nearest I'll ever come to sitting in the Algonquin hotel in 1920s New York, in a flapper dress and a cloche hat, smoking from a cigarette holder and drinking martinis with Dorothy Parker and her vicious circle.

'Ahh, come on, I really can't accept it as a gift, it's too much . . .'

'If you're determined to go on this collision course, at least be beautifully dressed.'

'Oh, Rachel . . .'

'I won't take no for an answer. You can call it an early birthday pressie if you want, but mark my words. If a husband is what you want and if you don't get one looking like that, you never will.'

I twirl around the changing room, high as a kite, giddy on the champagne, feeling hip and trendy and . . . there's no other word for it . . . *young*.

'Just be careful what you wish for, Amelia. That's all I'm asking.'

Chapter Five

Exes Revisited

Tracking down Greg Taylor, or 'the pig man' as Jamie has nicknamed him ('he's not quite a pig; he's not quite a man'), turns out to be an awful lot easier than I had anticipated. One big thing I have going in my favour is . . . this is Dublin. Probably the biggest village in the world. A city where, if you sneeze getting on a bus in Dalkey, by the time you get into Stephen's Green, someone will ask how your terrible dose of pneumonia is.

Everyone knows everyone. Now, this can either be a good thing or a bad thing, depending entirely on your point of view. As Rachel points out, Dublin can suddenly mushroom into a vast, sprawling metropolis if there's someone in particular you *want* to bump into, but rapidly shrinks to the size of a five-cent coin when there's someone you're trying to avoid.

OK. I need to give a bit of back story here. Greg's mother, when I knew him, was a very successful businesswoman. In the mid-1980s, when recession was rife and people were being made redundant right, left and centre, his father lost his job and had great difficulty in getting another. So his mum stepped up and launched her own, highly lucrative interior-design business, Teri Taylor Designs.

While the rest of the country was shrouded in deep economic gloom (Ireland in the mid-1980s was not a fun place to be), Teri was merrily kitting out the insides of Rolls-Royces for Arab sheikhs and doing up penthouses in five-star hotels, no expense spared. She was always appearing in glossy magazines giving advice on things like how to choose the correct lampshade colour for a north-facing sitting room, or why a peach bathroom suite with matching patterned border tiles would never, ever date. (Remember, this was at a time when the dado rail was considered the height of sophistication and people still used frilly crinoline dolls to cover up their toilet roll.)

Teri is even credited with being the person who first introduced feng shui to Ireland and at one point in the nineties ran a heavy advertising campaign offering a service whereby she'd come to your house and rearrange your furniture a bit, thereby shifting blocked energy and trans-forming your life. Or at least, that was the theory.

I can still hear Jamie sneering, 'So if I move the TV out of my southwest/relationship corner, then I'll find true love? And she'll make a fortune? So, basically, my loneliness is her conservatory.'

Come Monday morning, still nursing a roaring hangover from the previous Saturday, I arrive at my desk bright and early, coffee in hand, delighted to see that everyone else in the office has already gone over to the canteen for the cast and crew breakfast break.

A bit of privacy. Excellent. Believe you me, this is not a conversation I want anyone to overhear.

I whip out the Yellow Pages and there it is.

TERI TAYLOR DESIGNS
* MAKE YOUR HOME BEAUTIFUL
WITH OUR COMPLETE INTERIOR DESIGN SERVICE *
* BROWSE AROUND OUR EXQUISITE SHOWROOMS *
TO AVAIL OF OUR CONSULTATION SERVICE
CALL (01) 43381903/087 8677831

I pick up the phone and take a deep breath, then hang up the phone, then pick it up again, then do a quite creative visualization of me in the Vera Wang with my headless groom, then hang the phone up again.

Oh God, oh God, oh God, oh God.

Isn't there an easier way for me to find my husband? Maybe there's some internet chat room for the over thirty-fives that I don't know about? www.sadcow.com? Just then, my eye falls on a TV monitor in the corner of my office, with a live feed from the studio floor.

It's a full close-up of Cara O'Keefe with glycerine tears (an old actor's trick so you can get the wet-eyed look, minus the dribbly nose) streeling down her over-made-up face.

Cara, I should point out, is *Celtic Tigers*'s leading lady who plays the part of Glenda, a girl-next-door type of character, hugely popular with the audience, kind of our answer to Jennifer Aniston in *Friends*. But, unfortunately, life does not imitate art. In reality, she's vain, arrogant, self-obsessed and to call her a nightmare to work with would be an insult to nightmares. I'm not kidding, in interviews she describes herself as 'a diamond in the audience's dull grey lives'. You'd swear it was her job description. Her strops are terrifyingly regular and have become the stuff of legend upstairs in the production office, where the running gags among us are (*a*) that her scenes have to be shot at night so she can go back to her crypt in daylight, and (*b*) that she signs all her autographs in blood. We even have a nickname for her: 'Good Grief O'Keefe'.

'I just want to stay married to you, Sebastian,' she's saying, mouthing her lines in a way I swear she's copied directly from Julianne Moore. 'I want nothing more from this life than to be happily married to the right guy.'

It's a sign. Not a very well-acted sign, but it's a sign.

I turn the sound down on the monitor and pick up the phone again. How hard can this be? I'm a TV executive. When I was on current affairs, I used to produce shows that interviewed government ministers and asked them really difficult Jeremy Paxman-type questions. I'm not joking; we once had the Minister for Finance close to tears. Big ratings hit. OK, so I'm only deputizing on *Celtic Tigers* but I still make big important decisions about . . . oh, I dunno . . . cast coffee breaks and whether they should have digestive biscuits or Jaffa Cakes on said breaks, every day of the week.

My point is that if I can do all that, then I can make this one simple, albeit embarrassing phone call. If I'd put half the energy into finding my husband that I did into my career, I'd have been married years ago and now would probably be worrying about getting places for my kids in posh boarding schools.

Right. That's it. Decision made.

I'm poised, just about to dial, when my mobile rings.

'Hey, Amelia babes, just HAD to fess up and tell all about my close encounter of the nerd kind on Saturday.'

Jamie. Straight to the point, as always. There's never any kind of preamble on the phone with him, nothing as mundane as a 'hello' or a 'how are you', he just cuts right to the chase.

'So José Miguel asks me out for dinner after the audition and he takes me to that new fifties theme restaurant on Talbot

Street. Well, all I can say is, the Hard Rock Café has better crap.'

'Jamie, number one, I'm in work and number two, the Lovely Girls are barely speaking to you after you so callously stood us up on Saturday.'

'Oh dear, I was hoping the bitch fest would be over by now.'

I smile in spite of myself. It's impossible to stay mad at Jamie for very long; he just uses charm and humour to get around me. With one hundred per cent success every time.

'So we're sitting in this car crash of a restaurant eating chunky chips and cremated burgers and José Miguel says' – at this point he launches into a very passable impression of Manuel from *Fawlty Towers* – '"If I cast you, you must have *passion,* real *passion.*" So I say, "I *do*! I do have passion. I have passion for the play, I have passion for the part," and I'm about to say, I could very easily be persuaded into having passion for you, when he says, "No, no, you no understand. You must have *passion* with my English." Geddit?'

'Passion, passion . . .' I reply absently. 'Oh, he meant *patience.*'

I can almost hear the sound of Jamie's eyes rolling. 'You're like quicksilver. If I ever get on *Who Wants to be a Millionaire?* will you be my phone-a-friend?'

'So did you get the part?'

'Won't know till later today. I'll call you the minute. I think he fancies me though. Well, could you blame him? He's only human.'

'OK. You need to get off the phone now, honey. I'm about to call Teri Taylor and you're eroding my resolve.'

'Oh my Gowwwwd! And what'll you say if she answers the phone? Hi, remember me? Your son was my first boyfriend all of twenty years ago and I'm trying to track him down so I can figure out where I'm going wrong with all my exes. Be sure and tell her you're sane, won't you? She could so easily get the wrong idea.'

'I know, I know,' I reply, nervously doodling on the Yellow Pages in front of me. A bridal veil/headless groom doodle . . . 'I'm well aware of how it sounds, but if I don't do it now, I never will. Anyway, what's the worst that can happen? It's not like I'm ever going to see these people again.'

'Any idea of what Greg did after college?'

'Well, I did bump into Teri in the supermarket, years and years ago, and she said he'd gone to the States. Apparently he was working as the night manager of some flashy, posh hotel.'

'Nightwatchman, more like. So what will you do if he's still abroad?'

'I don't know. I'll think of something.'

'Have you really thought this through?'

'Yes. I mean no. I mean . . . Well, I don't have to meet up with him. I could just talk to him on the phone, couldn't I? Probably a lot easier too. Less embarrassing.'

'Honey, I've had rectal examinations that were less embarrassing than what you're about to do.'

'Well, I don't expect to come out of this smelling like guest-room soap, but it's worth a try.'

'So there's nothing I can do to talk you out of this?'

'No.'

'Great, because, if I'm honest, there's nothing I want to do. It's such fun being in the same century as you.'

'Hang up, I'll call you straight back.'

Jamie's right, of course. It has, after all, been over twenty years. Greg Taylor could be in any part of the world, doing anything for all I know. He was always smart and ambitious when I knew him; when he left school, he was voted 'Person most likely to do anything'. Happy, successful and married with a large family by now, most likely.

Come on, I tell myself sternly. Concentrate, regroup. What's my end goal? *A husband by the end of the year* . . . Yes, it's a tall order on the universe, I know, but if this is what it's going to take . . .

I pick up the phone and dial.

'Good morning, Teri Taylor Design Consultants, how may I direct your call?' A woman's voice, bright and chirpy.

'Hi, I wonder if you can help me. I'd like to speak to Mrs Taylor please.' *Keep it cool and businesslike*, I tell myself. *Try not to sound like a mumbling stroke victim* . . .

'Oh, I'm very sorry,' says the woman, sounding like she really means it, 'but Teri has retired. She does come into the showrooms to see us occasionally, but doesn't actually work here any more. Can anyone else on our design team be of any help to you?'

'Well, it's kind of personal really. Do you have an address where I can contact her?'

'You're very welcome to contact her care of this address. I'll make sure she gets it. Is she a friend of yours?'

What the hell, I figure; I've absolutely nothing to lose by being honest. 'Actually, it's her son Greg that I'm trying to contact. We've known each other since our school days.'

'And you're organizing a class reunion, are you?'

Brilliant! Why didn't I think of that? 'Yes, it's a kind of reunion. Of sorts. I don't suppose by any chance you know what corner of the globe he's in, do you?'

'Should be in Raheny by now.'

'What did you say?' In all my imagined scenarios of where Greg Taylor could possibly be living and working now, Raheny didn't figure at all.

'Yes, he's driving our delivery van and he had some curtains to drop off for a client there. He should be back in the office very shortly, though. Can I get him to contact you?'

Chapter Six

The Man Who Speaks Amelia

Great embarrassing places of our time where your mobile can go off.

1. While in a public loo.
2. While driving the car with a motorbike cop right beside you.
3. While in the middle of a crisis meeting with the head of television to discuss the sharply falling ratings on *Celtic Tigers* and, even more worryingly, the consequential drop in advertising revenue.

'The Axeman cometh,' Dave Bruton whispers to me as we all file into the television centre's very scary-looking boardroom for a last-minute emergency summit meeting. All the department heads have been hastily summoned; everyone's just had to drop everything. And by everyone, I really mean everyone. Scripting, design, wardrobe, make-up: they're all sitting round the table, with the same bewildered look of 'what's about to happen?'

The meeting is chaired by one Philip Burke, the head

of television, a man so important he's actually my boss's boss.

I've never met him before, although I know him by reputation as someone tough and uncompromising, slightly to the right of Attila the Hun. He's young to be doing such a huge job, no more than late thirties I'm guessing, slightly grey around the temples and with that washed-out, exhausted look all television executives seem to develop after a couple of years at the top. He's not handsome, he's not ugly, he's somewhere in between . . . Pugly. If he was played by a Hollywood actor it would have to be . . . Sean Penn.

I also note with interest that he's single.

It's almost like a reflex action with me now. Whenever I meet any semi-attractive man, my eye will instantly fall to the ring finger of their left hand to clock whether or not there's a wedding band. Which, in this case, there isn't. Well, can you blame a girl for keeping her options open?

He shoots straight from the hip. 'OK, people. Bad news and worse news. Which do you want first?'

There's a long silence. After all, there's direct and then there's stealth-missile direct. Eventually someone pipes up, 'Let's get the bad news out of the way, then.'

Philip Burke picks up a computer printout ratings sheet. 'The episode of *Celtic Tigers* broadcast last Saturday night attracted a viewership of fewer than four hundred thousand; that's an overall drop of *thirty per cent* on last month's Nielsen ratings. Not to put too fine a point on it, this trend is not good enough and can't be allowed to continue. Any ideas why this is happening?'

Sharon Quinn, head of marketing, pipes up. 'Well, Philip, we've recently experienced a lot of fundamental shifts in our audience demographic—'

'Coupled with the overall crappiness of the show, you mean,' he cuts right across her.

More surprised looks. We're not really used to straight talkers round here.

'I'm sorry,' he goes on, not raising his voice and being all the more effective for it, 'but aside from the Angelus and reruns of *The Little House on the Prairie*, this is now our lowest-rated programme. Did any of you people actually bother to watch Saturday night's transmission? One character comes out of a coma and half an hour later is engaged to his ex-wife's identical twin sister? Have you people lost all grip on reality?'

God, he's *really* scary . . .

'Excuse me, Philip,' Sharon retorts defensively. 'I agree with you that some of the plotlines are a tad far-fetched, but surely you accept that that's a conceit of soap opera? It's probably the only medium where characters can walk out of showers and we can claim the last few years have all been one big dream. All drama is about suspension of disbelief.'

'Not a good enough argument,' says Philip. 'Which one of you is Amelia Lockwood?'

I gingerly put my hand up.

'Oh, there you are, hi,' he says, as if he hadn't really noticed me before. 'OK, I know you're only babysitting the show till Jayne Lawler gets back, but as deputy producer, what are your thoughts?'

He's looking at me the way a scientist looks down a microscope and it flashes through my mind that he'd be a terrific boss on one of those reality TV shows like *The Apprentice*. A bit like Donald Trump, I'm half expecting him to swivel around in his leather chair and say, 'You're fired.'

I have to tread very carefully here because (*a*) I'm the new girl on the block; (*b*) the storylines have been in place for at least six months before I was drafted in, so in a way, I inherited all the I am-your-long-lost-twin-sister stuff which is being aired at the moment; and most importantly of all, (*c*) I actually find myself agreeing with Philip Burke. What he *doesn't* know is that there's even worse to come. Only last night I was reading ahead on next month's shooting scripts and found myself wincing at yet another outlandishly far-fetched plotline, this time involving one character who's convinced he's seen a UFO driving through the fog one night, but it turns out to be the lights from a late-night Multiplex cinema.

I roared laughing when I read it. For all the wrong reasons. 'OK, Philip,' I say tentatively, 'what I suggest is that we go right back to first principles. Entertain people. I think this show should be dramatic without being ludicrous, funny without being a sitcom and, well, you know . . . more . . . accessible to viewers.'

They're all looking at me. Yes, all of them. And not only has every head at the table turned my way, but there's also total silence. After all, I haven't been on the show that long; they're probably thinking, quite rightly: Who is yer one?

'Go on,' says Philip impassively.

I have two choices here. Plan A: I do what I'm supposed to do as a deputy producer, which is keep my eyes open and my head down, make sure the show ticks along without going over budget and try to prevent Good Grief O'Keefe from driving us all nutty in the meantime. Oh . . . and do my best not to drunkenly snog any more of the cast at wrap parties.

Hopefully, with a bit of luck, I'll be transferred back to my old stomping ground, the newsroom, before too long and I can go back to devising new ways of making ministers sweat.

Plan B: I actually *do* something. Yes, I'm only deputizing

on the show, but I do have one or two ideas. We used to do this on current affairs all the time: sit around a table and brainstorm. I'm well used to this, I can do it. And besides, it's something I've given a lot of thought to since I was first drafted on to *Celtic Tigers*. There's absolutely nothing to lose.

Well, except my job.

Right, time to explain myself a bit better.

'OK, if it were up to me, here's what I'd do. Firstly, I would introduce far more realistic storylines. Make *Celtic Tigers* less like a daytime show and more like a drama series. Remember *Eldorado* on BBC?'

A lot of nodding around the table.

'The reason it flopped was because viewers didn't want to come home from a hard day's work and watch characters living the high life in sunny Marbella. Rule one of television is know your audience. We have to reflect what's happening in society *now*. A successful drama is part soap, part serious drama and part sitcom. This show needs to straddle all three or we'll never get anywhere. And actors who could actually act would help.' I can't believe I actually said that out loud, but what the hell. I'm on a roll now. 'Honestly, that last plotline about the three vicious ex-drug dealers taking over the pub and then holding half the cast hostage? They were so brutal, they might as well have been called Snap, Crackle and Pop. I've seen head lice on my six-year-old goddaughter that were more threatening.'

There's a few titters and I'm aware that all eyes are still focused on me.

'I have to say, I think you're right,' says Dave Bruton. I smile at him, delighted he's backing me up. 'Personally, I thought that story wouldn't have looked out of place in a Coen brothers' movie.'

There's some ice-breaking laughter now, although Sharon

from marketing is looking at me with the blank expression of early man being told the meaning of fire.

'Good, good,' says Philip approvingly. 'What else?'

'Well, there's one tried and tested formula, proven to boost ratings,' I answer.

'And that is?' Philip is addressing the room, but looking at me.

'The death of a major character.'

Silence.

Then my mobile rings, loud and clear. That really irritating 'crazy frog' ring tone, which I only put on it to amuse Emma, Caroline's eldest.

'Sorry about that,' I say, blushing to my roots and snapping the phone off. 'I'll personally be torching whoever that was as soon as the meeting's over.'

More nervous titters, which Philip barrels over. 'So, pitch it to me in one line.'

'Less daytime, more primetime.'

'OK, Amelia Lockwood, here's the deal. The bad news is, I want you to stay on the show and I'm giving you exactly six months to get a result. And just so you're clear, by a result, I mean a steady viewership of one million. Otherwise, here's the worse news, folks, *Celtic Tigers* is history.'

Winston Churchill once observed acutely that a lie gets halfway around the world before the truth even has a chance to get out of bed and put its trousers on. And thus it is after the meeting. No sooner have I gone back to the production office than the rumour mill has gone into overdrive.

'Good Grief O'Keefe is for the chop. One hundred per cent, definite,' I can hear being hissed around the office, almost like Chinese whispers.

'Oh my God! Without television, she's nothing.'

'Not true. She's the drinking man's crumpet.'

'Serves her right. This is a woman who, when she's filling
out forms, under "Occupation" puts "Household Name".
Nothing like a good, long spell of unemployment to put
manners on her.'

I just smile, say nothing and head for my desk. That's one
fire I can pee on later, as Jamie would say. I take a deep
breath, slump down into my chair and frantically try to
regroup.

Six months to turn the show around.

Six months.

OK, this isn't so bad. Yes, I had hoped to get back to the
newsroom sooner, but that's not going to happen so I might
as well make the best of this and get on with it – with a good
attitude.

After all, what's the worst that can happen?

I could change the whole format of the show and it could
be a disaster and I could end up getting fired.

Shit.

No, I have to stay positive. If Philip Burke has confidence
in me then . . . then . . . Then I remember.

My mobile rang in the middle of the meeting. I fish it out
from the bottom of my overstuffed handbag and play back
the messages.

'Hi, Amelia, long time no hear. It's a blast from the past
here, Greg Taylor. The receptionist gave me your number
and said you'd called looking for me. Something about a
reunion?'

Oh dear God.

Ten minutes ago, I successfully persuaded the head of
television to grant *Celtic Tigers* a stay of execution, and now
the very sound of Greg Taylor's voice is turning my insides
to the consistency of a mushy pea.

It's OK, my rational inner voice says, *you don't have to return the call. It's never too late to run away and start a new life in the Outer Hebrides. No one will ever know just how insane I've been.*

Just then, Dave saunters over. 'Hey, Amelia, is this a bad time to talk?'

I bury the mobile phone under a mound of unsigned contracts and try my best to look busy and important. 'No, go ahead, Dave.'

'Just wanted to congratulate you. That was some performance you gave in there. Only for you, the Axeman would have had us all on our merry way to the dole queue by now. You were great, you know, you were really on the same wavelength as him. And I think your suggestions for the show are terrific. If I had to direct one more episode where a character says, "I love you Cherie, but ever since my sex-change, I love myself more," I'd have screamed.'

'Thanks, Dave, I appreciate it. You know, I don't want the show to turn into one where the most dramatic thing that happens is that someone buys a tin of Heinz beans, but I do think a little realism will go a long way.'

He whistles. 'Boy, do you have your work cut out for you, though. A million viewers in six months? Some target. Some deadline.'

'We can do it. We have a terrific team here. But there will have to be a fair few changes.' *Did that sound confident enough?*

'Well, you go, girl. If anyone can do it, you can.'

I smile up at him, really touched.

'I know the next few months will be tough on you, Amelia, but we're all behind you.'

'Thanks, Dave.'

'And you know the one really great thing you have going for you?'

'What's that?'

'You're single.'

'*Excuse me?*'

'Well, what I mean is, you're not like the rest of us. You can put in all the long hours and the working weekends. You have no ties or commitments. It's not like you're rushing home to a husband and family every night.'

I wait until he's out of the office before I pick up the phone and dial.

Chapter Seven

Of all the Gin Joints in all the Towns in all the World . . .

'Now, the minute you get in there, you're to order a large vodka and tonic and knock it right back.'

'Oh yeah, sure. That's what you want? My inhibitions lowered?'

I'm sitting in the car park of the Cabin theme pub/restaurant, on the phone to Jamie. To my utter astonishment, Greg has suggested we meet here for a drink this very evening, except now I can barely pluck up the courage physically to leave the safety of my car and go inside.

It's an odd place for him to have suggested. A bit dingy and, well, out of the way. The Greg I remember from twenty years ago would have gone for somewhere hip and trendy in town, the kind of place that has cool jazz music playing in the background and is filled with beautiful, thin people all wearing black and talking about obscure writers and beatnik poets I never even heard of.

This kind of feels like I'm about to meet George Clooney in a Taco Bell.

'Honey, switch the engine on and get the hell out of there.

This is not just any old date you're about to go on, it's the kamikaze of dates.'

'He was very friendly on the phone,' I say, trying to convince myself as much as Jamie. 'You know, sounded genuinely pleased to hear from me. And he was the one who wanted to meet up. Sooner rather than later, he said. Those are his words, not mine.'

OK, I'm playing for time now . . . a bit.

Well, a lot. Anything to postpone actually getting out of the car.

'It's sweet that he said that and sweet that you believe him.'

'I just can't believe he's driving the delivery van for his mother, can you? I thought he'd be running a whole chain of hotels by now, with one hand tied behind his back.'

'Well, maybe he got thrown out on his arse. Or, as he'd say, his elbow.'

'Ha ha, very funny. Greg was my first love, I'll have you know. There were some wonderful things about him.'

'Yes, the cheating particularly springs to mind. So what are you going to say to him when you get in there? Or have you learned nothing from your one-hour class?'

'Something will come to me. I'm good at talking shite. I work in television.'

'Right. Then go to it, girl. Get it over with. As I always say, if you're going to fail, you might as well fail gloriously.'

'OK, here goes nothing,' I say, giving my lipstick the final once-over before getting out of the car. 'If things go badly wrong, know that my last thoughts were of you . . .'

'Oh, that's so sweet!'

'Let me finish. Of you . . . blinding and torturing him if he turns out to be a complete arsehole.'

My apprehensions turn out to be quite well founded. The Cabin is dark, almost empty, with cheesy, nautically themed tat covering the walls: fishing nets and photocopies of the last menu served on the *Titanic*; that kind of crap. The music playing is awful too; the kind of stuff soccer hooligans listen to whenever they're feeling philosophical.

There are two middle-aged, overweight guys propping up the bar, nursing pints of Guinness as I walk past. Thankfully, they're both too engrossed in an Arsenal versus Manchester United soccer match that's on TV even to notice me. Still, though, I'm seriously beginning to regret my choice of outfit. The fab suede miniskirt and tight, low-cut jacket Rachel gave me just seem to be sending out the wrong signal in a place like this. I park myself at a table in a booth, under a galley-style oil lamp, so at least Greg will be able to spot me through the gloom when he gets here.

If he gets here.

The barman follows me over and asks what I'm having.

'White wine spritzer, thanks,' I say, by now really starting to feel self-conscious. I've always had a pet hate of meeting anyone in a pub when I'm on my own, but tonight's even worse. There's something about this place that makes me feel very much like a woman in her late thirties on the pull.

Ick.

I keep darting furtive glances over to the door, but still no sign. Nervously, I check my watch again. And again. And again.

Eight-twelve. Eight-fifteen.

OK, I figure, I'll give him till eight-thirty and then leave with my head held high. After all, apart from the two fatsos at the bar, there's no one else to witness my humiliation at being so unceremoniously stood up. Even desperadoes like me have to draw the line somewhere.

And then the unthinkable happens.

As the soccer match ends, fat balding guy number one

picks up his newspaper and saunters over to the men's toilets, which has a sign above it that says 'Sailors'. Fat guy number two also peels the bar stool from underneath him, stretches, spots me for the first time, then casually ambles over to where I'm nervously waiting.

Oh, sweet baby Jesus and the orphans, am I seeing things?

'Well, well, well, Amelia Lockwood. Look at you.'

My jaw almost falls to the floor. It's him. Greg Taylor. Except instead of the clean-cut, preppy, good-looking guy I knew, there's a 1980s snooker player standing in front of me. Red-faced and boozy, wearing jeans that are clearly a size too small and a T-shirt that only a nineteen-year-old with the physique of a US marine could carry off. *Even Mickey Rourke didn't age this badly!*

Eventually, I manage to close my jaw and get a sentence out. 'Greg. I honestly wouldn't have known you.'

'You look good,' he says, sitting in beside me, a little too close for comfort. He's wearing too much aftershave and it's kind of pongy.

The barman comes back with my spritzer and Greg orders a fresh pint of Guinness. 'I'm really glad to see you, Amelia. We've so much to catch up on. Don't you have some high-flying TV job now?'

'Ehh . . . well, I'm a producer.'

'On *Celtic Tigers*, right?'

'That's right, yeah.'

'Wow, big job.'

'It's not really,' I say, downplaying it. 'It's more like seven hundred small jobs. I can't believe you watch it.'

'Are you kidding? My ex-wife is your number one fan. She loves it. Last time I was leaving the kids over at her house, she had it on and I saw your name coming up on the credits. Fair play to you. Always knew you'd do well.'

'You're divorced then?'

'Separated.'

'Sorry to hear that.'

He sighs deeply and I really do feel sympathy for him. 'Yeah, well, these things happen.'

'And you're working for your mum's company now?'

'Got a family to support.'

'Oh? How many kids do you have?'

'Two, and one on the way.'

'Your ex-wife is pregnant?'

'No, my girlfriend is. Due in April.'

I take a sip of my drink, not really sure what to make of all this. He certainly hasn't been letting the grass grow under his feet, that's for sure.

'So, how long were you married for?' I ask, hoping I don't sound come across like Larry King interviewing someone. I can't help it; I'm just dying to know.

'Pretty much until my wife found out I had a girlfriend.'

He's sniggering now and I can't believe it. It's almost as if he thinks this is something to brag about, that he's some kind of super-stud. I'm saved from having to answer by the barman who comes back with Greg's pint.

'Good man, Tommy,' he says, taking the drink. The barman stands waiting to be paid as Greg turns to me. 'Would you mind getting this one? Thanks, I'm just a bit short.'

Flabbergasted, I pay for both drinks and wonder how quickly I can get the hell out of there.

Wait up, says my inner voice sternly, *you still haven't found out what you did wrong with him yet . . . Ten more minutes. You can do ten more minutes. That's all it'll take.*

I take another sip of wine and we chit-chat for a bit. Small talk mostly. Greg hasn't kept in contact with anyone from college and is astonished to hear that Caroline, Rachel and Jamie are still my best friends.

'And how are your parents?' he asks.

'Great, thanks. Dad's retired and he and Mum are living most of the year in Spain now. Just outside Alicante. They love it down there.'

'Well for you. At least when you go to visit them, you can get a suntan while you're at it.'

'Well, I hadn't quite thought of it like that, but . . . emm, yeah, I suppose so.'

After another few minutes of catching up, I decide to seize the bull by the horns. I don't want him to think that I'm looking to rekindle any kind of friendship; I just want to leave – and the sooner the better. I don't think I've ever felt so uncomfortable in my whole life and, God knows, that's really saying something.

'So, Greg, please don't think I'm being nosey, but I have to ask. You really had a girlfriend while you were married?'

He doesn't even have the good grace to look hangdog about it. 'For about two years, yeah.'

'*Two years?*'

'But – I know you'll understand, Amelia, because you've known me for so long – I think deep down I really wanted to be caught, you know what I mean?'

'No, Greg, I honestly don't.'

'I could handle having a wife; I could handle having a mistress at the same time. What I couldn't handle were the two dinners.'

I almost splurt out my drink. But there's worse to come. Before I've recovered myself, his hand is on my knee, all hot and clammy. *Oh dear God, is he making a move on me?*

'Really is great to see you again, Amelia. I was delighted

you tracked me down. I've thought about you a lot over the years, you know. So, tell me, do you have a boyfriend?'

Shit! The dreaded question. OK, time for damage limitation. 'Emm, well, no, I'm not actually seeing anyone right now – at the moment, I mean. I just got out of something long-term and . . . you see . . .' I'm trying my best so make it sound like I'm single out of choice and that there're loads of guys chasing after me and I'm failing miserably.

'You're on your own, so. Interesting. Did I tell you how well you're looking?'

'Greg,' I say, moving away and trying to sound cool, 'I think you might have got the wrong idea here . . .'

'Doesn't look like it to me,' he answers, grabbing my hand now. I try to pull away but he's having none of it. 'But don't worry, Amelia. Just because I'm technically involved with someone else, that's not any kind of problem, is it?'

'You don't understand . . .' I'm trying to keep the rising panic out of my voice.

'Oh, come on. You contact me again after all these years, agree to meet me, then walk in here all alone and looking hot and sexy? Bet you're living in some fantastic penthouse apartment now, with big leather couches and satin sheets on the bed . . . Why don't we go back to your place and take this a bit further?'

Chapter Eight

'Remind Me Again Why I Need a Man'

It's hard to believe that a week has passed and yet here I am, sitting in the front row of tutorial room 201, in full flow, virtually *ranting* at poor Ira Vandergelder about my experiences of the previous night.

'All I can say is, meeting my ex-boyfriend constituted one hour out of my life I'll never get back.'

The class titter.

'So what exactly happened?'

'OK, the nicest thing that happened all evening was that he covered his mouth when burping. This man has an ex-wife, a girlfriend – who by the way is pregnant, just for added entertainment value – and then he made a move on me. He had completely got the wrong idea as to why I'd contacted him and thought, in his own warped head, that because I was still single, therefore I was fair game. Can you believe the *arrogance*?'

'You wanna feel sorry for yourself or do you wanna get married?' says Ira.

I'd almost forgotten about the New York, take-no-prisoners directness. I can't answer her though; I'm too distracted by the rest of the class looking at me like I'm a few coupons short of a special offer.

'How old were you when you started dating him?' Ira ploughs on with the interrogation.

'Sixteen.'

'So, tell the class what it's taken you the guts of twenty years to learn.'

I pause for a minute and take a deep, calming breath. There comes a point when you've been so humiliated in front of a room full of complete strangers that you don't care any more. It can hardly get worse. 'My first boyfriend was a cheater when I knew him and he's still a cheater now. I suppose I've learned that people don't change.'

'There's something even more obvious than that.'

'What?' I'm genuinely stumped.

'We need to work on your screening process. Sounds to me, Amelia, as if you do not choose good men for yourself. Look at you, so pretty. You seem like a lovely person too, so what you need to ask yourself is this: Why would any man *not* want to be married to me? May I ask why you broke up with your most recent boyfriend?'

'The oldest story in the book. He said he loved me but couldn't commit to me.'

'Bullshit,' says Ira, rolling her eyes to heaven, as if she's heard this a thousand times before. 'When a man uses that "I'm commitment-phobic" line, let me translate it for you. It means he just doesn't want to commit to *you*. You are gonna learn to select better potential husbands, Amelia. Remember, you are not looking for a boyfriend; you are auditioning for a marriage partner. OK. Next.'

She moves on to the woman next to me and I find myself smarting, as I always do, at the very mention of *He-whose-name-shall-forever-remain-unspoken*. When we broke up, or, more correctly, when he finally had the guts to dump me, he'd said that it wasn't me, it was him. It wasn't that he didn't want to be with me any more, he didn't want to be with *anyone* and blah, blah, blah.

What Ira is saying makes a lot of sense. Maybe there's nothing fundamentally wrong with me, maybe I just make appalling choices . . . and have been doing so for over twenty years. It's an empowering thought and it cheers me up no end.

As the class goes on and everyone is vying to tell their stories, I'm almost starting to feel like I got off easily last night. Some of the other women's experiences would turn milk sour.

Swotty, red-haired girl (who I've since discovered is called Mags) tracked down her first proper boyfriend, who had a nice, sensible job in the civil service, only to discover that he was now driving a taxi around North Dublin and was happily married to a mail-order Russian who he'd bought over the internet.

'I was kind of half hoping it would be so romantic and that he'd tell me, after all these years, that he'd never stopped loving me,' she says, sniffing. 'But the truth is, he never started loving me in the first place. He couldn't even remember my name.'

At this point, I start to feel really sorry for poor Mags. Compared with that, my story is like something from a Disney cartoon.

The woman beside her found out her first ex-boyfriend is now in prison, doing ten years for drug-trafficking. 'And you know, it's funny,' she tells the stunned classroom, 'but whenever I'd go out on a date with him, there was always money missing from my bag.'

But the Olympic gold medal goes to this lovely-looking

woman at the back of the class who tearfully tells us she got in touch with her ex's family and asked how she could contact him. She said the hostility she met with was so forceful that she had to ask if she'd caused offence in any way just by looking for his contact number. It turned out he'd died in a car accident about five years ago, and no one had thought to tell her.

Ira patiently listens to each and every story and passes out good, rock-solid advice, mostly ending with her mantra: 'Good work. Now learn and move on.' Eventually she takes her position at the front of the class. 'OK, ladies, listen up,' she says, hands on hips. 'You have two assignments for next week. One is, you will get in touch with your second ex-boyfriend and find out what the hell went wrong there. Secondly, you will contact all of your married friends and ask for fix-ups.'

'Why married friends?' asks Mags.

'Because I want each of you ladies to change your reference group to reflect your desired status. You all wanna be married, right?'

There's nodding and murmurs of assent.

'And you're prepared to do *anything* to achieve that goal, right?'

More nodding and murmuring, although the way she emphasized the word 'anything' sends an alarm bell ringing in my head.

'Then you need to realize that your single friends, by and large, will want you to remain single. That way they'll have someone to talk to on the phone late at night and bitch about men while eating two-day-old cold pizza slices.'

I baulk a bit at this and have a brief mental picture of Rachel clocking her one, just for the cold-pizza remark alone.

But Ira ploughs on, 'Whereas your married friends tend to want you to be married too. That way they can go out in foursomes and have another couple to talk to when they've run out of things to say to each other.'

Bit of an unfair generalization, I think . . . but could she possibly be right about single people? Do they really want you to stay single?

'So, ladies, contact as many of your married friends as you can and ask them straight out. Tell them this is your year to get married and that you wanna be fixed up. Be *brave*. Remember you have nothing to lose. Their husbands must have single work colleagues, golf partners, football team-mates, whatever, and all you're asking your friend is to set you up on a date with one of them.'

'Ugh, I'd hate to go on a blind date,' says someone from the back.

'Then leave my class,' says Ira coolly. 'You are clearly not committed to finding a spouse. Of *course* it's a blind date. What is internet dating except blind dating with a fancy new name?'

Soon, too soon for my liking, it's nine o'clock and class is over.

'Go get results!' Ira calls out as everyone packs up and files out past her. I'm almost at the door when she calls me back. 'Amelia?'

'Yes?'

'A quick word. What I just said about getting your married friends to set you up with someone? That particularly applies to you.'

'How do you mean?'

'Seems to me like you make a lot of bad choices, honey. So, work the problem. See if one of your good friends can pick a better man for you, on your behalf.'

'Thanks.' I smile back at her. 'I'll certainly give it a shot.'

'Hope I wasn't too hard on you earlier.'

'No, not at all. In fact, you really lifted my spirits. I think you're right. I am lousy at choosing men. And I've also had a lot of very bad luck.'

'The thing to remember about bad luck,' Ira replies sagely, 'is that it always runs out.'

I get a clear, unequivocal sign later that night. I'm tucked up in bed, wading through some scene breakdowns I need to be on top of for a story meeting I've scheduled for first thing the following morning, when tiredness eventually gets the better of me. I switch on the TV by my bed and snuggle down to sleep. (Ask any single person: we all have little, idiosyncratic things we have to do to fill the void; mine just happens to be that I can't go to sleep without the TV on.)

The late night movie is on. *Top Gun*. The scene where Tom Cruise takes Kelly McGillis zooming off into the sunset on the back of his motorbike, as Berlin sing 'Take My Breath Away'. It triggers another memory, but this time for different reasons . . .

THE TIME: 13 February 1986. (I only remember the date so clearly because it was Valentine's Eve. Read on, you'll see why.)

THE PLACE: Blazes wine bar in Temple Bar before any of us knew it was Temple Bar. We just thought it a load of seedy side streets off the quays.

THE OCCASION: Jamie's newly formed band are making their highly anticipated debut. The Lovely Girls are, naturally, out in our finery to support him.

'Why are the band called Emergency Exit?' asks Rachel.

'So that their name will always be in lights,' I answer,

filling our glasses with the cheapest wine I could find, which is all we can afford.

'Ughhh!' says Caroline, spitting it out. 'Tastes like cat pee.'

'Oh, that is truly revolting,' says Rachel, spewing hers out too. 'In future, Amelia, you need to remember that wine should always cost more than milk.'

Blazes is packed with the UCD crowd, most of whom Jamie and his lead guitarist Pete Mooney have bullied into being there. They're both on stage (well, not really a stage, a big rostrum more like) tuning up, which involves Jamie screeching 'Two, two, two, one, two' into a mike at a decibel level that would shatter glass.

'I'd swear Jamie's wearing make-up, you know,' I say, squinting at him from where we're parked at a table on the far side of the stage.

'Yeah, I did it for him earlier,' says Rachel. 'He's going for a Boy George look, right down to the plaits. The Alison Moyet hat is mine too. Do you like it?'

'Alison Moyet? Crocodile Dundee, more like.'

'Oh, look, there's Celine, over by the bar,' says Caroline.

Celine is Jamie's girlfriend of about three weeks; an Annie Lennox lookalike, full-time English student, part-time rock chick.

'Will we invite her to join us?'

'No,' Rachel snaps. 'She should be Celine and not heard.'

'What's wrong with her?' asks Caroline. 'She seems really sweet and lovely.'

'So by that you mean thick.'

'Come on, Rachel,' I say, 'we should make an effort. She is Jamie's girlfriend.'

'Big deal, Jamie has a girlfriend. I have a pimple, but you don't hear me going on about it.'

91

'But they've been together for a few weeks now. That's quite serious, for our Jamie.'

'Oh, please, I have lumps of cheese in my fridge I've had longer relationships with.'

'Rachel,' I ask as gently as I can, 'what is up with you?' We're all used to her being brittle and caustic, but quite not to this extent.

'Nothing. I just happen to think the girl is a complete tea cloth. In fact, there are probably tea cloths out there with higher IQs than hers.'

Next thing, two really handsome preppy-looking guys saunter over to our table. 'Yes, before you ask, those seats *are* taken,' says Rachel, whose bad humour knew no bounds that evening. 'We're with the band.'

'Wish I could have said that,' I groan. 'I've waited my whole life just to be able to say, "We're with the band."'

'Didn't mean to interrupt,' says the taller one politely. 'I just wanted to ask your friend something.' He nods over to where Caroline is splurting out another gulp of the rancid wine.

'Sorry,' she says, looking up at them and giggling prettily.

'It's just that my friend here thinks you're the image of Selina Scott,' says the slightly cuter one of the two. 'That's before she started doing breakfast television and got all wrecked-looking. But I think you look really like Daryl Hannah in *Splash*. Except your hair's a bit shorter. We just wondered if you got asked this a lot.'

'Ignore them, they're pissed,' says Rachel.

Just then Emergency Exit launches into their first number, 'You're Nancy to my Ronald, you're Raisa to my Gorbachev, if I'm Scargill then you're Thatcher.'

Caroline doesn't ignore them though. By the time Jamie's band have shut up (about seven minutes later, Emergency

Exit's repertoire consists of only three songs), she is deep in conversation with the cuter one, who she blushingly introduces to us between songs as Mike, a third-year dentistry student at Trinity College.

Next thing, the torture's over and Jamie bounds over to us, demanding congratulations.

'Well done,' we all chorus. 'You were fab!'

Celine's over like a shot too, almost elbowing us out of her way to get to Jamie. 'Darling! Marvellous was not the word,' she says in her gravelly, sixty-fags-a-day voice.

'So you liked it, babe?' says Jamie, hugging her.

'I heard your music,' she says, deadly serious, 'and I was jealous. That's the best compliment I can give you.'

Rachel shoots me a significant I-told-you-to-watch-out-for-that-stupid-cow look and, for a moment, I feel maybe she's right. I shrug it off though, figuring: I'm sure Yoko Ono had to put up with this from Paul, George and Ringo all the time.

'I think Pete likes you,' Jamie says to me later on, once he's relaxed and happy with a Malibu and pineapple in his hand and Celine perched on his knee.

'Who's Pete?'

'Lead guitarist. Well, only guitarist. He wanted to know who your musical influences are. I told him Kraftwerk and Talking Heads. Could you imagine if he found out the horrible truth?'

'What horrible truth?'

'That you secretly like Sister Sledge and Bananarama. And you even have a Billy Joel LP lying around your house. No use to keep pretending it's your mother's, I have you sussed.'

Celine laughs, a bit cruelly I think, and I'm all set to defend myself when Pete himself joins us. 'Introduce me to him, quick,' I hiss at Jamie. 'I only have about an hour before my hair starts flattening.'

'Yeah,' says Jamie, clocking that at least three and a half cans of hairspray and mousse must have gone into my painstakingly backcombed hair that night. 'Take that, ozone layer.'

We all shake hands with Pete and offer congratulations, then he settles on a bar stool between Caroline, Mike and me. He's very cool-looking, beanpole tall and skeletally thin with hollow, sucked-in cheeks, kind of like Nick Cave's. He's head-to-toe in black and wearing heavy eye make-up too. Very New Order.

'So did you enjoy the gig?' he asks me.

'Yeah! You were *fantastic*!' I lie. (Well, it's been a long time since any guy cared about my musical influences. What can I say? I'm flattered.) 'You remind me of U2 when they first started out.'

'Don't mention those bastards. Adam Clayton stole one of my songs, you know.'

'What? Which one?'

'Sure, they only have two decent songs. "Pride in the Name of Love".'

'You wrote that?'

'Well, not exactly. I wrote a song called "I'm So Proud That You Love Me". But my brother was in the same class as Clayton and I'm telling you, he stole it. One minute, me and Jamie are jamming it in my dad's garage; next thing, before I even have a chance to record it on my double tape deck, U2 are on *Top of the Pops* singing it. Almost the same tune and everything. Bastards.'

'That's terrible.'

'That's the music business. What did you think of "Poison Yuppie"?'

I look at him blankly.

'The last song we sang? With me on lead vocals?'

'Oh, sorry, it was . . . emm . . . really, *really* great.'

'I wrote that.'

'You did? Wow.' I try to look suitably impressed.

'Yeah, when my ex-girlfriend left me for a guy with red braces and a filofax.'

We chat on for a bit, mostly – well, all about him, and eventually he says, 'Do you want to go and see Talking Heads?'

'Are they coming to Dublin? Do you have tickets?'

'No, I meant the film they're in, *Stop Making Sense*. It's on at the Ambassador.'

Just then, Caroline interrupts us. By now, I notice, she and Mike are holding hands. 'Are you both talking about going to a movie?' she asks. 'Because Mike's just asked me to see *Top Gun* with him tomorrow night. There's a special Valentine's night showing. Why don't we all go as a foursome?'

'Why not a sixsome?' says Jamie, arms tight around Celine.

It's only at this point I notice that Rachel has left.

Chapter Nine

The Set-up

'And please don't think I'm in any position to be picky. Just as long as they can stand erect and use a knife and fork, they're in with a chance. I'm completely inoculated from having any great expectations when it comes to men.'

I'm sitting in Caroline's elegantly appointed drawing room, sipping café au lait and filling her in on what's been happening in Ira's class/bitching about Greg Taylor/humbly begging to be set up with one of Mike's friends.

'Oh, sweetie,' says Caroline, cradling her sleeping four-year-old, Joshua, close. (You should just see the two of them. Throw in a star and three wise men and you're looking at a beautiful Madonna and child.) 'I'm racking my brains to think of any nice, eligible men Mike knows, who you haven't met yet, but I honestly can't. They're all either married or spoken for, every one of them. And besides, after the last few single guys we set you up with, I wouldn't blame you if you never went on a blind date ever again as long as you live, you poor thing.'

'I was kind of hoping you wouldn't bring them up.'

Over the years, I have, of course, badgered Caroline and

Mike into matching me up with anyone halfway suitable and . . . well . . . you don't need to have the consequences spelt out. Here I am, years on, still single, still sitting on her immaculate Louis XVIII two-seater, still looking for fix-ups.

'Do you remember the Oompa-Loompa?' Caroline giggles.

'Oh God, don't remind me!' I squeal.

The Oompa-Loompa was a work colleague of Mike's, an orthodontist, who Mike and Caroline had introduced me to years ago. In fact, that's probably the best thing I can say about him. He had a decent job. Otherwise he was arrogant and mean, the type who'd take me to dinner in a posh restaurant which I could ill afford, order three courses for himself while I'd nibble on a starter, insist on buying ludicrously expensive bottles of wine, then glug the entire bottle himself while I sipped on a thimbleful (I'd be the designated driver) and, finally, insist we split the bill fifty-fifty.

Then after we broke up, he became possessive to the point of virtually becoming a stalker. He would buzz the intercom at my apartment gates for hours at a time while I lay flat out on the living-room floor, terrified he'd see that I was home. It was Jamie who christened him the Oompa-Loompa, mainly because he was short with red hair. Jamie also did his best to start a rumour that the Oompa-Loompa had to buy all his clothes from kiddie departments, but it wasn't true, just Jamie being mean. Funny, but mean.

'He's married now, you know,' says Caroline.

'You see, if the Oompa-Loompa can find someone to marry, then so can I.'

'Well, sweetie, you know what I always say? These things are bigger than us. If Julia Roberts's movies have taught me nothing, it's that fate and serendipity will eventually lead you to Mr Right.'

'Caroline, I've waited thirty-seven years; can I help it if fate and serendipity need a kick up the bum?'

She starts giggling again. 'What was the name of that patient of Mike's you went out with? The one who took you to dinner in the Trocadero . . .'

'And when I asked for a mint tea—'

'He went, "Mint tea? La-di-dah!"'

'That wasn't the worst of it. His proudest boast was that he'd never been outside of Dublin in his life. Didn't even own a passport. He kept saying, "Sure, why would anyone want to leave the Phibsboro Road?" He was forty-two.'

'And he had boasted to Mike that he ran his own highly successful business . . .'

'But it turned out to be a sweet shop which he lived over.'

Suddenly Caroline goes quiet.

'What's up?' I ask.

'Amelia, do you remember what the nuns in school used to teach us?'

'That, sooner or later, everyone gets shot?'

She smiles. 'Stop messing.'

'What then?'

'Remember social studies class? Sister Hildegarde always used to say that you should go on at least three dates with a man before you rejected him. Do you think maybe you're not really giving these guys a real chance? That you're writing them all off for very superficial reasons? You know, like we tease Jamie for doing.'

'No I'm not. Am I? *Am I?*'

'I'll give you one example. Damien Delaney.'

I groan inwardly. She's got me there. Damien Delaney is a good friend of Mike's; they're in the same golf club and play together regularly. I have to tread carefully here as I know Caroline is very fond of him too.

'Now you tell me one thing that was wrong with Damien.'

I brace myself for the lie. The truth was, we only went on one date, just before I met *He-whose-name-shall-forever-remain-unspoken* and, although it wasn't disastrously awful, I did do the seatbelt manoeuvre when he drove me home. This is a handy move which Jamie and I have perfected over years of bad dating, whereby if a guy is driving you home and you've already decided you don't want to invite him in for coffee, you unlock your seatbelt just before you arrive at your destination, but hold it in place so it still looks locked. Then, once you're safely home, you can be out of the car in one swift movement, politely wishing him a very good night, and cleverly eliminating the embarrassment of any should-we-kiss-each-other-goodnight-or-not angst. One hundred per cent effective, every time.

'I know that he thinks you're lovely,' says Caroline. 'Anytime he's here, he always asks after you. Now, you give me one good reason why you won't see him again.'

I look at her sheepishly. There *is* no good reason and I'm beginning to feel she may have a point, that I do reject guys over inconsequential trifles. Damien was a lot older than me, about sixty, widowed with grown-up kids and now living back at home with his mother. He also had the same pen pal that he'd had since the age of seven and whom he'd never actually met. Now, ordinarily, I have a high tolerance level for the eccentricities of others, but even *I* thought that was a bit whacky. There was also the small matter of there being absolutely no chemistry between us . . . nothing . . . not even the tiniest smidge . . .

'I know what you're thinking,' says Caroline gently. 'OK, maybe he's not the funniest guy in the world, but just remember, you don't necessarily want to marry someone who's going to do stand-up routines every time you're out with him. You have Rachel and Jamie for that. But he's a good, solid man, who'd treat you well and look after you. Not the most exciting or glamorous, I know, but will you *please* give him one more whirl? For me?'

Just then, Mike bursts in, swinging Emma, their six-year-old, over his shoulders. All of a sudden, Joshua is awake and the whole room is happy and noisy, with both kids demanding sweets from soft Auntie Amelia's bottomless handbag. Mike looks as yummy as ever, getting more and more like Richard Gere every day and wearing Calvin Klein casual gear even better than Calvin Klein himself could. ('How does he do that to clothes?' Jamie's always moaning. 'Make them look so crisp and starched and immaculate all the time? He has two kids, for God's sake. The clothes should be covered in chocolate stains and congealed snot.')

I say my goodbyes and Caroline walks me downstairs to the front door.

'So?' she asks, hugging me. 'Will I ask Mike to set up another date for you?'

'Go for it,' I reply. 'As Ira Vandergelder would say, this is not a drill, people.'

'Good girl. There's the Dunkirk spirit. You'll see if I don't have you married off before the year is out.'

I hop into my car, drive away from her gorgeous Victorian doll's house and head for home. Caroline and I don't live too far from each other and within ten minutes I'm stepping out of the lift and into my toasty-warm apartment, dreaming about a long, hot bath and short crisp glass of Sancerre.

The phone in the hall is ringing and I answer. Jamie.

'Am I so undeserving of love?' he asks theatrically, cutting straight to the chase as usual.

'Oh dear,' I sigh. 'Are we talking about a certain Hispanic director with a limited grasp of the English language? Do I need a glass of wine in my hand for this?'

'A wine box more like, honey.'

'OK, you said it.'

I head to the kitchen, open the fridge (which is practically empty apart from wine), pour myself a very large glass and collapse on to the sofa while Jamie prattles on.

'So, José Miguel and I had lunch today and I asked if we were seeing each other exclusively and you know what he said? "I am like the wind." Can you *believe* it? That's the kind of answer you get when you punch up Google and key in "commitment-phobic bastard". It's at this point that my day starts to go downhill. Then he tells me I didn't get the part because – get this – I don't have *the X factor*. I said, "Oh great, thanks for the fantastic feedback! Because for a minute there I was afraid you were going to be vague."'

Just then my mobile beep-beeps loudly as a text message comes through.

'Whoever that is, ignore them,' Jamie demands. 'I'm not having anyone pulling focus away from my problem. Oh shit, curiosity just got the better of me. Go on, find out who it is that dares to interrupt.'

I haul myself up, walk back to where I'd flung my mobile on the kitchen table and read the text aloud. It's from Caroline. SPOKE TO DAMIEN. ALL SORTED. KEEP NEXT SAT NIGHT FREE, DINNER FOR THE 4 OF US?

'Hello? Explanation please? New readers begin here,' says Jamie.

'Now, don't overreact, OK? Caroline is setting me up again, with Damien Delaney. Remember him? Mike's golfing partner.'

'The old man?'

'In some cultures, early sixties is considered to be the prime of life,' I answer primly. 'OK, so he may not tick a lot of my boxes, but Caroline thinks he could be a grower.'

'A what?'

'You know, no fireworks, but a really sweet guy who slowly grows on you.'

'Well, don't look on him as old, honey. Look on him as younger than some buildings.'

'Ha ha. Very funny. I'd no idea you were so ageist.'

'Just think of it like this. In a way, you're living out your fantasy.'

'How?'

'You know how you always secretly fancied going out with a twenty-one-year-old? Well this way, it's like you're going out with three twenty-one-year-olds.'

Just then, there's a knock on my hall door.

'Oh, for God's sake, I was in mid-rant. Who's that?' says Jamie.

'Moany Moira Brady from downstairs probably. She's always thumping on the door whenever I walk around the wooden floors in my heels. Hang up and I'll call you when she's finished giving me an ear-bashing.'

'Get rid of Mrs Brady, old lady, and call me straight back. While she's tearing shreds off you, just mentally make a sentence out of the following words. Tip. Iceberg. You haven't even heard the half of yet.'

I whip off my shoes and tiptoe down the wooden corridor, bracing myself for the onslaught. 'I'm so sorry Mrs Brady—' I say, opening the door.

But it isn't her.

Instead it's the only other person I know who still has a key to my building.

He-whose-name-shall-forever-remain-unspoken.

'Amelia . . .' he says.

I have to grip tight on to the door frame, just to stop myself from passing out.

'I know you'll probably want to slam the door in my face, and I don't blame you, but . . .'

I can't speak. All I can do is stare at him in deep, total, shock. *Stop opening and closing your jaw*, my inner voice says. *You must look like a demented goldfish.*

' . . . it's just that . . . there's something you should know.'

Chapter Ten

Exactly How Much Closure Do You Need?

With the speed of light, four possible reasons as to what he was doing on my doorstep flash through my head.

1. He has an incurable disease and has six months to live.
2. *Oh God, far worse!* He has an incurable disease which he has passed on to me, and now I have six months to live.
3. He's come back for his CDs (which, actually, I'll be quite glad to get rid of; they're all Leonard Cohen and Johnny Cash excuse-me-while-I-just-open-a-vein type music).
4. Dare I even think this thought? He's back from Johannesburg . . . because, gulp, he misses me? Can't live without me? Loves me? Wants me back?

Spectacularly wrong, on all four counts.
'Amelia?'
I can't even answer him.
'Earth to Amelia?'

'What?'

'Sorry, but you'd done one of your drifting-off-into-space tricks there and I know how long your meandering little fantasies can last. So, are you going to ask me in?'

On mute, stunned autopilot, I lead him down the hallway and into my living room. He plonks down on his favourite armchair as if he'd never got out of it. 'Make yourself at home, why don't you,' I manage to say.

'Sorry, sorry. Force of habit.'

'It's OK.'

'It's good to see you, Amelia. You look well.'

'I am well.'

I'm aware that this sounds curt, but I'm no actress, and at this moment find myself unable to banter in meaningless pleasantries and small talk. Particularly when, if I'm brutally honest, I'd rather see him in a wheelchair than sitting in my apartment, cool as a breeze, as if he deserved a lovely, warm slippers-by-the-fire welcome, followed by a traditional Irish fry-up meal, fantastic sex and then a lift home.

After an awkward pause, where the penny seems to drop with him that he isn't going to get the red-carpet treatment, and nor am I about to stick a fatted calf into the micro-wave in celebration at his return, he eventually comes to the point. 'Look, Amelia, there's something I had to tell you myself, because I'd really hate for you to hear it from anyone else.'

Incurable disease?

'It's just that . . .' A deep, soul-searching sigh here. 'You know, this is so much harder than I thought it was going to be . . .'

'Give me the last sentence first.'

'OK, OK. The thing is . . . well, you and I have been broken up for a while now . . .'

Oh God, am I hearing things? Or is this actually his roundabout preamble to saying he wants us to get back together again?

I get another Walter Mitty head-rush fantasy, this time where the impossible dream has actually happened: he's grovelled/begged me for forgiveness/vowed never to mistreat me ever again . . . Next thing, we're happily reunited, having worked out all our differences and renewed our love while entwined round each other in the first-class cabin of a long-haul flight to the Fijian islands . . . (I've had quite a bit of practice with this particular flight of fancy, mainly because, in the first dark, dismal days of our break-up, I used to amuse myself by dreaming up all sorts of scenarios where he'd come crawling back. Believe me; the long winter nights just flew by.)

'How can I ever make it up to you for hurting you the way I did?' he's murmuring as we sip champagne cocktails by the infinity pool, whilst gazing out over the turquoise ocean from our tropical paradise hideaway . . .

'I'm getting married.'

'I'm sorry, what did you just say?'

'Amelia, I know this will come as a shock to you, but please understand I really wanted to be the one to tell you myself.'

'You're getting *married*? Am I hearing things?'

'I don't expect you to do your happy dance for me, but you see, the thing is . . .'

'*You're getting married?*'

'Yes.'

'But you said you never wanted to get married, not to me, not to anyone, ever. You said you were a born loner and that's the way you wanted to stay. You said you wanted to live out the rest of your days, alone, in your farmhouse in bloody stab city. Sorry, I mean Johannesburg. You'll forgive me for harping on, but please understand this particular subject is one which I have one hundred per cent recall on. I have spent some not inconsiderable time dwelling on the topic. Seeing as that was the main reason why we broke up.'

'I know, I know I said that, and that was true. Then. At that time. Before I met Poppy.'

'*Poppy?* You're marrying someone called Poppy?' I'm dimly aware that I'm repeating everything he says and am starting to sound like Dustin Hoffman in *Rain Man*, but guess what? I don't care.

'She's a lovely girl; I think you'll really get on with her when you meet her.'

Oh, for the love of God, is this why he's here? To invite me to his wedding?

'Of course, she's an awful lot younger than you and your friends . . .'

'How old?'

'Twenty-three. She's just out of college.'

By now, my head is beginning to spin.

'But, you know, she's not like you, Amelia. She's not chasing after a big, high-powered career. She just wants to get married and have a family. All the simple things in life, really. Meeting Poppy made me realize these are the things that I want too. A woman who wants to make a home.'

Now I'm starting to feel like I've just been hit by a stealth missile. When eventually I can get a sound out, my voice sounds tiny, as if it's coming from the room next door. 'But . . . but . . . those are all the things that I wanted. And still want.'

'I don't think so, Amelia. I never thought so. With all due respect, you're such an independent careerist, you haven't any time over for a partner. When we were together, I always figured your priorities were first, your friends, second, your big TV job and then last in line, me. At least with Poppy I know I come first.'

'Is that *really* what you thought?'

'Yeah, yeah, I really did. Now, don't get me wrong, Caroline's lovely but Rachel and Jamie can be very hard to take at times. I know for a fact Rachel calls me Shitface behind my back.'

I don't even attempt to deny this, although for the record what she actually calls him is Shitty from Stab City.

'They'll always come first with you, Amelia, and that's great for you, but not so good for any man you want to be with. Of course, it's fantastic that you have such support and that the four of you are all so unbelievably loyal to each other, but it always made me feel like an outsider. There's a bond between you that no man will ever come between.'

At this point, my stomach is starting to heave and I'm heartily wishing him gone so I can burst into tears without him seeing.

Calm down, says my cool, inner voice. *The torture has to be almost at an end. He's just told me the worst possible news I could ever want to hear . . . it can't exactly get much worse, can it?*

Anyway, Poppy is probably some South African who he met in stab city and who I'll never have to set eyes on as long as I live . . . he's only in Ireland briefly to tie up loose ends before he goes back to Johannesburg permanently with his bloody child bride. Yes, it's awful; yes, it's a shock; but at least I'll never have to worry about bumping into him in the supermarket on a Saturday morning, or, even worse, in Temple Bar on a Saturday night.

With Poppy.

While I'm still very much on my own.

Now that the initial shock has faded a bit, I'm starting to

feel the *unfairness* of it all. I know that sounds childish and petulant. I know that life isn't fair and I know that compared with some people I have it very easy. I could be living in the slums of Calcutta, with typhoid and leprosy. I could be sleeping rough. In Zimbabwe. Then I'd know all about pain and suffering. But it doesn't stop this burning urge I have to smack him across his smug look-at-me-I-just-got-engaged face. It's not like I don't want him to be happy, I just want to be happy first.

'So where did you meet her? In day care? Or maybe you were babysitting her?'

'Don't be like that, Amelia. It's not you.'

'You can see where I'm coming from, though. You and I were together for *three years*. Anyone you're with now is only supposed to be your transitional person, they're not meant to be The One.'

'All I want is for you to be happy for me.'

'And my hypnotherapy begins when?'

'I'm getting married because I'm in love with her.'

'Well, I didn't think you were getting married for all the lovely new kitchen appliances.'

He shook his head sadly. 'Look, Amelia, I think you're a fantastic person, I really do. There's no one who wants you to find happiness more than me. I mean it. But you must know, deep down, that you and I would never have worked out. I never expected to find the love of my life so soon after we split but, as Poppy says, you don't look for love; love looks for you.'

'And what are you doing back in Ireland?' *Here to sell his house and then get the hell out of my life for ever?*

'Poppy's family are throwing us an engagement party next week.'

I was about to beg heaven that he wasn't here to invite me,

when something struck . . . 'Poppy's family came over to Ireland with you?'

'No. They live here.'

'So . . . she's Irish.'

'Yeah, from Donnybrook. Just round the corner.'

I've never needed a brandy so badly in my life. I swear, if this was a plot on *Celtic Tigers*, no one would believe it.

'In fact, that's why I wanted to give you the news myself.'

'But you are going back to stab . . . I mean Johannesburg with what's-her-name, aren't you?'

'Why would you think I was going back to Jo'burg?'

'Because that's where you live. That's where you're from. That's your territory. This is *my* hemisphere, not yours.' By now, I'm on the point of calling a taxi for the airport and shoving him on to the first flight back. Anything, just to get him out of my apartment, out of Dublin and out of my life.

'Well, that's what I've come to tell you.'

'*WHAT exactly?* I don't want to appear rude, but I would have had less of a shock tonight if I'd just gone and stuck two fingers into an electric socket. Surely, for the love of God, you have nothing else to land on me?'

'Poppy's family are really wealthy, you see, and her parents naturally want her close by.'

'So?'

'So her father gave us an early wedding present.'

'I'm guessing it wasn't a set of steak knives.'

'No. It's the duplex right across the road from here. I really hope you're OK about this, Amelia, but you see, the thing is, we're going to be neighbours.'

Chapter Eleven

I Don't Sleep, I Vacuum

Seven-thirty a.m. the following morning and, I'm not joking, Jamie and Rachel are already pounding on my door, to see if I'm OK. Before I even open up, I can hear the pair of them in the hallway outside bickering.

'The best thing I can say about these flowers is that they aren't dead,' says Rachel.

'I know, I know, but what do you expect me to get at this ungodly hour?'

'Oh, I don't know, flowers that don't look like something you'd leave on the grave of an uncle that died and left you nothing in his will?'

The minute I let them in, they both hug me so tightly I almost have to come up for air.

'Are you OK, sweetie?' says Jamie, 'I mean really OK? Not just putting a brave face on for us? You can let it all out, baby, this isn't a Merchant Ivory movie.'

'Just so you know,' says Rachel, 'I had absolutely nothing to do with the flowers.'

Jamie hands over the sad-looking chrysanthemums apologetically. 'Sorry. I bought them from this poor homeless alcoholic who was selling them outside a garage. What can I say? I felt sorry for him.'

'You mean you didn't know him? I thought that was your agent.'

'Oh, shut up, Cruella.'

'I did, however, bring supplies,' Rachel goes on, holding up a paper bag from the deli down the road. 'You know, useful stuff. The fags are for me, the bagels are for you and the chocolate croissants are for Fat Boy Slim here.'

'Thanks,' I say dully, leading them down the corridor to the living room.

'Holy God!' they both exclaim in total shock when they see what I've been doing for the last seven hours.

'After he left, I couldn't sleep,' I explain, 'so I cleaned. Everything. All night long. There isn't a surface in this room that you couldn't perform an operation on. I had to stop myself when I ended up scouring the fake coal in the gas fire. I only wish I were joking.'

'Jesus, the smell of bleach in here,' says Rachel, waving her hand in front of her face in a futile attempt to dispel the fumes. 'Remind me not to light a ciggie or we'll all go up in flames.'

I slump wearily on to the sofa and Jamie hops into the kitchen. In no time, he's brewed up some incredibly colourless, watery instant coffee and handed me and Rachel a mug each. 'Drink that up, darling,' he says to me, really concerned. 'You look like you've just given three pints of blood.'

'Ughh,' says Rachel spitting hers back into the mug. 'Jamie! Will you look at the state of her! Go and make her something so strong she could trot a mouse over it. Irish it up if you have to. If this isn't an emergency, I don't know what is.'

'Sorry, Amelia, can't see straight,' he says, grabbing the mug from me. 'I think I'm still a bit drunk from last night. I was only coming in the door when I got your dawn distress call. I know, I know, feel free to call me a big dirty stop-out.'

'Where were you?' I ask automatically. Anything to divert the subject away from what we're inevitably going to have to talk about in minute, forensic detail.

'In a pub, then a club, then a tub with my sexy Spaniard.'

'A tub?' My questions are all lacklustre. Mechanical.

'He's staying at the Clarence and it has an outdoor hot tub. And you know how I'm a sucker for freebies. Well, freebies that other people end up paying for. It has a fabulous view.'

'Of what?'

'Marks and Spencer's loading bay.'

'Jamie,' I say, 'I know I'm functioning on very little sleep, but when we last spoke about this guy, all of – what? – ten hours ago, you distinctly said that you hated him.'

'What can I say? I'm complex.'

'You're pulling focus away from Amelia,' says Rachel threateningly. 'I hate to have to tell you to shut up, but shut up.'

He skulks back into my tiny galley kitchen to make some proper coffee this time, as my phone beep-beeps.

'It's Caroline,' I say, reading the text. 'Stuck in traffic on the school run. She'll be here in a half-hour.'

For about the millionth time in my life, I marvel at the pals I have. I can't remember who it was that said 'My glory was I had such friends', but at this moment I feel like having it engraved on my tombstone.

'You guys,' I say to Rachel, squeezing her hand. 'What would I do without you? I send out the SOS and here you all are.'

'With poppy-seed bagels,' Jamie shouts from the kitchen.

'Did you have to say poppy?'

'Ooops, sorry, I forgot.'

'Of course we're here for you, darling,' says Rachel, lighting a fag. 'You've done the same for us and will do again. The question is: What are we going to do?'

'I have something positive to contribute. Well, actually two things,' says Jamie, coming back in from the kitchen, having switched on my espresso maker.

'If you're able to put any kind of positive spin on this,' I say, 'then you should be in Downing Street, working for Tony Blair. There is absolutely no hope for any kind of happy outcome in this situation. For God's sake, I can see the house they're moving into from my bedroom window. I checked last night. About fifty times.'

'Just hear me out. Maybe he traded down from you.'

'*What?*'

'Well, here you are, great job, great friends, plenty of cash, lovely apartment, a size-ten figure and beautifully pretty without ever having recourse to botox jabs. How can Poppy possibly compete?'

'She doesn't need to compete, Jamie. She's *twenty-three*. She'll spend the rest of her life married to the man I thought destiny had intended for me and having lunch with the rest of her twenty-three-year-old friends, talking about twenty-three-year-old things, like, I dunno, boy bands and Jessica Simpson and all the Hollywood gossip that's in *Heat* magazine. The only thing I have on her is a job.'

'Yeah, but who gets married at twenty-three?' Jamie replies. 'Promised brides and cousins, that's who.'

'To him, she's probably just a brood mare, that's all,' says Rachel.

'Oh, come on guys, I may have hit the snooze button on my biological clock, but I can still have kids, can't I?'

'Of course you can, sweetie,' says Jamie, soothingly. 'You're only a spring chicken, fertility-wise. I read an article the other day about a woman in China who's pregnant with twins and she's sixty. Plus you could always have your eggs frozen. Loads of celebs are doing that now, you know. Career women just like you who want to put it off till later in life. Fertility slackers, they're calling them.'

'Thanks, Jamie. As if I didn't have enough to worry about.'

Rachel, thankfully, gets back to the more immediate matter in hand. 'Can I also point out that *He-whose-name-shall-forever-remain-unspoken* is moving into a house that her father bought?' she says, taking a bagel out of the bag and plonking it down in front of me. I know she means to be kind, but right now, even the smell of it is making my tummy churn. 'Is that how he's planning to spend the rest of his marriage?' she goes on. 'Under her daddy's thumb?'

'That's some men's fantasy,' I say. 'To have a partner who'll bankroll them for life.'

Jamie nods in agreement. 'It's certainly mine.'

'You could sell up and move,' Rachel goes on. 'You'd make a fortune on this place. And you're always saying you'd love to live in a house one day, as opposed to an apartment. Come on, it's not as if there're any nice single guys hanging around the car park outside, is it? Besides, doesn't the smell of microwaved dinners for one in the hallway outside drive you mental?'

'No,' I say firmly. 'I can't move. You know why? Because then he'll have won. I'm not going to be driven out of my home just to avoid them. I don't mean to sound stubborn and . . . oh, I dunno . . . like a squatter, but I was here first.'

'It mightn't be so bad,' says Jamie, the eternal optimist.

'Explain to me how.'

'Well, if you think about it, all it really means is that you won't be able to slip out on a Sunday morning to buy your papers in a slobby tracksuit any more. You're just going to have to wear make-up at all times. Now what's so awful about that?'

'Oh, Jamie,' I sigh, feeling a fresh bout of tears coming on. 'What's awful about this is that he's *marrying* her. Not living with her or even buying the bloody house with her, he's actually *getting married*. He was with me for years and the closest I ever got to a commitment from him was the time he bought me a goldfish. Which he then subsequently forgot to feed so it starved to death when I was away. I need you both to tell me honestly, as my best friends: is there something so fundamentally unmarriable about me?'

They soothe my battered self-esteem with a lot of 'Don't be so daft' and 'It's his loss, not yours' and 'What will he ever have in common with her?' And (my personal favourite) 'Just think, Amelia, when she's thirty, he'll be almost fifty. To her, he won't be just old, he'll be a hologram.'

But the thought still won't go away.

'I have some other news,' says Jamie, and from the foul look Rachel throws him, I correctly guess that they've been chatting about whatever it is in the car on their way here.

'Anything to distract me from the thought that I will probably die an old maid. With my ex-boyfriend and his lovely young wife for neighbours.'

'You know your find-a-husband course?'

'Yeah, what about it?'

'Well, stick a fake handlebar moustache on me and call me Hercule Poirot. You won't believe who I met in Café en Seine last night.'

'Give in.'

'Matt Coveney.'

'Who?'

'Matt? Oh, you remember him from college. Hunky and chunky type. Looks a bit like Simon Cowell?'

'Your point being?'

'He has no point,' says Rachel, shooting him a filthy look. 'He often has no point. Some say it's part of his charm.'

'I'm telling her this because I mean well,' he snaps back.

'Oppenheimer meant well. Pol Pot meant well.'

'Guys, I'm too tired to referee. Tell me whatever it is or I'll make both of you sit through a full episode of *Celtic Tigers*.'

'Well,' says Jamie, ignoring the bilious glares from Rachel, 'you know how Matt and I used to do loads of shows together in the drama society, back in the UCD days?'

'Oh, yeah, now I know who you mean. I think.'

'Well, he used to be really friendly with your old flame Pete Mooney way back then. So I asked him if he knew where he was now and, get this, they're still in touch with each other. So, Pete's in Belfast now, apparently, working as, oh God, you're going to love this, an *accountant*!'

'What's so funny about him being an accountant?'

'Nothing, just that when he so cruelly disbanded Emergency Exit, he told me that I had no talent and that he was going to be a megastar. And now I'm the one in showbiz while he's a humble bean-counter. It's not very often in this life that I get to say *HA HA*!'

'So he's up in Belfast now?'

'Yes, but here's the surprise, honey. Look what Papa has for you . . .' he says theatrically, producing a tatty bit of paper out of his pocket with the air of a conjurer.

'What's this?' I say, automatically taking it.

'Only Pete's home phone number. So you can do your homework for class next week and it'll hopefully distract you from *He-whose-name-shall-forever-remain-unspoken*. Aren't I just a national treasure?'

'If this Matt whatever-he's-called is still so friendly with Pete,' I ask, puzzled, 'didn't he wonder why you wanted his phone number? You and Pete haven't spoken in decades. Even the Beatles had a more amicable break-up than you pair.'

'Oh no, I explained to him that it was for you.'

'You *what?*'

'Well, I was telling Matt that you were doing this course where you hunt down all your exes which he thought was just hilarious. So then I said that you'd probably want to speak to Pete at some point—'

'Jamie! You told someone I barely know and that I haven't seen in twenty years that I'm trying to track down someone *else* I haven't seen in twenty years so that I can find a husband?'

'Well, I didn't think it was classified.'

'Do me a favour and kill him for me,' I say to Rachel icily. 'I'm jumping in the shower now, so if you could avoid bloodstains on the freshly vacuumed carpet, I'd be very grateful.'

'Why are you having a shower?' Rachel asks, surprised. 'You can't seriously be thinking of going into work?'

'I've a meeting with the senior script adviser at ten, which I scheduled, so welcome to the wonderful world of got no choice.'

'Amelia, you *cannot* go into work. Not today. I'm not letting you. Throw a sickie.'

'Well, if I do, then I'll just stay home all day and start disinfecting the furniture. Being busy is good. Having a focus is good. And anything that prevents me from physically hurling Jamie out the window right at this point in time can only be a good thing. Let Caroline in when she gets here, will you?'

I head for the bathroom but even as I close the door behind me I can hear Rachel tear strips off Jamie. Loud and clear. '*You fecking idiot!* I warned you not to tell her,' she rants at him. 'Why doesn't Rupert Murdoch just employ you and your big mouth? Save himself a fortune on Sky News.'

'There's one simple, basic tenet to being my friend,' Jamie answers defensively, 'and it's not my fault if you all keep forgetting. *Tell me nothing. I talk.*'

Oh dear. I'm no sooner in the shower than I feel another flashback coming on . . .

> *THE TIME: 31 December 1986.*
> *THE PLACE: Mike's student flat in Rathmines (or Rat mines, as we call it, mainly due to the low/non-existent standards of hygiene).*
> *THE OCCASION: A fancy dress, New Year's Eve party.*

I wouldn't mind, but we went to loads of trouble over our costumes. Myself and the other Lovely Girls have gone as Charlie's Angels. Caroline is Jill Monroe (except she looks even better in a jumpsuit), Rachel is Sabrina, I'm Kelly and Jamie is Charlie (any excuse for him to get into a dress suit).

The night does not get off to a good start.

'I'm breaking up with Pete Mooney. Tonight. For definite. Don't even try to talk me out of it.'

I'm sitting in Mike's tiny living room, chatting to Caroline, who's perched beside me on the edge of the moth-eaten sofa, still managing to look elegant even though she's drinking wine from a mug. Caroline rarely drinks but, believe me, in this flat you want to swig alcohol. It means there's a better chance of the germs being killed in whatever utensil you've been given to drink out of. The place is packed with all of Mike's dentistry student friends, doing vodka ice cubes, pissed drunk and all in full fancy dress, moshing to Jackie Wilson's 'Reet Petite'. It's hard to believe, but back in 1986, that song was all the go.

'Oh, honey, don't break it off with Pete tonight,' says Caroline. 'Not on New Year's Eve, that would be awful for him. Would you want to start off nineteen eighty-seven by being dumped?'

'No, but nor do I want to start off nineteen eighty-seven with a boyfriend who's driving me slowly up the wall.'

'That bad?'

'Caroline, I'm exhausted from trying to be cool enough for him. And guess what, I never will be. He's constantly criticizing me: the way I dress, the movies I want to see, the music I like. He came over for dinner last night and ended up having a go at my poor old mum because he caught her watching *Cagney and Lacey*. He told her it was the cheesiest series ever committed to celluloid and that it was fundamentally aimed at menopausal housewives.'

'You're kidding.'

'I wish. And Mum was doubly upset cos she'd gone to loads of bother over the meal. She'd defrosted quiche and every-thing. Then I thought Dad would physically fling Pete out of the house when he started having a go at his taste in films.'

'What films?'

'*Crocodile Dundee*. Dad's seen it twice.'

'I'm really sorry, Amelia. I didn't realize things were that bad. Didn't he take you to a movie just the other night?'

'Yeah, *Blue Velvet*. In the very first scene a human ear is found lying in a field . . . need I say more? I did my best to pretend to enjoy it, but he sees right through my act. Art-house stuff just isn't me. I would have been so happy just going to see *Hannah and Her Sisters*. And don't even get me started on the time he found out that I thought Che Guevara was one of the Rolling Stones. I still haven't heard the last of that one.'

'Have you told Jamie?'

'No. That's the other thing. He keeps putting Jamie down too. He's always giving out about him in the band. He says his singing is off key and that his songwriting is way too commercial. He wants Emergency Exit to head in a completely different direction. Experimental, electronic stuff, you know? I think Pete's idea of a successful song is one that gets them interviewed by Paula Yates on *The Tube* whereas Jamie—'

'Secretly wants to represent Ireland in the Eurovision Song Contest, I know.'

Just then Mike comes over and slips his arm protectively around Caroline's waist. That's the other thing that's upsetting me, although I'd never say it. They started going out the same night as myself and Pete, all of ten months ago, and are getting on so wonderfully well that it's almost highlighted the slow deterioration of my relationship. Put simply, Mike gave Caroline a string of pearls for Christmas (which he worked his arse off to earn the money for, at his part-time job in a garage) whereas Pete gave me . . . nothing. *Nada.* Not a thing.

Now, in his defence, he says he's fundamentally against the concept of exchanging gifts while there are people starving in Africa, but it's just that I went to loads of trouble over his present: a season ticket to the Fellini retrospective at the Adelphi Cinema, which I knew he'd love. Funny, but for someone opposed to giving gifts, he has no problem accepting them . . .

'So how're my two favourite Charlie's Angels?' asks Mike. 'And where've Sabrina and Charlie gone?'

'Dunno,' I reply. 'Last seen heading in the direction of the keg.'

'Doesn't he look handsome?' Caroline asks, looking up adoringly at him.

Mike has dressed up as Richard Gere in *An Officer and a Gentleman* (Caroline's Desert Island favourite movie) and looks like any woman's fantasy come true. I'm just about to ask them, Cinderella-style, how long to go till midnight when Pete himself sidles over.

'Oh, hi, Pete!' says Caroline warmly. 'So what have you come as?'

'A rock star.'

'Who?'

'Guess. Don't tell them, Amelia.'

'Ehh . . . Bon Jovi?' asks Mike.

'You think I'd dress up as *Bon Jovi*? Get lost.'

'Prince?'

'Not even close.'

'Give in.'

'Billy Idol. Thought that would have been, like, sooooo obvious.'

In fairness to both Caroline and Mike, it's not in the least bit obvious. The only difference between the way Pete looks now and the way he looks normally is that his hair is that bit spikier.

'Can you do something about the music?' he says to Mike. 'If I have to listen to Tina Turner singing "Private Dancer" any more, I'm leaving.'

'Give me a mo,' says Mike, politely hopping to.

'Oh, and I don't want to make a fuss, but could you get me something clean to drink out of?'

'Jeez,' says Mike, 'you said don't make a fuss.'

'So what do you think of our costumes?' Caroline asks Pete as Mike disappears into the crowd.

He doesn't answer; he just looks down at us in that

patronizing way he has which is *really* starting to bug me.

It takes more than a snotty look to deter our Caroline though, who's determined to extract a compliment from Pete if it kills him. 'Doesn't Amelia look gorgeous with her hair all backcombed, in the hot pants? Just like a 1950s cyberbabe.'

Pete just looks at me, searching for a suitably cutting witticism. 'She looks like . . . like . . . like a slutty American pin-up painted on to the fuselage of a bomber.' Then he swaggers off completely delighted and thinking himself the drollest man in the room.

'I'm sitting right here, you know!' I shout after him, boiling.

'I know. Think of it as a backhanded compliment.' And he's gone into the kitchen.

'Right, that's it. If you don't break up with him tonight,' says Caroline, smarting, 'I'll do it on your behalf. Just wait till after midnight.'

Just then Mike starts flashing the fluorescent light above on and off to grab everyone's attention. 'Two minutes to the countdown, everyone!' he calls out. 'Grab your partners!'

'Let me go and find Charlie and our missing angel,' I say to Caroline. 'At least let's all be together for the start of nineteen eighty-seven.'

Caroline smiles and rejoins her fella as I work my way through the throng, searching for the others. I scour the tiny, filthy kitchen and the hallway looking for them. No sign.

Then I spot Pete chatting to one of Mike's friends and he imperiously beckons me over, to be obediently by his side for the stroke of twelve.

Ughhhhh. As if. I shudder and am wondering how I can get out of that one when Mike switches off the music and starts the countdown. 'TEN–NINE–EIGHT–SEVEN–SIX . . .' they all start chanting.

I can see Pete coming through the crowd and moving closer to me. It's at this point I figure I have no choice.

'FIVE–FOUR–THREE–TWO . . .'

I open the bathroom door, not even caring if (*a*) there's anyone on the loo or (*b*) the bathroom is so dirty, it's a science project. This is an emergency.

And there they are.

It's one of those things that, if I hadn't seen it with my own two eyes, I'd never in a million years have believed it. Jamie and Rachel are having a snog, kissing the faces off each other with such reckless abandon that they hardly even notice that it's me, staring at them in deep, total shock.

'Emm . . . Oh God, if you'll excuse me, I'm just going back outside to gouge out my eyes,' I manage to stammer.

Then the whole place erupts. 'HAPPY NEW YEAR!'

Chapter Twelve

There's Nothing so Tragic, You Can't Find Something to Laugh at

I've said it once and I'll say it again. Thank God for work. Thank God for being busy and thank God for not having any time left over to think. I make it into the office and the morning flies by in a blurry haze of story meetings, script meetings and emergency meetings with the press office about how to prepare the media for the slimmed-down, tightened-up, new-look *Celtic Tigers* that will be coming shortly to a TV screen near you. It's well after two p.m. before I even get a chance to sit down at my desk, grab a sandwich and pick up my phone messages.

Nine missed calls. All from Jamie, all increasingly apologetic/grovelling/contrite to the point of . . . well, I'll let you hear for yourself.

'OK, sweetie, I know I've been a naughty boy, but you just have to forgive me. You know me, *in vino veritas*, and, besides, I was only thinking of you, my love. I'd never have dreamed of opening my big mouth about you and Pete Mooney and your night course if I hadn't thought I was helping—' *Beep.*

'Ooops, sorry, machine cut me off. Anyway, please don't judge me too harshly. I really, honestly thought I was doing you a favour or I'd never, ever have breathed a syllable about your course, which, for the record, I think is fantastic for you, honey. I know how much you want to be a Sadie, Sadie, married lady and fair play to you. You're actually going out there and doing something about it—' *Beep.*

'Sorry, bloody machine again. Are you still in meetings? Ring me when you get this. I sort of have an idea about how I can make this up to you. Love you, mean it.' *Beep.*

'OK, OK, it's midday now and you still haven't returned my calls, which means you're either in a major snot with me or you're still trying to figure out a way of making your show more popular than *Nip/Tuck* . . . I hate to sound needy or anything, but call me, call me, call me!' *Beep.*

'Hmm, twelve-twenty-two. Now I'm worried that Good Grief O'Keefe has found out she might be for the chop and has sprinkled anthrax in your coffee. If I don't hear from you soon, honey, I'm calling all the hospitals within a twelve-mile radius . . .' *Beep.*

'Oh God, now I've got visions of you in some emergency room with that cute doctor from *ER* giving you CPR and saying, "No! This can't be happening! This woman is too young and beautiful to die!" And then that awful hospital administrator with the red hair and the walking stick that they all hate says, "Sure, tough break. Wouldn't you think her best friends would be here?"' *Beep.*

'Right. Here's the deal. I've made an executive decision on your behalf. While you have actively NOT been return-ing my calls, I've had a lightning bolt of inspiration. I have a cunning plan which cannot fail. Now, pay attention, Bond. I'm going to call Pete Mooney and I'll tell him that he may just be hearing from you and not to be surprised if he does;

it's because you're doing research for a new character that's coming into your show who by day is a mild-mannered accountant but by night plays in a 1980s nostalgia band. Brilliant, eh? He'll never suspect a thing. Pete was always thick as a plank. Don't bother thanking me, it's the least I can do. If you're not in an intensive-care unit, call me straight back. Love you up to the sky!' *Beep.*

'OK, you'd better be sitting down for this one. I rang Pete. Now, you're not to get annoyed with me, promise? The good news is that he actually sounded so humongously pleased to hear from me, you'd have sworn I was Graham Norton calling. We chatted for ages, got on like a house on fire; you'd never have thought there was a cross word spoken between us. So then your name came up and I was saying wouldn't it be great if we had an Emergency Exit reunion for old times' sake and that you'd have to come along too, seeing as how you were our number-one groupie—' *Beep.*

'So here's the *fabulous* news! Are you sitting comfortably? You'll just never guess what, so don't even try. As luck or serendipity or fate would have it, Pete's at a wedding this weekend *IN DUBLIN*! I nearly had to have a lie-down when he told me. So, the wedding is on Saturday and I said why not meet up for a drink if he had any free time over the weekend. Then, totally unprompted, he says he's planning to come to Dublin on Friday evening and how about we meet up then? Tomorrow! So are you thrilled? Aren't I just your golden boy? And more importantly, am I back in your good books again?' *Beep.*

'My final message. Promise. I may have exaggerated the *teeniest* little bit about what I was doing now . . . and . . . well . . . I might just need your help.'

★   ★   ★

Between one thing and another, the rest of the week flies by. Meetings, more meetings, scripting sessions that go on till all hours, bickering with actors' agents . . . you name it, I dealt with it. I must have clocked up an eighty-hour week and, for once, it doesn't bother me.

As I say, nothing like hard work to take your mind off things.

And still no sign of *He-whose-name-shall-forever-remain-unspoken* and the pre-teen fiancée moving in.

It's not that I've been checking every day or anything, but I do have to drive by their new house with the 'Sold' sign nailed to the ground in front of it, taunting me, every time I go outside the bloody door.

But somehow, I've made it through the week and now it's Friday and I can't believe it. It's the weekend and I'm going out for the night, like normal people do. Well, except that, in my case, it's to meet up with an ex-boyfriend I haven't seen in nineteen years . . .

Did you ever find yourself in a situation so surreal that all you can do is wonder how the hell you ever got there in the first place? It's the only way I can describe how I feel as I find myself sharing a taxi with Jamie on our way into town. In all honesty though, I have to admit that it's actually really nice to have the bit of moral support. I'm feeling absolutely none of the awful anxiety attacks I went through before I met up with stinky old Greg Taylor. This time, I've brought an ally.

The taxi picks me up first, then we head for Jamie's flat and get there punctually on the dot of eight, but, as usual, he's not ready. He never is. After a twenty-minute wait, punctuated with Jamie sticking his head out of his bathroom window every moment he gets and shouting down at the taxi, 'Nearly there! I promise, sweetie! Bit of a hair gel emergency!' eventually he plonks down into the passenger seat beside me.

'Pooh! What is that aftershave?' I ask. I have to roll the window down, the smell is so overwhelming.

'It's my lucky blend, darling. I invented it myself. It's a subtle mixture of Route du Thé from Barneys in New York—'

'And what? Harpic toilet bleach?'

'Smell is a critical part of chemical attraction, you know. Don't you like it?'

I can't even answer, I'm too busy spluttering.

'Well, it is Friday night. And we are meeting in my favourite haunt, the Dragon bar on George's Street.'

'*Jamie!* You arranged to meet Pete in a gay bar?'

'Oh, put your claws in, Ena Sharples. I didn't suggest it, he did.'

'But he doesn't even live in Dublin. How is he supposed to know it's a gay bar?'

'Relax. It's one of the most famous pubs in town; it's practically a landmark, that's the only reason he knows it. Besides, the front part of it is mixed, so you'll be fine. So do you want to know the good news, oh single one?'

'After the week I've had, all good news is gratefully received.'

'Now don't get over-excited, but I think Pete could be single too. I was on the phone to him for ages and he never once mentioned a wife or dependent kids. Nor did he even mention the dreaded GF word.'

'GF?'

'Girlfriend, idiot.'

'Jamie, it doesn't matter if he's a practising Mormon with seven wives. This is not a date. This is about as far from a date as you can get. I'm not meeting him because I want to get back with him; the only reason I'm here is to try to learn from the mistakes of my past.'

'You didn't make any mistakes with Pete. He was a total arsehole back then. The only honourable course of action open to you was to drop him off in dumpsville.'

'Well, as Ira Vandergelder says, I'm clearly doing something wrong.'

'Explain.'

'OK. Let me put it to you like this. Suppose I go on one job interview and I don't get the gig.'

'I can certainly relate to that.'

'Well then, it's fair to assume that I just wasn't what they were looking for. But supposing I spend the best twenty years of my life doing interviews and at the end of all that, I *still* don't have a job to show for it. Then guess what? Chances are *I'm* the problem. Same with dating.'

'Oh, sweetie, you and I both have that in common. It's time to shut the revolving door of losers and hold out for something better.'

'You're dead right,' I say, squeezing his arm. 'It's like that Samuel Beckett line about the harder you try, the better you fail.'

'And for the record? I totally understand this burning need to have to be married. At least it'll save you having to go out on any more crap dates.'

We're just outside the Dragon bar by now and the taxi pulls over. I fish about in my handbag for the money to pay the driver and Jamie hops out.

'Thanks for paying, darling,' he coos. 'You know me, I'm like the Queen. I don't carry cash.'

The taxi speeds off and I take a deep, calming breath.

'Oh, come on, honey,' says Jamie, linking my arm, 'just think. After tonight, three down and only seven to go.'

The Dragon is truly awful: crowded, noisy and full of Friday-night poseurs. We battle our way to the bar, order drinks and look around for anyone who even closely resembles Pete: i.e., tall, thin, beanpole, weedy types. Kind of like John Cleese, except in his late thirties.

'OK, when he gets here,' Jamie shouts in my ear (he has to, the noise is deafening), 'you're to ask me if I've decided whether or not to do the Spielberg movie.'

'Jamie, what exactly have you been telling him?'

'I didn't lie. Well, not exactly. I just tweaked the truth a bit. Oh, and if my mobile phone rings, you're to say, "Don't tell me that's your LA agent ringing you *again*. Doesn't he understand that this is your downtime?"'

'I'll never remember.'

'Yes you will. And if I mention Colin, you're to tell Pete I'm talking about Colin Farrell. Likewise, Marty is Martin Scorsese and Bobby is Robert de Niro. OK?'

Pete is very late. So late that I've almost decided to abandon the plan and bolt for the safety of home. Some of the looks I'm getting are starting to make me feel a bit self-conscious. Plus, I'm the only woman here. At least, I think I'm the only woman here. Some of the blokes have such fabulous bone structure, you wouldn't be too sure . . . Anyway. We've been here for over a half an hour now, and still no sign. *Bugger it. I've had enough drama for one week, haven't I?*

'How pissed off with me would you be if I left you here and ran away?' I eventually pluck up the courage to ask Jamie.

'On a scale of one to ten, stratospheric. What's wrong, honey?'

'Number one, I'm the only person here carrying a handbag and number two, some of these guys obviously have far better skincare regimes than I do. I'm about as conspicuous here as you would be at a speed-dating night in Jury's Inn.'

'One more drink, that's all I ask. Then at least you'll have given it a try and can retreat with honour.'

I'm just about to call up another order, when an eerily familiar voice shouts over the noise at Jamie.

'Well, well, well, Dr Livingstone, I presume?'

It's him. It's Pete. For definite. And the weird thing is that he's hardly changed a bit. Still skeletally thin, still hollow-cheeked, still with the ghostly pallor of the night-dweller; the only notable difference is that his clothes have dramatically improved. We all hug and air-kiss and greet each other and I try my best to act casual and relaxed as if I frequent gay bars every night of the week.

He and Jamie have hit it off goodo and are chatting away like they're best buddies.

'I was so pleased you called,' Pete says to him. 'You won't believe this but I often used to think about you with such a *shamingly* guilty conscience. I can't believe I ever said that your talents were end-of-pier.'

'All in the past, let it go.'

'And you're an actor now? Would I have seen you in anything?'

Jamie is very well-prepared for this one. Boy, has he done his homework. 'I do a lot of art-house movies mostly. Limited release stuff, you know. I'm very reluctant to sell out my art and do more commercial films, you know, the way Colin has.'

'Oh . . . ehh . . . that's Colin Farrell he means,' I dutifully chip in, making a mental note to slag the hell out of Jamie later for actually using the phrase, 'my art'.

'It's an ongoing battle between me and my LA representation,' he rattles on, beaming. 'They're always pushing me to do big blockbuster movies, whereas I've always felt my first love was the theatre. So I'm reading a lot of scripts at the moment, just biding my time, waiting for the right part to come along.'

Pete is suitably impressed by all this shite and the two of them chat on.

And by the two of them, I really do mean the two of them.

We order another round of drinks and half an hour later, well, I'm starting to feel very much like a third wheel. After another few minutes of Jamie giving the best performance I've seen him do in a long, long time, eventually he excuses himself to go to the loo.

'Back in a mo,' he says cheerily, tossing his mobile phone at me. I only think he's gone a bit too far when he says, 'If Brad or Angelina call, just take a message, will you? Tell them I'll get my people to call their people and we'll all meet up really soon, stateside.'

There's an awkward pause as both Pete and I sip on our drinks and I frantically rack my brains wondering how I can bring up the big subject.

Eventually, a tactic strikes me. 'So, Pete,' I begin, hoping Jamie will be gone for ages, which he normally is. I never know what he does in there, but he takes far longer than any girl in the loo. 'Can you believe it's been *nineteen* years? You've hardly changed a bit, you know, I'd have recognized you anywhere.'

'Well, thanks,' says Pete, delighted. 'It's so great to catch up with both of you again, after all this time. And isn't it wonderful how well Jamie is doing in his career? But then he did always have a big gaping hole in his character which could only be filled by applause, didn't he?'

What am I supposed to say to that? Half of it sounded like a compliment and the other half sounded like an insult . . .

'So, are you single at the moment?' Pete asks me, apropos of nothing.

OK, this is good, this is great. Now I'm back on track. I'm actually delighted he's asked, as this gives me a much-needed chink of opportunity to talk about when he and I used to date. Pete, however, doesn't even give me a chance to draw breath.

'Because I am at the moment,' he barrels on. 'Just broke up with someone.'

Oh shit . . . There's an awful, awkward moment where we both just look at each other. He's single, I'm single and now I'm thinking: *Please, dear God, don't let him ask me out. I don't think I even liked him when we were dating, I just fancied him which is a completely different thing and now that I see him almost twenty years on I'm beginning to think I might need my head examined.*

Pete is happily warbling away though; blithely unaware of what's going through my head, which at least is something.

'You see, I was the dumpee, not the dumper and that's never a barrel of laughs,' he's saying. 'I'm not joking; before Jamie called, I was sitting at home, all by myself, crying so hard, I could barely iron my underpants. In fact, do you mind me asking you something, Amelia?'

'Ehhh . . . of course not. Fire away.'

'It's kind of personal.'

Oh God, here we go, he wants to ask me out. Right, nothing for it but to brace myself for a good, stout lie. I have to say I'm seeing someone.

No, he'd never believe that because then what would I be doing in a gay bar with Jamie on a Friday night?

OK, here's the plan. I'll say I'm seeing someone who's either (a) a long-haul pilot (b) in the army peace corps serving in the Lebanon or (c) in a coma.

'Are you Jamie's hag?' he asks me straight out.

I almost choke on my drink, but there's even better to

come. *Because right then, ladies and gentlemen, we heard an alarm bell. Possibly the loudest, clearest alarm bell ever heard this side of Big Ben.*

'Do you know if *Jamie's* seeing anyone right now?'

'Why do you ask?'

'Well, just that if he's free, I'd *love* to ask him to this boring old wedding with me tomorrow. I don't think either of the grooms would mind me bringing a last-minute date; Jack and Dave are both really cool about things like that. I know I haven't seen him in such a long time, but . . . do you think he might be interested?'

Chapter Thirteen

Supposing This Is as Good as it Gets . . .

'So, to make a very long story short, not only is Pete Mooney gay but for added entertainment value, he hit on Jamie. I swear, if you saw this in a movie, you'd say it was far-fetched.'

The next morning is one of those bright, sunny Saturdays that really make you feel as if you could fall for Dublin. I've volunteered to drive Rachel to the airport (*a*) so that I can fill her in on all the high jinks of last night and (*b*) because I won't see her for almost a week now, as she's jetting off to the Peter O'Brien couture show in Paris followed by meetings with all of the big Italian buyers in Milan. She really looks the part too, with her Jackie O sunglasses and Hermès scarf casually knotted over a beautifully cut black cashmere coat.

OK, so maybe Jackie O wouldn't be sucking cigarettes out of the car window, as Rachel is now doing, but you get the picture.

'Am I blind or just plain thick not to have seen this coming?' I storm on. 'I honestly thought that the only reason Pete suggested meeting in a gay bar was because he didn't know Dublin very well. You're right to all nickname me Miss Magoo, I really *am* that short-sighted.'

'Honey, with hindsight, you could have seen the signs from space.'

'He told Jamie he only discovered he was gay in nineteen ninety-five.'

'In that case, he was the last to find out.'

'Do you think?'

'For God's sake, even leaving the gay issue aside, I could never understand what you saw in him back in college. He was always so pretentious and up-his-own-arse. That type never un-dorkulate.'

'It's hard to describe. I suppose I thought he was very cultured.'

'A yoghurt has more culture than him.'

'Ring Jamie, will you?' I ask, as I take the turn-off marked 'Dublin airport'. 'I'm dying to know what happened after I left last night.'

'What time did you leave at?'

'As soon as I could reasonably get the hell out of there without actually leaving either skid marks or a cloud of dust behind me.'

Rachel fishes around the bottom of her bag for her phone, dials his number, then snaps the phone shut. 'What am I thinking?' she says in exasperation. 'It's only ten in the morning. He's never up before the crack of lunch.' Then she turns to me, whipping off her sunglasses and looking at me as intently as a Jehovah's Witness. 'So, Pollyanna, has this experience finally made you see the light about this ridiculous quest of yours? Are you finally ready to rejoin the ranks of the sane? Or is there more to come?'

'Do you derive self-esteem from denigrating my misfortunes?'

'I prefer to call it good, old-fashioned tough love. Anything that'll encourage you to give up that infernal night course.'

'You can laugh all you like,' I say firmly, 'but I'm actually looking forward to going back to Ira Vandergelder next week, just to hear what she makes of Pete Mooney. I could be in danger of becoming the class clown when they all hear this latest.'

'You've had quite enough drama for one week, sweetie,' says Rachel. 'I wish you'd just tell Ira what's-her-face where to get off and give yourself a well-deserved break.'

'I'd never give up the course,' I answer, trying to sound jokey and not defensive. 'Just look at all the fantastic progress I'm making. Number one ex-boyfriend wanted me to be his bit on the side, number two referred to me as a hag, and skipping forward to number ten, let's remind ourselves that he's getting married to someone who wasn't even born when we were doing the Leaving Cert. Why would I quit the course? Look at the hours of fun and laughter it's given us all.'

'I'm being serious, Amelia. If I die in a plane crash, my last thoughts will be: Why did I stand back and allow my best friend to put herself through all that self-inflicted torture?'

'You already know the answer to that one,' I say, pulling the car over at the entrance to the departures hall. 'Because I don't want to be alone.'

'Answer me one thing, and I would really like you to give this some thought. *Why not?* What is so terrible about being alone? You need to shift your attitude, honey, and focus on all the positives about being single.'

'Name me one.'

She turns to me with that mad glint in her eyes she sometimes gets when there's devilment afoot. 'OK, off the top of my head, here's one. Get on the plane with me right now and come to Paris for the weekend.'

'*What?*'

'Why not? What's to stop you? You could come to the show with me this afternoon if you wanted, or if not you could do the galleries and museums and we'll meet up for a bottle of Bolly tonight . . . brunch on the Champs Elysées tomorrow . . . dinner in the Hôtel du Crillon. What do you say?'

'Oh, Rach, I'd love nothing more,' I say, really touched at her kind offer. 'But . . . emm . . . you see, I can't.'

'Better be a very good excuse.'

'I don't know if it's a good excuse, but it's an excuse. I have a date.' Which, if Caroline hadn't called first thing that morning to remind me, I would have clean forgotten. Damien Delaney.

'Ughh, the aul' fella?' says Rachel as we hug goodbye. 'I won't say have fun but do keep me posted.'

'I'm not expecting it to be a dance around the maypole, but who am I to turn down a decent bloke, just because he's a bit, well . . . advanced in years?'

Now, at this stage in my long and spectacularly un-successful dating career, whenever I first come face to face with any date/fix-up/potential husband, my mind operates almost like a computer screen, split right down the middle. On the left, I see the pros for each guy so clearly they could almost be written in neon graphics, and on the right, I see the cons. And thus it is with Damien.

Caroline has invited both him and me for dinner at seven, but naturally I'm at her house a good hour earlier, mainly so I can gossip about last night.

'Fab, you're early!' she says as she throws open the hall door and hugs me tight. 'It'll be great to have our own private chat before the boys get here. Oh, you shouldn't have, you angel!' she says, gratefully taking a big bunch of stargazer lilies I brought for her, along with a bottle of Bollinger.

'Thought that might be a good ice-breaker,' I say, handing it over.

'You're a pet. Come on, let's get a glass of this into you and you can tell me all about Pete Mooney. I'm still in shock that he invited Jamie to a gay wedding! And I'm even more shocked that Jamie didn't go.'

'I think the only reason he wouldn't go is because he told so many lies about his acting career, he said he'd never be able to remember them all when he sobered up. Oh, Caroline, if you'd seen the Dragon bar last night, you'd have fallen over. I'm not joking, trying to find another straight woman in there was like trying to find a clock in a Las Vegas casino.'

She roars laughing and leads me downstairs to the beautiful Victorian kitchen, which is so big it takes up most of the basement floor. A beautiful aroma of garlic and ginger is wafting from the Aga in the corner and Felix, Emma's cat, is fast asleep on the armchair beside it. The whole scene looks like something out of a really posh interiors magazine.

I plonk down on a stool at the breakfast bar, oooing and aahing at all the yummy dinner smells. 'Caroline, your entire life is one big glossy magazine. Do you realize how much *Homes and Gardens* would pay to get shots of this house?'

'Yeah, right, you just wait and see it five minutes after the kids get home,' she laughs, sticking the champagne in the fridge and producing another, pre-chilled bottle. 'Here's one I prepared earlier.'

'Good woman. Where are the little cherubs anyway? I was thinking the house was unusually quiet.'

'Please don't judge me, but they're at McDonald's with the au pair. I know, I know, I'm a bad mother for letting them eat crap, but I work on a bribe system with them, especially Emma. On special occasions like this, they get hamburgers and fries in return for good behaviour.'

Just then, the doorbell rings.

'It can't be them already,' says Caroline, utterly dismayed. 'It's only just gone six. Wait here, will you, pet, and let me get rid of whoever it is. I don't want anything interrupting our private chat.'

Two minutes later, she leads Damien through to the kitchen, full of apologies for being so early. It seemed that he and Mike had to cut their golf game short, as Mike, who's on call this weekend, got unexpectedly called in to do an emergency surgery, so Damien came straight to the house, with promises that Mike wouldn't be long behind him. And that's when the computer graphics in my mind's eye kick in.

After all, he could just turn out to be my headless groom . . .

PRO:

It's ages since I've seen Damien, but I'm reminded again of what a sweet, nice guy he seems to be as he kisses me warmly on the hand, just like Trevor Howard would have done in a 1940s black and white B movie. He then presents Caroline with a lovely, tall potted pink orchid.

'I never bring wine to a dinner party, my dear,' he says to her. 'It's considered very bad etiquette, you know. Presumes that the host or hostess hasn't put thought or consideration into choosing the correct wines to serve with each course.'

CON:

That's the kind of thing my grandad, God rest him, would have come out with. I smile gamely though and resist the temptation to start messing and say something like, 'In that case, never come to dinner in my house. I don't care what plonk I serve up to my unfortunate guests as long as it's fermented and distracts them from my atrocious/non-existent cooking skills.'

PRO:

He's really made an effort with his appearance tonight and I have to admit, does look really well. For a man of his age . . .

CON:

Oh, who am I kidding? He looks so old that I actually feel cheeky calling him by his first name.

PRO:

After a few minutes of chit-chat, the door bursts open and in barge the kids, high on E numbers from McDonald's and swinging freebie novelty toys they've got for us all to see.

Damien, I can't help noticing, is really great with them, giving them both piggy-back rides on his shoulders and shelling out cash for them to buy treats with tomorrow. The analytical part of my mind that I'm slowly training to filter potential husbands from potential losers instantly notes what a great dad he'd make.

CON:

Well, that fantasy didn't last long. Caroline sweetly asks him how his grandchildren are. Turns out he has five, ranging in age from ten to eighteen. *Eighteen!* That's almost old enough for Jamie to hit on . . .

There was a time, long ago, when my mother would jokingly ask me if I'd met the father of my children yet. Then, as the years passed and I still had no man to show for myself, the question morphed into 'Have you met the father of your stepchildren yet?' Now, it's the father of my step-*grand*children . . .

PRO:

No sooner have the kids been ushered into the TV room by the au pair than poor Damien collapses on to a kitchen chair, knackered. It flashes through my mind that, in a million years, he'd never have the *energy* to cheat on me.

CON:

Oh my God, I can't believe I just listed that as a pro . . .

As soon as Mike gets home, the four of us troop upstairs to the dining room, which Caroline has laid out beautifully with linen napkins and all the good Louise Kennedy crystal glasses. Dinner is up to her usual five-star standards (she's gone for a wonderful Asian theme tonight: Malaysian noodle soup with coconut and prawns to start, followed by stir-fried pork with aubergine for mains. Unbelievably yummy – so much so that by dessert I think I'll have to roll home.)

It's actually a really enjoyable evening, and Caroline and Mike never once have to resort to prodding either myself or Damien into chatting to each other. In fact, it hardly feels like we're being set up at all. He's very easy and relaxed and seems genuinely interested in my TV work. I entertain the table with a few choice anecdotes about Good Grief O'Keefe and some of her worse excesses and he encourages me to tell a few more tales out of school. In return, I ask him all about being retired and all the free time he has on his hands. Turns out he spends all of it either playing golf or else looking after his mother, who he lives with.

Once again, my mind's off . . .

PRO:

This is a good thing.

All the self-help books proudly boast that if you want an instant handle on a guy, all you have to do is casually ask him how he gets on with his mom. The rule of thumb being that nice guys tend to have very good relationships with their mothers whereas the losers, my normal targets, tend not to. Given that Damien is well into his sixties, the mother must be in her eighties at least, so, I figure, isn't it sweet that he's so devoted to her?

CON:

He spends so long talking about her, all I can think of is Norman Bates in *Psycho*. I even find myself wondering if he has creepy stuffed birds in his house . . .

After dessert, Caroline asks me to give her hand with the coffee, winking surreptitiously at me from the corner of her eye to follow her. We gather up a load of plates between us and trundle downstairs to the kitchen, leaving the boys to talk about their golf handicaps.

'Well, what do you think?' she asks as soon as the door's safely shut. 'I know the mother thing is a bit of a turn-off, but apart from that?'

I smile at her. That's the great thing about Caroline; you never have to tell her what you're thinking. She always knows. 'On paper, he's perfect,' I say, loading up the dishwasher for her. 'But in practice . . . oh, Caroline, I hate saying this when you've gone to so much bother, but there's just no spark between us. Nothing. I've seen more chemistry in a bad episode of *Celtic Tigers*, and God knows that's saying something.'

'Give him a chance, that's all I'm asking. He'd take you out to lovely restaurants and treat you like a queen and who knows? Maybe you'll kiss him and sparks will fly. Better an old man's darling than a young man's slave, as my mum always says. Anyway, I'm very proud of you for coming out tonight. It was brave of you, considering the week you've had.'

'That's one good thing about Damien,' I say, shuddering, as we head back to the dining room, 'he's the complete antithesis of *He-whose-name-shall-forever-remain-unspoken*.'

Pretty soon after coffee, the grandfather clock in the hallway chimes ten and Damien makes his excuses to leave. 'Goodness, I had no idea it was so late,' he says. 'I'm afraid I really must be off or Mummy will wonder where I am. Besides, I always take her to early Mass on Sunday mornings, so I really ought to call it a night.'

The tiniest, barely perceptible look of he's-a-nice-guy-so-just-ignore-that-comment-and-give-him-a-proper-chance from Caroline.

'You really are a most charming young lady,' Damien says, affectionately kissing my hand as he makes to leave. 'I do hope we meet again. Perhaps you'd do me the honour of having afternoon tea with me some day?'

I hesitate for a nanosecond and then clock Caroline and Mike looking at me, dying to know what I'll say. *Headless groom, Vera Wang, headless groom, Vera Wang . . .* 'That would be lovely, thanks, Damien.'

'Wonderful. I'll tell Mummy we can expect you then. I think you'll both get along very well.'

The three of us dutifully wave him off and then, I'm sorry to say, I get a bit giddy. 'Afternoon tea? Now I know how it feels to be courted like a Jane Austen heroine.'

'Damien's a great guy,' says Mike, shutting the door and yawning. 'I'd never have got into Portmarnock Golf Club without him.'

Hours later, when I'm tucked up in bed, I can't resist the temptation to call Rachel in her hotel in Paris to tell her all about it.

'Oh God.' She laughs so hard I can hear her spluttering on a cigarette. 'So what did his wife die of? Boredom?'

'Shut up. Caroline says I have to give him a proper chance, so I'll do the whole tea with Mummy thing and report back—'

She interrupts me with a loud cackle.

'What?'

'Nothing, I just did a mental calculation.'

'Your point being?'

'If you persist in that half-assed night course of yours, then, in strict chronological order, do you realize who your next target will be?'

I almost drop the phone.

My silence says it all.

'Yes,' says Rachel. 'I might just have to come with you for this one. Over my dead body am I letting you meet up with *him* on your own.'

Chapter Fourteen
The One that Got Away

Oh, this'll be good. Of the entire parade of losers I call my ex-boyfriends, this one I'm actually looking forward to tracking down. First, though, I should give you a little bit of deep background.

Number four is called Tony Irwin and although I'd known him since my schooldays, we didn't start going out with each other till we were both well into second year at college. Tony was amazing, a really, stunningly wonderful all-rounder of a guy. If his life was ever made into a Hollywood movie, he would have to be played by . . . Jude Law.

He went to St Andrew's College, the boys' school around the corner from us, and was something of a lust object/ pin-up/yardstick against which to measure all other men for each and every girl in my class. Apart from his looks (tall, blond, blue-eyed Aryan, the type I'm sure Oscar Wilde would have had in mind when he wrote *The Picture of Dorian Gray*), he really was the man who had it all.

Gifted athletically as well as academically, he was head boy at his school and then went on to read History and English at UCD. He was one of those rare people who the Gods smile

147

on and save all their best gifts for and, as if this wasn't enough, he was easily the nicest and best-liked man I've ever met, before or since. As we say in television: he was so popular, he was practically lowest common denominator. Everyone loved him and absolutely no one had a bad word to say about him.

To give an example of his phenomenal charisma, let me just say that, after all these years, Rachel and I still maintain that he's the only man, living or dead, real or fictitious, that we'd ever physically fight over.

It was circumstances that broke us up, or so I like to think: he won a rugby scholarship to Glasgow University in Scotland and so, to my complete devastation, we had to part. Even though we were both only nineteen, if it had been up to me, I'd have married him. No question. But we lost touch, as you do, and the strain of keeping up a long-distance relationship took its toll, as it inevitably does. So, after a couple of months of romantic letter writing (which seems prehistoric now, in this age of email and five-cent texts and cheapie Ryanair flights to Glasgow Prestwick airport, but back at the end of 1987, a good, old-fashioned pen and paper was all we had, quite apart from the fact that my dad would have crucified me if I'd run up the phone bill on long-distance calls) and after much weeping and wailing and gnashing of teeth on my part, we eventually had to call it a day. That's the trouble with being nineteen; you think the Tony Irwins of this world grow on trees. It was only when I got older that I realized what a rare diamond I'd let slip through my fingers.

But there's one thing no one can ever take from me. For six, happy, glorious months, back in the Hilary and Trinity terms of 1987, I was Tony Irwin's girlfriend.

As soon as she gets back from her trip, Rachel volunteers to do all the detective work for me, which I'm very grateful for, as my work load on *Celtic Tigers* has virtually gone stratospheric.

I even find myself having to slip into the office on Sunday, to play catch-up in editing the production week we've just filmed, and also frantically to read ahead on the coming week's shooting scripts. However, I still manage to find time to call Rachel in Paris and we plot a rudimentary track-Tony-Irwin-down strategy. Now, it may not exactly be Desert Storm, but it's the best we have. OK. Let me explain the chain . . .

1. When Rachel split up with hubbie number two (or shit features, as she calls him) she sold both of her engagement rings and used the money as a deposit on a bijou, dinky little villa by the sea in Dalkey, County Dublin. Her reasoning at the time had been: 'I've been engaged more times than a switchboard, I might as well have something pretty to show for it.'

2. Not long afterwards, she went for broke and bought Urban Chic in the city centre, which came with a fully fitted luxury apartment above the shop, in turn-key condition and with stunning views over the River Liffey. Now, for a city chick like our Rachel, the lure of living in the heart of town was too much to resist, so she rented out the villa and moved lock, stock and barrel into her new bachelor-girl bolthole.

3. It just so happened that when Rachel came to rent out the house, the estate agent sent out another St Andrews's past pupil and an old classmate of Tony's to take care of the place, the unfortunately named Michael Brick, or Mick Brick. Not exactly the brightest candle on the tree, we'd all known him for years – but by his nickname, Thickie Brickie.

4. So this, in a nutshell, is the plan. First thing in the morning, Rachel is going to ring Thickie Brickie on the thinly veiled pretext of discussing the lease on her

villa, which by a stroke of very good luck, is up for renewal at the end of next month. Her tenants are great and she fully intends to let them have the place for as long as they want, but we're hoping Thickie Brickie will live up to his name and not realize that her calling him is only a ruse to dig for information about his old friend Tony. There is, of course, the likelihood that (*a*) Thickie doesn't have the first clue where Tony is or what he's up to or (*b*) he knows where Tony is all right, but is too dim to remember . . .

As Rachel very wisely says, though, we'll just cross that bridge when we come to it.

The TV station is deserted and without the distraction of phones ringing and actors throwing strops, I get loads of work done, although sitting in an empty office on a Sunday afternoon all on your own has to be one of the most surreally lonely experiences you'll ever have. Dave Bruton's words come back to me, that this is the perfect job for someone single, but right now, much as I enjoy the work, I'd prefer to be sweeping the streets or stacking the shelves in SuperValu if it meant that I could go home to a loving husband at the end of a long, tiring day . . .

It's late, almost heading for eight o'clock by the time I'm trudging to the car park to plod my weary way home. I'm fantasizing about whether to order in Chinese, Indian or just to chicken out, call Caroline and ask her if I'm too late to stick my name in the pot for her usual big Sunday family roast, when I hear footsteps behind me.

Through the darkness, I see Philip Burke, also alone and also heading for his car. *Shit.*

OK. Given that this is not only my boss but also the most

intimidating man in television, my first instinct is to run for the hills and hope against hope that he didn't see me, but the car park is practically deserted, so the chances of that are slim. He spots me, waves and strides over. I walk towards him, silently praying that he doesn't ask me any hard questions about our ratings-boosting strategy on *Celtic Tigers*. I'm way too exhausted to do all my hard work any justice right now.

No such luck. Without any preamble or reference to the fact that we seem to be the only two people in the whole station working on a Sunday, he cuts straight to the chase with his usual hawk-like focus. 'Amelia, there you are. I watched the episode broadcast last night, you know, and I have to say that Rob Richards's performance was lazy to the point of coma-inducing even by his standards.'

Double shit. He does want an impromptu work discussion. And believe me, this guy is so scary that just talking to him makes you feel like you're treading on eggshells, in a banana skin factory, in an earthquake.

What I want to say back to him is: 'So you stayed in and watched TV on a Saturday night then, did you, Philip? My, what a full life you lead,' but, unfortunately, I need this job. I take a deep breath. 'Philip, ever since our last meeting, we've made a lot of major production changes, but given that the episode you're talking about was shot weeks before I even came on board—'

'Calm down, I'm not giving you a hard time over this, I'm just pointing out that if you are planning on doing a cast culling, there's your prime target.'

'As it happens, we have had story meetings to figure out a quick, effective way of losing the dead wood from the show—'

'Plane crash? Pub explodes? Alien abduction? *Celtic Tigers* is known for taking chances on crap, as we all know. So what's it to be?'

'We haven't made a final decision yet, but don't worry, I'm on top of it.'

'Glad to hear it. Cut away the fat. Just like a boxer sheds useless flab before winning a world heavyweight title.'

'Emm, yeah.' Philip Burke may be the youngest-ever head of television, but his social skills are up his bum. I'm not sure what to answer to that; I'm too busy thinking: Did he just say that? There's more to come, though.

'I know it must feel like you're flogging a haggard old nag to the gates of the boneyard right now,' he goes on, 'but it'll be worth it. Trust me. I want to see changes on that show and I want to see them fast.'

'You will.'

'When?'

As always, when cornered, I resort to joking to get me out of a tight spot. 'Faster than a Britney Spears marriage.'

The gag is lost on the humourless Philip Burke, however, and he bids me a brisk goodnight. We head for our respective cars and I find myself wondering if he too is going home to a cold, empty apartment.

We're both about to hop into our cars when he calls after me, 'Oh, and Amelia? FYI? That's my parking space you took.'

One thing's for certain though; if Philip Burke isn't actually gay, I'll put money on the fact that he hasn't had a girlfriend in a very long time. There's no woman on earth who wouldn't gladly have thumped that lack of finesse out of him.

I spend the entire journey home full of smart-alec indignation at all the things I wish I'd said.

Now, as it happens, we are actually bringing a new family into *Celtic Tigers*: the Kennedys. Normal, ordinary people who will reflect the normal, ordinary hopes and aspirations of our target audience. He's a doctor, she's a primary-school teacher and they have two teenage daughters who will hopefully generate romantic stories amongst the younger male characters in the show.

Bright and early Monday morning, I'm just rushing into a meeting with our casting director when my mobile rings. Rachel.

'Well, darling, I have *fabulous* news that'll haul you out of your sorrow cycle.'

'Sweetie, I'm just about to go into a meeting, can I call you back?'

'You'd better. The FBI couldn't have done a better number on Thickie Brickie than I just have.'

I glance over my shoulder to make sure no one can overhear. 'EEEEEEK! What did he say?'

'It was like shooting fish in a barrel. He sang like a canary, if you'll pardon my mixed metaphors.'

'So where is Tony now?'

'Get this. He's teaching English and History in Glenstal Abbey. I never bothered asking whether he was married or not, because even Thickie Brickie might have copped on to that one. We'll find out soon enough.'

'Do you mean Glenstal Abbey in Limerick?'

Glenstal Abbey is one of the poshest and most prestigious boarding schools in the country. You practically have to build a library wing and pledge an AstroTurf pitch just to get your child on the waiting list. Its past alumni are so esteemed that they're virtually guaranteed seats in the cabinet or at the very least a government ministry if they so choose.

'Glenstal Abbey in County Limerick, the very one. So how are you fixed for a Thelma-and-Louise-style road trip this weekend?'

Chapter Fifteen
There is no Oz without Kansas

So much has happened in the week since my last class that I take up almost ten full minutes of Ira Vandergelder's time. Nor am I the only one battling for airtime. In fact, you can hardly shut any of us up. Everyone is bursting to tell their stories about the previous week's adventures in the dating field and when my turn eventually comes, I seize the day.

My instincts, for once, are totally on the money. I *am* in danger of becoming the class comedienne. Worst part is, though, I'm not trying to be funny. I'm just telling the truth. I'm in the middle of relating to them all the saga of Pete Mooney and poor Mags beside me has to hold her sides, she's laughing so hard. 'Your description of the Dragon bar alone should get a slot on *Saturday Night Live*,' she guffaws at me. And I wasn't even exaggerating.

'Pete wasn't just a slightly camp friend of Dorothy's, he *broadcast* gay. By the end of the night, he'd hit on my friend Jamie. He even referred to me as Jamie's hag.'

More raucous laughter.

'When you were dating him, did you see any signs that he might be gay?' Ira asks, peering at me from under her glasses, the only person in the room who's not finding this hysterical.

'Well, apart from the fact that he wore glittery jackets and eyeliner and would spend more time in the bathroom than me, no. But then this was back in nineteen eighty-six. Not even Boy George had come out then and don't get me started on all the teenage years I wasted lusting after George Michael, thinking that he was straight. For God's sake, even Elton John had a wife back then.'

'Then it clearly wasn't your fault, Amelia. That time. But the lesson for you here is that you've gotta develop and hone those instincts of yours. If there's something weird that you can't quite put your finger on about any guy you're dating, get out quick. Cut your losses. A smart dater doesn't waste precious time on a relationship that's not moving forward. Did you do your assignment? Did you ask a friend for a fix-up?'

'Yes,' I say, delighted that at least I've done something right. 'With a really sweet man.'

'Why do I sense that there's a but coming?'

'Too old. No chemistry.'

'How old is too old?'

I'm aware Ira will probably say a good man is a good man at any age and that I should be thankful he's not living in an old folks' home that smells of wee, so I know I have to tread carefully here. Either that or make a joke of it. 'Well, it's all relative. To anyone born during the Napoleonic era, I'm sure he's a spring chicken.'

'Do you always use humour as a defence, Amelia?'

This shuts me up. God, Ira's good, to see through me so easily. I'm really amazed. Talk about laser-like penetration . . .

'But then, as I always tell my students, if there's no spark,

155

there's no spark,' she goes on, addressing the packed class-room. Then, to my complete surprise, she adds, 'There is no compromise in my class, nor is there room for desperation. Do not fall into the trap of thinking: What right have I to reject a perfectly good man just because I'm not attracted to him; at my age, I should take what I can get and be thankful for that. You all wanna be happily married to a man you truly love and you all should settle for nothing less. But there is something you *can* do, Amelia,' she says, turning her focus back to me.

'Yeah?'

'OK, so this older man didn't exactly light your fire, but your friend who fixed you up must think very highly of him.'

'Yes, she does. He's a dote of a man really, sweet and attentive and knows how to treat women well.'

'Are you familiar with the phrase "One man's meat is another man's poison"?'

There's a lot of mutterings from the back row.

'What I mean,' says Ira, 'is that in a few weeks' time, we are gonna throw ourselves a class party. I will be asking one of you ladies to host it and the rest of you to provide food and wine. But there's a catch. Each of you will have to bring along a date; but not your normal type of date. A single, straight guy who you've personally vetted to make sure that they're good, decent people, but who you yourself are not attracted to at all. Maybe one of your classmates will fall madly in love with him, who knows? In the United States, we call this a treasure-or-trash party. Amelia, I strongly suggest that you bring along this older guy of yours. Just because you weren't keen, doesn't mean one of these other lovely ladies won't be.'

Genius. Fab idea.

I'm just silently glancing over at Mags and idly wondering whether she finds men in their sixties who still live with their mothers attractive when Ira moves on to the woman on my left. I really want to say, 'Wait! Please! I wasn't finished!' but, in fairness, I've already hogged quite enough of her time. Besides, the story about *He-whose-name-shall-forever-remain-unspoken* is so mind-bogglingly far-fetched, who in the class would even believe me?

Some of the other fix-up stories are a scream. A woman called Sheila sitting behind me said she was matched up with a guy who her best friend did meals-on-wheels with. She very naturally jumped to the conclusion that this meant he was a kind, considerate, civic-minded member of the public. Turned out he was doing meals-on-wheels as part of his community service.

'What's good about this,' says Ira, 'is that you're getting back into the dating zone. OK, so this man wasn't for you, but who's to say the next man won't be?'

To my shock, in no time at all, it's almost nine o'clock and Ira is already giving us our homework for next week. What is it about this class that seems to make time stand still?

'Number one assignment: you are all to get to work on tracking down your next ex-boyfriend and see what you can learn from him,' she commands.

I'm well ahead of you there, I think to myself smugly, absolutely dying to get in touch with the lovely Tony Irwin. He has to be married by now, I reckon, how could he not be? Whoever she is, though, there's one thing for certain. Mrs Tony Irwin has to be the luckiest woman alive . . .

'Number two: I want you all to write out your personal matrix and then figure out a way to expand it.'

A lot of 'Huh?'s and what's-she-on-about looks. I'm inclined to forget that Ira is, first and foremost, a marketer.

'OK,' she says. 'I want all of you ladies to cast a wider net, or, in other words, to expand your market. I give these classes the world over and I'm constantly amazed at the number of single women whose list of criteria they need in a potential husband is so long, you wonder if such a man even exists. Fact: the odds of finding a husband over thirty-five change. Quite simply, women outnumber men. So we need to figure out a way of meeting a whole new range of eligible guys. This means you all gotta forget about your "type". In my class, that's a dirty word. You're gonna learn to be flexible. Your future husband may be shorter than you, he may not earn as much as you, he may not love the theatre the way you do. But if he's a really wonderful person and you could truly love him, should you really overlook him just because of a few trivial details?'

Someone from the back asks a question. 'Ira, what's a matrix?'

'Let me explain. When cell phones first came on the market, they were designed for business people on the move. That was the primary market. But then the phone companies got smart. They realized they could make a lot more money by expanding their target market to include secondary buyers, like teenagers or busy moms. Smart move, I think you'll all agree; that's where they made their fortune. And that's what all of you ladies are gonna do. For next week's assignment, I want you all to write out your matrix, and then figure out how you can expand it.'

By way of explanation, she whips out a red marker and starts drawing a chart on the whiteboard. It looks a bit like this:

Remind Me Again Why I Need a Man

	My Type	Cast My Net Wider
Age		
Profession		
Background/education		
Height/physique		
Interests/hobbies		
Personality type		
Income		
Marital status		

'From this day on, ladies,' she continues, 'you *have* no type. I want you all to fill out this matrix and really give thought to the kind of guy who's *not* your type. Remember this is only an experiment, I'm not asking you to compromise yourselves in any way. All you're doing is learning to cast your net wider.'

Class has run way over time by now and eventually Ira wraps it up.

I purposely loiter behind, dying for a quick, private chat with her. Pretty soon, the room empties and I go for it. 'Ira, I'm sure you're dying to get home, but could I have a minute of your time?'

'Sure, honey, fire away.'

I find myself telling her all about *He-whose-name-shall-forever-remain-unspoken*, the unedited version, right the way up to his impending marriage and plans to move across the road from me. I don't even know why I'm telling her except that (*a*) I'm dying to know what she thinks and (*b*) in a million years, there's no way I'd be up to discussing this in front of the class.

Even Ira, with all her boundless energy, has to grab a seat for this one. 'Wow, that's some tale,' she says, shaking her head.

159

'I suppose I really just wanted to tell you that you were right,' I say. 'You told me that when a man doesn't want to commit, all it means is that he doesn't want to commit to you. And you were right.'

'You poor girl, I really feel bad for you,' she says. 'I don't ever believe in putting men down, but what an asshole.'

'Don't worry, that's mild. You should hear what my friends have to say about him.'

'In all the time you were together, did you ever get signs that he wasn't for you?'

'Honestly?'

'Yes, honestly.'

'Loads of them. So many signs, I've lost count,' I say, remembering things like the time he was to come to Spain with me for my dad's surprise seventieth birthday and let me down at the last minute (for absolutely no good reason); the year he completely ignored Christmas; then there was one occasion when he was moody and rude to me at his friend's wedding where I knew absolutely no one . . . it's quite a list.

He was also someone who needed what I can only describe as the uninterrupted ego-massaging normally associated with heirs to the throne in ancient civilizations. You know: the type of guy who thinks that everything centres on him, at all times, always.

Funny how a bit of perspective from a failed relationship can make you feel like a total idiot. When I think what I put up with, in the name of love . . .

'All I can say in my defence is that I really, honestly adored him. I thought he'd change and that I could make it work. Plus, if I have one talent, it's bashing square pegs into round holes.'

'Never think you can change a man, sweetheart,' says Ira,

kindly. 'Biggest mistake you'll ever make. If you want my opinion . . .'

'Yes, please.'

'I think the best thing you can do is stick with this course. You have to stop dating dumb and learn to date smart. If you'd been in my class when this guy first started mistreating you, I'd have ordered you to dump him right there and then. There is no point in throwing good time after bad. Good luck to him and his bride-to-be. There's someone so much better out there for you and we are gonna find him and you, my dear, are gonna have the happiest ending. Where I come from we have an old saying: "There is no Oz without Kansas."'

'What does that mean?'

'It means that you can only really appreciate all the wonderful guys in this world when you've been through the shits. I know what I'm taking about, Amelia. I've been married three times.'

'Wow!'

'And after all that, I still believe in love and happiness. You know, there's a metaphysical word to describe what you're going through. Chemicalization. Ever heard of it?'

'No, never.'

'Put simply, it means that when the universe sends you something awful like you've just experienced, the converse is only around the corner. And this wonderful thing that's waiting for you will be the perfect counterbalance to what you're going through right now. The universe is very fair like that.' She clocks my puzzled look and takes me by the arm. 'It means go home and crack out the champagne, Amelia. Your prince is almost here.'

Chapter Sixteen

The Frenaissance

The rest of the working week goes by in such a blur of meetings, castings, hirings and firings that I almost can't believe it when I wake up at six a.m. on Saturday morning (force of habit; *Celtic Tigers* starts shooting at seven) and then realize that this is the one morning of the week when I can actually sleep on.

I doze off and have the craziest dream . . .

I'm living in a mud hut in Johannesburg with *He-whose-name-shall-forever-remain-unspoken*, barefoot and pregnant, when Ira Vandergelder swoops down in a helicopter, throws a rope ladder over the side, and rescues me.

Figure that one out, Dr Freud.

I'm in the deepest, soundest sleep when the phone on my bedside table rings. Rachel, putting on a truly awful Southern accent. 'Hi, Thelma, it's me, Louise! Get your lazy arse out of the bed and look out the window.'

'Oh God, what's the time?' I ask, groggily dragging myself out of bed.

'Time we were on the road, sleeping beauty. It's eleven-thirty.'

I haul myself like a sleepwalker over to the balcony window, throw back the curtains and there they are: Rachel and Jamie, sitting in the front seat of her convertible with the roof down, waving at me like a pair of demented loonies. Rachel is looking very Audrey Hepburn today, in a 1960s-style shift dress and big, dark sunglasses, and Jamie looks like he always does, as if he just fell out of an early house pub down the docks.

Suddenly I'm wide awake. I fling open the French windows and stage whisper down to them, mindful that (*a*) my neighbours are all night owls who, chances are, could still be asleep and (*b*) *He-whose-name-shall-forever-remain-unspoken* might have moved in across the road: 'Jamie! Are you coming with us?'

'Course I am. I was starting to feel really left out of all the fun. If you pair are going to be Thelma and Louise on this road trip, then I'm Brad Pitt. You know, the sexy, super-cool drifter they pick up. Don't you think that would be good casting for me?'

'You have exactly five minutes to get your tush down here,' says Rachel, ignoring him. It's a three-hour drive and I plan on a good stiff cocktail before we get to Glenstal.'

'Booze hound,' says Jamie.

'People in glass houses,' she snaps back. 'The smell of stale drink off you, I'm only thankful we can take the top down on the car. You must have been locked out of your head last night.'

'Do you mind? I prefer tipple happy.'

To avoid them entertaining the neighbours any further, I manage to persuade them to come up to the flat for a lightning-quick coffee while I jump in the shower, and then decide on a suitable outfit for, fingers crossed, meeting Tony Irwin in.

163

'Now remember, he's a schoolteacher,' Jamie advises me as I'm standing in front of my wardrobe in a bath towel, frantically trying to root out something. 'So nothing too overtly sexy. Dress like you would for a garden party and you won't go too far wrong. You know, vicar's-wife type vibe.'

I settle on a long, floaty skirt and a sweet little pink cashmere twin set which is on extended loan from Rachel and, five minutes later, we're on the road.

Caroline calls and we put her on the car speakerphone so we can all chat/squeal at her.

'Have fun, you guys,' she says. 'Think of me stuck at home all weekend!'

'Where's Mike?' I ask.

'Don't get me started,' she says, a bit crossly, for her. 'He's at a conference in London. Which means he'll spend ten minutes talking to sales reps and the rest of the time out on a golf course. Won't be back till Monday. So ring me all the time and keep me in the loop. Otherwise I'll go off my head looking at Barney DVDs and scraping porridge off the walls. Oh, and will you do me a favour?'

'The answer is yes, what is the question?'

'Will you ask Tony if he has any pull getting boys into Glenstal Abbey? I'd so love to enrol Joshua there. Wouldn't he look so sweet in that lovely navy-blue uniform?'

'Consider it done,' I say. 'In fact, it might even be good cover for us going down there in the first place. Sure as hell beats my explanation of, "Oh, hi there, Tony, long time no see, we were just passing, don't suppose by any miracle you're still single?"'

She laughs and we all say goodbye and promise to keep her fully posted.

'OK, girlies,' says Jamie, 'we have a gruelling, three-hour

journey ahead of us, so that should just about give us enough time for me to tell you about my date last night.'

'Don't tell me you actually met up with Pete Mooney?' I ask, horrified at the very thought.

'Like I'd ever do that to you? Even I have standards, you know. Besides, that is *soooo* last Friday's news. Try to keep up.'

'With your Spaniard?' Rachel asks innocently.

'No, that's mucho finito.'

'Since when?'

'Since he stopped calling over a week ago. You know me, I'm not needy but I do require the reassurance of constant attention and if he can't provide that, then let him see how dull and boring life is in a Jamie-free universe.'

'This is the twenty-first century, don't tell me guys still do that?' says Rachel, wrinkling her nose in disgust, as if she'd just driven past a silage plant. 'Just stop calling you and then expect you to psychically deduce that you've been dumped? And what's the statute of limitations these days anyway?'

'Stop using long words. Explain. Slowly. I'm *very* hung over.'

'I mean, thicko, if a man stops calling, then how long do you give it before you accept that he's the dumper and you're the dumpee?'

'Depends,' says Jamie. 'With me, there's usually a forty-eight-hour rule. And a text message doesn't count. That's just what guys do when they couldn't be arsed picking up the phone to you. No full-on phone contact, no Jamie. Look at me, Amelia, and learn by example.'

'When I was married to shit features number two,' Rachel chips in, 'and he was working late and wouldn't call me, I used to think either he was having an affair or lying on the side of the road in a coma. Funny, but I think I actually would have preferred the coma option.'

'I'm really sorry to hear about your Spaniard,' I say. 'It would have been nice if things had worked out for you.'

'Yeah, well, it would have been nice if Hitler had channelled all his energies into opening a nice chain of vegetarian restaurants instead of the Third Reich, but guess what? That didn't happen either.'

'So what poor unfortunate freak-o-saurus were you dating last night?' Rachel asks.

'This guy I met on the internet. Now, normally, I'm not one to kiss and tell, but . . . Oh, who am I kidding? Well, girlies, you'd have howled. From his profile, I expected to meet a guy with the swarthy good looks of a young John Cusack and the charisma of that guy who won American *Pop Idol*. What I actually got was a middle-aged man who looked like one of the judges on *Pop Idol*, with all the charisma of a Heinz ketchup bottle. I wanted to say to him, "Do you *have* a full-length mirror in your house?" The difference between him and his Gaydar profile was so unbelievably huge, you'd think he was leading a double life. You know, kind of like Bruce Wayne and Batman. Except this guy looked more like the aul' fella that's the butler.'

'Just out of curiosity,' I ask, 'what does your Gaydar profile say?'

'Actor, Buddhist, gym bunny, muscle Mary. OK, maybe I've only been a Buddhist for twenty minutes but, apart from that, it's all true. I'm far too honest about myself online, that's my trouble.'

Just then, his mobile beep-beeps for about the fourth time. 'Oh shit, it's him again,' says Jamie, glancing at the text message, then snapping the phone shut. 'He's got a bad case of Jamie-itis. How am I going to let him down gently? What would you do, Amelia? You repel men all the time.'

'Stop taking your hangover out on me. For a Buddhist, you have a very nasty streak.'

We've just bypassed Naas when naturally enough the chat turns to Tony Irwin.

'Now, don't pass out,' says Rachel, 'but if by any miracle he's still single, then, baby, you've got yourself some competition. My legs are waxed and I'm match fit, if you get my drift.'

'Well, stop the presses,' says Jamie, sticking his head between us from the back seat of the car, suddenly as excited as a puppy that needs the loo badly. 'Can this be Rachel speaking? The same Rachel who has forsworn all men, love, romance and all that jazz?'

'Doesn't surprise me in the least,' I say. 'This is Tony Irwin, after all. The only man we ever fought over in eighteen years.'

'You better watch out, sweetie,' says Jamie, patting my arm, 'she might just deploy the lethal Rachel pheromone.'

'Ladies, we have to be realistic here,' I say.

'One hour away from meeting someone you haven't seen in eighteen years and now you want to get realistic, because . . . remind me again? Oh yes, because you think this will get you a husband this year,' says Jamie.

'Why don't you find a parade and then go and rain on it,' Rachel snaps at him. 'Could you imagine if we had to track down all of your exes? It would take a lifetime.'

'I know,' he agrees, taking it as a compliment. 'I am to dating what—'

'Cholera is to Senegal,' she finishes his sentence for him.

'I was about to say that we should realistically accept that Tony is happily married with a large family by now,' I go on, ignoring their bickering, which always blows over like a tropical storm. 'So you deploy the lethal Rachel pheromone all you like and we can fight over him all we want, but I think we both know that if either one of us actually got him, it would be way too good to be true. Chances are some other lucky bitch has got there light years ahead of us.'

'Yeah, you're probably right,' says Rachel grudgingly. 'He couldn't possibly be still single. Life isn't like that, is it?'

I nod in agreement and we drive on in silence, the mood in the car having cooled down considerably.

To this day, I can never understand how a guy like Tony picked someone like me over Rachel.

And then I remember . . .

THE TIME: Spring 1987.
THE PLACE: The Carlton Cinema, O'Connell Street,
  Dublin.
THE OCCASION: Tony and I have just been to see
  Withnail and I *with Rachel and Jamie who are, get this, a*
  couple.

'Isn't Tony just the sweetest, loveliest man ever?' I shout at Rachel over the toilet cubicle that's separating us. 'I think I've met the love of my life and I'm only n-n-n-n-nineteen.'

'Shut up, I hate that bloody song,' she barks, flushing the loo.

'Sorry, but I really think this is THE ONE. He's so adorable; he even apologized for all the bad language in the film. There're not many guys who would come out with something like that.' I come out of the cubicle and head over to where Rachel is frantically putting on even more blusher and lip gloss in front of the mirror. 'I love your hair in the bob,' I say to her admiringly. 'You look just like Holly Hunter.'

'Tell that to my boyfriend.'

I'm only half listening as I'm so anxious to get back to Tony. You know when you're so mad about someone that even running to the loo seems like an eternity to be apart?

'Are you nearly ready Rachel? The lads said they'd wait outside for us and then Tony's talking about getting the bus back out to the Belfield bar for a nightcap.'

'Do I look OK to you? You know, normal? Attractive? Not repulsive?' she suddenly asks me, out of nowhere.

'You look like any man's fantasy.'

It's the truth. In fact, I might as well be honest here. I have a niggling, sneaking suspicion that the only reason I had the great good fortune to land my lovely, wonderful Tony is because Rachel was otherwise occupied with Jamie . . .

'I went to loads of trouble to look well tonight,' she says. 'I've three tins of mousse in my hair, this outfit cost all of my Saturday job money and my shoulder pads are miles bigger than anyone else's here.'

'Rachel,' I say gently, 'what's up?' She's been in bad form all evening, but this is the first time she's hinted at the reason why. It's not like her to show any kind of chink in her armour.

'Jamie. My so-called boyfriend. That's what's up.'

'Tell me.'

'I don't know. All I know is that whenever I'm with him, I feel like the unsexiest girl in college. He won't lay a finger on me and it's driving me nuts. Apart from a few chaste kisses, with no tongues, that's it.'

'Oh, honey, are you OK?'

'No actually, I'm not.'

'Maybe he just wants to take things slowly. He's such a good friend—'

'My arse. Amelia, everyone in UCD is doing it except me. My parents were out last night and he came over to watch a video of *9½ Weeks*, which I'd rented specially, thinking it would get him in the mood. Then he spent the whole night talking about Mickey Rourke and did I think he'd look as well as him if he started taking aerobics classes. I'm telling you, my patience is wearing very thin.'

'Just because he's not a fast mover doesn't exactly make him a minion of the Antichrist. You're one of his closest friends; it's hard for him. Maybe he just needs a bit of encouragement.'

'I drip-fed him six cans of West Coast cooler, put on a nice, romantic Lloyd Cole and the Commotions record, sat on his knee and practically threw myself at him.'

'What happened?'

'He said he was feeling really flabby and that the crappy lighting was doing nothing to help. And then he started giving out about the music, leaped up and put on Bronski Beat instead. Not exactly what you might call smooch music.'

'Have you tried talking to him about it?'

'Course I have. I started to explain to him that I was a normal, hormonal teenager with needs and desires and you know what he said?'

'What?'

'He said, "Why are you telling me this? Are you dying?"'

'Oh, Rachel, I'm really sorry. I don't know what to say.'

'You'll laugh when I tell you what else he said. That he *respects* me too much. Can you believe that? Most nineteen-year-old men would basically do it with a tree and I'm dating frigid bloody Fred. You mark my words. There's something wrong with that fella.'

'OK, now I'm officially bored,' says Jamie, stretching out on the back seat of the car. 'Are we there yet?'

'Behave yourself,' says Rachel. 'Not much longer.'

'What are you smirking at, Amelia?'

'Oh nothing, just remembering something.'

'Spit it out. I'm practically comatose and my bum feels like a bag of spanners.'

'Well, it's just that when I was seeing Tony, do you remember? You pair were having the fling, or rather the non-fling of the century.'

'Oh dear God, did you have to remind me?' says Rachel.

'Shut up. Easy for you to be disparaging. You made me gay.'

'Well, darling, in that case you're on a road trip with the Gaymaker and the Man-Repeller,' says Rachel. 'Be sure to include that on your internet profile, won't you?'

I've booked for the three of us to stay at Limerick's Dromoland Castle, a fabulous five-star hotel, conveniently close to Glenstal Abbey. My treat, as Rachel did all the driving and, while Jamie enjoys the life of luxury, he never has any money to finance it.

However, seeing as how we're on something of a mission, we decide to hit Glenstal first, ask where Tony lives and maybe even get a phone number. The plan is to go back to Dromoland afterwards, freshen up a bit, get in some alcoholic fortification and then (gulp) call him and see if he's free to meet up with us.

What seems like an eternity later, we're finally pulling through the gate of Glenstal Abbey and zooming up the long driveway. As it's a Saturday afternoon, the rugby pitch is in use, with boys training, working out and generally making Jamie salivate out of the window at them.

'If you persist in making a show of us I'll kill you,' Rachel snaps at him. 'Down, boy.'

'I'm only looking. What did I do to piss you off today anyway, Narky Nellie?'

'Well, you got out of bed, didn't you?'

We park the car on the huge, gravelled forecourt and haul ourselves out, stretching after the long journey. It's a fabulous, sunny afternoon and I'm surprised to find that I'm not in the least bit nervous about meeting Tony again. In fact, I can hardly wait.

'All set?' says Rachel, linking arms with me as we totter up the stone steps to the front door.

'Sure I am. What's the worst that can happen? Even if he turns out to be married, it'll still be great to see him. And who knows, maybe we'll even become good friends again. Every girl should have a Tony Irwin in her life. Guys like that are such rare diamonds.'

'I'm right behind you and I heard that and I just want you to know that I'm not jealous,' says Jamie.

We rap on the heavy oak door and wait for ages for someone to answer.

'I can't bear the suspense,' says Jamie. 'I think I might pollute my jeans with excitement.'

Eventually, an elderly monk, bent double with age, opens up. Not surprising as the school is run by the Benedictine order.

'Hello, Father,' I say, trying to sound casual and normal.

'Brother,' he answers.

'Oh, sorry, that's what I mean, Brother. And also, sorry for barging in on you like this, but we were just passing by and you see, we think that, or what I mean to say is . . . we were told that . . . Well, you see, the thing is, this guy we used to know years ago told us that this *other* guy that we haven't seen in ages—'

'We've come to see an old friend of ours,' says Rachel, assertively taking the reins and thankfully cutting me off in mid-ramble. 'He's an English and History teacher here. Maybe you could tell us where to find him? His name is Tony Irwin.'

The monk looks a bit puzzled. 'Emm, let me see, did you say Tony Irwin?'

'Yes. If it's not too much trouble. If you even had his phone number, that would do us just fine.'

The elderly monk still looks a bit baffled. 'I'm trying to think now, my dear, we have so many staff here, do you see . . .'

'It's TONY IRWIN,' says Jamie, speaking as if the man was stone deaf. 'He'd be about our age. Tallish, brown hair . . .'

'Oh, yes indeed,' says the monk, all smiles. 'You mean Brother Anthony. He's at vespers now with the senior boys in the chapel. Would you like to come inside and wait for him? I'm sure he'll be delighted to see you.'

Chapter Seventeen

Me and My Matrix

'There, there, there,' says Rachel soothingly. 'You just drink up. Lovely gin will soon obliterate the memory.'

The three of us are sitting in the bar of Dromoland Castle, all a bit shell-shocked at this latest turn of events.

'Thanks,' I say, trying not to slur my words. 'I think there's a tiny danger there might be some blood in my alcohol.'

'Who'd have thought,' says Jamie for about the thousandth time that night. 'Brother Anthony. Never write your autobiography, Amelia. In a million years, no one would ever believe it.'

'I'll say this for him,' says Rachel dismally. 'He looked really well. Don't you think he looked well?'

'Yeah, suppose,' I answer morosely.

'What I mean is, the monastic life must really suit him. We can't even console ourselves by saying "what a waste" because he seemed genuinely happy. He had that serene, far-away look in his eyes that elderly nuns always get.'

'And not a line on his face, lucky bastard,' says Jamie.

'Is this meant to cheer me up? That he has a good skincare regime?'

'Sorry,' says Jamie. 'My mouth sometimes works independently of my brain. I just meant, well, what else improves that well with age after . . . what, eighteen years?'

'Only three other things in this world,' Rachel replies. 'U2, Madonna and *The Simpsons*.'

No one answers. We're all too busy gazing out into the middle distance, still trying to take it all in . . .

Our stay at Glenstal Abbey was mercifully short and sweet. We were shown into the visitors' parlour, a beautiful, vaulted Gothic room, almost Tolkienesque. In fact, I'm half expecting to see Gandalf and the Hobbits coming out from behind the curtains. The heavy, dark stone walls are stuffed with pictures of rugby teams and past pupils who went on to be the president, that kind of thing. There's also an incongruous-looking platinum CD, wall mounted, which looks completely out of place beside a photo of the Pope. We're all three of us drawn to it and Jamie reads the caption below out loud: '"For the monks of Glenstal Abbey. For the remarkable achievement of sales figures over one million copies. Sony Records."'

'Oh yeah,' I say, remembering. 'Didn't the Benedictine monks release a CD of Gregorian chant music a few years ago? I think they may even have had a number one.'

'Ironic, isn't it?' Rachel says to Jamie. 'You were the one who was in a boy band and yet all Tony Irwin had to do was become a monk and he still managed to have a more successful career in the music industry than you.'

'Oh, shut up. Emergency Exit broke up because of artistic differences.'

'Really? I thought it was because you sounded like a bag of cats being doctored without anaesthetic.'

I'm about to shush the pair of them up when the door opens and Tony – sorry, I mean Brother Anthony – strides in, in the long, flowing brown robes, the crucifix, with his head shaved, the full works. Still the same, gorgeous, warm, friendly Tony; still the same magnetic charisma.

In an instant, I revert back to being a giddy teenager with a crush, and Rachel is the very same. We're both staring at him as if we've just met Jesus. In fact, if they were ever remaking the Jesus of Nazareth story, the casting department need look no further than Tony. I swear, the blue eyes alone would burn through celluloid.

He's delighted to see us, shakes all of us by the hand and asks how each of us are doing with the great, unaffected sincerity that made him so irresistible all those years ago. He never refers to the fact that he's become a monk, as if it would be too vulgar even to presume that we didn't already know all along.

I can't help myself though. I'm dying to find out. So, after some polite chit-chatting and general catching-up, I go for it. 'So, Tony, sorry Brother Anthony—'

He smiles. 'It's OK, you're grand. Tony will do me just fine.'

'I hope you don't mind me asking you, but . . .'

'But what am I doing here?'

Rachel, Jamie and I all titter nervously.

'It's OK,' he says, laughing. 'I get asked that all the time. I think I realized I had a latent vocation about ten years ago. I used to come here on retreat quite a lot and the Benedictines helped me to realize that this was my true calling. I suppose I just fell in love with the spiritual life and with the solitude here. Have you ever felt that strongly about something, Amelia?'

He's looking me right in the eye now, in that way he has which makes you feel like you're the only person in the room.

'Do you know what I mean? That you've finally found the one true path God wants you to follow?'

Coming from Tony, this didn't even sound cheesy, like a door-to-door bible salesman. In fact, he's so persuasively sincere that five more minutes with him and he'd probably have had me thinking I should really have been a nun. A distant bell rings though, and he excuses himself, saying that it's time for evening Mass and that he has to be on his way.

'Matins, lauds, terce, Mass, compline, it's all go here, you know.' He smiles again.

'It's certainly not what you might call happy-clappy, is it?' says Jamie.

Tony – sorry Brother Anthony – takes it in good spirits. 'You're very welcome to come and stay with us, you know. We have a guesthouse here for weekend visitors. If you ever want to recharge your spiritual batteries, the offer is there. Ordered calm and contemplation can be a gateway to the spirit.'

He asks us to stay in touch and then blesses us, which I can see out of the corner of my eye is making Rachel giggle like a schoolgirl and Jamie react as though he was the Antichrist and had just had holy water sprinkled on him.

But it makes me feel better.

Back in the bar at Dromoland, we're all three of us well on the way to being completely sozzled. Particularly Jamie, who's been drinking doubles and who's always crap at holding his drink anyway.

'Shhho what'shhh up next then?' he asks me. 'You braaave little footsholdier.'

'Next up,' I answer, trying to sound positive, 'I have to work out my own personal matrix.'

'Your whatshhh?'

'It's about expanding my target market and casting my net wider and . . . oh, forget it, you'll only laugh.'

'After the day we've had, I think we could all do with a laugh,' says Rachel, knocking back the dregs of her G and T, sober as a judge. 'Who's for another round? Come on, when you're out, you're out.'

'You and your hollow legs,' I say to her enviously. Rachel can drink anyone, male or female, under any table, easy as eggs.

'Go back to the . . . whasssit . . . oh shit . . . that movie with Keanu Reeves . . .' says Jamie, clicking his fingers.

'Matrix,' I answer.

'Explanation, please.'

'Simple. What you do is think about the type of fella you'd normally go for, then expand your market. You divide it all up into separate categories – you know, age, profession, income, hobbies; all of that – and then you figure how to cast your net a bit wider. The idea is that I start looking at blokes who might have been invisible to me before.'

'HAAAAAAAAAAA, ha, ha, are you listening to that?' says Jamie, prodding Rachel in the ribs. 'Shoooo? Would that make you look at Gormless Gordon in a whole new light, my serially celibate one?'

'PISS RIGHT OFF,' Rachel snarls back at him. 'I only wish to God he *was* invisible.'

I should explain. Gordon (nicknamed 'Gormless Gordon' by who else but Jamie) owns the bistro right across the road from her boutique and is a living, breathing example of the devastating havoc the lethal Rachel pheromone can wreak. Every week he asks her out; every week she shoots him down and the following week he's bounced right back and is hanging around the boutique, desperately trying to date her again. There's nothing wrong with the guy, he's perfectly normal in every other way apart from this huge, life-threatening crush he has on our Rachel.

'You have to feel a bit sorry for him,' I say, sadly.

'Poor kamikaze bashhtard,' slurs Jamie.

'To call Gormless Gordon thick is an insult to thick people everywhere,' snaps Rachel. 'Now can we please change the subject?'

'I'd kill to have a lovely fella chasing after me, asking me out all the time,' I say. 'Even if I wasn't interested, at least it's marginally better than what I have going on at the moment, which is a big fat nothing.'

'It's not any kind of ego boost, believe me,' says Rachel. 'The guy is just too dim to take no for an answer. May I remind you that this is the man who once said he thought Apollo Creed was the first man on the moon.'

Jamie starts to snort into his glass. 'And remember when he said tsunami was an actual place somewhere.'

'Enough said,' says Rachel. 'He's the only person on earth who could make Bob the Builder sound like Nietzsche.'

'But the queshhtion under dishcussion is, what ish Amelia's normal type?' Jamie refocuses. 'Shoo, lemmmme see. I know you like 'em tall, successful, independent, you know, someone who won't be hanging out of you all the shtime . . .'

'Let's take a moment to recap, shall we, children? Here's an update of my type to date,' I say. 'A serial cheater, a closet gay, a self-confessed commitment-phobe who then gets engaged to the first girl he meets after he breaks up with me and, last but not least, a perfectly lovely man who unfortunately had a latent vocation. If anyone could do with expanding their horizons a bit, it's me, you have to admit. At the age of thirty-seven, I'm finally having to accept that not only have I not found great love, I haven't exactly inspired any of the men I've been with either.'

Jamie immediately bursts into song, warbling a few lines from the old Marianne Faithfull number 'The Ballad of Lucy Jordan'.

'Don't,' Rachel and I say together.

'Why? Whattttshhhh's wrong with that song?'

'Just the line about her being thirty-seven and realizing that "she'll never ride through Paris in a sports car . . ."'

'I know,' says Rachel. 'That song always gets me too and I never know why.' She squeezes my shoulder affectionately. 'I agree with you, sweetie, you may not have a great track record,' she continues, on her way up to the bar, 'but at least you don't have Gormless Gordon the moron plaguing you morning, noon and night. Besides, as D:Ream would say, things can only get better.'

'What is it with me?' I say to Jamie as Rachel shouts in another order for us. 'I hate to sound whiney, but how come some women find it really easy to find husbands and partners and men chasing after them whereas to me, it's completely elusive, like . . .'

'Me trying to break into movies?'

I smile. 'Kind of, yeah. All I want to figure out is: What am I doing wrong?'

'You, my daaarling one, have been very busy concentrashing on your career, shat's all that's wrong. And you're shooo shhhuccessful, Miss Big Shhhot Producer Pants . . . and I'm shoooooo proud of you.'

'Bless you. That's the nicest thing I've heard all day.'

'Now gimme a job.'

'Stop harassing her for work,' says Rachel, plonking back down again. 'OK. Get out a pen and paper, Amelia. We're going to figure how to widen your matrix.'

'Here? Now?'

'Either do it without the attitude or don't do it at all. If you have to do this, then we may as well have a bit of fun while we're at it.'

An hour later and the three of us are hysterical with laughter, the perfect antidote to the day we've had. We've scribbled my matrix all over a couple of paper napkins and it reads something like this.

AGE, MY OLD ATTITUDE:

In an ideal world, my ideal type of man would be aged somewhere between thirty-five and forty-five. Fifty's kind of getting on a bit and I'm afraid that if I went out with anyone younger than thirty, there's a good chance I could be mistaken for his mother.

MY NEW IMPROVED ATTITUDE:

From here on in, any heterosexual male aged between eighteen and eighty is within my target age range. As Jamie says, if a man has his own breathing apparatus, that's considered a bonus. Even if he has a bus pass, a pension and has to go everywhere with a nurse in tow, so be it.

PROFESSION, MY OLD ATTITUDE:

Work is an important part of my life and if I'm really honest I would have to admit that I like a man who enjoys what he does and is good at it. In my experience, they tend to be the best adjusted ones. Besides, let's be brutally honest. As Rachel says, would I really have anything in common with the man who sweeps the streets?

MY NEW IMPROVED ATTITUDE:

From now on, the man who, although trained to dig a hole in the road, is now reduced to holding up the 'STOP/GO' sign at roadworks is on the menu.

EDUCATION, MY OLD ATTITUDE:
Being completely upfront, I have to admit that I do like a guy
to have a few letters after his name.

MY NEW IMPROVED ATTITUDE:
As long as a guy has letters *in* his name, he's a potential
husband.

INTERESTS/HOBBIES, MY OLD ATTITUDE:
I'm a great theatre-goer (even, in fact, especially if Jamie *isn't*
in a particular show I want to see) so I love a man who I
can share that pastime with. Also it's great if he's sporty
and athletic, enjoys reading, eating out, fine wines, holidays
abroad, weekend breaks at home, old black-and-white
movies, Monty Python, music, literature and art . . . but apart
from all that, I'm not in the least bit picky.

MY NEW IMPROVED ATTITUDE:
If his interests include getting out of bed, switching on the
telly and reading the back of a Cornflakes box while burping
out the national anthem, he's in with a chance.

'So all you're basically doing is taking your standards and
then lowering them beyond all recognition?' Rachel asks.

'No, that's not it. I'm not settling, just trying to be a bit
more flexible, that's all. Suppose there's someone wonderful
right under my nose that I'm not looking at in a romantic
light just because he's not six feet tall with a great job and
sings light opera in his spare time?'

'I have to shay,' slurs Jamie, 'looking at your old me/new
me lisshhhts . . . there's nothing in the "new me" column
that'd put me off any guy. I shhon't care what he is or does,
once he's mad about *this* boy. And has a nice tight arse.'

'Well, that's just fantastic,' I say. 'I'm stuck in a homo-sexual man's matrix.'

Not surprisingly, the drive home the next day is a far more sombre affair than the journey down. All three of us are nursing such colossal hangovers from the night before that Rachel and I are silent for most of the journey while Jamie fills in the background with his babbling. You never even have to answer him when he goes off on these stream-of-consciousness monologues and I'm grateful for this as it gives me much-needed head space to think about the week ahead, which, even by *Celtic Tigers* standards, is exhausting. More meetings, more casting sessions and one other, deeply un-pleasant task which lies ahead . . .

'Now shut me up if I'm boring you girlies,' says Jamie from the back of the car, 'but it really helps my creative visualization process when I talk aloud like this. So, pay attention, universe. I want to be such a big star that I can strut around film sets and say things like, "Make me five iced frappuccinos and bring me the best, frothiest, foamiest one." Or, "Bring me a bowl of M and Ms but take out all the red ones." You know, basic high-maintenance shite-ology.'

I'm so lost in thought that in what feels like half the time it took to get to Limerick, Rachel is already driving through the security gates to my apartment complex. And there it is. A lovely welcome-home surprise waiting for me.

Two cars are parked outside the duplex that *He-whose-name-shall-forever-remain-unspoken* is moving into. The front door is open and a tall, willowy blonde girl is busy unloading boxes from the boot of one car. She's utterly gorgeous, in a leggy, doe-eyed, Carolyn-Bessette-Kennedy way, the type who was just made to model Calvin Klein jeans. Through the open hall door, I can just about catch a glimpse of *He-whose-name-shall-forever-remain-unspoken* on his way back outside to unload more boxes.

Suddenly, all three of us in the car are wide awake.

'I don't suppose there's the slightest chance you didn't see that?' Rachel asks.

'*Bastard!*' says Jamie. 'Do you want me to sort him out for you, Amelia? Just give me the nod and I'll take him out.'

'You'll *take him out*?' says Rachel. 'Oh, please, where do you think you are? Chicago? Nineteen twenty-two?'

'Drive,' I say in a hoarse whisper, slumping down in the seat in the hope that I won't be seen. 'Just drive the car.'

Rachel almost chokes the engine, she revs past the house so fast. Then she pulls up outside my building, which is literally one hundred metres down the road.

'Are you OK?' they both say, patting my arm, really concerned.

I take a deep breath and try to sound cool and rational. After all, it's not like I didn't know this was coming. In fact, I've been dreading this for so long, that now that it's actually happened, in a weird way it's almost a relief. 'OK. I have two clear choices. Either I can go upstairs, drown myself in Sancerre and spend the rest of my life feeling sorry for myself, or I can accept the situation, deal with it and move on. Just remind me to set my alarm for half an hour earlier tomorrow morning, so I can at least drive past their house with make-up on and freshly washed hair.'

'Good girl,' says Jamie. 'Come out fighting. She's not all that good-looking either. I know I only had a quick glimpse, but I'd swear I saw acne scarring.'

'Like we said last night,' says Rachel, 'things can only get better.'

'You guys. What would I do without you?'

Chapter Eighteen

An Iron Fist in a Velvet Glove . . .

OK. I don't particularly like Mondays at the best of times, but today is really going to be a howler. I've hardly slept a wink with the knot of tension that's in my tummy. I might as well have had the *Celtic Tigers* logo tattooed on to the insides of my eyelids, I spent so much time in bed last night tossing and turning, tummy churning in dread of the next day.

Two grim Herculean labours lie ahead. I have to impart news about future plans for each of their characters to (*a*) Good Grief O'Keefe and (*b*) Rob Richards. I've scheduled both meetings for as early on Monday morning as possible, mainly to get them over and done with as soon as I can.

Eventually, I realize that I'm not going to get any sleep, so I get up at dawn, jump in the shower, throw on my only ironed pair of trousers with a smart black cashmere sweater and lash on a bit of make-up.

Up until last night, you understand, I'd never have dreamed of going to all this much trouble just to go into the office, but you never know who you might meet on the way there.

It's still dark when I jump into my car and head for the security gates. I can't resist taking a peek as I drive past. Yes, there's *He-whose-name-shall-forever-remain-unspoken*'s house, two his-and-hers jeeps parked outside, curtains drawn and in pitch darkness.

Obviously not morning people then.

Good.

There's very little traffic at that hour, but even though it's early when I get into the office, pretty much everyone's here. And there's a distinctly gallows-like atmosphere about the place. It's almost as if everyone knew it would be pistols at dawn and came in extra early so as not to miss out on any of it.

'Good luck this morning, Amelia!' hisses Suzy, our lovely production secretary to me as I make my way through the main office and on into the more private conference room which I've commandeered for the time being. I close the door, take a deep breath and plonk down on a swivel chair. A text comes through on my mobile and the beep-beep almost makes me jump out of my skin, I'm that edgy.

Jamie. On his way home from a club, probably. TAKE NO PRISONERS TODAY DEAREST GIRL BUT IN CASE OF EMERGENCY JUST TEXT ME AND I WILL BRING VODKA.

I'm just about to reply when, without even knocking, the door bursts open and in she comes: all five feet nothing of Good Grief O'Keefe. Bang on the dot of seven-thirty, which is probably the only time this season she's been on time for anything.

She's absolutely tiny, just like a doll, with the face of an angel, a figure like Kylie Minogue's and an attitude that would make J-Lo seem like a meek, sweet-natured pushover. Her tactic is clear as crystal: suck up to the producer as much as is humanly possible, lay on the charm offensive and hope that's all that's needed to ensure her long-term survival on *Celtic Tigers*.

'Amelia!' she says, air-kissing me and plonking a cappuccino down in front of me. 'I thought you might be gasping for a coffee, so I got you this. Look at *you*! You look FAB! How do you always manage to look so stunning at this hour of the morning?'

I'm not looking in the least bit fab, but it doesn't stop her rabbiting on about the outfit that I'm wearing, my hair and make-up, then moving on to eulogize what a wonderful producer she thinks I am. In a nutshell, her sycophantic carry-on would be considered nauseous in LA, but in Dublin, it's little short of projectile-vomit-inducing.

'Have a seat,' I say, mentally reminding myself to call her by her proper name, Cara, and not Good Grief O'Keefe.

'Anything you say, you're the boss and can I just say, you're by far the best producer I've *ever* worked with, Amelia. I hope you're not going to leave us now for the bright lights of Hollywood!'

Don't get sucked into all the toadying, says my inner voice, *just come straight to the point and get it over with. Oh, and try to avoid the coffee, it could be spiked.*

'Cara, I just wanted to have a chat with you about the storyline we have planned for your character.'

'Fantastic,' she says, looking a bit relieved that she's not for the chop. 'You know me, I'm a pro to my fingertips. I'm happy to play out any storyline you have, whatever it involves.'

'Well, that's good to hear. OK. As you know I've had a lot of intensive meetings with the story team over the past couple of weeks, and I think we all feel that we've gone about as far as we can down the sex-kitten, glamorous, femme-fatale

187

route with your character, Glenda. So we've decided to send her off in a completely different direction . . .'

She's looking at me, face frozen, but with her mouth parted in shock, and it flashes through my mind what a great silent-movie actress she would have made. You know, the ones that had captions underneath them in the 1920s: this one would be 'STAR FEIGNS HORROR'.

'Basically, what happens is this. Glenda finally walks out on Sebastian, sick to the gills of all of his cheating and mistreating her. She loses pretty much everything: her home, car and flashy lifestyle. Times get tough for her, but she refuses to take a penny from her family or friends; instead she's determined to forge a brand-new life for herself, without being dependent on any man ever again. She's too proud to accept any help from all her old friends and pretty soon, they start to dwindle away.'

'And then what?' Good Grief O'Keefe asks; the eyes like slits.

'Obviously she needs money and isn't exactly qualified to do much, so Sam gives her a part-time job in the café, to help get her back on her feet again.'

'Waitressing? You want Glenda to be a *waitress*?'

This silent-movie caption would be 'STAR DOES DEEP SHOCK'.

'Nothing so grand, I'm afraid. No, she ends up working in the kitchen and Sam very kindly lets her rent a room in the flat above the café.'

'Oh dear God, you have got to be kidding me.' ('STAR DOES DISGUST'.) 'Please tell me this is April Fool's Day.'

'Listen, Cara, this is a wonderful storyline for you; it's a fantastic opportunity for you to really get your teeth into something meaty. You've played the glamour girl for years, now here's your chance to let the audience see a whole new side of Glenda. There are actors out there who would *kill* for a storyline like this.' I take a breath. I hadn't wanted to resort to this, but now I may not have a choice. 'Of course, Cara, if you don't want to do it . . .'

It's unspoken between us. This is what's happening irrespective of whether you like it or not; now, do you want the gig or do you want to leave the show?

A pause. 'STAR PONDERS DEEPLY'.

'Right then,' she eventually says with a tortured expression on her face, as if she's having an excruciatingly painful bowel movement. 'But just don't think for one second that I'll be caught dead wearing a hairnet.'

She storms out and I barely have time to catch my breath before Rob Richards comes thundering in, all guns blazing.

'I don't know what you just said to Cara, but she's downstairs bawling her eyes out!' he shouts at me. 'That's how you get your kicks, is it? Reducing people to tears?'

It's intimidating and awful when a man shouts at you and I really have to try my best to stay calm. The minute you get emotional in any argument, I remind myself, you've lost. This is going to be dreadful enough without resorting to raising my voice back at him.

'Sit down, Rob, I have some news for you and I thought it would be better coming from me than from your agent. I feel it's the least we owe you, after all your years here.'

He grunts and sits down and I find myself vowing never, ever, on pain of death by electrocution, to have a drunken fling with anyone I work with for as long as I live . . .

I launch into pretty much the same patter I said to Good Grief O'Keefe earlier and he rudely cuts across me.

'Yeah, yeah, yeah, show's going in a new direction, blah blah. I get it; it's not a subtle point you're trying to make. Can I please just have the last sentence first?'

Still maintaining the same measured tone, I break it to him, far more gently than he deserves. 'Both myself and the story team feel that we've come to the end of the road with your character, Sebastian. You have a marriage break-up story coming up in the next few weeks, where Glenda leaves him to make her own way in the world.'

'Then what?'

'He tries to persuade her to give the marriage another shot, to no avail, so . . .'

'So?'

I brace myself. In his shoes, I'd hate to be on the receiving end of this news too, so I try to make it as quick and painless as possible for him. 'So Sebastian leaves the country. He sells the house and decides to follow his dream. He buys a vineyard in Provence and makes up his mind to spend as much time there as he possibly can, away from his old life and all the constant reminders of happier times with Glenda.'

Rob just glares at me in mute stupefaction.

'Look, Rob, I know this is hard for you to hear, but the good news is that we're not killing off your character. Maybe in a year or two Sebastian could come back to the show. I'm not ruling anything out for the future of this character and neither should you.'

There's an awful silence. I'm studying his face, waiting for the volcano to erupt, when without warning he picks up the cappuccino on my desk and hurls it at me. He misses, but destroys a bundle of scripts I had spread out in front of me. 'You're nothing but a *bitch*!' he roars. 'Who do you think you are, firing me?'

It's a terrifying display but, somehow, I keep cool. 'Rob, I told you, you're not being fired, we're just sidelining your involvement in the show for the foreseeable future and, to be quite honest, if you think behaviour like this is doing you any favours, you're mistaken.'

It's getting harder to stay composed as he's standing right in front of me now, shouting at the top of his voice. 'You have *no show* without me, do you realize that, you blow-in? What am I even doing here, listening to you? You're only a dried-up, frustrated old *spinster*.'

And he's gone. I slump back into the chair and really have to fight back the tears. After a few minutes, there's another, gentler knock on the door. I look up, although I'm still trembling. It's Suzy.

'Are you OK?' she asks me, genuinely concerned. 'God, that was awful. How *dare* Rob Richards speak to you like that? You could hear the shouting from the other end of the office. You could have him up for harassment for that, you know.'

'Oh, Suzy, let's just be glad he's gone. God, I really hate my job sometimes. Do you think I might get lucky and that they'd transfer me back to current affairs? Fallujah would be a breeze compared with this. Right now I'd happily welcome any war zone as if it were an all-inclusive stay at the Ritz-Carlton.'

'I don't blame you. Do you want anything from the canteen?'

'Not unless they've started serving fun-sized packets of morphine to go.'

I'm just beginning to breathe normally again when the internal phone rings.

Philip Burke. *Oh God, what does he want?*

'Amelia,' he says, gruff as ever. 'Can you come up to my office, please? Immediately is good for me.' He doesn't even wait for me to reply, just hangs up.

Five minutes later, I'm knocking on the door of his office, which is the penthouse, three floors above mine.

'Get in here,' he says, so in I troop.

It's a fabulous, spacious room, with floor-to-ceiling windows on two sides and a panoramic view of, well, the car park mainly. I've only ever been here once before, when the station first gave me a contract, all of ten years ago. People only ever come in here to be either hired or fired and I'm just wondering what Philip has in store for me when I notice that he's watching an episode of *Celtic Tigers* on the monitor beside his desk. It's the episode which was broadcast last night, which is the first one I had a hand in. He's analysing it so closely that he doesn't even seem to notice that I'm actually standing right in front of his desk.

I, however, have dealt with quite enough rudeness for one morning, so I do a loud 'ahem, ahem?'

He motions at me to sit down, but doesn't lift his eyes from the screen.

'Wow, Philip, the Zapruder film wasn't studied that closely.'

He laughs, puts the show on freeze-frame and looks up. 'Great, Amelia, there you are. I'm just watching the show and I have to say there is a marked improvement.'

'Thanks. That's good to hear.'

'Are you OK then? You're not going to flood the floor with tears on me, I hope?'

I look at him quizzically, wondering how he knew I was shaken. I thought I was putting on such a good act of 'I'm a producer, I get shouted at and abused every day of the week, I'm well used to it; in fact, in a warped way, I kind of enjoy it.'

'I just had Rob Richards in here telling me what happened, or rather his side of what happened.'

I stand tall, determined not to let someone like Rob Richards and his bully-boy tactics get to me. 'It got ugly,

192

Philip, I'll be honest. He didn't quite throw furniture at me, but wasn't far off it.'

'I see, I see,' he says, his full focus on me. 'He came the heavy with me too. Said that no one in the show was more popular than him and that he had a following.'

'Well, I'm sure both of them can visit him at home.'

He snorts. 'In fact, I'm half expecting Cara O'Keefe to come barging in any second, hot on his heels, to see if she can flirt her way out of this one.'

'And long may she rave.'

'As long as you're all right,' he says, giving me the final once-over, then swivelling back to the TV and switching the 'Play' button on the remote. It's a very dismissive gesture so I take the not-so-subtle hint and head for the door.

He doesn't even bother saying goodbye so I don't either. Philip Burke's people skills – or lack of them – are no concern of mine, thankfully.

I'm almost gone when he stops me.

'So, don't you want to know what I said to Rob Richards?'

I turn around, but he's still engrossed in the TV. 'What?'

'I may not be as witty as you, but I am proud of this one.'

'*Dead Man Walking*?' It's lame, but it's the best I can come up with . . .

'No, I told him to go home and wait for a phone call from the Royal Shakespeare Company. That's the best performance I've seen him give in years.'

Chapter Nineteen

Mr Intense

I'm still so shaken by the day's events that I'm only too delighted to accept Caroline's sweet suggestion to leave work early and pop in to her for a glass of vino on the way home. I really need to be around happy, normal, non–actor–type people right now. She opens the door and wordlessly hands me a lovely, chilled glass of Sancerre.

'Angel from on high,' I say, taking it gratefully.

'Thought you could use a bit of alcoholic fortification,' she says, leading me upstairs to the drawing room. 'If I wasn't pregnant, I'd join you. My darling babies have a sixth sense and start acting the maggot in direct proportion to how exhausted I am.' Just then, murderous screams can clearly be heard from the playroom. 'See what I mean?'

Then Ulrika, the Norwegian nanny, shouts upstairs to us, 'I so sorry, Caroline. I tell Joshua it velly rude for him to pick his nose and he smack me on the head.'

Caroline looks at me in weary exasperation. 'You don't ever need to have kids, you know. You can just have one of mine. If my son persists in picking his nose, he'll end up with nostrils bigger than the port tunnel. Please give me news about life in the outside world. Anything to distract me from the fact that I'll shortly have to go downstairs and cut chewing gum out of Emma's hair. Hubba Bubba too, the stickiest kind. Believe me, I know these things.'

I fill her in on the day's events, sparing no detail. Caroline is suitably shocked, particularly at Rob Richards's shouting-roaring, bully-boy carry-on.

'Can you *believe* him? Yes, it's awful for him to be written out of the show, of course it is, but there's absolutely no need to take it out on you. If he was here now, I'd tear strips off him. And this is not what you needed, you know, not after the shock of Tony Irwin at the weekend . . .'

She chats on and I'm thinking how she's just so fab, like a mother tiger protecting her cubs, whenever any of her friends are being got at. Which is quite a lot, if I'm being honest.

'Let's just say I'm glad it's all over and I'd trade places with you any day,' I say, sinking into the deep, cushiony-soft armchair and taking a big relaxing gulp of vino.

'Be careful what you wish for,' she says with a wry smile. 'May I just remind you that while you were all having fun and games in Dromoland Castle, I was stuck here trying to scrape jam out of the inside of the DVD player. Joshua's latest trick.'

Suddenly I feel guilty. 'Hon, were you OK on your own over the weekend?'

'Oh, you know, I missed you guys. I was exhausted. I missed Mike. But then he goes off on these conferences and plays eighteen holes a day, so at least one of us is having a whale of a time. Besides, would you blame him for needing a break from this house? Rachel says I should have a sign on the door saying "Twinned with Beirut".'

More screeches from downstairs.

'You'll notice I'm choosing to ignore that,' she goes on, visibly wincing. 'I need the adult chat too badly. Ulrika is great, though, she even stayed over Saturday, so at least I managed to have a lie-in. You have to understand that to a parent, that's the equivalent of winning six numbers on the national lottery. Oh, and guess who came to see me yesterday? Asking for you very fondly?'

'I'm too punch-drunk with tiredness to guess . . . Oh, wait a sec, it has to be Damien Delaney.'

'Got it in one. I think he really likes you, Amelia. He says he's going to call you this week to arrange the tea date so you can meet his mum. *Do not* roll your eyes up to heaven,' she goes on, suddenly switching to her cross Mummy voice, the way only parents can. 'I thought we agreed you were going to give this guy a whirl. A proper whirl.'

'I know. I will. I promise.'

'That's the girl. Oh, and I have more news. In fact, this should have been the first item of news. Wow, I'm starting to feel like the latest edition of something, which is a new experience for me. Normally I'm so dependent on you guys to keep me in the know.'

'Oh, I love news. Especially if it's about other people.'

'Two words for you. Mr Intense.'

'*What!*'

'I know exactly what he's been doing all these years. Even better, I think I know *how you can contact him*!'

'How did you . . . ? What do you . . . ? But I thought . . . ?'

Just then, we hear Joshua bawling from the playroom downstairs, followed by Emma screaming at Ulrika, 'I never even touched him, hardly at all. That's tomato sauce, not blood on his face.'

In a trice, Caroline's up and gone off to troubleshoot. 'Do not move from that armchair. I'll be right back and I'll fill you in. Don't suppose you'd care to adopt one of my children, by any chance? I'll pay you cash.'

Oh dear. I really am going to have to go on rhinoceros tranquillizers or some other max-strength medication to stop all these flashbacks . . .

THE TIME: December 1987.
THE PLACE: Dramsoc, the UCD drama society's rehearsal
  space.
THE OCCASION: The annual college fashion show, which
  we're all out in force for, because this year, Caroline is
  modelling in it, along with my boyfriend, who I call Simon,
  but who everyone else calls Mr Intense.

Jamie and I get there early, which turns out to be not such a good idea as we end up sitting beside Mrs Egan, Caroline's mother. Did I tell you about Mrs Egan? She's like a cross between Margaret Thatcher and Lady Bracknell, with shades of Edwina Currie thrown in for good measure. Scary, scary lady, ferociously proud of her beautiful daughter and basically of the opinion that no man is good enough for her. Not even the lovely Mike, who's sitting further down the row from us.

'Another few minutes and you'd have been late,' she sniffs as we take our seats beside her.

'Sorry, Mrs Egan,' we both mumble, instantly regressing back to a pair of ten-year-olds. I don't know what it is; she just has that effect on people. Jamie says that I should console myself, smug in the knowledge that I once peed into the water feature in her immaculate garden when I was seven.

'Oh, there's Mike.' I nudge Jamie, waving down to him. 'Hi! Isn't this just so exciting?'

Mike nods and smiles back at us, but looks a bit put off by

Mrs Egan's frostiness too. In fairness, you couldn't really blame him.

'A dentistry student,' she mutters sotto voce, but clearly intended for Mike to overhear. 'If I've told Caroline once, I've told her a thousand times. A dentist will always be one down from a doctor.'

We're all far too scared of her to answer back, but the sting is fully felt, especially by poor Mike, who visibly reddens, but stays furiously focused on the catwalk ahead.

'*Bonsoir, mes amis,*' says Rachel, breezing in and looking breathtakingly amazing in a fanny-pelmet leather mini and an oversized black leather jacket, a black beret, fishnet tights and stilettos.

'Everyone, this is Christian; Christian, this is everyone,' she says, carelessly introducing us to the guy she has in tow. He's utterly gorgeous, handsome in a Mediterranean way, with black eyes, olive skin and a Kevin Costner haircut. Very, very sexy. We all shake hands, unable to take our eyes off him, particularly Jamie.

'Where are you from?' Mrs Egan asks him imperiously, with this killer glance she has that can kill at ten paces.

'He's Parisian, but you're wasting your time talking to him,' Rachel answers on his behalf. 'He doesn't speak a word of English. Well, hardly any.'

'Then how on earth do you communicate with him?'

'Oh, I don't. We just have fantastic sex and I can assure you, Mrs Egan, his vocabulary when he's shagging me is surprisingly adequate.'

Rachel, I should point out, is the only one of us who was ever remotely able to handle Mrs Egan, who just stares right back at her, with a face that would stop a clock.

'I didn't know she was bringing a date,' Jamie hisses at me, really pissed off. 'Did you know she was bringing a date?

Great. Now I'm the only one here with no date. Jamie heaven.'

'She never told me she was bringing anyone either. He's very good-looking, isn't he?'

'He's all right. Look at the state of her though. All she's short of is a bike, a stripy T-shirt and a string of onions around her neck singing "Frère Jacques". And he doesn't speak English, gimme a break. Does he come with subtitles?'

'Don't get narky, you can hang out with me and Simon afterwards if you want.'

'Mr Intense? Thanks but I'd rather chew tinfoil.'

'Stop having a go. What is wrong with him anyway? He's about to model in a fashion show, don't you think that's really cool?'

'You have to stop using the word cool when you're talking about Mr Intense. He is, without a doubt, the uncoolest person in the whole of UCD and that's really saying something.'

'Jamie, emm . . . Let me see, how can I put this . . . SHUT UP.'

On cue, the house lights are dimmed and the show starts. Kraftwerk's song 'The Model' is played and out comes Caroline, striding down the catwalk as to the manner born. She's modelling a tartan suit with big shoulder pads and a micro-mini, with her hair all backcombed and a black Alice band holding it in place. The lyrics of the song really seem to suit her too; certainly the line about her being a model and she's looking good. I glance back at Mike, who's beaming up at her, transfixed.

'Isn't she stunning?' I say to no one in particular.

'Oh, don't be so ridiculous, Amelia,' snaps Mrs Egan, patting her helmet-hair. 'She looks like a Ukrainian prostitute. I would blush to be seen with her in public dressed in that outrageous get-up.'

Then the lads come on, led by Mr Intense . . . sorry, I mean, Simon, my fella of, oh, going on for two months now. We met after an L and H debate (the Literary and Historical Society) that I was speaking in. He came up to me afterwards and started giving me tips on how I could improve my debating skills, right down to some vocal exercises he recommended for me, which I thought was just so . . . *sweet* of him. You know, considerate and thoughtful.

And not a bit controlling at all, in spite of what Jamie said at the time. I really *hate* that the others all call him Mr Intense . . .

Tonight, he's wearing tartan too, baggy tartan pants and a yellow matching tartan waistcoat, worn over a bare chest. I wave at him and I'm sure he sees me as I'm in the front row, but he ignores me and keeps that modelly admire-me-from-a-distance-but-if-you-come-near-me-I'll-kick-your-teeth-in smouldering glare he has going on.

'Doesn't he look cute?' I say to Jamie.

'Cute? Constipated, more like.'

'OK, he may not be your favourite person, but you have to admit he is bloody gorgeous-looking.'

'Yes, I'm sure his smile brings dead puppies back to life.'

'Your jealousy is very transparent. You'd love to be up there, strutting your stuff, admit it. What have you got against Simon anyway?'

'Hmm, let me see. He's weird, he's conceited, he's up his own arse and he's obsessive. But apart from that, I'm sure he's an absolute sweetheart.'

'Lay off, Jamie. You're only saying that because he rearranged all the clothes in my wardrobe. I wouldn't mind, but I only told you that story because I thought you'd get a laugh out of it.'

'And?'

'He can only fall asleep if he's facing due east. Perfectly normal behaviour.'

'And?'

'And he colour-codes the towels in his bathroom.'

'Which have to . . . ?'

I sigh. I knew it was a big mistake telling the Lovely Girls about Simon's idiosyncrasies. Now I'll never hear the end of it. What can I say? My will to gossip is just too overwhelming. 'Which have to hang exactly twelve inches from the towel rail.'

'And you don't see anything wrong with any of this? Any normal person would have run a mile by now. You can do a lot better for yourself, Amelia. You're not that ugly.'

By now, the music has changed to Marvin Gaye's 'I Heard It Through the Grapevine' and all the models come out wearing Levi's 501 jeans, just like in the TV ad. And then I notice something. While all the other models are looking designer-scruffy, Simon's jeans are immaculately creased down the front. Eagle-eyed Jamie spots it too and shoots me a significant told-you-so look . . .

There's a party afterwards and we all stand around drinking warm white wine out of plastic beakers and thinking ourselves very sophisticated. Over by the bar, Christian is blatantly feeling up Rachel, who's doing absolutely nothing to stop him, while Jamie, Mike and I stand around making tense small talk with Mrs Egan.

And then something occurs to me. It's almost as if Rachel is going out of her way to flaunt her new fella under Jamie's nose to annoy him and it's working and now he's taking his appalling bad humour out on me. I decide to let it go, though. After all, this is Caroline's night, not mine . . .

Eventually, the star of the show herself emerges breathlessly from the makeshift dressing room, carrying a huge bouquet of roses, which are obviously from Mike. She pecks her mother demurely on the cheek and gives Mike a bear hug and they look so adorable together that I whisper to Jamie, 'Do you think they'll ever get married?'

Mrs Egan, who could hear the grass grow in her sleep, immediately snaps back, 'With a sense of humour like that, Amelia, you really should consider a career in stand-up comedy. *No one* marries their college boyfriend.'

'I certainly hope *you* don't,' Jamie mutters to me. 'Have you noticed how Mr Intense is the very last to leave the dressing room? He's probably still staring in the mirror checking his hair hasn't moved one-eighth of a degree.'

'Give me a break, Jamie. OK, so he has his odd little ways, but I have fun with him.'

'Oh, please, there are prisoners on death row with more *joie de vivre* than him.'

'He's smart.'

'Get real. There are more intelligent forms of life floating around in ponds.'

'OK, so he might be a little bit intense, but so are a lot of very gifted people like . . . emm . . .'

'Hitler? Stalin?'

'Why are you picking on my boyfriend? Why don't you pick on Rachel's? Cut me some slack.'

'I only met . . . whatever his name is . . . Christian, an hour ago. Give me time.'

We're interrupted by Mr Intense, who accepts all our congratulations as though he's just won a Nobel prize.

'Yeah, I really think I may just pursue a full-time career in modelling,' he says modestly. 'Everyone says I'm a born natural.'

Jamie mouths something which looks like: 'Born wanker, more like,' but I ignore it and offer to buy a round of drinks, leaving Simon chatting, or rather talking about himself to my pals.

I'm waiting ages at the bar and fall into casual conversation with Tom O'Gorman, a really nice guy in my class. We're both doing our final year theses and are swapping notes on our subjects and the real reasons versus the interview reasons why we chose them.

'Mine's on Jane Austen,' I'm telling him. 'Interview reason: because I love the early-nineteenth-century novel form; real reason: I get to watch a lot of movie adaptations of her books all day long, which sure as hell beats working for a living.'

Tom laughs. 'I can top that. Mine's on late-eighteenth-century men's costume. Interview reason: because I'm fascinated by the playwrights Congreve, Goldsmith and Sheridan; real reason: because it's such an obscure topic, I can get away with murder. No one knows very much about it so I reckon all I'll need to do is read about two books and I'm home and dry.'

'Genius! Wish I'd thought of that.' I laugh.

I'm just about to pay for the drinks when Mr Intense . . . sorry, I mean Simon comes over, face like thunder. I introduce him to Tom and then instantly regret it.

'So who are you then?' Simon asks him, so rudely that Tom looks back at him, a bit dumbfounded.

'Tom's in my class,' I say, puzzled by this behaviour.

'Did you tell him that you have a boyfriend?'

'*What* did you say?'

Tom quite rightly senses an almighty row brewing and moves off the minute his pint is ready.

'Amelia, the guy was chatting you up and you were letting him. I was watching you. You were flirting your head off.'

His tone is low and – well, there's no other way to describe it – *menacing*. For a split second, I don't know whether to laugh or not. He has to be messing . . . hasn't he?

'Is it actually possible that you're being serious? I barely know the guy; we were only talking about our theses for a few minutes while we were waiting for the drinks.'

'Eleven minutes.'

'You *timed* me?'

'Amelia, the only reason you're getting annoyed is because you were found out. You've probably been seeing him behind my back for weeks, haven't you?'

He's gripping my arm tightly now, and it's hurting. Instinctively, I look around to see where my friends are. Not too far. Good. I'm starting to feel a bit scared. 'Simon,' I say, shaking him loose and rubbing my arm, 'can you just *hear* yourself?'

'I can only think of one reason why you're being so defensive. You're sleeping with him.'

'Never, never, never have kids,' says Caroline, wearily coming back into the drawing room. 'Take it from me, sterilization is the answer. I nearly had to throw a bucket of water over the pair of them.'

'Oh dear. Worse than the new-car row?'

This was a famous occasion a few months back where Emma was perched on the bonnet of Mike's brand-new Mercedes with a flinty stone in one hand. She absent-mindedly etched her name into the paintwork: 'Emma'. Then she realized what she'd done and changed it to 'Emma is a pig', so Joshua would get all the blame. When the truth was discovered, the ensuing row lasted for days.

'God knows how they'll react to a new arrival,' Caroline goes on, patting her tummy and sitting back down. 'So? Aren't you dying to know how I figured the chain between us and Mr Intense? I'm not bragging, but I am particularly proud of this bit of detective work.'

'It's been almost eighteen years and, you know, if Jamie heard we were trying to track him down, he'd still vomit.'

'Never mind Jamie. I did this for *you*. Easy peasy, really. I did the maths and figured that after poor Tony Irwin, Mr Intense . . . sorry, I mean Simon was next on the hit list, so to speak. Now. Do you remember Phoebe Smyth?'

'That you used to model with?'

'That's the one. Well, her daughter is in Emma's class and I bumped into her this morning and we just got chit-chatting about the old days. And then I remembered that Mr Intense did a bit of modelling with the same agency as myself and Phoebe. So I asked her if she ever saw any of the old gang and casually dropped Mr Intense's name. Turns out he's still working for the same agency now, but as a bookings manager.'

'And you have the number of the agency?'

'Right here in my address book.'

'Caroline, if I've said it once I've said it a thousand times: You're an angel sent from on high.'

We both look at each other.

'Are you thinking what I'm thinking?' Caroline asks.

'What are you thinking?'

'Let's ring him now. It's only just gone five-thirty; the agency would still be open. Come on, Amelia, you and Jamie and Rachel have all the fun; this would be the most exciting thing that's happened to me all day. Apart from the U-bend in the downstairs loo getting blocked.'

205

'You're on. Just let me finish this glass of wine. Dutch courage is better than no courage.'

A few minutes later, the pair of us are rolling around laughing, with the speakerphone switched on. I take a deep breath and dial. It rings.

'Hello, Catwalk modelling agency, how may I help you?'

'Ahem. Hello. I'd like to speak to . . .' Shit, I'm so used to hearing everyone call him Mr Intense I have to rack my brains to remember what his real name is. 'Oh, yes, Simon Byrne please.'

Caroline gives me the two-thumbs-up sign. If I say so myself I do sound very confident, but then, I've had quite a bit of practice over the last few weeks . . .

The receptionist falters a bit. 'Is it a personal call?'

'Yes, that's right.'

'OK. Well, Simon actually left here some time ago, but I still have his mobile number, is that any help to you?'

'That would be great, thanks.' I scribble the number on the back of my hand and hang up, delighted.

Caroline is on the edge of her seat.

'Right,' I say, 'now for the hard bit.'

'Oh God, my nerves,' squeals Caroline. 'Are you sure you want to do this now?'

'No time like the present,' I answer firmly, bracing myself. I dial the mobile number. Caroline has to stuff a tissue in her mouth to stop herself laughing out loud.

It rings. And rings. Eventually a woman's voice answers. Caroline and I look nervously across at each other. Could this be his wife?

I take the bull by the horns. 'Hello, is that Simon's phone?'

'Ehh . . . yes. Who's this?'

'Amelia Lockwood. I'm a friend of his from college. Could I have a quick word with him, do you think?'

'Oh. You're a friend of his?'

'Ehh . . . yeah.' I pull a face at Caroline. A total exaggeration, but what choice have I?

'Well, maybe you'd like to come and visit him then?'

I think on my feet. Yes, isn't this the whole object of the exercise? 'I'd love to, if that's all right.'

'Great. I'll tell him to expect you. It's just that of all our patients, Simon hardly gets any visitors, you know.'

This time, Caroline and I look at each other in horror.

'Emm, I'm sorry but . . . where exactly is Simon?'

'Here in St Moluag's psychiatric home, St Killian's ward. Any time tomorrow would be great. If you come to the main reception desk and just ask for me. Nurse Sarah O'Loughlin.'

Chapter Twenty
The Cuckoo's Nest

There's no getting out of it. I have to go and visit poor old Simon and that's all there is to it. It's a mad busy day for me in work, but I make up my mind to go and see him at lunchtime, when things in the office are slightly less manic. Even Caroline gently admits that it's the right and proper thing to do.

'You have to. Especially after the nurse told him to expect a visit from you,' she says during a sneaky phone call when I'm meant to be holed up in the conference room reading scripts. 'I'm just not very happy about you going on your own. Do you have to go at lunchtime? I have a check-up at one, but if you could wait till later in the afternoon, I'll come with you.'

'Bless you for that, but I'm in meetings for the rest of the bloody day. It's lunchtime or never, I'm afraid. Besides, better to get it over with sooner rather than later. If I leave it till tomorrow, there's a very good chance I'll think about what I'm about to do and then not do it and then run in the opposite direction, very, very fast.'

'OK, well, keep safe and remember I'm only on the other end of a phone if you need me.'

I decide not to tell Jamie about this latest turn of events as (*a*) to say he never liked Simon is a big understatement and (*b*) he's got an interview for a big commercial this morning, and is up to the ceiling about it. He won't tell any of us what the ad is for on the grounds that it's bad luck; all he'll say is that, if he gets the gig, he'll be able to repay all the money he owes us. I keep my fingers crossed for him because he *needs* this. It would be so good for his self-esteem right now. Plus, with the amount of money he owes me alone, I could treat all the Lovely Girls to a five-star round-the-world cruise on the *Queen Mary*. One p.m. comes and I'm into my car and out of the station like a hot snot, when Rachel calls.

'Well, well, well. I take my eye off you for two minutes and this is what happens.'

'Hi, hon!'

'Caroline told me exactly what you're up to, so don't even *attempt* to deny it.'

'It has to be done,' I say, pulling out on to the motorway. 'No way out of this one.'

'Just make sure you wear a T-shirt that says "sane", won't you? I don't have time to come and bail you out later.'

'Ha bloody ha. When I get married, I'm making you wear lemon-yellow chiffon as my chief bridesmaid and it'll serve you right.'

'Shit, hold on one sec.' She covers the mouthpiece with her hand but, although it's a bit muffled, I can still hear the unmistakable sound of Gormless Gordon asking her out to lunch. 'No thanks,' she's telling him crisply, 'I don't do wheat, dairy, gluten or any kind of meat product so there's no point really.'

'Maybe you'd come for coffee later on?' I can hear him saying.

'Don't do caffeine either,' she snaps back. 'Sorry.'

'Poor kamikaze bastard,' I say when she comes back to the phone.

'People in glass houses. Look at what you're about to do and then judge me, if you dare.'

Point taken.

Anyway, St Moluag's isn't too far from work and about ten minutes later I'm pulling up the long, oak-lined driveway which leads to the hospital. Except that it doesn't look remotely like a hospital, more like a big, posh country hotel. The grounds are fabulous, beautifully maintained, and there's even a tennis court, I notice as I park the car in the visitors' car park. I hop out and scrunch up the gravelled driveway, taking nice, deep, calming breaths as I head for the main entrance.

Nothing scary; no one in straitjackets being chased by men in white coats; no one wandering around the grounds thinking that they're chickens; so far, so good. I make my way inside, walk up to the main reception desk and ask a very friendly-looking nurse where I can find Simon.

'Oh yes, he's been expecting a visitor,' she says, smiling prettily. 'I think he's waiting in the canteen. It's just round the corner, I'll show you.'

'Ehh . . . thanks,' I say, bracing myself.

'Just one thing, Miss . . . emm . . . ?'

'Amelia.'

'Amelia. Would you mind if I had a quick look in your handbag?'

'Sorry?'

'Don't worry, it's nothing like the security checks at Dublin airport.' She grins cheerily as I hand my bag over. 'I just need to make sure you don't have anything sharp in there.'

I obviously pass the test as she slides my handbag back to

me and tells me to enjoy my visit, as if I was expecting it to be anything other than a barrel of laughs. Gulping, I make for the canteen, which is busy, naturally enough, this being lunchtime, but I spot Simon straight away. In fact, it's hard to miss him.

He's sitting at a table on his own, still outrageously good-looking, but somehow without that aloof, reserved aura he always used to have about him; that quality he had which, at aged twenty, I mistook for a nervous, passionate, highly-strung temperament but which was actually just plain weird. The only other tiny difference the years have wrought is that he's put on a bit of weight, but otherwise there's no mistaking him. He spots me and waves over for me to join him.

'Hey,' he says, pecking me warmly on each cheek, 'Amelia Lockwood, as I live and breathe. You look fantastic – great outfit! Smart casual is a good look for you.' He hardly gives me a chance to ask how he is; in fact, he seems so delighted to see me that he barely draws breath. 'I was so pleased when they said you were coming to see me. A Big Successful TV Producer like you.'

'Oh, you knew I worked in television?'

'Are you kidding? When *Celtic Tigers* is on, it's about the only time of the day that there's total silence in the recreation room here.'

I smile and he suggests we grab some take-out coffees and sit outside to chat, since it's such a lovely day. I buy us two cappuccinos the colour and strength of dishwater and he jokes that I'll have to pay for them as he's not allowed to have cash in here. Part of me is so relieved at how calm and relaxed he seems that, as soon as we get out to the garden, I find myself wondering, well, what's he *doing* here?

We sit on a bench in a quite peaceful spot and I sip on my

coffee as he roots around in his pocket for a packet of Marlboro Lights. The silence is comfortable, easy. We smile at each other and then . . . wouldn't you know it? My big mouth takes over.

'So, Simon . . . I hope you don't think I'm being cheeky but I was just wondering . . .'

'What in the name of God I'm in here for?'

I laugh. 'You took the words right out of my mouth. You just seem so . . .' I'm about to say normal, but I check myself just in time. 'So, so . . . healthy and well.'

He looks me straight in the eye. 'I don't know that you'd understand, Amelia, because you were always very together and goal-orientated, but have you ever felt so stressed out that you just can't cope with any more pressure?'

'Every day. And it must have been doubly hard for you, working in the modelling business. Caroline always used to say it was like a pressure cooker.'

'The modelling business?'

'Yeah. Isn't that where you work? At the agency? That's how I got your phone number.'

'Amelia, Catwalk let me go, as I think the phrase politely goes, almost a year ago.'

'Oh. I had no idea.' I'm really starting to feel sorry for him now. Who wouldn't?

'Yeah, well, I was getting panic attacks, so I dropped out for a bit and didn't really do anything. I was on the dole for so long, I was surprised they didn't ask me to their staff Christmas party.'

'And how are you feeling now?'

'Much better. Greatly improved. The rest in here has done me the power of good. I've spent a long time confronting my demons and I think I'm just about ready to turn a corner. I've a fantastic psychiatrist, Dr Simpson, and he's helped me come to terms with a lot of recurring behavioural patterns I had.'

I look at him, a bit puzzled.

'Oh, come on, Amelia, even when you and I were dating, you must have noticed some, shall we say, aberrations in my behaviour.'

I giggle nervously, not sure whether to contradict him or not. 'Well, I suppose . . .'

'There's no need to be polite.' He smiles. 'I was insufferable back then and I'm only glad to have a chance to apologize. I don't know how you put up with me.'

'It . . . was a little bit intense all right,' I say, embarrassed.

'So I've been told.' He laughs. 'Therapy has helped me realize that my particular obsessive compulsive disorder was my need to control others around me, particularly girlfriends. I've dated a lot of women in my time and the ones who allowed me to control them became my enablers. Not you, I hasten to add,' he says, catching my surprised look, 'you were always too focused on getting what you wanted out of life. Plus you had very good friends around you at the time, who I don't exactly think were big fans of mine.'

I tell him that the Lovely Girls are still my nearest and dearest friends and he doesn't seem in the least surprised.

'Just beware of getting too co-dependent, Amelia. It can happen so easily with cosy quartets like yours. You can create a defensive space around the group which others are wary of inviting themselves into.'

Politeness prevents me from contradicting him, but this is the only time that what he's saying sounds like complete and utter psychobabble.

Apart from that one blip, Simon comes across as saner than I am myself and certainly an awful lot lower maintenance than most of the actors I have to work with on *Celtic Tigers*.

In fact, we're getting on better now than we ever did when we were dating.

Another comfortable silence.

'Now it's my turn to ask *you* something, Amelia,' he says. 'Is that OK?'

'Sure.'

'Are you with anyone at the moment?'

Now, ordinarily, a direct question like that immediately has me groping for a good, fat lie such as, 'I just came out of something long-term and I *really* want to be on my own for a bit,' or, quoting Rachel, 'What people don't realize is how fantastic it is being single. I'm having the time of my life right now,' but somehow, with Simon, I just can't bring myself to tell such blatant whoppers. He's been honest with me; the least I can do is be honest back.

'Yes, I'm single,' I answer simply.

'So why aren't you married? I think it's fairly obvious why I'm not, unless there's some nice bipolar manic depressive in ward five that would do me, but there are guys out there who'd kill to be with someone like you.'

'It's not for the want of trying on my part, let me tell you. But at this stage, even my mother has given up asking why there's no man on the scene. She keeps saying things like, "Cheer up, Amelia. Look at Condoleeza Rice. There's a great example of what a woman can achieve if she stays on her own." She even sent me an article about having your eggs frozen. I don't think it's exactly what she and poor old dad had planned for me; their only hope of ever having grand-children stuck in a deep freeze somewhere.'

He laughs again. 'Oh God, you have no idea how good it is to talk to someone who doesn't speak to me in a special-needs voice. So . . .'

'So?'

'So would it be terrible if you and I had a drink sometime? When I'm back home again?'

I look at him fondly. No, it wouldn't be so terrible to see him again at all. He's changed so much over the years since I knew him; he's almost like a different person.

'I'd really like that. Thanks.'

'Great. I've a lovely pagan altar in my flat, strewn with human remains. You'd love it. We could watch a movie, drink blood from skulls . . . Gotcha! You are so gullible.'

Now I'm laughing with him. 'You messer! For a minute there I thought you were going to start rearranging all my clothes again.'

'I told you, my days of controlling women are long past.'

Yet another comfortable silence. It's really great how unembarrassed he is by the whole situation. And after all, I remind myself, what's to be embarrassed about? He had a bit of a breakdown and came here to get well.

I can't help smiling, though. Just wait till tonight and my next class with Ira Vandergelder. I came to a psychiatric home to visit my ex-boyfriend and ended up leaving with the promise of a date. Now if that's not getting out of my matrix, what is?

Just then, a doctor comes round the corner, white coat flapping in the breeze, and sits down beside us.

'Hey! Doc Simpson, how's it going?' says Simon, introducing me. 'This is an old girlfriend of mine, who . . . well, who hasn't given up on me.'

I smile and shake hands. Dr Simpson is mid-fifties, I'm guessing, grey-haired and sallow-skinned, with warm, friendly eyes, the type who could almost have come from central casting if you were looking for a kindly, twinkly-eyed doctor.

'Yes, Simon,' he says, 'I heard you had a visitor. That's

why I'm here.' Then, turning to me, he says, 'It's very good of you to come. I hate to interrupt, but do you think I could have a quick word with you in private?'

I'm a bit surprised at this and Simon looks . . . well, put out, but waits on the bench as Dr Simpson leads me down the path and towards a rockery, well out of earshot. 'Please don't think me rude, Amelia,' he says, 'but why exactly did you come here?'

Oh dear. If I tell him the truth, I'm half afraid he'll lock me up in the women's ward and throw away the key. I'm fumbling around for a good lie when Dr Simpson interrupts me.

'I don't want you to misinterpret my question, it's just that we're at quite a critical stage in Simon's treatment, you see. It's wonderful for him to have a friend who'll come to see him, but what I need to know is: do you plan on coming to visit regularly?'

'Oh, well . . . I suppose . . .'

'Let me explain. Simon is in a place where he needs routine and recurrent patterns in all external stimuli around him.'

'I'm sorry?'

'What I mean is, if you're planning on visiting him on a regular basis, then we need to set up a weekly meeting slot for you. That way, he knows you're coming, he knows to expect you and in time he will grow to trust the fact that there are people out there who won't let him down. From Simon's point of view, the worst thing you could do is come and see him a couple of times and then not return. Giving up on him could set his recovery back months. Of course, no one is forcing you to keep up regular visits; if you never want to return after today, that's absolutely fine. My concern, you understand, is with my patient and his wellbeing. I'm only looking out for him.'

I think for a second. Simon has changed so much since I knew him, I've actually *enjoyed* meeting up with him again. Of course I want him to get well. And I'm delighted he's asked me out. And if it means coming to see him regularly every week, that's fine by me. It's the very least I can do, isn't it?

'I'd be delighted to come back again, doctor,' I say. 'I'm sure I can set up a weekly time slot with you. Lunchtimes are good during the week, or I could come at weekends if you feel that would be better for Simon?'

'Well done,' he says, looking at me with what I can only describe as admiration. 'That's wonderful news. I'll let you get back to Simon, but perhaps you could come by my office before you leave? I'll need to sort out a visitor's pass for you.'

'Of course,' I say as we stroll back to where Simon is still sitting on the park bench, smoking.

I shake hands with Dr Simpson and sit back down again.

'It was nice to meet you,' he says.

'And you.'

'My office is on the second floor. Just ask at reception and they'll direct you,' he says, going back inside.

I glance down at my watch. Almost two-thirty p.m.

'Sorry about this Simon,' I say, 'but I'm going to have to get back to work. I've a meeting with the finance director at three, so—'

'So you're going upstairs to see your boyfriend then, are you?'

'*What* did you say?'

'I saw you. You were flirting with Simpson. Practically threw yourself at him.' His tone has totally changed. Now he sounds cutting, intense, *scary*.

'Simon? He was asking me about you. He wanted me to come and see you regularly, that's all.'

'One minute you agree to go out with me; the next you're hitting on my doctor. Even making arrangements to go up to his office to see him privately. What kind of person are you, Amelia? What kind of person does that?'

OK, now I'm actually frightened. 'Let's just clear this up right now,' I say, trying to sound calm and measured. 'All I was doing was—'

'You were nothing but a slut when I knew you and you still haven't changed. Bet you're sleeping with him, aren't you?'

Chapter Twenty-One

My Own, Personal, Tailor-made
Emotional-pension-plan Man

I'm late for class and I hate being late for class. Not my fault. Well, not entirely. Firstly, a production meeting I had with Janet Taylor, the set designer on *Celtic Tigers*, ran way over time. (We were sitting in the canteen, poring over the preliminary sketches for this new family that are about to join the show, the Duffys. More anon.) Janet's great, dead easy to work with and a real pro. The set designs are absolutely spot-on; they hit just the right balance between interior-designed tastefulness and nouveau riche.

I was in the middle of throwing in my two cents' worth when I realized that it was after eight p.m. 'Janet, would you mind if we took this from here in the morning?' I asked, frantically packing up my things.

'Sure, of course . . . what's the mad rush?'

I'm sure I must look like a rabbit caught in the headlamps. 'It's . . . emm . . . it's a long story . . . Emm . . . let's just say I have to be somewhere.'

'Say no more, Amelia.' She grins at me. 'Dark horse, aren't you?'

'What?'

'You can't fool me. You've got a fella, haven't you?'

'I'm neither confirming nor denying . . .' I laugh, doing a really crap impersonation of a government minister.

'Oh, spare me the current affairs spiel. Just go and enjoy yourself. And if he happens to have any single mates, let me know. See you bright and early.'

Then, as I'm driving down the motorway to UCD, my mobile rings. It's not a number I recognize, so I let the machine take it.

Damien Delaney.

Shit.

I'd almost forgotten about him. I play back the message.

'Hello, Amelia dear. It's Damien here. Just wondered if we could have tea soon? I've told Mummy all about you and she's so looking forward to meeting you. Do give me a call. Take care now, and God bless.'

Instantly, I think: *Oh no! Do I have to?* Then I remember I promised Caroline I'd give him a whirl. A proper whirl. Double shit. I really, really, *really* don't want to call him back. An image of me in my Vera Wang with my headless groom comes back. Don't I want to be married within the year? I ask myself sternly. Yes, that's the whole point.

Brainwave. I'll text him.

Then I think he's probably too old to understand about texting – and I do have a clear recollection of him complaining about how he's not able to read small print on menus and contracts and stuff like that any more. Then I banish that thought on the grounds that it's mean and it's like the trivial kind of thing I'd slag Jamie off for saying. Then I realize I've already missed half the class and I'd better get a bloody move on or I'll miss the whole thing.

I save his voice message though. If Ira gives me a hard time about not getting out of my dating matrix, I'll play this back to her as proof.

I make my way to the classroom, slip inside and look around for a free seat, trying not to draw any attention to myself. Ira waves at me and so does Mags, who's saved me a seat beside her.

'Thanks a million,' I mouth at her.

'I was afraid you weren't coming,' she hisses back at me. 'We could all do with a good laugh.'

As usual, everyone is battling to get their stories out and the snippets of conversation I'm overhearing make me doubly furious with myself for being late.

'. . . meeting up with my ex made me realize that, to paraphrase Princess Diana, there were three of us in this relationship. Me, him and the television . . .'

'. . . dating after thirty-five is such a high-stakes game, they can practically *smell* the wedding seating plan from you . . .'

'. . . my ex said to me, "There are a million reasons why you could have dumped me, so which one did you pick?"'

'. . . for God's sake, his name was Travis. Well, I now learned a new rule. It's probably not a good idea to go out with anyone whose name is Travis . . .'

'. . . I really don't know what to do here, Ira. Let's face it, my plan of waiting until divorcees came back on to the market again has been a spectacular failure . . .'

By the end of it all, my neck is sore from nodding in agreement.

Funny, I think, how we see other people's stuff with such clarity, it's just our own that gets a bit foggy. You should just see these women. They're all lovely. There's absolutely nothing wrong with any of them, they've just made bad choices over the years, and now time is running out and we're all getting panicky.

Right, that's it. I'm ringing Damien Delaney straight after class. And I'll do the afternoon tea thing with his mother and I'll be on my best behaviour and not curse or anything in front of her.

Or introduce her to either Jamie or Rachel and their bad talk. Could you imagine if the poor woman had a heart attack and it was all my fault?

'Amelia? Would you care to join us?' Ira's peering over her glasses at me and suddenly I'm aware of how quiet the class has gone.

'Ehh . . . sorry?'

'You had drifted off there. I was asking you how you'd progressed this week.'

They're all looking at me. That's the downside of having a reputation as the class comedian: everyone expects you to perform on demand and be effortlessly hilarious. I'm just not sure I'm up to this after the week I've had . . .

'You don't want to know, Ira, trust me.'

'Come on, share with us. How bad can it be?'

How bad can it be? 'Ira, like so much in my life, if you put the story of my last two exes in a book, no one would believe it. Not in a million years.'

'Spit it out. We're all in the same boat and we're all here to contribute.'

Right, well you asked for it. 'OK, then. Here goes. I managed to trace two exes this week. One is in a monastery and the other one is in a psychiatric home.'

They all roar laughing, but I wasn't trying to be funny.

'Don't get me wrong, they're both very happy where they are.'

More giggles.

'Amelia, be serious,' says Ira sternly.

'You think I'm making this up? How could you make this up?'

She looks at me in that assessing way she has, weighing up whether I'm messing or not. Nor can I blame her, this is *very* far-fetched. 'What have I said to you before about your screening process, Amelia? Now, I'm sure you were young when you dated these guys and of course you can't be held responsible for what became of them in the meantime. But I think you need to focus on the fact that you pursue un-suitable partners.'

'I agree. So far my dating history could almost be a manual in what not to do.'

'Are you gonna make wisecracks or are you gonna try to turn a negative into a positive? Before the week is out I want you to have made contact with one ex-boyfriend that you can really learn from. Otherwise, lemme tell you right now, you will never achieve your end goal. All you're doing is wasting your time and mine.'

Wow. Harsh stuff. Talk about your NYC tough love. I can see some of my classmates are thinking the same thing, because it's gone very quiet and everyone's eyes are looking down, just like in school when the class messer gets a rap on the knuckles for going that bit too far.

Ira goes back to the front of the class and starts asking everyone about their matrix. I drift off again, doodling on a piece of paper in front of me. A normal ex-boyfriend . . . tall order.

And then I get a flash of inspiration. Jack Keating. *Genius! Why didn't I think of him before?*

OK. There's something I need to explain.

Claudia Carroll

THE TIME: *July 1988.*

THE PLACE: *Boston, MA. Me and the other Lovely Girls have just finished our finals in college and are spending the summer in the States, working (legally) under the student visa program.*

THE OCCASION: *One of those dinner parties that everyone had in the 80s, where we'd all dress up, eat crap food, drink cheap wine and, basically, try to ape our parents' lifestyle as much as possible, thinking ourselves fierce posh altogether.*

Caroline, Rachel and I are in the galley kitchen of the house we're all renting, frantically trying to throw a posh-looking dinner together and failing miserably. None of us is a cook. In fact, this whole summer-working-in-America experience has been unbelievably eye-opening for all of us. Not only are we all worse than useless in the kitchen, none of us has the first clue about washing, ironing, laundry, housekeeping . . . you name it, we can't do it.

What can I say? Back in Ireland, we all live at home with our mammies who do everything for us and, as Rachel says, this is only playing at being grown-up anyway, isn't it?

There are three guys sharing the house with us and, if possible, they're even messier than we girls.

Jamie's here, of course, but we always knew he'd be disastrously unhousetrained. Bei-rut-al. So far, his only contribution to the laundry was the time he washed all of our white work shirts with a bright red pair of his own pyjamas, so that everything ended up a disgusting pinky-grey. Since then, he's given up on washing anything at all, claiming to have figured out a way to make the same pair of underpants last for a four-day minimum.

Then there's Mike, whose idea of hygiene is to use

whatever toothbrush first comes to hand in the bathroom.

And then there's Jack Keating.

And it's entirely my fault that he's here.

OK, allow me to give you some background info. Back in Dublin, Jack is my next-door neighbour; we pretty much grew up together. We're exactly the same age, both only children and therefore destined to be playmates from a very early age. His nickname for me is girl-next-door and mine for him is boy-next-door. Sweet, isn't it . . . ? Or so you'd think . . .

Anyway, Jack is lovely, absolutely lovely, very good-looking, great fun, the brother I never had and, likewise, I'm the sister he never wanted to have. As kids we fought and scrapped with each other, as teenagers we fancied each other's friends and now as almost-college-graduates we're sharing this house together in Boston, at my invitation.

But there's one thing you need to know about Jack. He's a natural-born flirt. Can't help himself. It's just the way he communicates with women. And boy, do they fall for him. In droves, like you wouldn't believe. James Bond wouldn't have as many notches on his bedpost as Jack. You know the type, men want to be him, women want to change him. Not me, I hasten to add, I'm kind of immune to the Jack Keating charm offensive. I don't fancy him and I never did, he's too much like a brother to me. But from the age of fourteen, Jack has pretty much always had a girlfriend; he just goes effortlessly from one to the next. He doesn't even go to the bother of chasing them, they flock to him. Moths to a flame.

And tonight's dinner party is no exception . . .

'Right. No one ate their starters,' says Rachel, dumping some very green-looking melon balls into the bin. 'How's the spaghetti bolognese doing?'

'Shit,' I answer, using all my strength to stir the congealed glob of pasta from round the edges of the saucepan. 'That's what it looks like and that's what they're all going to say it tastes like when we serve it.'

'Do you smell burning?' asks Rachel.

'Eh . . . yeah, sorry, that's me too,' I answer apologetically. 'The mincemeat's all gone black. Come on, girlies, what'll we do?'

'Plan A, we scrape off the unburned bits and serve it up and hope they won't notice,' says Caroline helpfully.

'Or plan B,' I say, 'we open another bottle of Blue Nun, force it down their throats and hope they'll all be too sloshed to notice.'

'Brilliant,' says Rachel, striding for the fridge and whipping out another bottle. 'At least the dessert will be impressive. You can't beat a Black Forest gateau. And the fact that it's shop-bought means at least one of the courses will be edible.'

Then Jamie squeezes himself into the tiny kitchen, bursting for a good gossip. 'Apart from all of you lovelies,' he says, 'there are three other single women at the table.'

'I'm not single!' says Caroline.

'Neither am I!' snaps Rachel.

We all turn to look at her. 'OK, I mightn't have heard from Christian for a while, but the post from Paris is really slow,' she says defensively.

I busy myself with the burned spaghetti and Jamie suddenly starts folding paper napkins with a vengeance.

There's a horrible silence.

She and Christian are 'on a break' as the phrase goes at the moment and, well, it's just not a subject to be discussed in front of Rachel. Not unless you want your teeth kicked in.

'That's the only reason he hasn't written in ages,' says

Rachel, raising her voice now. 'Christian would be here if he could, you know!'

'Shh, shhh,' says Caroline, giving her a soothing hug. 'We know.'

'You are in love with being in love, that's all that's wrong with you, Rachel,' says Jamie.

'Piss off,' she almost spits at him.

'Oh cool down, Saliva Dolittle. I only came in to fill you in on our resident live-in Lothario.'

'Jack?' I say. 'What's up with him?'

'Nothing. It's just that I've been studying human behaviour in the dining room and, darlings, it's a scream. Of the other three ladies present, one is an ex-girlfriend and she doesn't know it, one's a present girlfriend and she doesn't know it and one's a future girlfriend and she doesn't know it either. And don't get me started on his stupid, put-on American accent. Hilarious. Irritating as hell, but hilarious. We've only been living here for a month and he's starting to sound like Ted Danson.'

'So, Jack's flirting,' I say. 'Jack always flirts. You must fancy one of those girls yourself, Jamie, or you wouldn't be in here giving out about him.'

'I don't, is the odd thing.'

'What's wrong with them?' Molly, Sarah and Kate all work as chambermaids in the hotel Caroline and I got jobs in. Well, until I got fired.

'There's nothing wrong with them. They're just . . . not my type.'

'How do you mean?'

'Well, look at them. They're like the three little maids from school in a Gilbert and Sullivan light opera. They're a pussy posse. Indistinguishable. Right up Jack Keating's alley, but not mine.'

In a funny way, I can see what Jamie means. We all troop back out and valiantly try to pass off the coagulated spaghetti bolognese as a cordon bleu meal. Molly, Kate and Sarah are all very pretty, very tanned, very blonde and are all clustered around Jack, hanging on his every word. Everyone's giddy on the Blue Nun and, in no time, Rachel brightens up. Soon she's back to her old self. Alcohol always does the trick with her. Well, either alcohol or a long-distance phone call from Christian.

'Amelia, I've lost count,' she asks me. 'How many jobs have you had again?'

'OK, let's see. First there was the waitressing job in À La Carte . . .'

'Which you nicknamed À La Cockroach,' says Mike, helpfully topping up everyone's glass.

'Then you worked with me in the temping agency,' says Rachel.

'Where they invented the slogan "We are Flexible, Available, Reliable Temporaries Incorporated"!'

'Or FARTI girls,' she snorts.

'I have to say, I'm loving my summer job,' says Jamie, who's working in Filene's bargain basement store. 'I've learned more about the craft of acting than I would have in four years of RADA training. All that ringing up early in the mornings, pretending to be too sick to go in.'

'You know, we'll never have this freedom again,' says Jack. 'Just think, we'll be home in a few weeks, home to our final exam results . . .'

'Home to the real world . . .'

'Having to get proper jobs . . .'

'And act like grown-ups . . . You know, *responsible* . . .'

There's a silence. Even Jack's three adoring soubrettes have stopped their twittering. It's a sobering thought all right.

'So what are we going to do with ourselves?'

'Or an even better question is, where do we all want to be by the age of, say, thirty-five?' Jack asks the table.

'Easy,' says Jamie. 'I'll be living in the Hollywood hills, polishing my Oscars. Plural.'

'I'd love to be a hard-hitting journalist,' I say thoughtfully. 'You know, like Kate Adie on the BBC. Going into war zones and reporting live with gunfire all around me.'

'And you'd look great in the jumpsuits she always wears,' says Jack.

'This is Amelia Lockwood for the BBC, reporting to you live from Iran,' I say, mimicking Kate Adie's deep voice, with a fork in my hand, pretending it's a microphone.

'I want to be living abroad,' says Rachel. 'France maybe, or a country where they've at least heard of cappuccino. So that's basically anywhere except Ireland.'

'I want to stick with the modelling for a bit,' says Caroline.

'But you can't do that beyond thirty,' says Jamie.

'Sure, we'll be married by then,' Caroline and I answer in unison.

'Yes, but married to who, Caroline dearest?' Jamie asks cheekily.

Mike goes a bit red, but says nothing.

'Oops, sorry, guys,' says Jamie. 'Have you two not had "the chat" yet? Am I embarrassing you?'

'Shuttup,' Rachel snarls at him.

'I think thirty-five's a really good age to get married at,' says Jack. 'Whaddya say Amelia?'

Jamie's right, I'm thinking. *The American accent is starting to sound very affected* . . .

'Amelia?'

'Sorry . . . what was that?'

'I was proposing.'

229

'*What!*'

Everyone's laughing now. Well, everyone except the Three Degrees clustered down Jack's end of the table.

'Come on, Amelia. We've known each other all our lives and we've never once had a cross word. I think we should make a pact. If we're both single by the age of thirty-five, then we get married. Whaddya think? . . . Amelia? . . . Amelia?'

'*Amelia?*'

I come back down to earth with a shudder. The whole class has gone quiet and Ira is standing right in front of me.

'Sorry . . . what was that?'

'Nice of you to rejoin us. We were discussing plans for our class party next weekend. I was looking for a volunteer to host the party.'

'I'd love to,' says Mags beside me, 'but I've got the builders in. I don't even have running water at the moment.'

'Well, I'll host it,' I say, mortified at being caught day-dreaming twice in the one class. 'If none of you objects to my atrocious cooking.'

'Good,' says Ira, nodding at me approvingly. 'But no need to go to any trouble. Just providing the venue is great. Remember, ladies, this is not just any old party. This is a strategic networking event to gather single men and women together in a room so you can pump up the volume of eligible, available men that you all know.'

'Sounds about as much fun as a bikini wax,' I mutter, but they all hear and laugh.

Ira suppresses the giggles with one of her killer glares. 'Remember the rules, ladies. This party is about creating new prospects for yourself and for your classmates. It's also a goodwill gesture. You've all got old dates or good male friends who may not have clicked with you, but who may fall madly in love with one of your classmates. Then, down the road, hopefully that classmate will repay the favour by introducing you to someone else in return. The golden rule is each of you must bring a man who is single, straight and in the marriage market. Understood?'

The minute I get in the door that night, I take firm and decisive action. In fact, driving by *He-whose-name-shall-forever-remain-unspoken*'s house and seeing the two jeeps parked cosily side by side with all the curtains drawn only spurs me on more.

Firstly, I ring Damien Delaney, but it's his voicemail. Well, it is almost ten, he's probably in bed with a mug of Horlicks that his mother made for him. I try to sound as bright and chirpy as I can. 'Hi, Damien, it's Amelia. Sorry to have missed you earlier. I was just wondering . . . how would you like to come to a party in my flat next Saturday night?'

Right.

Now comes the tricky part . . .

Chapter Twenty-Two
Let's Face the Music and Dance

Ten p.m. and one glass of Sancerre later.

> **From:** amelialockwood@eircom.net
> **To:** jackkeating@hotmail.com
> **Subject:** How the hell are you?
>
> Hey Jack!
> How's it going? It's been weeks since I've heard
> from you, just wondered how you were? Still making
> your millions at the law firm in Boston, Mr Big Fat
> I've-just-been-made-partner Pants? Listen, when you're
> home next, maybe we could meet up? You must be
> due a trip home soon . . . I'd love if we could have a
> bite to eat??? Or go to one of your rugger-bugger pubs
> and have a few drinks – whatever you fancy. Lots to
> tell you and lots to hear . . .

I reread, then hit the delete button. Too needy, too eager.
Not casual enough. Needs to be . . . lighter. 'Whatever you
fancy'? . . . I can't believe I even wrote that.

I never suggest meeting up with Jack; he always calls me whenever he's in Dublin, which is maybe four times a year, and he's *always* the one to invite me out.

He knows me too well – he'd read this and run a mile. I do not want to be part of the Jack Keating pussy posse, I want a husband; I have to be really cool and behave exactly the same way I always have done.

If *Cosmo*, *Marie Claire* and magazines of that sort have taught me nothing, it's that you should treat a guy you fancy exactly the way you'd treat a guy you don't fancy.

Not, I have to stress, that I fancy Jack Keating. We just had a deal. Which was his idea, not mine. And we're both well over the thirty-five mark now . . .

At least he would be one relatively normal ex-boyfriend, or rather non-ex-boyfriend, that I could tell Ira Vandergelder about.

OK. Draft two.

Ten-thirty p.m. Second glass of Sancerre. Haven't eaten a scrap since lunch, so am now feeling deliciously woozy.

From: amelialockwood@eircom.net
To: jackkeating@hotmail.com
Subject: (No Subject)

Jx

How are you?

Ax

Delete, delete, delete.
Too cool by half. I get up from my desk and pace around

a bit, then go over to the mantelpiece and pick up a photo of me and Jack. It was taken the night of my thirtieth birthday, all of seven years ago. There's a big gang of us clustered around a restaurant table, all wearing party hats with streamers hanging out of us. For some reason, Caroline, Jamie and Rachel are wearing those fun furry angels' wings and look like they're on the way to a raucous hen night in Temple Bar. Jack has both his arms around me and is squeezing me tight.

He had flown in from Boston just that morning especially for the party as a birthday surprise for me. I smile to myself, putting the photo back in its place. He'd gone to so much bother too. He even called my mobile from outside the restaurant door, pretending to be in the States, raging he couldn't be there, then walked up to me, phone in hand, singing happy birthday and almost giving me a cardiac arrest. This photo was taken immediately afterwards and you can just see the glow of happiness on my face because he came. My wonderful friend Jack.

OK, I am bending the rules a bit here, I know. It's not as if Jack and I ever dated. Or even kissed. But a deal's a deal. We are each other's matrimonial back-up plan. He even reminded me on the night of my thirtieth. I'll never forget it. It was about five a.m., when we all fell out of Lillie's Bordello, giddy on the champagne we'd been skulling back all night. Caroline and Mike hopped into one taxi, Jamie and Rachel staggered on to an early opening pub down on the docks and Jack, ever the gentleman, walked me home.

To all intents and purposes, we must have looked like a couple; he even took off his jacket and slipped it around my freezing shoulders, as if we'd just been to a debs ball together.

'Thanks for coming,' I said, linking arms with him. 'That was the best birthday present I could have asked for.'

'A pleasure. Wouldn't have missed it for the world. I just can't believe you're thirty.' Then he put on a voice like a ham actor in a Victorian melodrama. 'Five more years and you shall be *MINE*!'

'You're only saying that because you're between girlfriends now.'

'No I'm not. We made a pact. If we're both still single by thirty-five, I'm carting you down that aisle, whether you like it or not.'

OK. When I worked in the newsroom and had to script a difficult piece, this is what my executive producer used to tell me. Write down exactly what you want to say in layman's terms so that the sense is there, then gloss it up and throw in all the long, TV-speak phrases you want.

Right. Here goes.

Midnight. Fourth glass of Sancerre and I've bypassed woozy and am now starting to feel drrruuuunnnnkkkkk. Ah, what the hell. Life's short.

OK. Here's the message I want to get across, in draft one form.

From: amelialockwood@eircom.net
To: jackkeating@hotmail.com
Subject: Way too bizarre to fit into the subject box. Just read on . . .

Hello, Jack

You will be surprised to hear from me. It's been, what, two months now? Hope all's well with you in Boston. I know myself and the other Lovely Girls are always saying we'll have to pop over to see you and do a bit of shopping, but I really mean it this time. To come over to see you, I mean, not just to shop.

I've so much news to tell you and it's all bad. So horrific, I will put it in bullet-point form, for easy digestion.

1. You will remember the emotional car crash that was *He-whose-name-shall-forever-remain-unmentioned*? Well, the curse of Amelia strikes again. Not only is he getting married, but he and his fiancée are virtually my new next-door neighbours. As your mother used to say, me nerves are in flitters.

2. I've been transferred on to the crappiest TV drama show in history, kind of like Ireland's answer to *Days of our Lives*, and told to revamp it and double the audience numbers. This is akin to turning an episode of *Cell Block H* into *The Shawshank Redemption*. And while we're on the subject of prison dramas, I could never understand why there weren't more break-outs in *Cell Block H*. For God's sake, all they had to do was kick down the shaky scenery. Oh dear, I'm rambling . . . As your mother also used to say, me brains are mince.

3. So Caroline's pregnant again, Jamie's dating a different fella every night of the week, Rachel is Rachel and I'm on my own. The only avenue I have open to me is an old, old man who I really don't fancy.

4. Jack, it's like this. When you're chronically single and romantically unloved, something inside you starts to shrivel up. I'm slowly starting to despair of ever meeting anyone. In fact I really think I've more chance of winning the Eurolottery. I mean, do you

realize how unbelievably slim the odds are? That I'll walk into a club or a pub, meet someone, like the look of him, hope he likes me back, that he'll be single and straight, that he'll want to date me, will call when he says he'll call, be a reasonably decent guy who won't cheat, then, eventually, that he'll make a commitment to me without my having to resort to any shit-or-get-off-the-pot tactics, which are just so humiliating on so many levels.

5. So what do I do? Accept that this is it, this is my life? In fairness, the universe has sent me lots of other fantastic blessings, just not the one thing that I really, really want above everything else . . .

6. Or you and I could resurrect the idea of our pact. I don't mean to sound pushy or anything, but we're both single and thirty-seven and I'm sure you have a string of girlfriends over in the Old Colonial (remember you used to call them Jack's Angels and I used to say they should all have T-shirts printed?!), but, maybe, if you thought it was still an OK idea . . . can we at least talk about this . . . ?

7. Please???

Twelve-forty-five. The wine has really hit me now and I'm semi-comatose. I press the 'Send Later' key and decide to hit the bed, get up bright and early and try and compose a less terrifying, needy, reeking-of-desperation email to send Jack. It feels good though to have draft one safely filed and out of the way; now all I have to do is rewrite from here. Something upbeat and confident, I think, rubbing my eyes sleepily. Kind of 'Hi, Jack! Hey, if you're still single, then next time you're home, why don't you and I give it a whirl? We're always talking about it, why not go for it? What's the worst that can happen?' Except not as . . . direct.

Oh shit, this could take another seventeen drafts.

I yawn and stretch, then pad barefoot into the bathroom to go through the motions of taking off make-up, most of which has almost completely worn off by now anyway.

Something makes me stop dead in my tracks.

That was the 'Send Later' key I pressed, wasn't it?

Wasn't it?

I leg it back into the study, switch the computer back on and check my email account. No saved email. I'm starting to feel weak . . .

With a trembling hand I click on 'Sent Items' and there it is, safely delivered . . .

OK, now I want to throw up . . . It's about seven in the evening in Boston now, *and Jack Keating is reading my email* . . .

Chapter Twenty-Three

Treasure or Trash?

It's going to be so busy in work the following morning I know I'll barely have time to go to the loo, so there's nothing else for it. This is a damage-limitation exercise. There *IS* no other choice.

From: amelialockwood@eircom.net
To: jackkeating@hotmail.com
Subject: Major bite of humble pie. Major.

I think I may have accidentally sent you an email that I shouldn't have, very late last night with more than a few glasses of vino in me. Please ignore. Long story. Will explain all later. Am v. sorry if I terrified you. Be assured it wasn't intentional.

Axxx

OK, OK, OK, I think on the drive into work. At least this buys me a bit of time so I can hopefully think up some plausible excuse to get me out of this.

So far, I've come up with three: (*a*) I'm on very heavy medication; (*b*) I only sent that email for a bet/joke/dare; or (*c*) the truth, i.e., I was drunk, I was lonely and what can I say? It sounded normal in my head.

Jamie. I need Jamie. He's absolutely brilliant at thinking up excuses. I glance at the clock in the car. Just seven a.m. on the dot. Probably isn't even home from wherever he was last night yet, but no matter, I'll call him in a few hours' time. He's usually up and about by the crack of lunch as Rachel always says.

I park the car and head into the canteen for a badly needed max-strength coffee before I haul myself up to the office to start the day proper. I'm just at the till, about to pay, when a familiar voice from behind almost makes me jump out of my skin.

'Good episode last night. It's the first time I've actually *wanted* to stay in to watch *Celtic Tigers*.'

Philip Burke, with a heaving plate of bacon, rashers and sausages on a tray in front of him and a side plate piled high with buttery toast. Great start to the day, just what I need. Thank you, universe.

'Hi, Philip, how are you?' I ask, trying to sound bright and breezy. Awkward pause. 'Not on a diet then, I see.'

Did I just say that to the head of television?

'Not that you need to be on a diet . . . that's not what I meant at all. You're very . . .' *Very what?* '. . . emm . . . trim. Just like Michelangelo's David, if he was doing Atkins.' *Shut up Amelia. Shut up and run, while you still can.*

Thankfully he ignores my ramblings, but it's my own bloody fault to begin with. Why do I always forget this man doesn't do pleasantries?

'Very well scripted,' he says, paying the cashier. 'Tight. The acting wasn't too bad either. No long-drawn-out sighing before each line or looking directly into the camera, which certainly makes a change.'

I pay for my coffee. 'Thanks, I'm glad you thought so.'

I look at him for a moment, but that's it. You never can be sure with him whether a conversation is actually finished or not.

I decide that it is and move off. 'Well, have a good day, Philip.'

'Yeah, one more thing. Just so you're aware, that's the last compliment you'll get from me. I don't do positive feedback. When the show's doing well, you'll hear nothing from me. But rest assured, if I'm not happy, then you'll know all about it.'

I don't even attempt to answer this, I just leave. *Unbelievable. The man is unbelievable. Not quite a sociopath, but only a degree or two away from it . . .*

I text Jamie: RING ME THE MINUTE U SURFACE. HAVE DONE SOMETHING STUPID. NOT UNUSUAL 4 ME BUT THIS IS REALLY BAD. NEED YR HELP. URGENT. AX

Later that morning, I'm in the actors' dressing rooms welcoming a new cast member on board, when Jamie texts back. AM IN WORK, BARELY IN LAND OF THE LIVING AFTER LAST PM. RING ME WHEN U CAN TALK. R U OK? SHOULD I BRING U VODKA? JX. PS MET A HOTTIE IN THE DRAGON BAR LAST NIGHT. HE'S MR ALTERNATIVE IRELAND. I'M NOT MESSING.

'Sorry about that, I have to head back to the office,' I say to Sadie Smyth, who's just been cast as Good Grief O'Keefe's birth mother Mrs Duffy, a new central character in the show. God love her, it's her first day in studio today and she's as nervous as a kitten. She's a highly respected theatre actress, but hasn't done a huge amount of TV and is white in the face with apprehension.

I give her a warm smile and shake hands with her. 'You'll

be brilliant, Sadie, there's absolutely nothing to worry about. You did an amazing audition and we're very lucky to have you in the show. I know you'll be fantastic in the part. Knock 'em dead.'

'Thanks, Amelia,' she says, gripping my hand tight.

'And remember, if you've any problems, just come up to the office and find me, any time.'

She laughed. 'Wow. It's been a long time since anyone I've worked for has been this *nice* to me.'

Wish I could say the same, I think to myself, with Philip's legendary rudeness not far from my thoughts. Extraordinary how he can have scaled the heights of the corporate ladder with absolutely no people skills whatsoever . . .

I take the precaution of calling Jamie from the privacy of the conference room, which has pretty much become my office now, so I can fill him in properly.

'Oh, Amelia,' he says sadly. 'Where is your impulse control? Have I taught you nothing?'

'I was kind of hoping you'd say something like: "OK, so that's the problem, now let's figure out a way to solve it. Oh, and don't fret yourself, Amelia, it's not nearly as bad as you think."'

'I won't lie to you, it's even worse. To tell an ordinary, normal guy that you're single and panicking and now you'd like to hold him to a seventeen-year-old pact and get married to him is bad enough, but to a guy like Jack Keating? We'll be lucky if he hasn't run screaming across the border into Canada. He's probably changed his name by now, in case you hop on a flight and come after him, wearing your Vera Wang and clutching a bouquet.'

'Gee, thanks for the help. What a great spin doctor you'd have made.'

'No need to get ratty. It's not my fault if you broke one of my three golden commandments. Don't get intexticated, don't drink and dial, and never, ever get e-drunk and email when you've had a few over your e-limit.'

'Jamie, they are *not* your three golden commandments. You're always ringing people you fancy whenever you've had a few. The last night we were out, you drank five margaritas and made what I can only describe as an abusive phone call to your agent.'

'Oh, who are you, my biographer? Besides, my agent needed that kick up the arse. If he doesn't get one of his clients a decent job soon, he'll have to go full time on the checkout in Tesco's.'

'Sorry. Well, all I can say is I've learned my lesson the way I seem to learn all my lessons in life. The hard way.'

'Are you near your computer?'

'Yup.'

'OK. Forward the offending article on to me and I'll forensically examine it for any evidence that'll get you out of this. PMS is considered a defence in some states under federal law, you know.'

'You're a sweetheart, I owe you big time,' I say, logging on to my laptop and bringing up the emails. I can't even bear to look at it again, so I send it straight on to Jamie. 'OK. It's sent. Just please don't judge me when you read it.'

'I have seen the inside of your bathroom cupboard, filthy bitch. We have no secrets.'

'Oh shit, that reminds me.'

'What?'

'I'll have to call my cleaning lady. As if I didn't have enough to do, I'm hosting a party for my class this Saturday and before you even ask, no, you can't come.'

'Am I allowed to ask why not?'

'Because you're neither a single woman over thirty-five

who's actively pursuing a husband, nor are you an eligible straight man who's in the marriage market.'

'No, but I could be a really good party caterer for the night. I could certainly do with earning a few extra quid.'

'Jamie, no offence, but you've never catered before in your life.'

'How hard can it be to open a few trays of Marks and Spencer's party packs? Come on, Amelia, I need the cash and you're time poor. I'll do a great job. Trust me.'

'I have deodorant that I trust more than you.'

'Relax. Have I ever let you down?'

The day drags on. This isn't helped by the fact that I keep checking my emails every chance I get between meetings, in case, just in case, Jack has got back to me.

By three in the afternoon, mid-morning in Boston, still nothing.

That's it then. He's read it, thinks I'm insane and I'll probably never hear from him again, ever, as long as I live.

The only emotional pension plan that I had going for me, and I had to go and blow it.

Six p.m. Sadie Smyth has just given such a towering perform-ance in the last scene she shot that I have to run on to the studio floor to congratulate her. Even up in the production office, people were clustered around TV monitors, glued to the screen. On the floor, the crew burst into spontaneous applause and Good Grief O'Keefe, who shared the big mother-and-child reunion scene with her, is quietly fuming in the corner looking (there's no other word to describe it) pole-axed.

'Can we shoot that again?' she pleads with the floor manager. 'I just wasn't prepared for how *emotionally* she was going to play it. I know Sadie's my birth mother and she's explaining why she gave me up for adoption and everything, but did she have to burst into tears? It's not like she's dying of a tumour or anything.'

If she'd come right out and said, '*I* do the tears on this show,' her jealousy couldn't have been more transparent.

'Thank you, everyone, that is a wrap for today, see you all in the morning,' the floor manager calls, completely ignoring her.

'Sadie, you were *terrific!*' I say and she gives me a huge bear hug.

'Thanks, Amelia, for all your encouragement.'

'Any time. Keep up the good work!'

I can still hear the crew congratulating her as I leave the floor and go back to the office.

'What an entrance, the audience are going to love her.'

'What can I say? A star is born.'

I check my emails for about the thousandth time that day. Still nothing. Then I check my voicemail. Four new messages.

The first one's from Jamie: 'Oh, you poor misguided fool. I'm just home and I've read the email. Dear God, what were you drinking? Methylated spirits? I can't believe you actually used the phrase "when you're chronically single, something inside you starts to shrivel" without irony. Off the top of my head, the best thing I can suggest is that you tell him you've been sucked into a religious cult and are now going through a very painful deprogramming which is making you act like a crazy lady.' *Beep.*

Jamie again: 'Machine cut me off. Ring the second you get this. Don't even bother playing the end of the message.' *Beep.*

Rachel: 'I heard what you did last night and I know you're probably in a state but here's my two cents' worth. Ignore, ignore, ignore. Walk away from the problem and be thankful there's the Atlantic Ocean between you and Jack Keating. Ring me when you've finished work and we'll meet up to discuss further.' *Beep.*

Then, a warm, friendly voice I haven't heard in a long, long time: 'Hey, Amelia, howya doing? Thanks for your email, which I . . . emm . . . read . . . with . . . emmmm . . . well, it sure made an interesting read. Look, as it happens, I'm coming home for my parents' fortieth wedding anniversary next week, why don't we meet up then?

'Oh, it's Jack here, by the way.'

Chapter Twenty-Four
The Social Event of the Year . . . Not

In the end, I'm delighted I took Jamie up on his suggestion that he cater for the party. Although it's Saturday, it's still a filming day on *Celtic Tigers* so it's almost seven p.m. before I even get home.

I'd never have had the time to do everything he's done. The apartment looks immaculate. The wooden floors are gleaming; there are fresh long-stemmed lilies dotted about the place; scented candles glowing; the dining table is beautifully laid out with glasses and bottles of red wine, uncorked and breathing and just crying out to be drunk. Jamie emerges from the kitchen in his work uniform with an apron tied around his waist, like a French waiter.

'Well, hi, honey,' he says, hands on hips, camping it up, 'how was your day at the office, dear? Don't you feel like we're in a role-reversal nineteen-fifties American sitcom, starring me as the stay-home housewife?'

'Jamie, whatever you're charging me, you're worth far more. I can't get over how *fab* the apartment looks!'

'You may not say that when you see the bill. I spent like a wise guy.'

'Well worth it. Just look at this place!'

'Everything's done. The white wine is chilling; I even bought a nice bottle of champagne for you and me, just to get us in the party mood.'

'You're a treasure. If I can dust down an old chestnut, if you were straight, I'd marry you.'

'If I had five euro for every time I heard that. Oh, and I feng shui'd your bedroom for you too.'

Jamie, I should tell you, once read a magazine article about feng shui which said that ninety per cent of it is just plain old-fashioned decluttering. The result now is he uses the phrase to be synonymous with the word 'tidy', i.e.: 'I'd better go and feng shui all those dirty dishes out of the sink.'

I'm over the moon. As would anyone be who'd seen the state of my bedroom this morning. 'Jamie! You're amazing! You should be a full-time party organizer!'

'Well, there's going to be nothing but single men here, who's to say you won't score? Oh, that's unless your teacher has put you on some "rules" thing where you can't sleep with a guy for at least three months.'

'No, most definitely not.'

'That's the spirit. You take what you can get, honey. Go! Go have a look at your room, then jump in the shower and I'll have a nice chilled glass of bubbly sitting on your dressing table for you to knock back while you're pampering. Hurry, babe, there's less than an hour to show time.'

Half an hour later and I'm as ready as I'll ever be. I'm wearing my 'serial result' little black number with my hair loose around my shoulders and just the lightest bit of make-up. 'Whaddya think?' I say, twirling in front of Jamie.

'Any man's fantasy come true. A thirty-something Meryl Streep.'

'You're lying, but bless you anyway.'

'Here,' he says, topping up my glass.

'Thanks,' I say, taking a gulp. 'I'm nervous.'

'Oh, please, what's to be nervous about?'

I take a nice, soothing deep breath. 'OK. My present panic attack stems from the following, in no particular order: (*a*) Damien Delaney is coming, which is good news, but he may cop on that this is a treasure/trash party and that I only invited him so I could try to pawn him off on someone else, which makes it bad news; (*b*) I'm afraid that all the boys will cluster around one end of the living room and the girls around the other and no one will talk to anyone and it'll be like a parish dance hall in rural Ireland circa nineteen forty; (*c*) aside from one girl called Mags, I barely know anyone in my class, let alone any of the fellas they're all bringing. I've basically invited a bunch of total strangers to my flat and all we have in common is that we're single. How do I know they won't rob me?'

Just then, the phone rings and Jamie leaps to answer it, putting on a John-Gielgud-type accent. 'Good evening, Miss Lockwood's residence, the butler speaking. Whom shall I say is calling?'

I make an I'll-slit-your-bloody-throat gesture as I snatch the phone away from him. 'Hi, Amelia here.'

'Amelia, this is Ira Vandergelder calling. Wow, I'm so impressed that you have your very own personal Paul Burrell.'

'Oh, hi, Ira, emm . . . no, that was the caterer, actually.'

'Caterers? Didn't I tell you not to go to any trouble?'

'Well, it's just finger food mostly. And *lots* of drinks.'

'Good. Lowers the inhibitions. I just called to wish you luck. Now remember, mingle. Rediscover your inner flirt. Remind yourself that you have nothing to lose but your single status.'

I'm half annoyed I didn't put her on speakerphone so Jamie could hear the way she goes on, just to prove I wasn't exaggerating about her. Then the panic hits. 'Sorry, Ira, did you say that you weren't coming tonight?'

'I never go to these parties, honey. I find my being there tends to make my ladies a little nervous, which defeats the whole point of the exercise.'

'Oh, rats. I was hoping you could help me to winnow out the decent guys from the messers.'

'What have I told you about honing those rusty instincts of yours? Have a wonderful party and I'll see you at class next week.'

And she's gone.

Eight p.m. Bang on the dot, the doorbell rings. Jamie hops behind the makeshift bar/dining table and wishes me luck as I go to answer it.

I'm dying to know who it is; none of my friends ever comes to a party on time. I open the door, hoping my smile doesn't make me look too much like the desperado I am: Damien Delaney, carrying a magnificent potted pink orchid.

'Good evening, Amelia my dear, how very pretty you're looking.'

'Emm, thanks,' I say as we peck each other politely on each cheek. I don't know how he does it, but there's just something about the way he speaks that makes me feel as if I should be wearing Victorian crinolines and clutching a phial of smelling salts.

'This is for you,' he says, handing over the orchid, which is encased in cellophane.

'Thank you so much,' I say, really touched. 'It's my favourite plant. And the only one that I'm actually able to keep alive.'

'Yes, I spoke to Caroline, she told me. Of course, I would never dream of bringing fresh-cut flowers to a party. Dreadful breach of etiquette. It presumes that the hostess has not put any thought into her floral arrangements.'

'Oh . . . emm . . . really? Imagine that.'

OK, so that may have sounded a bit stuffy and old-fashioned, but he's fundamentally a very nice guy, I remind myself, silently blessing Jamie for buying all the beautiful lilies and arranging them as elegantly as only a gay man can.

I usher Damien into the living room and automatically go to introduce them both, but Damien beats me to it. 'Yes, of course, Jamie and I have met before. In Caroline and Mike's beautiful home. I almost didn't recognize you . . .'

'With all my clothes on?' says Jamie cheekily.

A hint of a blush from Damien and a furious glare from me.

'I was about to say, in your charming uniform.'

'Thanks. I like it cos it accentuates my ass.'

Jamie has a really bad habit of reverting back to a bold schoolboy whenever he comes up against anyone whose manners are . . . a little more formal, and right now he's behaving like the Artful Dodger.

'What can I get you to drink, Damien?'

'I'm driving, unfortunately, so perhaps just a mineral water. Still, please.'

'Oh, come on, it's a Saturday night. I'm always saying to Amelia that Saturday nights are all about getting drunk and getting laid.'

I could *kill* Jamie . . .

Nine p.m. I could *hug* Jamie . . .

Everyone's here and the party's in full swing.

Jamie was worth his weight in gold when they all arrived.

He whirled around the room like a dervish on acid, getting people drinks, taking coats and even putting on boppy salsa music to swing things along a bit. Meanwhile I did my best to introduce people I barely knew to people I'd never met before in my life.

In fairness, they all seem really nice. Any initial awkwardness is quickly done away with as soon as the wine begins to loosen everyone up. The girls seem to be doing most of the work, introducing the guys they've brought and chatting away, although occasionally you can spot one of them scanning the room faux casually, thinking: So who or what has everyone *else* brought?

Just like I'm doing right now.

Yes, bingo, target identified.

Now, I know it's never a good idea to assess men solely in terms of looks; it's bad enough that guys do that to we girls, but you should just see this fella. He's tall, very tanned, Nordic blond and is standing over in the far corner chatting away to a small, round guy with Gucci glasses who's holding a plate of sausage rolls and eating all of them. Sexy-looking guy looks really bored. Brilliant. Now's my chance.

I sidle over to where Jamie is frantically scooping ice cubes from a freezer tray into an ice bucket and pick up two bottles, one red, one white, just to be on the safe side.

'Do I look OK?' I hiss at him. 'I've just identified a possible target. Twelve o'clock. Over by the balcony. Act natural.'

'Mmm . . . yes, hot, hot, hot, in a Viking-warrior-type way. Doesn't look Irish.'

'I love being the hostess. Remind me to do this every week. Perfect way to sidle up to him and ask him what he'd like to drink without arousing suspicion.'

'You see that guy over there by the fireplace? The one

with the boiled potato head? Gay and doesn't know it yet.'

'Jamie! You and your gaydar.'

'Where's Damien? Remember Damien? Your date – or rather your non-date, except he doesn't know it yet.'

'Oh shit,' I say, suddenly overwhelmed with guilt. 'I've hardly said two words to him all night.'

'Relax. Go flirt. I'll mind him for you. Maybe even turn him, who knows?'

'Behave yourself.'

'I've always secretly fancied the idea of having a rich older guy to lavish gifts on me and take care of me. You know, the way Frank Sinatra and Sammy Davis Junior used to take care of Liza Minelli . . .'

I roll my eyes at him and head back into the throng. Yes, there's my cute Viking, all on his own now and still looking bored. I make my way over to him, topping up glasses as I go.

Now, I know I'm chronically single and am in absolutely no position to criticize anyone else who's in the same boat, but, to be honest, if Ira overheard some of the snippets of conversation that I'm hearing now, she'd pass out.

One tall, stooping guy with really bad dandruff falling down the back of his crumpled linen suit is chatting to a particularly stunning girl from the class, who I think is called Emily. 'Of course I didn't mean to insult you,' he's saying. 'It's just that I'm a consultant anaesthetist and I thought maybe you'd had breast-augmentation surgery. I only meant to compliment your surgeon, whoever he is. He did a great job. They're very realistic.'

Emily catches my eye and for a second I think she's going to slap him one across the face.

Then I pause briefly to top up the glass of another man

who looks like a young fogey, the type who'd end up leading the Conservative Party, a bit like William Hague. He's talking to Sarah, a very pretty plumpish blonde girl.

'And what do you do?' he asks her.

'I'm an air hostess with Aer Lingus.' She smiles brightly. 'I work on the transatlantic route.'

'Really?' He nods sagely. 'I had a cousin who was an air hostess. Very unsociable hours, I hear. Is that why you find it so difficult to meet men?'

Sarah's looking at him, dumbfounded.

'What's your last name?' he continues, undeterred by her stunned silence. 'Just in case I ever need an upgrade.'

Nor is it just some of the men who are coming out with howlers. I pause for a moment to top up the glass of another girl who has buttonholed a very bored-looking guy. She's got him up against a wall; he's an awful lot younger than her and is basically looking anywhere in the room except directly at her.

'Do you remember when Prince Charles said that Camilla was not a negotiable part of his life?' she's asking him sadly. 'Well, why can't I meet a man who'll say that about me? Is that too much to ask?'

Viking man is all on his own, glancing at his watch, when I make my move. I'm just about to offer him a top-up when Jamie shouts across to me from the bar where he's trying to pour about six drinks at once. 'Amelia? Can you get the door? I would, but I'm snowed under here.'

OK, bad timing, but I can always approach Viking man in a minute. I catch his eye, pull a would-you-excuse-me? smile at him and head back out to the hall.

By now, Sarah has made her escape from the young fogey and now he's chatting to a girl I don't recognize at all.

'It's not that I want to get married per se,' he's droning on, 'it's just that I think a wife would be a really good asset to my career.'

I slip down the hallway and open the door, wondering who the late arrival could be.

It's Mags, looking absolutely lovely in a cream cashmere coat which sets off her red hair to perfection. 'I'm so sorry I'm late,' she says, hugging me and presenting me with a bottle of champagne. 'I'd left your address on a scrap of paper at home and we had to go all the way back to get it.'

'Oh, don't worry a bit; I'm just so glad you're here. You look *amazing*.'

'Thanks! All I've done is take off the glasses and wear my lenses for a change. How's it going?' she asks as I help her take off the good coat.

'Well, everyone's chatting away, so at least that's something. I've so far identified one cute guy and one to be avoided like the Black Death.' Then it strikes me. 'Did you come on your own, Mags?'

'Oh no.' She smiles. 'I'm with an old friend. He's just the fussiest man you ever met about where to park his car. Can't park under a tree in case a bird poos on it; can't be too close to another car in case they scrape off it. I just came on ahead to apologize to you.'

I'm about to say there's absolutely no need for apologies and usher her inside for a nice, relaxing drink when the lift door glides open.

Philip Burke.

Nine-o-four p.m. I had a silent bet with myself to see how long it would be until he came out with a Philip Burkeism. Exactly four minutes, which must be a record, even for him.

'This is Amelia that I've been telling you all about,' Mags

says cheerily as Philip comes in. 'You'll love her; she's just such a *hoot*. She always has the class in stitches.'

No! Now he knows I'm on a course to find a husband and, what's even worse, Mags has probably told him some of my ex-boyfriend stories . . .

I'm a bit shell-shocked, but I compose myself enough to shake his hand and say, 'Yeah, actually, we work together. Philip, please come in, you're very welcome.'

'You just said the party was in some girl called Amelia's house,' Philip says to Mags. 'You never said it was Amelia Lockwood.'

The implication is clear enough; if you had, there's no way I'd have bothered coming.

'Sure, I'd no idea you worked in television.' Mags smiles at me. 'Let alone your last name. That's the funny thing about our course. All we really know about each other is that we're all single.'

Oh God, this can't get any more embarrassing, can it? Yes, this is my life. Of course it can. There is always room for further embarrassment.

I bring them both into the living room and the first person we bump into is Damien. I'm just about to introduce them all when Philip says, 'Hi there. Nice to meet you. Are you Amelia's father?'

Eleven p.m. Disastrous night. Just awful.

I've spent the last two hours stuck in a corner, collared by Philip, and all he can talk about is *Celtic Tigers*. Most people have left by now, including cute Viking man, who I never even got to speak to. I don't even know who he came with and I can hardly go into class next week and make an announcement saying, 'Excuse me, girls, hands up who here brought the guy who looks like an extra from *Conan the Barbarian*.'

Mags is sitting on the sofa chatting away to Damien, but apart from them there's only a handful of people left, none of whom I even know.

Jamie comes over to us, offering to top up our glasses. Philip's not drinking but I bloody well am.

Then I do something a bit below the belt. I'm not very proud of it, but needs must. Tonight was supposed to be about meeting single guys, not being stuck talking shop in the corner with my boss.

'Jamie, did I introduce you to Philip Burke?'

'No, hi, how are you?' says Jamie, shaking hands indifferently.

'Philip is the head of television.'

For a second, Jamie almost looks like a character from a cartoon with a lightbulb suddenly flashing brightly over his head. 'The head of television? Amelia! Are you telling me that the man who could change the entire course of my career has been under the same roof as me all this time and you never even told me? Philip, it really is an honour to meet you. I'm an actor, you know. But I also have a wonderful idea for a screenplay, or a sitcom, it could be either. Do you have a sec?'

I leave them to it and drift away.

'Amelia?' says Mags as I walk past the sofa. 'Could you show me where the bathroom is please?'

'Sure, it's this way. Excuse us for a moment, Damien.'

I take her down the hallway and show her where the main bathroom is, but there's someone in it. 'Not to worry,' I say, 'there's an en suite off my room. Here, I'll show you.'

No sooner are we in my bedroom than she bangs the door shut and plonks down on the bed. 'I didn't need the loo at all. I just need to talk to you privately.'

I sit down beside her. 'Is everything all right?'

'Couldn't be better. I just wanted to run something by you. I'm really getting along well with Damien. He's so sweet and . . . gentle and . . . like a big teddy.'

'Yeah, I know what you mean, he kind of is, isn't he?' I laugh.

'Look, I know he's the guy you brought tonight, but the thing is he's offered to drive me home and I just wondered if that was OK with you?'

'Mags, I'm thrilled! I was hoping you two would hit it off. This is *fabulous* news.'

'So, do you mind me asking you something else?'

'Is it about Philip?'

She sighs. 'I wish you'd give him a chance, Amelia. He really is a lovely man. I've known him for years and years. I know he has a habit of saying the wrong thing at the wrong time, but it's nothing that can't be sanded down and worked on over time. You've got so much in common with him.'

I want to say to her, what exactly do you think I have in common with that oddball? But then I have to remind myself that he is Mags's friend and I am the hostess and have to be ultra-polite and not slag off the guests.

Right then, think of a polite comment . . . Ooh, I know . . .

'How do you know each other?'

'He went out with a friend of mine for ages and he and I always got on. She met someone else while she was still seeing Philip and ended up going to Australia with this other guy. She's married to him now and I think they've a few kids. Poor Philip; you've never seen anyone so devastated when she upped and left him. So, I was his shoulder to cry on and we ended up being great friends.'

Somehow the idea of Philip Burke being cast as the heartbroken jilted lover just doesn't ring true.

'So, what do you think, Amelia? Come on, as Ira is always telling us, you have to cast your net wide.'

'Emm, well, I don't really think he's interested in me. Honestly, we were just talking shop.'

'You're not answering the question. If he asked you out, would you say yes?'

I'm saved by the bell.

Literally.

The doorbell rings and I excuse myself to go and answer it.

'Sorry about this, Mags. Probably my moany neighbour to tell me to turn down the music. I won't be a sec.'

She follows me out to the hall and we bump into Philip, searching for his coat at the hatstand with Jamie still bending his ear.

'So can I send my CV and headshot straight to you then, Philip? Or I could drop it into your office on Monday, if that would suit you better . . .'

'I have to go,' Philip says to me, ignoring Jamie. 'It's been a very . . . interesting evening.'

The doorbell goes again and I answer.

Am I seeing things? He-whose-name-shall-forever-remain-unspoken. Looking cool and casual, as if I'd been expecting him all along.

'Hi there. You're having a party then?'

I can't answer him. I'm too shocked.

'What do you want?' says Jamie in an ice-cold tone. He puts a protective arm around my waist for good measure and I find myself clinging to him.

'Jamie, good to see you, how are you, man?'

'I said, *what do you WANT?*'

God, Jamie's good when he's angry. Even I'm a bit intimidated.

'Hey, take it easy, I didn't mean to interrupt, I just saw that you had people over and I wondered if I could borrow a corkscrew. If it's not too much bother.'

Now, I've always said that I'd be better in a fight than Jamie any day, but now I have to admit that I was one hundred per cent wrong. Jamie reacts as if he'd been asked for the loan of a kidney. 'Is there a sign above the door that says "lying, cheating, bastard ex-boyfriends welcome"?', he snarls. 'I don't think so. Now get the hell out of here or I'll kick you all the way back to stab city. You are not welcome here. Do you understand? The reason God invented dead-bolts, spyholes and intercom systems was to keep people like you away. Got it? Good.'

And with that, Jamie slams the door in his face. 'Jeez, Amelia, I just thought you needed a hand with the catering. Didn't think I'd end up doing bouncer as well. I should charge extra.'

Chapter Twenty-Five

When They're Interested, They're Interested, and When They're Not, They're Not

Caroline has invited us all over for Sunday lunch the next day, bless her, so we can all catch up on what's been happening in each other's lives over the last few days. Or, more correctly, so we can all have a good laugh at my disastrous treasure/trash party, I think, depressed beyond all reason as I pull the duvet over my head.

Now, ordinarily I'd be first in the queue to tell funny stories about last night and some of the shenanigans that went on, were it not for the last few, excruciating minutes of the evening.

Oh God.

I honestly don't know which is worse. That *He-whose-name-shall-forever-remain-unspoken* seems to think it's absolutely OK casually to drop into my apartment looking for cork-screws at eleven o'clock at night or that Jamie had to come the heavy just to get rid of him.

In front of Philip Burke.

He probably thought he'd walked in on a traveller wedding by accident.

The phone rings and it's Caroline. 'Hi, pet, I know I'll be seeing you later on but just a quick word to the wise. Absolutely no one is to say *anything* to Rachel about *anything* and I specifically told Jamie he's to back off and leave her alone. What she got up to last night is entirely her own affair—'

'*What?*'

'JOSHUA!' she screams. 'Take your fingers out of that plug socket THIS MINUTE! I have to go, honey, emergency, I'll see you at one.'

Then my mobile rings. Jamie. 'Well, sweetie, it's your lucky day. It seems you will not be the sole focus of attention over lunch later on.'

'What is going on? Did something happen to Rachel? Is she OK?'

'Put it this way. Our dearest, acid-tongued friend is seriously straining to do some explaining this morning.'

OK, now I'm starting to think she was in a drugs bust last night . . . 'Jamie, stop talking in sound bites. Tell me everything!'

'Gormless Gordon scored a home run. For definite.'

'*WHAT?*'

'Too true, my angel. I called her ten minutes ago and he answered her landline.'

'Oh, come on, Jamie, that doesn't mean anything . . . does it? You've put two and two together and made five thousand.'

'My beautiful idiotic innocent, will you let me finish? She was in the shower so I did a KGB on him and got the full low-down. The poor kamikaze bastard said he'd managed to drag her to a pub after work yesterday and then went back to her place for a nightcap and *then* he said they had a physical connection which I'm guessing didn't involve working out together.'

'You are *joking*!'

'How could you make this up? So I said to him, "Well, you're about to find out what it's like to have slept with a praying mantis. When it comes to Rachel's men, the survivors envy the dead."'

'I can't believe it. I'm in total shock.'

'Ring her if you don't believe me. Oh, and can you pick me up on your way to Caroline's?'

'What? Oh . . . ehh . . . sure.' I hang up, stunned. Naturally, Rachel's not answering her phone, and I'm wide awake now anyway, so I get up. Besides, I'm unable to start into the big apartment clean-up without (*a*) a very strong coffee inside me and (*b*) a quick scan of the Sunday papers. In between trying to call Rachel every two minutes, that is.

Eventually she answers her mobile.

'Just give me a one-word answer,' I say. 'Is it true?'

'I will plaster Jamie's brains all over a wall for spreading this,' she snarls. 'I was drunk; I had nothing better on last night; it was only sex; if he ever comes near me again, I'll set fire to him.'

'Who, Jamie or Gorm— sorry, I mean Gordon.'

'Either of them. Tell me honestly,' she says and I can hear her lighting up a fag, 'is everyone talking about this?'

'Jamie's talking, everyone's listening.'

'Right. Hang up, I have to go. Damage limitation. See you at one.' And she's gone.

This is *unbelievable*. This is *shocking*. This is . . . oh God, this is one of those days that I really miss having a partner: Sundays and bank holidays, and occasions when there's super-hot gossip to be discussed; especially when my friend scored last night and I didn't. It's the little things, you know, like waking up in someone's arms, taking turns to make brekkie, playfully bickering over whose turn it is to get out of bed and go and get the papers. All the normal stuff.

Life is not designed to be gone through alone; you're *supposed* to have a partner. Even if it's someone you're initially not interested in, like Gormless Gordon, who is actually all right, it's just that Jamie saddled him with that horrific moniker and now it's stuck.

No wonder I'm going a bit off my head, I think, pulling on my jeans and a T-shirt and running out of the door.

I head for my local Italian deli, Dunne and Crezenci's, which is one of those fab places that every single person should have right on their doorstep. It caters absolutely one hundred per cent for people like me who, although we have state-of-the-art kitchens, only ever seem to use the micro-wave. Or else just eat out all the time.

I'm barely in the door when the aroma of deep-flavoured Italian coffee hits me. Yummmmmm. That and the very cheering sight of Giorgio, the drop-dead-gorgeous manager, who looks like he's just stepped off a catwalk in Milan during fashion week. Double yummmmmmmm.

I often think it would be worth my while to get caught shoplifting, just so he could feel me up. By now, I must look a bit like Homer Simpson with drool coming down the side of my mouth as I grab the papers and order a ham and melted cheese croissant with a cappuccino to go.

I glance at the headlines as I'm waiting to pay. 'PLIGHT OF LOTTO WINNER. "SINCE I WON THREE MILLION, MEN ARE PLAGUING ME TO WED. I HAD THREE PROPOSALS LAST WEEK ALONE."'

'Don't suppose you sell Lotto tickets, do you, Giorgio?' I ask, hopefully.

'Sorry, Amelia, try the newsagent's next door.' He laughs.

'So you wanna be a millionaire and have men chase you like that lady?' he asks, glancing down at my paper.

I smile at him in what I hope is a beguiling/mysterious way, but which I'm afraid only makes me look like a consumptive in dire need of a blood transfusion, because then he asks me if I'm feeling all right and did I have a very late night last night?

'Yeah, yeah,' I mutter, mortified, 'I had *way* too much to drink, you know. Anyway, thanks for brekkie. See you soon!'

I scarper out of the door and barely get three paces down the road when a jeep pulls up. A black jeep.

Where have I seen that car before?

Oh no, no, no, fate couldn't be that cruel, could it? Lightning doesn't strike twice on the same weekend – does it?

Unfortunately, in my life, the answer always seems to be yes . . .

'Hey, Amelia, good morning!'

It's him. *He-whose-name-shall-forever-remain-unspoken,* all dressed in Sunday morning casual jeans and denim shirt, as cool and relaxed as if we were the best of buddies, about to go on a fun-filled hiking day out up the Sugarloaf mountain.

Then a hot flush of anger and frustration comes over me. I swear to God, sometimes I know how it must feel to have an anger stroke coming on . . . The raw-faced, brazen *cheek* of him just to pull up outside of Dunne and Crezenci's as if he owned the place.

I hate to sound petulant and sulky but *I* was the one who introduced him to this place and if he and I had been married and if there had been a divorce settlement, then the right to frequent Dunne and Crezenci's would have been mine, particularly early on a Sunday morning, when he knows I'm always in there. Is that so unreasonable?

Bastard.

I mutter a greeting and quicken my pace to get out of there. *Does he even remember last night?*

'Amelia, don't walk off. I was kind of hoping I'd bump into you here this morning.'

I stop dead in my tracks.

'I wanted to apologize to you for yesterday evening. For arriving at your apartment unannounced, I mean. I really am sorry, I shouldn't have. I just noticed that you were having a party and it looked like you were all having a great time.'

If you only knew the truth, I think to myself, but say nothing.

'I was on my own last night, you see, not that that excuses anything,' he adds, seeing the look of yeah–right–like–I–care flitter across my face. I'm trying to keep my expression bored and deadpan, but probably look more like a moody, hormonal teenager.

Another silence.

'Well, anyway, it just looked like you and all your friends were really enjoying yourselves,' he trails off. 'Certainly more fun than sitting at home on a Saturday night, drinking wine on your own.'

Now, this is the point where I should have bid him a polite, frosty good day and elegantly strolled away, dignity intact, the high moral ground effortlessly maintained. But sometimes I'm just too bloody nosey for my own good. I'm incapable of quitting when I'm ahead. 'So where was your fiancée?'

He looks a bit shifty. 'In Lillie's Bordello with her friends. They'd asked me along, but . . . well . . . it just isn't really my scene. Too old and too tired for all that. Half the time, I don't even understand what they're all talking about. And it really embarrasses me to have to go up to a bar and ask for a round of alcopops.'

Boy oh boy, aren't you in for a wonderful marriage . . .

'Anyway, Amelia, I just want to say sorry. It won't happen again.' Then he looks at me hopefully. 'Unless you want it to?'

I'm hearing things; I have to be hearing things . . . 'Can we just get one thing straight?' I say, desperately trying to keep the wobble of emotion out of my voice. 'I don't think you and I will ever have the kind of neighbourly relationship where we call into each other's homes borrowing cups of sugar.'

'It was a corkscrew actually.'

'Can I please finish? I really don't care if it's five in the morning and you need to borrow my car to drive yourself to an intensive-care unit, I'm not your twenty-four-hour, on-call, girl next door, who you can just land in on whenever your bride-to-be is out at a rave with all the other Leaving Cert students. Not now, not anytime in the future. I didn't choose this situation, I didn't ask you to buy the house across the road from me; all I am asking is to be left in peace. OK?'

I walk off and try not to slop my cappuccino all over the pavement, I'm shaking that much. He doesn't even go into Dunne and Crezenci's, he just gets back into the jeep and drives off. I have a strong urge to shout after him, 'Mind you don't drive over any landmines, now,' but I manage to restrain myself.

I've had quite enough for one weekend.

Unbelievable, just unbelievable.

An image flashes through my head: the day we finally broke up. I had come home early from work to find two packed suitcases sitting neatly in the hallway. He was wearing an overcoat, standing in the living room, scanning it as if double-checking to make sure he'd left nothing behind. To this day I still wonder what would have happened if I hadn't chanced to come home early. I think he hoped I'd just notice that all his stuff was gone and then cop on that we were finished without any discussion/post-mortem/explanation or any of those conversations men hate so much.

Cowardly bloody bastard had everything planned except his speech. 'It's not you, it's me,' he kept repeating, like a hackneyed cliché you wouldn't even hear on *Celtic Tigers*. 'I need to be on my own right now.' And my personal favourite, 'It's not that I don't want to commit to you, I don't want to commit to *anyone*.'

Then his taxi arrived and he was gone. It was that quick.

This is the man who ripped out my heart, flung it against a wall and now thinks it's absolutely OK to come back late at night looking for a loan of household appliances.

My mind races on the brisk walk home as I force myself to put him out of my head and think only positive, happy thoughts.

Right. Here goes. Deep, cleansing breath.

Good things going on in my life right now
Shit, shit, shit, I really have to think hard.

Yes. There *is* one. My emotional-pension-plan man. In spite of my hysterical email to Jack Keating, he didn't run a mile. He's home next week and I'll hook up with him then.

Bad things going on in my life right now
I will have to go out of my way to prove to him that I am a normal, serenely contented woman and that, furthermore, one deranged late-night email does not a bunny boiler make. Yes, I had remembered our pact and if I drunkenly alluded to it and caused him any undue stress or worry, then I will apologize unreservedly.

Unless he's still single.

Then, I'm sorry, but he's fair game.

Good thing

Must think positive, happy thoughts about other people and be less self-absorbed in my own dramas. OK. Yes, I have one. Mags is a really lovely girl and if one good thing came out of last night, it's that she seemed to really hit it off with Damien Delaney. I really do hope things work out there. They'd be such a sweet couple . . .

Bad thing

I'm the one who's going to have to explain to Caroline and Mike that in spite of their best-laid matchmaking plans, I have now officially let Damien slip through my fingers.

Good thing

Schadenfreude. In the first dismal days after my break-up with *He-whose-name-shall-forever-remain-unspoken,* you could barely have picked me up off the floor. When I heard he was getting married, if it weren't for my friends I honestly think I'd have had an emotional collapse.

It's horrible of me to admit this, but from where I'm standing, now it looks like the age gap between him and Poppy (or whatever her MTV name is) is finally starting to show. If he's staying home at weekends while she goes out clubbing with her mates . . . what does that tell you about the cracks in their relationship? And why is he calling round to my apartment like we're old friends and it's absolutely OK?

I give that marriage six months tops.

I just have one more comment to make and then I'll shut up on the subject for ever.

HA, HA, HA, HA, HA, HA . . .

There's a great story about the Beatles, when they were famously turned down by a record producer from Decca, who, in 1962, proudly declared that guitar bands were on the way out. A journalist remarked to John Lennon that the guy must be kicking himself. 'Good,' replied Lennon. 'I hope he kicks himself to death.'

Not very charitable, I know, but you can see where I'm coming from.

By the time I get home, I'm feeling an awful lot better and am just about to hop back into bed with the papers when my mobile rings. Not a number I recognize, which is odd.

'Hello?'

'Amelia?'

The line isn't great and I can't quite place the voice . . . 'Yes?'

'Philip Burke here. Hope you don't mind me phoning you on a Sunday?'

'Oh . . . hi. No, of course I don't mind.' *Like I'm going to do a big 'How dare you? This is my one and only day off' number on the head of television?*

'Mags said I should call you.'

'Oh, right.' *To thank me for the party? Or . . . oh gulp . . . to ask me out?* Neither, it would seem.

He chats on about, surprise, surprise, *Celtic Tigers* for a bit; he'd seen a rough cut of Sadie Smyth's first few scenes and is as impressed with her as I was. I'm just waiting for the Philip Burkeism to come and sure enough, right on cue, it does. 'So who was that guy who tried to gatecrash the party at the end of the night?'

'It's a long story.'

'Is he South African?'

I grunt in reply. It's not very polite, but it's the best I can manage.

'Yeah, I thought I recognized the accent.'

I don't answer. The least said about that incident the better.

'Ex-boyfriend, I gather.'

Again, I'm silent. Philip seems to take the hint that this isn't an area I want to be drawn in on, and changes the subject. 'You know, Mags thinks you and I should go out on a date.'

Typical of him, bloody typical. Was that him asking me out just there or not? A normal bloke would come out with, 'Would you like to go to a movie/dinner/meet for a drink?' Simple, straightforward and we all know where we stand. But then, this is certainly no normal bloke . . . 'Mags thinks you and I should go out on a date' is putting the entire onus on me and now I don't know what to say. If I answer, 'Yes, please, thank you, that would be lovely,' then I look too eager, but if I just umm and ahh and sound non-committal, then it looks like I'm being rude to my boss's boss.

'So, what do you think?' he says. 'Good idea, bad idea?'

I don't know, is the honest answer. I don't know what I think.

The only reason we're even having this highly embarrassing conversation is because we're both single, that's all. I don't fancy him and I'm pretty certain he doesn't fancy me either. We're just at the age where the club/pub pick-up scene is all just getting too *exhausting* and this just happens to be convenient.

But then . . . he is Mags's friend, so that says a lot in his favour. The recurrent image of my headless groom comes back into my mind. Yes, OK, he's not perfect and he's only trying me on for size because his friend told him to, but then,

I do want to be married, don't I? Before the end of the year? And I'm the girl who woke up this morning longing for a partner, I remind myself. As Ira always says, you have to pump up the dating volume or you'll never get anywhere. And Philip was very considerate over the whole Rob Richards/Good Grief O'Keefe debacle, calling me up to his office just to see if I was OK . . . wasn't he?

Then I think about Rachel scoring last night. Yes, she'll probably kick my teeth in for saying it, but in fairness to Gorm— sorry, I mean Gordon, he is now living proof that persistence pays. In this life, you have to take risks.

Just as I'm wavering, Philip comes out with one of his classic howlers. 'Look, Amelia, I realize that asking a single, late-thirty-something woman out is a bit like throwing fish-heads at a starving piranha: you normally get your hand snapped off, they're so eager to say yes. So, come on, what would you say to a drink after work some night during the week?'

'*What* did you just say?'

'Sorry, did that come out wrong? It was only a joke. Oh shit, I really should rehearse conversations with women beforehand, shouldn't I? You'll have to forgive me, I'm a bit out of practice.'

I can't make head nor tail of this guy. One minute he's so rude you want to put the phone down on him, the next, he's actually being . . . almost *endearing* . . .

'Philip, please don't feel you have to ask me out just because Mags told you to. It's very sweet of you, but you really don't have to.'

'So that's a no then?'

'We *work* together.'

'Your point being?'

'It would be . . . awkward.'

'Rubbish. Just be direct with me, Amelia. What's going on here?'

Right, well he asked for it . . . 'I hate to appear nit-picky, but you were the one who presented me with a six-month ultimatum: turn *Celtic Tigers* around or else face the axe. You'll forgive me for bringing it up, but the idea of going on a date with the man who could propel me to the back of a dole queue in a few months' time is a slightly intimidating one. This may sound surprising, but I'm actually *not* trying to get fired.'

There's a crackly silence and I'm not even sure if he's still on the phone.

'Hello? Philip?'

'Yeah, still here. Right. Well, at least it wasn't a flaky excuse, I'll give you that much. Last time I asked a girl out, she said she had to stay home to do her VAT returns. If you change your mind, call me. Just remember, I'm rich, male and in my late thirties. I'm the one who's in a buyers' market.'

He hangs up and I slump back on to the pillow.

This is neither a good thing nor a bad thing. It's a terrifying thing.

Chapter Twenty-Six
My Knight in Flabby Armour

OK, I admit it; I'm a dirty big cheat. I've made an executive decision. I'm skipping my next ex-boyfriend on the list. Yes, I know Ira will go mental; yes, I know I'm bending the rules here; yes, I know that cowardice has got the better of me, but if you knew the sad, awful truth, you'd do exactly the same.

I should explain.

THE TIME: The Christmas holidays 1991.
THE PLACE: The long, slushy, foggy, ice-bound road from Dublin to Monaghan.
THE OCCASION: Tim Singen-Underwood, my wonderful, gorgeous boyfriend, has invited me to spend the new year at his family's county estate. This is the first time in my life that I've ever been formally invited to meet any boyfriend's parents, let alone his entire family, and I'm experiencing a whole kaleidoscope of emotions. I'm flattered, overwhelmed, knickers mad about my boyfriend, desperately eager to make a good impression on his family but most of all . . . I'm shit scared.

First of all, there was the drama about what to wear.

'You need to strike exactly the right chord,' says Caroline as she and I pilfer through the collective bounty of her, Rachel's and my own wardrobe combined. The three of us by now are all sharing a dotey little townhouse, which is great because it's like having twenty-four-hour access to two other girls' wardrobes as well as your own. Jamie has semi-moved in too and spends most nights on our pull-out sofa mattress, rent free. This is also very handy, as (*a*) he's the only one of us who's remotely able to cook and (*b*) it's like living with your own personal stylist.

'Remember the Singed-Underwears are proper, west-Brit aristos,' says Jamie, coming into Caroline's bedroom, wearing only a pair of boxer shorts and eating toast.

'Singen-Underwood, not Singed-Underwear,' I say.

'Whatever. My point is you don't want to wear anything that looks either too new or flashy. Old and tatty is the look you're going for. Think Nancy Mitford and you won't go far wrong. Posh, but broke.'

'What about this?' I ask, holding up a high-necked, very modest-looking cream blouse.

'Ughhhh . . . have mercy, put it away. Too Rose of Tralee.'

'I bet they dress for dinner in the evenings too,' says Caroline, fishing out a little black number from the darkest recesses of her wardrobe and holding it up. 'Just like in Agatha Christie. What about this?'

'Too sexy,' says Jamie. 'They're Protestants; they'll probably have the vicar over for dinner too. You need to think demure. We may even have to put you in pearls and a Hermès scarf.'

'I don't own a Hermès scarf,' I squeal in desperation. 'What am I going to do? All my clothes are too . . . too . . .'

'Too-girl-about-town,' says Caroline, sweetly finishing the sentence for me. 'A great look for an up-and-coming journalist like you, but maybe not quite for this trip. What about this?' She brandishes a Chanel-type suit in front of us, which would be lovely except for all the medals and gold chains hanging off the shoulder pads.

'Caroline, you should be ashamed of yourself,' says Jamie sternly. 'Newsflash for you; the eighties are dead and gone. All your suits, shoulder pads and Ivana Trump pastel gear should be flung into the nearest Oxfam. That's if they'll even take it. I'm sorry, girlies, but we only have one option.'

The three of us look at each other.

'We can't,' says Caroline firmly.

'She'd kill us,' I agree. 'I'm still paying her back for the laddered Woolford tights fiasco.'

'Besides, we promised her we wouldn't,' Caroline says firmly. 'We'd be breaking our word.'

'Those are noble sentiments, ladies, but for once in your lives, can't you just be cool? Rachel is in Paris having great sex with Christian and she won't be back for another two weeks. Do you really think she's worrying about her designer collection at this point in time? Besides, if this isn't an emergency, I don't know what is.'

Caroline and I have no choice but to reluctantly agree as we sneak into Rachel's room, like the Three Stooges. Even opening her wardrobe is like going into the Garden of Eden; while we're still dressing like students, apart from the odd freebie Caroline gets from the fashion shows she models in, Rachel is now a junior manager at the Irish fashion centre and, boy, does she dress the part. Every stitch belonging to her is by a well-known designer and everything in her wardrobe is immaculately swathed in protective zip-up bags, the kind they put dead bodies in on *Prime Suspect*.

'Now this is more like it,' says Jamie, triumphantly producing a tweed box jacket (Paul Costelloe) and a matching
pair of beige jodhpurs (Ralph Lauren). Not that Rachel
would know one end of a horse from another, any more than
I would myself, but this just happens to be a very hot look at
the moment.

'Bingo,' says Jamie. 'That with a crisp, white cotton shirt
and a string of pearls and you're home and dry.'

'Just remember to get it all dry-cleaned before she gets
back,' says Caroline, worried. 'And don't make the same
mistake I made last time. For the love of God, you have to
take all the safety pins out when you get her stuff back from
the cleaners. I swear, she checks these things.'

'And we'll have to get the Hoover out of the utility room
and give the bedroom carpet a quick going over,' I add, a
bit panicky. 'You know what she's like. She'll notice the
footprints.'

'We have a utility room?' says Jamie.

'Yeah. Downstairs. You know, where we keep all the
Christmas decorations.'

Ten minutes later, I'm kitted out, with a stuffed, packed
suitcase, all filched from Rachel's bottomless wardrobe.

'Fabulous,' says Jamie, 'great look. This says to the parents,
"Hello, I'm Amelia, I'm perfect daughter-in-law material."'

'And it also says, "I may be a city chick, but I can
adapt to the life of a country girl, no problem,"' says
Caroline.

'Promise me I don't look like Sarah Ferguson?' I ask,
gazing at myself uncertainly in the mirror.

'NO!' they both chime. 'Definitely not!'

'You're every inch a Sloane Ranger,' says Jamie. 'Wait till
you see; you'll fit in beautifully. I'd be surprised if you don't
come back engaged.'

The phone on the hall table rings and I almost jump out of my skin.

'If that's my student loan officer, I'm not in,' says Jamie, going into the bathroom and banging the door behind him.

But it's Tim. To say he's on his way.

OK, here comes the panic . . .

Colossal social faux pas number one:

First of all I have to say that Tim is sensational and I'm madly in love with him. Yes, he's much posher than me, but I just love and adore all his west-Brit quirky ways: his cut-glass accent; the fact that he has all his clothes specially made by a tailor in London (I've tried to introduce him to the wonderful, and much cheaper, world of discount shopping but to no avail); the way he has a preferred brand of single malt whisky; and the fact that he's a member of a gentlemen's club in Dublin. And he's only twenty-seven.

Now, Jamie says the club is men only so they can have strippers in, but I've actually been there on ladies night a few times, and as far as I can see, it's just full of old men on Zimmer frames and, somehow, it always smells of cabbage.

Anyway, I love Tim and on the long, wintry drive up to Monaghan, all I can think of is how vitally important this weekend is for us as a couple. I don't mean to exaggerate, but my entire future happiness depends on the next seventy-two hours.

And my behaviour around his family.

And the fantastic impression I'm determined to make.

Mrs Singen-Underwood. Doesn't that sound fab? Mrs Amelia Singen-Underwood . . . The Singen-Underwoods are at home . . .

'Are you hungry?'

'Sorry, Tim, what did you say?'

'You'd drifted off on me there for a moment, old girl. Just wondered if you fancied a spot of nosebag?'

'Oh . . . yeah . . . great, that'd be lovely.'

That's the other thing about Tim. He likes his food. I mean, really likes his food. He's a big guy, and has to eat breakfast (a fry-up, usually), lunch (three courses), afternoon tea and that's all before his main meal of the day at night (another three and sometimes four courses). Not including snacks. When we first got together, all of six months ago, I couldn't quite get my head around the sheer amount of food he'd get through. He'd eat a colossal breakfast and then an hour later would wonder what our plans were for lunch. I've given up saying, 'But you just ate!' Anyway, as Caroline wisely says, I can't expect a grown man to survive on bags of lettuce from Marks and Spencer's, as I would normally do.

So we stop off at a roadside café and Tim orders lunch. No light snacks for my Tim here, he goes for the full works: soup and a baguette, chicken in a basket, chips, mushy peas and a side order of jacket potatoes, swimming in sour cream.

Now, I haven't eaten a thing all morning (I'm too uptight) and really just want a coffee, but Tim insists on my having something. I know he hates it when I just chase a piece of cheese around a plate and he's always telling me that I could do with putting a bit of meat on me, so I go for the chicken too. It's a bit pink in the middle, but I force myself to munch as much of it as I can stomach.

Eughhhhh.

We get back into the car and hit the long, potholed road to Ashton Hall, the family home. We're easily another hour in the car and the combination of my nervousness, the revolting, undercooked chicken and the bumpy road is now really starting to make me feel queasy . . . That and the sight of Ashton Hall.

It's one of those huge, gothic buildings with stone gargoyles glowering down at you, almost daring you to go inside. My stomach is churning and I'm starting to feel light-headed, but I take Tim's hand as he leads me up the steps to the main entrance door. We knock and wait and I try to steady my nerves.

Remember, you only get one chance to make a first impression, my inner voice says . . .

A middle-aged woman in a wax jacket and a woolly hat answers the door.

'Hello, Mrs Singen-Underwood, what a pleasure to meet you . . .' I say, going to shake her hand.

'I'm the housekeeper,' she growls and Tim roars laughing at my mistake.

'This is Sheila,' he says introducing me.

'Hi there.' I smile at her nervously, desperately eager for her to like me and at the same time dying to ask her where the nearest bathroom is. The dark, dank hallway stinks of damp and the smell isn't doing my poor sick tummy any good. It's also colder inside the house than outside and Sheila's woolly hat is now starting to make a lot of sense.

'Sheila's our Mrs Danvers,' Tim whispers to me as we trot after her down one long twisting corridor after another.

'Where's your bags?' she grunts.

'In the car boot. I'll bring them in later,' says Tim. 'I say, are we in time for tea? I'm absolutely starving.'

My stomach does another churn at the very thought of food. On top of everything else, now I'm feeling faint and light-headed, as if I might keel over.

'Do you mind if I use the bathroom?' I ask in a tiny, embarrassed voice, but either they don't hear me or they both ignore me.

'They're all in the library,' says Sheila. 'Florence is in there too.'

'Now there's a lovely surprise,' says Tim brightly. 'I didn't think Flo was spending the weekend with us too.' He takes me by the hand and leads me down the mankiest, filthiest carpet I have ever seen, past suits of armour and busts of long dead Singen-Underwoods.

'Who's Florence?' I ask innocently. A family friend? A relation he hasn't mentioned before?

'Oh, you'll simply love her,' says Tim, striding on ahead of me, dying to get to the tea and sandwiches. 'Everyone loves Florence. Old girlfriend of mine, you know.' He throws open the great double doors of the library and thrusts me in.

The room is absolutely enormous and it's packed. There must be twenty people here, all dressed in jeans and super-thick jumpers, all munching on sandwiches and holding cups and saucers. I don't have to wonder for very much longer about Florence as she shoots over to Tim faster than a bullet, throwing her arms around his neck and squealing like a girlie-girlie teenager.

'Timmy! Bet you didn't expect to see me! Your mother told me you were bringing a new girlfriend so I just had to hack over to check her out.'

Florence is about my age, milk-maid blonde (natural – I may be feeling queasy but I still checked), tall and, to put it politely, a very, very big girl.

'Flo, darling!' he says, hugging her. 'How wonderful you're looking! I love a woman I can really squeeze on to.'

Unlike this bag of bones I'm going out with, was the clear implication there, I think, as he introduces us.

'Dear Lord, you are skinny,' Florence exclaims. 'Tim, you and I will simply have to fatten her up a bit when she's here. Do you ride?'

'Sorry?'

'You're wearing jodhpurs.'

'Oh, no, I just borrowed these from my flatmate. It's a look . . .' I trail off lamely.

She laughs, a bit cruelly. 'You look just like a Thelwell cartoon, if you ask me.'

'Florence, I don't mean to be rude, but do you think you could show me where the bathroom is, please? I'm actually not feeling a hundred per cent . . .'

'Well, we're all riding to hounds tomorrow, you *have* to join us. Tell her, Timmy.'

Tim, however, is far too engrossed in a plate of sandwiches he's grabbed from one of the side tables.

'Oh, do give me one, Timmy, you great oaf!' Florence says, playfully punching him and helping herself to a good-sized fistful. 'Would you like one?' she asks, brandishing them under my nose. 'Yum yum, my absolute fave. Sheila's such a doll to remember. Hard-boiled egg and tripe.'

It's all too much for me. I put my hand over my mouth in a frantic attempt to cover up what's coming, but it's too late.

I throw up all over Florence's feet.

Colossal social faux pas number two:

Dinner is served punctually at eight p.m. (none of the Singen-Underwoods like to be kept waiting on meals, it seems) but I'm too ill to join them.

I've got the worst dose of food poisoning I've ever had in my entire life. It's not just the nausea; by now I'm shaking all over and in a cold sweat. Tim is sweet and very under-standing about it; he showed me to my room, tucked me in and said he'd make my apologies to everyone, but the minute the dinner gong goes, he's out of there like a scalded cat.

The room is filthy, damp and so cold that I have to sleep

with all my clothes on. From the dining room below, I can hear them all roaring with laughter, in top form, having a fantastic time . . . and then another wave of nausea sweeps over me.

This is not helped by the one thought I can't escape from. I should be down there with them all now, trying my best to be the perfect, charming, intelligent, witty house guest/girlfriend/prospective daughter-in-law. I'd even re-hearsed.

Caroline, who's brilliant at this stuff, gave me a crash course in how to make a boyfriend's parents fall in love with you: i.e., pay very careful attention to everything the mother says, ask loads of questions about her fabulous hairdo/clothes/ housekeeping tips and, most importantly of all, keep compli-menting her on what a wonderful son she has. With the father, you want to appear fun and playful, a good sport, a great bit of crack: in short, the type of girl who'd be a great addition to any family gathering.

Jamie even gave me a book for Christmas, called *Not a Lot of People Know That: 1000 Interesting Facts About Country Life*, and urged me to memorize a few. 'The Singed-Underwears will immediately think you're one of them,' he said, 'plus it's the kind of stuff that'll come in very handy for pub quizzes.'

OK, it may not have made for the most scintillating of conversation (I can now tell you exactly how many acres are in a hectare and the correct type of bridle to put on a two-year-old mare, that type of thing) but the point is that I really made an effort and now they all probably think I'm some sort of Elizabeth-Barrett-Browning type, pale and sickly and bedridden. Absolutely no fun and most *definitely not* daughter-in-law material.

Oh God. A fresh bout of queasiness comes over me and I know I have to get to a bathroom in double quick time. I've puked up on quite enough carpets for one day. I run out on to the corridor and try the room next door to me.

No joy, it's a linen cupboard.

So, I work my way down through all the doors to my left and right, knocking gingerly on each one and each time failing to find a loo.

By now, dinner's over and I can hear them all drifting from the dining room into the drawing room, chatting and laughing, everyone full of the holiday spirit. Just then, a tall, blonde, middle-aged woman, who kind of has a look of Tim about her, comes striding down the corridor towards me.

'Excuse me,' I ask, stopping her in her tracks, 'could you show me where the bathroom is, please?'

Now, I have absolutely no idea who this woman is. The minute I threw up all over the library floor earlier, I was ushered upstairs and haven't actually met any of the family. Plus, there's an awful lot of them and they all look a bit alike.

'Are you the girl Tim brought?' blondie woman asks me bossily. 'The one who vomited all over poor Florence?'

'Emm, yes, that's me.'

'She was making us all laugh over dinner with that story. Right then, you'd better have a barf in my bathroom if you want. It's through here.'

'Thanks,' I say weakly, following her into a bedroom and straight on through to her en suite.

What follows isn't pleasant and I'm in there for ages. When I emerge, I presume that blondie woman will have gone back downstairs to rejoin the others, but she hasn't. She's in the bed, completely naked with a very dark-haired, younger-looking moustached man, kissing the face off him.

'Oh, I'm really sorry,' I say, speeding through the bedroom as fast as I can, but they completely ignore me, as if they've far better things to get on with than exchanging pleasantries with a food-poisoned house guest . . .

I presume that this is her husband/lover/partner/boyfriend and leg it back to my own room, feeling a whole lot better.

Breakfast the next morning is buffet-style and, thank God, I'm actually able to eat again. Only a thin bit of toast, much to Tim's annoyance, but at least it's something. He and I are the first downstairs and have just plonked ourselves at the dining table when my blonde-haired guardian angel from last night comes in, with the moustached man I'd seen her with the night before, followed by another, much older, silver-haired man. *Tim's father, maybe?*

Before Tim even has a chance to introduce us, I'm in like Flynn.

'I owe you such a big thank you for letting me use your en suite bathroom last night,' I gush at blondie woman, 'you really saved my life. In more ways than one.'

'Absolutely all right, don't mention it,' she says as the three of them help themselves to rashers, sausages and scrambled eggs from the huge platters groaning on the sideboard.

'Feeling better, then?' asks moustached man, very casually.

'Much better, thanks.'

Now, if I'd had the good sense to leave it at that, perhaps all would have been well, but guess what? I don't have the social discretion that God gave a fruit fly. 'Oh and, by the way, I must apologize for walking in on you both last night.' I smile at moustached man in what I hope is a friendly, I'm-a-woman-of-the-world-type way.

Then I whisper to blondie woman, 'I hope I didn't embarrass you?'

With that, the older, silver-haired man, who's standing right beside them, gives me a furious look and storms out of the breakfast room.

That alone should have sent alarm bells ringing in my head. None of the Singen–Underwoods ever walk away from food, ever.

Moustached man turns to Tim and growls, 'Can't you teach your girlfriend some manners?'

Tim covers his face with his hands, shoves his food away (another alarm bell) and hisses at me. 'You idiot, Amelia! Don't you realize what you've just done?'

'What?' I say, desperately panicking. 'What did I say?'

'Aunt Mabel has been having an affair with George Newman for years. We all know about it, everyone *knows*. It's just not spoken of in front of her husband, by any of us, ever. Do you realize the irreparable damage you almost certainly have caused?'

Colossal social faux pas number three:

Later that morning, they're all going hunting but I opt to stay in the safety of my room. My eyes are still all red and puffy from the awful row I had with Tim.

I must have apologized about twenty thousand times; I tried my best to defend myself and, in fairness, how was I supposed to know who's having an affair with who? Let alone what's to be spoken about and, more importantly, what's not to be spoken about . . . honestly, it's like a real–life game of Cluedo.

'You could have just kept your big mouth shut,' Tim snapped at me, slamming the bedroom door behind him.

He's barely gone when there's another rap at the door: Florence, impeccably turned out in her hunting gear, neat blazer and gleaming black riding boots. 'You poor sausage, I've just heard about your horrific gaffe,' she says. 'It's all over the house.'

Terrific, I think. *Just terrific.*

'But I bring a ray of hope,' she goes on. 'The thing is . . . I've come to offer you a way out.'

Ten minutes later, we're outside in the paddock, and she's saddling up a very scary-looking animal, eagerly persuading me to join them on the hunt and absolutely not taking no for an answer.

'But, Florence,' I protest, 'I can't ride a horse.'

'But yesterday, you said you did.'

No, I want to shout at her, were you even listening to me? You asked me if I could ride because you happened to see me wearing jodhpurs and now you've jumped to the conclusion that I'm an Olympic three-day eventer.

Right. Time to nip this in the bud. I've had quite enough humiliation for one morning. 'Florence, I have a confession. The last time I came close to any four-legged animal was at the under-fives donkey derby my dad entered me into on a beach in Wexford. Which I came last in. Sorry to let you down, but I really think it's better for me to be honest.'

'Now just look here. I'm trying to do you a favour. I practically grew up with Timmy and I'm going to give you a piece of advice. The worst thing you could do is spend the morning moping about in your room, hiding away from everyone. If it's one thing the Singen-Underwoods really appreciate it's a house guest who'll muck in. Put this morning behind you and show that you're one of us.'

'But, Florence . . .'

'Now, I'm only going to put you up on Ginny. Gentle Ginny we call her. She's Mrs Singen-Underwood's absolute fave and she's just a dream to ride. All you have to do is sit there and she'll do all the work.'

'But suppose she gallops off with me?' I ask, a terrified vision flashing through my head that I'll end up clinging on to her mane, being dragged through gorse bushes for miles, and eventually be thrown into a stinking, putrid septic tank by Mrs Singen-Underwood's favourite horse.

'Ginny? Gallop?' Florence roars with laughter. 'She's about fourteen years old and has never as much as cantered in her whole life. Look, just come with us for a bit. You can always hack back if you get scared.'

She has a point. I should at least appear to make an effort to be a good house guest and good house guests/prospective daughters-in-law muck in, as Florence puts it. And Tim knows I don't ride, so he'll appreciate the effort I'm making in getting up on a horse all the more, won't he?

She helps me up on to Ginny, tosses me a riding hat and leads me round to the front of the house, where the rest of them are all mounted, having a good, strong stirrup cup before the off.

This feels OK, not too scary at all. Maybe, just maybe I can pull this off . . .

There's an awful silence as they all take in what they're seeing. It's very surreal. The only way I can describe it is that it feels as if about twenty pairs of beady Singen-Underwood eyes are all focused on me. Next thing, Tim rides over to where I am, red with fury. 'Amelia, that's my mother's favourite racehorse. Ginny is a *racehorse*, not a hunter. Do you even understand the difference? She's running at the Curragh next week and under no circumstances should be out jumping over fields today. Take her back to the paddock at once, please. We're already late starting off.'

'But Florence said that . . .' I begin, with tears stinging my eyes.

'I'm so sorry, Mrs Singen-Underwood,' I can hear Florence saying to yet another big blonde woman sitting on a horse that looks ready to do the Grand National. 'She absolutely insisted. I tried to stop her, but she just hopped up on Ginny anyway.'

Bitch. Bad, bloody malevolent bitch. She's nothing but a pig in knickers.

I swear I can hear twenty Singen-Underwood tongues clicking in exasperation as I trot round the side of the house, scarlet in the face.

Just then, the horn sounds the off and Ginny's ears prick up. It's all too much for her. She sees all the other hunters chasing the hounds down the driveway and, oh dear God, in a second, she's off. I'm clinging on for all I'm worth, screaming at the top of my voice for her to stop, when a dog shoots out in front of us, Ginny rears up and suddenly, I'm thrown off.

I'm fine, I think. I'm shocked and winded, but I don't think I've broken anything. Tim, Florence and I presume his mother ride back to where we are, but to my surprise they all cluster around where Ginny is now peacefully grazing on the grass verge, completely ignoring me.

'Limping,' says Florence, shaking her head gravely. 'Oh dear, this could be serious.'

'No, I think I'm OK,' I say, picking myself up off the gravel and dusting myself down. The three of them look at me furiously and for a moment I almost wish I had broken a collar bone, fractured a leg or, at the very least, was stretched out on the ground, unconscious.

'Not *you*,' snaps Florence. 'Ginny.'

'Call the vet,' the mother barks at Tim. 'And get that bloody girl out of my house.'

'Are you happy now?' Tim asks me viciously as he dismounts. 'Ginny's seriously injured; she could even be lame. There'll be no steeplechasing her for months, possibly never again.'

'Tim, I'm so sorry, I didn't do it on purpose, it was an accident . . .'

'I really think the best thing all round is if you left. Immediately. You must understand that your presence is no longer welcome in this house.'

At times like this, you really know who your friends are. I phoned home and Caroline came to my rescue. She borrowed her mother's car, cancelled all her plans and she and Jamie drove the whole three-hour, pot-holed journey to collect me. I think I bawled the whole way home.

Chapter Twenty-Seven

Is this Night Course about as Much Use to Me as a Chocolate Teapot?

. . . I wonder as I drive into UCD for the following week's class. Or, to put it more plainly, am I completely and utterly wasting my time?

I arrive in the classroom and the girls all give me a big round of applause as a thank you for hosting last Saturday's shindig. I smile and wave and grab a free seat in the back row, right beside Sarah, the pretty blonde air hostess, who got stuck with that awful guy at the party.

Ira is doing her usual, working her way down through everybody, asking them in a very businesslike manner (*a*) did they meet anyone at my flat (*b*) how many new, single men they spoke to there and (*c*) did they get a phone number and if not, why not?

Mags is the star pupil this week, by a mile. She glowingly tells us all about her budding *relationship* (her word, not mine; I think I've only ever used the 'R' word twice in my whole life) with Damien Delaney. The works. How she asked him loads of questions about himself at the party (which you're supposed to do: get the guy talking about himself and he'll talk to you all night is the theory); how she had two glasses of wine on purpose so she'd relax and not come over as too uptight; and finally, the pièce de résistance, when she discovered they both lived in the same part of town, she asked would it be too much trouble for him to drive her home?

One hundred per cent success. They kissed, he took her number and has been calling her every day since.

The only man who calls me every day is Jamie and half the time that's just because he's looking for me to give him a job.

'He's just wonderful,' says Mags. 'He's even invited me to have tea with his mother.'

'I am very proud of you,' says Ira and Mags blushes to her roots, beaming.

'The rest of my class have a lot to learn from you. You put yourself right outside of your own personal matrix, you smartened up your appearance, just as you would if you were going after any big job, you took a chance and you got a result. Now, you seem to be with a man who truly likes you. Well done. Keep me posted on what happens and keep up the good work. Ladies, a round of applause for Mags!'

'Thanks,' says Mags, as we all politely clap her. 'Although if it weren't for Amelia, none of this would have happened.'

'We'll come to Amelia, don't you worry,' says Ira, moving on to Sarah, beside me.

The class titter just at the anticipation of the mad stories they're all expecting me to tell. Oh dear . . . Sarah, however, takes the focus off me for a bit as it seems she didn't have nearly such a good week of it as Mags.

'I got all dressed up for the party,' she tells us disappointedly. 'I even had my hair and nails done. And what happened? Nothing. No offence to any of the guys you all brought along, but I didn't even *like* any of the men I got talking to and not one of them showed the slightest interest in me. Apart from wanting upgrades on my flights. So then I did something I'm not very proud of.'

'What's that, honey?' asks Ira, concerned.

'I'm so annoyed with myself.'

'Tell us. We're all here to help you.'

'Well, I went home in the depths of depression, you know the way you do when you've really made an effort and you feel you're looking OK and then you come home having met no one and . . . well, I got intexticated.'

'Excuse me?'

'I started texting my ex. My big ex. The exest of them all. I know, I know, I'm a total idiot . . .'

Poor old Sarah, I think, really feeling for her. Haven't we all been there? The fatal cup, I call it. You know, when you just have that one drink too many, which sets you over the edge? Next thing you know, you're home alone, deciding it's a great idea to pick up the phone to the man you think is the love of your life, in spite of the fact that he was the one who broke up with you and hasn't even bothered contacting you to see how you're doing. There but for the grace of God . . .

'Honey, let me stop you right there,' Ira says to her, gently but firmly. 'You need to ask yourself this. Does this man ever get intexticated, as you say, and contact you? Does he call *you* late at night when he's lonely and missing you?'

'Never.' Sarah sniffs. 'Not once.'

'So what does that tell you? Ladies, you must always remember my femininity rule. While you're all learning to position yourselves in the marriage market, a certain amount of good, old-fashioned restraint still applies. Put simply, when a man is interested in you, he'll call you, and when he's not, he won't. Men like to be the pursuers. They like to feel that they've somehow won you. This means you gotta box clever.

You're learning to sift potential husbands from time-wasters, but without aggressively hounding down any man you've targeted. There's no surer way to scare him off.'

Five hands immediately shoot up in the air and Ira is hit by a barrage of questions. When should you call? How long should you wait before you realize a man isn't calling you? Isn't the whole let-him-be-the-one-to-do-the-phoning/chasing/pursuing/rules notion obsolete in the twenty-first century?

I drift off again, doodling on the notepad in front of me as Ira clarifies herself and attempts to calm down all the ruffled feathers.

You'll never guess what my doodle is . . . yes. Me in my Vera Wang with my headless groom by my side . . .

It's all very well and good my feeling sorry for Sarah, but if I'm really honest, I haven't exactly been a model student myself up until this, have I? I've been doing this course for weeks now and am about as far away from my goal as I ever was. And it's not as if I'm learning a huge amount from my past mistakes, is it? Unless my life lesson is that the past is destined to repeat itself ad nauseam?

OK. To recap. In chronological order.

Number 1: was a cheater at the age of eighteen and is a cheater now.
Lesson: I make bad choices.
Number 2: was always a bit self-absorbed when I knew him and is now, officially, out and out gay. Oh, and he hit on Jamie who turned him down.
Lesson: I still make bad choices and Jamie's screening process is miles better than mine any day. (Mind you, in my defence, he does have an awful lot more practice with gay men than I do.)

Number 3: *He-whose-name-shall-forever-remain-unspoken.*
Yes, strictly speaking, he is my most recent ex, but
this is when he chose to foist himself back into my
life. Oh, and, for added entertainment value, on to
my road.

Lesson: This is the man I really, honestly thought I was
going to marry. He dumped me claiming that he
couldn't commit to anyone, not just me, then six
months later is engaged to a teeny-bopper. The only
lesson I can deduct here is that my instincts are up
my bum.

Number 4: fell in love with the spiritual life and became
a monk.

Lesson: Not to be too hard on myself. Even if I'd been
St Thérèse the Little Flower, I wouldn't have stood
much of a chance here.

Number 5: was a tad possessive and creepy when I dated
him and is now in a psychiatric home.

Lesson: Yes, I make crap choices, but occasionally I do
have the odd lucky escape.

Number 6: my emotional-pension-plan man. I'm
cheating as I haven't actually dated him, but fingers
crossed he's still single . . .

Lesson: No lesson here. I haven't had a chance to mess
this one up. Yet. Thank God for him, though. The
thought of seeing him again is just about the only
thing that's keeping me sane these days.

Number seven: Tim Singed-Underwear—

'Amelia? Would you care to join us?' says Ira.

'Oh . . . emm . . . sorry . . . I was . . . ehh . . .'

'Daydreaming?'

'No . . . I was . . .' I pick up the piece of paper I've been scribbling on as proof that I haven't been snoozing at the back of the class. 'I was just . . . recapping.'

'Recapping? Good. So tell us about the ex-boyfriend you spoke to this week.'

The class are all looking at me, grinning, dying for a good laugh.

'Well, Ira, you see, the thing is, I didn't actually make steps to contact him. Nor would you, if you knew the story. I was afraid he and his family would set a team of highly trained Alsatians on me.'

'Can't be worse than what you told us last week. Come on. We're all in the same boat and we're all here to share.'

I tell them about Tim in edited form. And, predictably enough, they howl.

'Why aren't you producing comedy shows?' asks Sarah beside me. 'You'd be a natural.'

'Sounds like that movie *Gosford Park*,' someone else from the front laughs.

'Amelia, there is no easy way out in this class,' says Ira crossly. 'Do you wanna entertain everyone or do you wanna find a husband? Are you on my program or aren't you?'

Well, I'm sitting here, aren't I? I want to shout at her in frustration, but instead, coward that I am, I opt for ummming and ahhhing under my breath instead. Thank God I have an emotional pension plan, that's all I can think. It's a lovely, warm, smug feeling, to know that at least I have one trump card up my sleeve . . .

'Amelia? Are you listening?'

'Emm . . . yeah.'

'You must contact this Singen-Underwood man so you can learn from your mistakes. Otherwise, all you've got for me is that it didn't work out because he came from a different social background. How is that going to help you?'

I look at her in silence.

'How did you do at the party? I know you were the hostess, but I still expect you to have a result for me.'

'Oh, disaster,' I start, warming up for a good story-telling session. 'I did identify one potential target – that is to say, I clocked a dishy bloke I really fancied, but just as I was about to chat him up, my boss arrives. So we pretty much ended up talking about work for most of the night.'

I look up to the front of the class and see Mags waving her hand in the air. 'Ira, can I just interrupt here, please?' she asks.

'Go ahead.'

'His name is Philip Burke and I brought him. He's an old friend. I just want to say for the record that I think he likes Amelia. And there's something else . . .'

'Yes?' asks Ira.

Mags and I look at each other and all of a sudden it's like being back in primary school and the class swot is about to rat me out.

'He told me he called Amelia to ask her out and that she turned him down.'

'Mags!' I shout at her. 'Thanks a bunch!'

Mags folds her arms, resolutely sticking to her guns. 'I'm sorry, Amelia, but this is for your own good. You helped me and I want to return the favour. He's a good guy,' she adds to Ira, as if I was about to tell the class he was an axe-wielding sociopath.

'Is this true?' Ira asks me, glaring over her glasses and making me feel very small. 'You rejected a perfectly good man?'

'Emm . . . well, you see, it's not that simple, he's my boss and . . . well . . .' I glare over at Mags again.

'Well what?' says Ira.

'He can be a little bit hard to talk to,' I say in a small voice.

'Some of the clangers he comes out with, you're left there thinking: Did he *really* just say that? The last conversation we had, he compared a single woman in her late thirties to a starving piranha fish.'

'I know,' Mags agrees. 'You just tune that stuff out after a while.'

'Well then, Miss Amelia,' says Ira looking down at me triumphantly. 'Your homework for the coming week couldn't be more clear-cut. You are to contact this aristocratic ex of yours' – the class are already giggling – 'you are to track down your next ex-boyfriend, but most importantly of all, you are to arrange a date with Mr Philip Burke. Otherwise, don't bother coming back to my class next week.'

Mags is polite but firm as we trundle back downstairs when the torture's finally over. 'One date won't kill you,' she says. 'Bet you'll end up having a great time with him.'

I'm too gutted to answer her.

How in the name of God am I going to manage this? Bad enough to have to ask a guy out in the first place, but *Philip Burke*? I can't even lie and pretend to the class that he's away or that he's emigrated or that he's suddenly going out with someone else, because Mags will land me in it all over again. However, as we walk back outside to the wet, drizzly car park, I do see something that gives me just the kick up my backside I need.

There's a car parked, right beside us, waiting. The window rolls down and I see that it's Damien. 'Mags, dear!' he calls. 'I so worried about you out in this awful rain. I was terrified you'd catch your death so I came to collect you. Oh, hello there, Amelia. Thank you so much for a most delightful party.'

Mags waves me goodbye, hops elegantly into the passenger seat and kisses him lightly on the cheek.

'Let me take you out to dinner, my dear,' I hear Damien say before she bangs the door shut with an expensive clunk. 'I want to hear all about your day.'

As I make my rain-drenched way to my car, alone, I make up my mind. I'll do Ira's bloody homework. I'll go on the bloody date with Philip weirdo. I'll bloody well contact Tim Singed-Underwear and I'll do my best with number eight on my hit list. I'll stick with the course, even though to date I have absolutely nothing to show for it. If Mags can have a perfectly good fella patiently waiting to take her out after class, then you know something?

So can I.

Chapter Twenty-Eight
Heaven in Blue Jeans

Right. To work. With a fresh spring in my step, I get into work and get cracking. I call directory enquiries and get the number for Ashton Hall, Co. Monaghan.

'Would you like to be connected to the number?' asks an irritating, automated voice.

'Yes, thanks,' I answer chirpily. What the hell: even if Tim is living on the Falkland Islands tending sheep, at least some of his family still have to be living in that awful barracks of a house and they can put me in touch with him. At least, that's the plan.

As the call goes through and the phone rings and rings and rings, I remember back to when I contacted my first ex, Greg lying, cheating Taylor, all those weeks ago. I'm almost snorting at how nervous I was then, whereas now I'm so used to the whole drill, you'd swear I was best friends with every single ex-boyfriend I ever had in my whole life. Embarrassment wears off remarkably quickly when desperation is snapping at your heels. Next thing, I'll be having them all over for Christmas dinner.

'Hello, Ashton Hall, how can I help you?' An elderly-sounding woman's voice, which seems familiar, some-how.

'Hello. Emm . . . that's not . . . Sheila, the housekeeper, by any chance?' I ask. No, it can't be. Sheila would be well past retirement age by now . . . wouldn't she?

'Yes, it is. Who's speaking please?'

'Hi, Sheila, I thought I recognized the voice. I'm sure you don't remember me, but my name's Amelia Lockwood. We met, oh, a hundred years ago.' I'm about to say, 'I can't believe you're still working,' but I stop myself just in time.

'Amelia Lockwood? Of course I remember you. Sure, every time I see your name coming up on the credits after *Celtic Tigers* I say, "I once cleaned up her vomit."'

'Emm . . . yeah, I'm really sorry. I was kind of half hoping you'd forgotten about that little . . . emm . . . episode.'

'Did you want to book a room? Is that why you're phoning?'

Book a room? I'm thinking. *Are the Singed-Underwears, sorry I mean Singen-Underwoods running a bed and breakfast now? You mean they're actually charging people to stay there?* 'Ehh . . . no, I was just wondering if I could speak to Tim? That's if he's still living at the Hall?'

'If he's still living here?' She laughs. 'Sure, isn't he the general manager! Hang on, I'll get him for you.'

General Manager? Well, maybe after all these years, they've finally done a massive renovation on the kip and now it's a five-star palace and all of Hollywood want to have their weddings there . . . Odd, though, that there's no switchboard or proper reception or muzak for me to listen to while I'm waiting to speak to Tim . . .

Then I hear Sheila screech at the top of her voice, '*TIM! Get down here you big oaf! You're wanted! It's Amelia Lockwood!*'

Right. Obviously not being run as a five-star hotel then.

Then Sheila picks up the phone again. 'Tell me this and tell me no more,' she says, 'just as I have you there. What happens between Glenda and Sebastian on *Celtic Tigers*? I nearly died when they broke up, you know. Couldn't believe it. Especially after that big fancy wedding they had. I'll tell you who's great though, is that new one that's Glenda's mother. What's this her name is? Oh yeah, Sadie Smyth. Now *there's* an actress. Will you tell her I think she plays a great part. Now, how in the name of God do they learn all them lines? Sure, God love them altogether.'

Then I hear Tim's voice. Unmistakably him. 'Give me that phone, you silly woman. Hello? Amelia Lockwood? Is that really you?'

The same plummy tones, the same Robert Morley-style inflections: it's Tim all right. 'Hey, Tim, how are you?'

'Bloody glad to hear from you, old thing. Perfect timing.'

'Sorry?'

'There I was the other night watching one of those documentary things on the telly box about my cousins across the pond, the Woolseys. Couldn't believe it. Old William Woolsey, swearing and cursing into the cameras, giving out about how he hasn't got a bean to keep the old stately pile going.'

'Yes, I think I saw that show too,' I say, although how in a million years I did, I couldn't tell you. *The Weird and Whacky World of the Woolseys* it was called, basic fly-on-the-wall stuff about an aristocratic family and their struggles to keep the family home afloat. Interesting that William Woolsey and Tim are cousins I think . . . although I have to admit, they do look a bit alike. The same portly Hanoverian gait, the Habsburg jaw, that slightly . . . well, over-bred look about them. (Sorry, that sounds awful, but there's no other way of describing it.)

'Delighted you saw it too, old thing,' Tim goes on. 'Do you know it's absolute serendipity that you just phoned now?'

'Why's that?'

'Well, after the show, I instantly remembered that you were working as a big TV producer, so I turned to old Flo and I said—'

'Sorry . . . do you mean Florence? The same Florence that I met all those years ago?'

'Yes, of course. You must remember Flo.'

He's married to her, my inner voice says. *He has to be. She'd never in a million years have let another woman even approach the airspace around him, or if she did, she'd then go out of her way to make sure that woman's life was a living hell.*

'Yes, I remember Florence.'

Like I could forget?

'So I turned to her after the TV show and said, "What a wonderful idea for a programme! This is exactly the type of thing the licence payer is absolutely gagging to see! Why don't we get an Irish crew to come here and film Ashton Hall? We could certainly do with the cash, old thing. Roof's about to fall in on us any day now, you know." Then I said, "Do you know who I bet would steer us in the right direction? Good old Amelia Lockwood, that's who."'

'Yes, it's certainly an . . . interesting idea, Tim, but you see I'm working over in drama now, you know, so it's not really my thing.'

'Well, you must know somebody who you could suggest the idea to. Be a big ratings winner, you know. I'd even be prepared to let my family appear, how's that for a nice juicy carrot?'

His family? Makes sense. He and Florence must have a load of kids by now . . .

Oh, bugger it, I have to find out. Why else am I making this highly uncomfortable phone call?

'So how long have you been mar—'

'Or here's another pitch for you,' he barrels over me. 'You know all those ghastly *Big Brother*-type shows? We set one here, a *Big Brother is Haunting You* sort of thing. You get the idea.'

'Tim, I'll certainly pass on your suggestions, but, as I say, it isn't really my department. So, changing the subject, how many children do you and Flo—'

'Oh, I've got it in one,' he says and I swear I can hear him smacking his podgy hand off his forehead. 'You do one of those *Celtic Tigers* Halloween specials and you film it here at Ashton! There's plenty of room for the entire cast, you know, and I've always had a bit of a thing for that scrummy Cara O'Keefe. I very much know what I should like to do to her if she ever came to stay . . . I say, is she single? Do you think she'd give me a whirl?'

'*Tim?* Aren't you married? What would Florence say?'

'Dear me, no. You are funny! Did you really think that old Flo and I were married? No, not by a long shot, old thing. Still a bachelor, me, I'm afraid. I've had heaps of girlfriends over the years, but you know how it is, I just never seemed to find the right one. They all come to stay here, meet the family, meet Flo and then that invariably seems to be the end of them, somehow. There's not many of my GFs that can survive the Flo test, you know. Can't imagine why.'

Towards the end of the day, however, events take a dramatic turn for the better. I'd wound up an exhausting script meeting and popped over to the canteen for a quick take-out cappuccino. I'm just paying for it, looking over my shoulder all the while for Philip Burke (no sign . . . phew!), when Suzy, our lovely production secretary, calls my mobile.

'Hey, Amelia, are you done with the script department for the day?'

'Yeah, just finished. Is everything OK?'

'Ummmmm . . . yeeeeeees,' she says, drawing out the 'yes' for so long, it set off an alarm bell in my head. 'So you're on your way back up to the office, then?'

'Yeah, I just stopped off for a coffee. I think I'll be burning the midnight oil tonight, so anything to keep me awake. Do you want me to get you one?'

'No thanks,' she almost sings down the phone. 'OK, so your plan is to work late tonight?'

'Yeah, I need to check the edited episode we shot last week. Emm, why do you ask?'

'Oh nothing, nothing. Just . . . well, your plans could easily change, that's all.'

I go back upstairs and gingerly open the office door, half expecting to find Philip Burke sitting there and not quite being able to figure out how I feel about this. But it's not Philip at all.

It's the only person I know who could (*a*) put the beam back on my face and (*b*) make me doubly thankful that I washed my hair that morning and am wearing make-up.

Jack Keating.

My very own emotional-pension-plan man.

'Well, hello, gorgeous,' he says, as smooth as ever, swivelling around in Suzy's office chair and looking a million dollars himself, all casual in jeans and a T-shirt that shows off how muscly he's got since I saw him last.

'Jack!' I almost throw myself at him, I'm that delighted to see him.

'Well, well, well, let me look at you,' he says, jumping up and swirling me around. 'Jesus, you're stunning. You must be in love to look this well. Who is he? I'll beat the crap out of him. Do you think I'll stand by and let another man make you happy?'

He's messing, of course, but by now half the office are watching the happy reunion side show, probably wondering, Who's this big ride that Amelia secretly has on the go? There's a bunch of red roses plonked on the desk, which Jack presents to me theatrically, on bended knee.

Another great font of gossip for the office. I playfully pretend to hit him across the head with the flowers and they all laugh.

'Come on then, babes, let's leave them all guessing and let me take you to dinner,' he says, grabbing my hand. 'Catch you later.' He winks at Suzy on our way out. She grins back at him, bats the eyelids and gives me a huge thumbs-up sign the minute his back is turned. But then Jack's been provoking that kind of reaction in women since he was about six.

Work is forgotten about and *Celtic Tigers* could go down the toilet in the morning for all I care, I'm so ecstatic as I swan out of the office, roses in one hand, Jack Keating in the other.

Once in a while good things *do* happen.

He takes me to Peploe's, an über-trendy restaurant in town, the kind of place you practically have to give a blood sample just to get a table. In spite of all my feeble protests about our not having a reservation, Jack just does his thing. He makes a beeline for the hostess on duty, releases the full megawatt force of the Jack Keating charm offensive and, within ten minutes, we're sitting at the best table in the house. The King of Spain could have been left standing at the bar moaning to Pope Benedict about how long the wait is for a table, but not my Jack.

As we're glancing at our menus, I realize that it's impera- tive that I keep my head and not get drunk and, most importantly of all, not refer to my by now infamous email. There's no point in my continuously blaming myself, not when I can just blame myself once and move on.

Baby steps. First of all, I need to find out if he's single.

I decide what I'm ordering, put the menu down and smile at him with what I hope is an inscrutable mask.

But Jack knows me far too well. 'Are you OK?' he asks.

'Of course I am. Why?'

'You have a very pained-looking expression. You don't need to run to the loo or anything, do you?'

'Ehh, no. Definitely not.' *Shit. So much for my inscrutable mask.*

'OK, what do you say we cut to the chase here?' He smiles. 'It's kind of like there's a big pink elephant in the middle of the room that we're both ignoring. Why don't we just get the awkward bit out of the way and then I can go back to having a good night out with my old pal Amelia. What do you say?'

I smile up at him, kind of relieved, although I do think: Did he just say old pal? This does not augur well . . .

Then comes the sentence I've been dreading.

'OK, bull-by-the-horns time,' Jack begins. 'I read your email with great interest. After I'd picked myself up off the floor, that is.'

I cover my face with my hands, mortified, but at least now it's out in the open. 'Do I need a brandy in my hand for what's coming?' I ask, half-messing, half-serious.

'The thing is,' he says, lowering his voice so that I have to lean forward to hear him. 'I've thought about you a lot. About our friendship, I mean. You know how it is with me, Amelia, women come and go but you're always there. You're a constant in my life and I love that.'

OK, I think, *so far so good . . .*

'And of course I remembered our pact. Here we both are, late thirties and still unmarried. So . . .'

'So?'

I have to take a very deep breath and an equally big slug of wine. Not to over-dramatize things or anything, but the next sentence out of him could change the entire course of my life.

Jack, however, doesn't seem to have a nerve in his body. In fact, the waitress (who, by the way, is very pretty) comes over with the wine list just at that point and he automatically starts flirting with her. She falls for it and flirts right back and I almost feel sorry for her, because I'm thinking: You think he means it but he doesn't. This is just the way he communicates with all women. He can't help himself, it's practically encoded in his DNA.

Then I have a flash forward . . .

TIME: The not-too-distant future. I hope . . .
THE PLACE: The National Maternity Hospital, Holles
    Street, Dublin.
THE OCCASION: I'm in the delivery ward, legs in
    stirrups, about to give birth to my first-born.

'Come on, Mrs Keating,' the midwife is barking at me, 'nearly there. One big push and it'll all be over.'

'*Aghhhhhhhhhhhhhh! I can't do this!*' I'm screeching at the top of my voice. 'More drugs, gimme more drugs!'

'You can have one more mouthful of gas, Amelia,' says my gynaecologist from underneath the greeny-coloured sheet thing that's covering my modesty. 'But that's your lot, I'm afraid. You've had quite enough. I don't want the baby coming out stoned.'

'*Bastard!* Is there anyone with a uterus in this room who

will find a vein and help me?' I scream at him viciously (mainly because, in my head, he looks an awful lot like my old headmaster in school, who I hated). 'Spinal tap me now!' I snarl. 'I don't care if I give birth to Jimi Hendrix! I need maximum-dosage pain relief.'

'Baby's crowning,' says my headmaster, sorry, I mean gynaecologist. 'Quick, get the husband.'

But Jack isn't at my side, mopping my fevered brow and saying things like, 'There, there now, darling, you still look beautiful to me,' as fathers-to-be are supposed to . . . he's in the corner, chatting up the very pretty nurse.

In my fantasy/nightmare, she's like a Benny Hill caricature, all tits and ass and lip gloss, giggling at Jack's jokes and pointing her boobs in his face.

'Yeah, I've always had a thing about nurses' uniforms,' he's saying, totally ignoring my wails from the bedside. 'Very, very sexy. Where did you say you were from again? Tipperary? Fabulous accent, I just love it. So what time does your shift finish at?'

'South Tipperary, actually,' she giggles inanely. 'So, are you ready to order yet or would you and your girlfriend like a bit more time?'

What! Oh yeah. Reality. Sorry about that.

'Oh, and by the way, the special tonight is grilled guinea fowl with spinach purée and a tarragon-butter sauce. It's really delish.' The waitress licks her lips a bit and looks coyly at Jack as if to say, '*You're* really delish.'

'Great, thanks,' says Jack, looking up at her all twinkly-eyed. 'Oh, and FYI?' he winks after her. 'She's not my girlfriend.'

OK. It's not very often I get reality checks, but here comes a biggie . . .

I can't do it. I can't. I couldn't marry Jack even if he loved me romantically, which he doesn't. I'd never be happy. I just know I wouldn't. I love him dearly and I know he loves me too but neither of us is in love with the other and there's a very good chance we could end up ruining a fantastic, lifelong friendship.

In the end, we both say it at exactly the same time.

'We're better off as friends.'

Then we burst out laughing and, all of a sudden, we're back to being the old Jack and Amelia, pre-pact. Having fun. Loving each other's company. Buddies.

Hours later, as we're drunkenly pouring ourselves into a taxi outside Lillie's Bordello, Jack suddenly goes all quiet on me.

'What's up?' I ask, sensing the change in his mood. 'Are you worried that you haven't collected enough girls' phone numbers for one night, is that it, Mr Lothario?'

'No,' he says, mock serious. 'I just had an idea.'

'Whasssssup?'

'Here we both are, late thirties and single. What do you say we make a fresh, brand-new, revised pact? If we're both forty-five and still single, we get married, you and me. Good plan?'

I don't even answer him. I just pretend to smack him on the back of his head with the flowers he gave me and we both collapse in a drunken, hysterical fit of giggles.

Chapter Twenty-Nine
A Very Twentieth-century Way of Being Dumped

You might not have thought so, but after years and years of getting out there, getting rejected, getting up off the ground and going out there again, eventually, the unthinkable happened.

Jamie got a job.

A proper one, in a proper, posh 'frock' show.

It's the stage adaptation of Jane Austen's *Pride and Prejudice* and he's been cast as Mr Collins, the slightly ridiculous rector who wants to marry the heroine, Lizzy Bennet, but has to make do with her best friend Charlotte Lucas instead. It's the Christmas show at Dublin's prestigious Gate Theatre, all set to open on 1 December 1994.

Two things about Jamie, however. One, he decided it would make him far too nervous to have all us Lovely Girls sitting pretty in the front row on his opening night, so he asked us to come to his first preview instead. 'And I'll do my best to make you all proud,' he said. 'Or, at least, less ashamed.'

'You're going to be wonderful in the part,' I said to him at the time, bursting with pride. 'I've never seen you work so hard.'

'You've never seen me work, full stop.'

Secondly and more importantly, Jamie has officially 'come out'. This is after weeks/months/years of him dragging us all into gay haunts and then strenuously denying that there was any ulterior motive.

'No, darlings,' he'd protest, 'it's just that you haven't lived until you've been to Sunday afternoon bingo in the George pub. Especially when Miss Panti is the hostess.'

In due course, the inevitable came to pass. 'You'll all be deeply shocked to know that . . . drum roll, pause for dramatic effect . . . yes! I'm out!' was his way of breaking the news to us. 'I know it's a tired old cliché, I went into showbiz and found love in my own locker room, but hey! Welcome to the theatre!'

So Caroline and I dutifully trooped along to the Gate, minus Rachel who's living in Paris by now, but who has sent the biggest bouquet of flowers you ever saw, along with a bottle of champagne to toast Jamie's success and to mark the launch of what we all hope will be a glittering career. His name in lights, fantastic reviews, agents bickering over him and all of his performances making the news, just like when Laurence Olivier started out.

But life isn't like that, is it?

He made his grand entrance in the third scene, where all the cast dance a quadrille at the Netherfield ball. Caroline and I both collectively held our breath as an invisible string quartet struck up and . . . disaster.

Jamie, clad in heeled Regency buckle shoes that he wasn't quite used to, went to do a very fancy-looking twirl (think Nureyev meets Nijinsky) and fell over, dragging both Lydia

Bennet and Caroline Bingley all the way down as far as the footlights with him.

He got into the papers all right, but just not in the 'review' section.

ACTOR'S UNLUCKY BREAK

James French, making his debut at Dublin's Gate Theatre last night, suffered an onstage fall which brought the show to a complete halt. An understudy will take over the role for opening night as Mr French recovers in hospital from a fractured ankle and two cracked ribs.

Which brings me neatly to ex-boyfriend number eight on my hit list. Or, as I like to call him, Mr Non-Closure . . .

And I wouldn't mind, but it all started out so romantically . . .

> *THE TIME: The curtain went up at eight p.m. and barely one hour later, we're all in the Accident and Emergency department.*
> *THE PLACE: Saint Vincent's Hospital, Dublin.*
> *THE OCCASION: Caroline and I are both nervously clustered around the tiny little bed that they've put Jamie in, when suddenly a curtain swishes back and into the cubicle walks Johnny . . .*

OK. His proper name is Johnny Allen. Dr Johnny Allen to be precise. Tall, broad, prematurely balding and newly qualified as a junior doctor; he looks like a younger version of Kelsey Grammer crossed with the toothiness of a Kennedy brother. He bounds in, full of energy and not at all like someone who's been working a one-hundred-hour week and functioning on next to no sleep.

313

We start flirting immediately.

'OK, Jamie,' he says cheerfully, 'good news and bad news. Which do you want first?'

'You mean there's *good news*?' Jamie snarls from the bed as Caroline and I do our best to calm him down. 'The only positive outcome to this is if my agent comes around that curtain right now to say either that *Pride and Prejudice* can go ahead with Mr Collins on crutches, or that there's a load of interesting offers in for an actor in a wheelchair. All the parts that Daniel Day-Lewis turned down,' he almost wails, bitterly disappointed and in acute pain.

'No, sorry, not quite what I was getting at,' says Johnny, sounding a tad hesitant, as would anyone who wasn't used to Jamie's hissy fits. 'The good news is that I'm letting you go home, but the bad news is we're going to have to put you in plaster for at least six weeks. No opening night for you, I'm afraid.'

'*You have to be kidding me!* I can't believe that I've gone almost three minutes without saying "*Bastard bloody universe! Why me?*"' Jamie continues to screech.

Now, Caroline in her infinite wisdom is always lecturing me that there are five distinct categories whereby it's possible for me to meet men. We even have them categorized, a bit like the way they classify hurricanes in the States.

Category 1: Your friends and, by extension, your friends' friends. OK, at this point, we're almost into 1995 and I've still had no joy here . . .

Category 2: Work. I've just started working as an investigative journalist for the *Irish Record*. It's a fab job and I absolutely love it, it's just that there's a downside. The only eligible men I'm meeting through work these days are either drug barons, crime lords or gangland criminals. Not exactly what you might call suitable husband material . . .

Category 3: Socializing. Clubs, pubs, you name it, I've been trawling through them all and here I am, twenty-six years of age and no sign of Mr Right. Caroline is engaged now and is sporting a rock on her finger bigger than the Hope diamond and while there's nobody happier for her than I am, I just wish it was my turn.

Yes, I want to have a successful career. Yes, I want to work in television, the Holy Grail. I would just like to get married first, that's all . . .

Category 4: Activities and hobbies. I regularly go to the theatre and the movies but still no joy. I know this is a numbers game and that you have to go to every dog fight you're invited to and I do, I *really* do.

Anyway I'm not *actively* looking to find my man when I'm on a night out with my friends . . . mainly because everyone says this is the surest way to meet someone. I.e., by not looking.

Category 5: Accident. Let me explain. When Caroline first mooted this to me, I presumed she meant if you spot a guy you fancy, you should reverse your car into his – that type of accident. But no. This category effectively covers those rare and wondrous occasions when you meet someone unexpectedly, unplanned, out of nowhere.

She catches my eye from the other side of the bed and silently mouths 'Cat. five'.

Hint taken.

I flick into full flirtation mode.

'Sorry about this, doctor,' I say, gazing into his lovely blue eyes, 'it's just that this was a really big career opportunity for Jamie. Do you ever go to the theatre? Tonight's show looked really interesting – well, the ten minutes of it that we saw. It's just that if you wanted to come with us when we go back . . .'

'Ughhh!' groans Jamie from the bed. 'Heterosexual politics, thank God I'm out of that arena. Look, Dr Whatever-your-name-is, she's single. She's not bad to look at. From her demented ramblings I'm guessing she wouldn't mind seeing you outside of this public-health hell-hole. Have you the slightest interest?'

I glare at Jamie thunderously. 'Remind me again which is the bad leg?' I ask him. 'Just so I can bang my handbag down on it?'

'Sorry, I'm just trying to save both of you a lot of time.'

'Now, now, Jamie,' says Caroline, 'don't take it out on Amelia just because she's able-bodied.'

Dr Johnny, however, spares my blushes. 'Sounds great. I'd love to take you out,' he says simply.

'Good. Just don't think of going to see *Pride and Prejudice*, that's all,' says Jamie warningly. 'If you value my friendship, you'll boycott all theatre until I'm back in the game.'

'How about a film?' Caroline tactfully suggests, bless her.

'Sounds good to me,' says Johnny. 'The last movie I saw was a colonoscopy.'

And thus it came to pass . . .

Remind Me Again Why I Need a Man

THE TIME: Flash forward to about six months later, June 1995.

THE PLACE: The townhouse I'm still sharing with Caroline and Jamie. Well, until Caroline gets married, at least.

THE OCCASION: Rachel's home for the weekend from Paris, where she now lives with Christian, and she and I are having a night in to catch up on each other's lives. Caroline's out with Mike's family, Jamie's on a date and this is the first time I've actually had Rachel all to myself. After a bottle of wine, I blurt out the whole, sad tale of me and Dr Johnny . . .

Ten p.m. 'Right, now that the other two are out of the way, tell me honestly,' Rachel asks me as she lights a fag and takes a deep drag, 'when was the last time he called?'

'Let's see now,' I say, topping up our wine glasses. 'This is Friday, so . . . emm . . . it would have been . . . almost three weeks ago.'

'And no row? No other woman on the scene? No signs that this was coming? No reason for this?'

'No, that's what has me on the verge of turning into a stalker. Everything was going really well. He treated me well, took me out to lovely places, I got on with all his friends, he got on with Caroline and Jamie. Then, about three weeks ago, he took me to see *Braveheart*, dropped me back here, stayed over, went to work the next morning, said he'd call and then . . . big, fat nothing.'

'That has to be the world's greatest lie: "I'll call you."'

'No, the world's greatest lie is "You know I love you."'

'Whatever. He's a bastard. If Christian dropped me without having the balls to say it to my face, I swear on his future grave I'd rip out his goolies.' Then she clocks the hurt look on my face. 'Sorry, darling. Are you not ready for me to start slagging him off? Give me the nod as soon as you are. I'm your girl.'

'It mightn't be so bad,' I say. 'I called his direct line at the hospital earlier and the ward sister said he's definitely on the night shift tonight. She said she'd give him the message and get him to call as soon as he gets a break.'

Rachel arches an elegantly plucked eyebrow. I swear she can do it even better than Roger Moore. She doesn't need to say anything, her message is plain.

'I know, I know,' I say, 'I shouldn't have called him at work, but oh, Rachel, the whole thing is driving me mental. I've already left about five messages for him at his house and he's ignored every one of them. Am I still going out with him or is it all off? That's all I want to know. I can handle being dumped, I've been there before and will be again. What's killing me is the not knowing.'

Silence from Rachel.

'I know what you're thinking,' I say, 'but I just need to give it this one last chance. If he doesn't call me back tonight, then that's it. Finito.'

Midnight. We're on to our second bottle of wine and still no call.

The phone is sitting on the table between us, actively not ringing.

'Which would you prefer to have?' Rachel asks, slurring her words only a tiny bit. 'A bionic arm or a bionic leg? Just say if you had to choose.'

'Jamie could do with a bionic leg,' I reply. 'They should hurry up and invent them.'

'Yeah, he's still a bit Sir Limps-a-lot, isn't he?'

'Naaaa, he's loving all the attention. Ever since he started physio, he's turned into a grade A hypochondriac. I can't stop him from going to doctors, healers, herbalists, acupuncturists, you name it. He says it's great to be able to talk about himself in a surgery for a full hour uninterrupted. He woke me up the other night because he had chest pains and he thought he was having a heart attack, but it turned out to be a packet of Revels he ate before he went to bed.'

Rachel nearly chokes on her wine she's guffawing so much and I have to thump her on the back. 'Wine went up my nose. Sorry.'

'You OK?'

'Yeah. I just miss all this so much,' she says. 'The messing and the crack and the staying up all night talking about fellas. I never thought I'd say this, but I miss Dublin.'

'Dublin misses you.'

'Everything's changing,' she says, suddenly serious. 'Caroline's getting married, I'm living in Paris . . .'

'Some things are still the same. I'm still single. There are some things you can always rely on. It was ever thus and probably always will be.'

And still the deafening sound of the phone not ringing . . .

Two a.m. Now the tears have started.

'He couldn't have not got six messages in a row,' I sob drunkenly.

'Well, sweetie, if I can just dust down an old chestnut, what a shithead and I hope he dies roaring for a priest.'

'You know, maybe he's just really, really busy tonight and he hasn't had time to call . . . yet.'

Rachel just does her eyebrow thing and lights up another fag.

'I know, you're right,' I say, despondently. 'I would have had more respect for him if he'd just told me to fuck off.'

319

★   ★   ★

Four a.m. Rachel's fast asleep now, stretched out on the sofa like an elegant Persian cat . . . And still no call.

I stay up a bit longer though.

Waiting, waiting, waiting . . .

Anyway. Back to the present.

After work next day, I go home, kick off my shoes and get straight down to business.

Tracking down Mr Non-Closure turns out to be the easiest one yet. I didn't mention it, but in the ten years since we dated, he's actually become quite famous. He's now a consultant cardiologist and is always in the papers, giving advice on things like 'Why the Atkins diet is keeping coronary bypass surgeons in business' or 'A forty-minute cardiovascular workout every day plus a half glass of red wine and you'll never end up on my table'.

Best of all, he's still working in St Vincent's Hospital, which makes my job as easy as pie. Brave as you like, I pick up the phone and ask to be put through to his direct line.

His secretary answers. 'Dr Allen's office, may I help you?'

I ask if I can speak to Johnny, fully expecting to be told that he's not available. And I'm right.

'He's actually in theatre at the moment, but I'm expecting him back to his rooms in about an hour's time. Can I get him to return your call?'

'Yes thanks,' I say, trying not to sound like I'm ringing up to arrange an angiogram. I tell her it's a personal call, leave my name and number and say that I'll be at that number for the rest of the evening.

Phew. Apart from asking out Philip Burke, which is another day's work, that's pretty much this week's home-work taken care of.

I'm just about to pour a nice glass of Sancerre when there's a buzz at my apartment door. 'Who is it?' I ask a bit gingerly, just in case it's *He-whose-name-shall-forever-remain-unspoken*. But, thank God, it's Rachel.

'Just on my way home and I thought I'd pop by to catch up with you. Is that the blissful sound of a bottle of vino being opened that I hear?'

Just the treat I need. I buzz her in and an hour later we're both stretched out on the sofa, with an empty pizza box and a half-drunk bottle of wine in front of us. 'It's such a treat for me to have a conversation with one of the Lovely Girls that doesn't involve slagging me rotten over Gormless Gordon,' she says, lighting a fag. 'The most ill-judged one-night stand of the century. I swear, if Jamie *dares* bring up the subject one more time, over twenty years of friendship will count for naught. There will be bloodshed. It's bad enough that the Gormless gobshite is practically stalking me outside the shop at this stage. If this goes on, I may have to change my mobile phone number.'

'We've all made fools of ourselves in the name of love,' I say. Then I fill her in on Mr Non-Closure and she roars laughing.

'Can you just *believe* how needy and pathetic I was back then?' I snort. 'Waiting in on a guy to call me who clearly had no interest in me? I don't know what Dr Johnny was in, but it certainly wasn't my face.'

'Yeah.' She laughs. 'We'd no finesse in those days.'

'Or pride.'

'Yeah.'

'What time is it now?'

'Half-eight. What time did you ring the hospital?'

'Sevenish.'

We look at each other.

'He's probably really busy. You know the way surgeons work,' she says. 'I'm sure he'll ring back in an hour or so.'

'Yeah, course he will.'

But he doesn't.

Eleven p.m. and still no call.

Midnight . . .

'He was probably exhausted after operating and went straight home,' I try to convince myself. 'Bet he'll ring tomorrow.'

'Yeah, course he will,' says Rachel, yawning. 'Keep me in the loop, won't you?'

But he never calls.

Not the next day, nor the one after and now I'm starting to run out of excuses for him. It seems the twenty-first century way of being dumped/ignored isn't all that different from the last century, is it?

Plus ça change . . .

Chapter Thirty

A Rush of Blood to the Head

So far, so good. I'm well on track to have all my homework done for Ira's class this week and with a bit of luck to oust Mags from her lofty position as the class golden girl. OK, so Mr Non-Closure never called me back, which is hardly my fault, is it? But at least I did make the call.

And then Tim Singed-Underwear only spoke to me so he could pitch an idea for a documentary series, but that's hardly my fault either, is it?

However, I still have one major obstacle to negotiate before I dare cross the threshold of that classroom: Philip Burke.

Since the last class I've found myself actually looking around for him in the canteen, the car park, in a lift or just walking down a corridor, but no joy.

I kind of have a speech rehearsed in my head to say to him. Now, it may not exactly be worthy of Prince Hamlet of Denmark, but it's the best I can come up with, given that (*a*) I don't even fancy him and (*b*) I'm only doing this because I have to.

'Oh, hi, Philip, haven't seen you for ages!' (This to be

delivered in a casual, throwaway manner.) 'Are you free over the next few days? We should have a drink and a chat.' You may not think it, but this particular piece of doggerel actually went through several rough drafts in my head before I even got this far.

Anyway. As my mother would say: Ah sure, it'll fecking well do.

Then, however, fate takes over in a way I could never have predicted . . .

I'm rushing into the production office to grab a bunch of scripts I need for a meeting with our script editor when an ashen-faced Suzy stops me in my tracks. 'Oh, Amelia, I was just coming to look for you. Philip Burke rang and says you're to drop whatever it is you're doing and get straight up to his office now. That it's urgent.'

'*What?*'

'That's what he said.'

She looks petrified, like a rabbit caught in the headlamps and I don't blame her one bit. There are only two reasons why anyone gets called upstairs to that office. Either to be hired or fired.

I deliberately play it cool in front of poor old Suzy, who's probably thinking that *Celtic Tigers* is for the chop and that she'll be out of a job by the end of the week. Not for nothing is Philip called 'The Axeman' behind his back.

'Right. I better get this over with then,' I say crisply.

'Oh shit, Amelia, I can't lose this job. I just got a mortgage! And a cat!'

'Shhh, shhh, calm down. Let's just see what he has to say first, will we? And we'll take the rest from there. OK?'

I give her a big, confident, encouraging smile, go back outside, get into the lift and . . . here comes the panic . . . I almost have a palpitation.

Thank God I have Rescue Remedy in my bag. I don't even bother with the dropper thingy; I just unscrew the lid and knock it all back in one gulp.

OK, I can think of two reasons why he needs to see me so urgently. One: he's axing *Celtic Tigers*. After all my hard work. After my turning the show around. Not blowing my own trumpet, but our ratings have gone up by 150% since I came on board, and we're now attracting an audience of 800,000. The sponsors are thrilled and the advertisers are queuing up. Yes, OK, I know we're still shy of the one million target he set me, but my six-month deadline isn't up yet. We're getting there. That's the point and if he pulls the plug now . . .

Then a second reason strikes me. He's not going to axe *Celtic Tigers*, just me. *I'm* for the chop. I haven't met my target yet, he's not happy with my performance and now he's firing me.

My mind races ahead in double-quick time and by the time I get out of the lift, I'm playing out a scenario in my head. I'm up in court and the judge is saying to me, 'So, Miss Lockwood. You, the plaintiff, are taking this case against the head of television on the grounds of unfair dismissal and all you have to say in your defence is that you think it's personal? Because he asked you on a date and you refused? Do you really think this man capable of such bitterness? Do you really believe that you could inspire such levels of vengeance from a spurned would-be lover? Do you think you're that good-looking or something?'

Either way, I think, rapping on the heavy oak door of his office, what a bastard.

I go in all guns blazing, but he doesn't even look up at me. The lunchtime news is coming up and he's glued to the flat-screen TV beside his desk. 'Amelia. There you are,' he says. 'Just wanted to—'

I don't even give him the chance to get his sentence out. 'Philip, can I just say that we have all put in a huge amount of work on the show and to pull it now or to terminate my contract would be a supreme act of . . . well . . . well . . . you'd be mad. You'd be off your head.'

He turns to look at me as if I'm a few sandwiches short of a picnic. 'Is that why you think I wanted to see you? To fire you?'

'You mean you're not?'

Shit. That means the show is for the scrapheap . . .

'No, you're not fired.'

'Then what about *Celtic Tigers*?'

'What about it?'

'Are you going to axe it?'

'Why would I do that?'

'Because . . .' I stop myself from saying, 'Because it's the kind of thing that you would do. It's what you're famous for. Even the stray dogs hanging round the back of the canteen know that your nickname is The Axeman.'

'Amelia, the reason I asked you up here is because there's something coming up on the news that I want you to see.'

'On the news?'

'Yes.'

'That you want me to see.'

'Yes. Please don't feel you have to repeat everything I say. You're starting to remind me of Geoffrey Rush in *Shine*.'

It's a Philip Burkeism, but I let it pass because (*a*) I'm so relieved that everything's OK and (*b*) I'm dying to know what it is.

I don't have long to wait.

The lunchtime news comes on, the dun–dun–dun–dun theme is blaring and the announcer reads out the head-lines. 'Peace talks continue in the North . . . A post office is raided in South Dublin . . . The annual shin-kicking contest opens in Listowel . . . A monkey at the zoo gives birth to twins . . .'

'Slow news day,' I say, remembering back to my time in current affairs when I'd dread days like this.

Philip waves his hand imperiously for me to shut up.

And then it comes.

'And on a lighter note, it's just been announced that the flagship drama series *Celtic Tigers* has been nominated in the best entertainment category at the prestigious annual television awards ceremony to be held next week. The show's producer, Amelia Lockwood, credited with its recent meteoric rise in popularity, is also nominated in the best producer category. The ceremony will be televised live from the Four Seasons Hotel in Dublin.'

Philip zaps the TV off and turns to me. 'So, what do you think of that?'

I'm stunned, shocked, bewitched, bothered and be-wildered . . . you name it, I'm feeling it.

'Amelia? Do you want to sit down? Are you all right?'

'Is this a joke?' is all I can say. 'Am I on candid camera?'

'No. I put your name forward for this a few days ago.'

'Oh.' I still don't know which I'm more shocked at. That he would do that, or that I'm not fired.

'Jeez, don't lose the run of yourself thanking me or anything.'

'Oh, sorry, thanks. I just . . . well, I can't believe this.'

'You deserve it. You're a bloody good producer. Keep this up and you could end up doing my job in a few years.'

'I'm lost for words. This is unbelievable.'

'Yes, you've already said that.'

'Thank you so much . . . This is . . . Oh my God!'

'You're welcome. Is that it, then?'

'Ehh . . . yeah, I think so.'

'Right, well, you'd better go back to spending the licence payers' money then.'

Another Philip Burkeish way of dismissing me, which is fine because I'm dying to get out of there. I need to walk around the block a few times. I need to sit down. I need a brandy.

Shit!

I need to ask him out.

'Emm . . . Philip?'

'Yup?' It's as though I've already left the room. His head is buried in a pile of boring-looking financial returns and he doesn't even look up.

OK, I say to myself sternly. See the image of my headless groom and just go for it. What's the worst that can happen? The one good thing I will say about Philip is that he's as batty as I am myself, so even if he says no, chances are he'll genuinely have forgotten in about three minutes' time . . .

Deep breath.

'I don't suppose you . . . I don't suppose that it . . . Well, it's just that . . .'

Now he is looking at me. 'Give me the last sentence first.'

Headless groom, Vera Wang, headless groom, Vera Wang . . .
Go for it.

'Do you want to come to the awards with me? It's absolutely fine if you don't, I completely understand, I just thought . . . well . . . Well, for starters, you'll know everyone there, won't you? And . . . then, it's an awards do, isn't it? It's bound to be a great laugh. Not for me, of course, I'll probably have my head down the loo for most of the night, throwing up with nerves . . . which I realize doesn't make me sound exactly like the most fun person you would choose to be there with . . . In fact, now that I think of it, you've probably got someone else in mind that you could bring . . . another date, I mean, so please just disregard everything I've just said as the deranged ramblings of a woman who's just been nominated for an *award* . . .'

'Yeah, OK, why not?' he says, shrugging.

'Sorry.'

'I'll go to the awards with you. Anything to shut you up.'

'Oh. Right. OK then. Emm . . . thanks, I think.'

'That's unless you want to take that South African bloke who gatecrashed your party.'

'Very definitely not.'

'Right. That's a date then.'

I leave his office, completely stunned. I honestly don't know which is the most overwhelming. That I'm up for a big, flashy award or that I just asked Philip out. And he said yes. And, considering that he's barmy, it was remarkably easy.

This mightn't be too bad . . . Who knows? It may even turn out to be fun . . .

By the time I get back downstairs, the word's out. It seems that everyone in the whole production office either saw the news or heard about it on some mysterious tom-tom. Suzy throws her arms around me and squeals congratulations, then asks me if I'd like a loan of her good Catherine Walker evening dress, bless her. The production team give me a spontaneous round of applause and I almost have tears in my eyes.

'Good on you, girl, no one deserves it more than you!' says Dave Bruton, giving me one of his trademark bear hugs.

Everyone's standing up now and the atmosphere is just amazing.

'Thank you so much, all of you,' I say tearily, still in shock that none of us is out of a job. 'You've all worked so hard for this. I'm just proud to be on this fantastic team. I know that sounds schmaltzy, but I really mean it.'

They clap again and then someone from the back of the office shouts, 'Hey, Amelia! Is there any room in that production budget for champagne?'

'Too bloody right there is!' I say and they all laugh. 'Let me just ring the office hotline to Berry Brothers and Rudd and I'll be right back. Crack out those plastic beakers!'

There's more laughter and I go into the conference room and slump into the chair, still trembling.

Best producer.

Oh my God.

Never in my wildest dreams, and I'm a pretty big dreamer, did I see this one coming.

The phone rings. Rachel. Sounding even more stunned than I am myself. 'Darling, I have never been prouder in my whole life. Caroline just rang me to say she saw it on the lunchtime news. Sweet Enola Gay . . . this is *unbelievable*! Now, you do realize that from here on in, it's all going to be about the dress, right?'

'Rachel, I'm knocked for six here. And that's not the half of it. What the lunchtime news didn't tell you is that I asked Philip—' The phone beep-beeps as another call comes through. 'Can I put you on hold? I've another call.'

'Sure, Miss Best Producer Nominee,' says Rachel. 'But before you go, I've made an executive decision. I'm going to be your personal stylist for the night so you just leave all your wardrobe considerations to me. No arguments. Silver, I don't know why but I'm seeing you in a long silver bugle-beaded gown, with your hair in a chignon. Oh! You'll be so gorgeous! Call me straight back!'

'Hello?' I click on to the call that's waiting.

Caroline, sounding strastospheric. 'I nearly died; I almost

passed out when I saw the news! Amelia! You're up for an award! I have to go and ring everyone I know. Pet, I can't breathe. This is the most exciting thing I can ever remember . . . Oh, hang up, darling, that's Mike ringing my mobile. I rang him with the news as well as Jamie and Rachel . . . I'll call you back in two minutes!'

No sooner does she hang up than the phone rings again. Jamie. Straight to the chase as always. 'I'd like to thank all the members of the Academy for this overwhelming award; I'd like to thank my parents for having me, my agent, publicist, colonic irrigationist, herbalist and mentalist. I'd like to thank my boyfriend – Oh wait a minute, I forgot, I don't have one. I love you all and I know one thing for sure. You like me! You really, really like me!'

'Jamie! You sound like Sally Field. It's not the Oscars.'

'Do you realize that you are now living out my fantasy? Ever since I became an actor I've practised my acceptance speech in the bathroom mirror every day. All part of the creative visualization, baby. OK, so it's happened to you instead of me, but hey! Maybe I'm next.'

'I'm in total shock. I thought Philip was going to axe either me or the show or both.'

'OK, honey, here's the plan. I'm going to be your speechwriter, if you win. By the time I'm finished with you, your acceptance speech will brim with boiling eloquence. Think Winston Churchill. For no extra charge, I'll also coach you in your facial expressions, just in case you lose.'

'Facial expressions?'

'Vitally important. You have to look dignified and gracious in defeat, but at the same time really pleased for the bitch who did win. Then, of course, if you *do* win you need a really good sound bite for the press – you know, like Emma

Thompson saying she was going to keep her Oscar in the downstairs loo. The papers love that kind of thing.'

'I don't have a downstairs loo.'

'We may need to work on your stair technique too.'

'My what?'

'Think about it. You'll be in high heels and you'll have to negotiate steps, both up and down, in a gown with a train. This could take hours of rehearsal to get just right.'

'Jamie, I'm able to walk up and down stairs. I'm not ready for a stairlift just yet.'

He's on a roll, though. 'Getting in and out of a limo, that's another thing; you don't want a tabloid getting a shot of your knickers. Then we need to discuss your make-up . . .'

Oh God, I think as he rabbits on. I haven't even had a chance to tell them I'm bringing Philip Burke.

What have I let myself in for?

Chapter Thirty-One
Look Back in Languor

If I thought I was going to get any kind of effort cup in class this week, I was very much mistaken.

Star pupil is a lovely woman called Emily, who I remember from the party but haven't seen since. Turns out, get this, she got back with one of her exes, went on a reconciliation holiday with him to Tuscany and came back . . . engaged.

Now that's what you call a result.

'I can't thank you enough, Ira. This is all down to you. Meeting up with my first three exes helped me to realize what I'd been doing wrong all along. All three of them said I came across as, well, a bit . . . intimidating and emotionally cold.'

'Tough feedback for you to hear,' says Ira. 'What's great is that you learned from that and turned it to your advantage, just like any good marketer would.'

'Well, you see, by the time I contacted Nick, my fiancé' – she smirks a bit at this and flashes the ring at us all. Again – 'I realized that I was giving off signals that I wasn't interested, when all the time I really was. Just down to nerves on my part, really. So I made a conscious effort with Nick to relax, open up and try to let the real me come through. He said he'd missed me a lot since we broke up, then it turned out we both had last week off work, so we booked the holiday. It went brilliantly; we got on like a house on fire. Then he proposed in this really romantic little taverna on our last night. I didn't even have to think about it. I said, "Yes, please, I'll marry you tomorrow."'

'May I be the first to congratulate you, Emily,' says a delighted Ira. 'I wish you and Nick a long and happy life together. You see, ladies? For all you Doubting Thomases sitting here, here's the proof. My program *works*. A round of applause for Emily, please!'

We all clap her and before I know where I am, it's my go.

'Shhhhh,' says Mags. 'Amelia's stories are always the funniest.'

And tonight is no exception.

I tell Ira about Tim Singed-Underwear and the awful Florence, not forgetting to leave out the bit where he wanted me to shoot a documentary series in his house.

'So what did you learn?' asks Ira.

'I don't know really, apart from the fact that it's unlikely any woman will get him *near* an altar so long as bloody Florence is glued to his side like Mrs Danvers.' Then I can't resist going for a gag. They're all looking at me so expectantly. 'But, on the plus side, as my friend Jamie says, at least now we know what happened to Baby Jane.'

Laughter from everyone in the room except Ira.

'And who else did you contact?'

I fill her in about Mr Non-Closure. 'I don't know what I did wrong there and now I never will. What can I do? He still hasn't returned my call. All I've learned there is either (*a*) that he doesn't even deem me worthy of a phone call or (*b*) that he's the rudest git on the planet. My friend Rachel says it's a double shame because it's always handy to know a doctor. I've always had a terrible phobia that I'd end up dying on a hospital trolley.'

'Your friend this, your friend that, your friend the other,' Ira says. 'You won't like the next thing I'm about to say to you, Amelia.'

'What's that?' *Can't be much worse than some of the stuff you've said to me over the past few weeks.*

'Just a word to the wise, that's all. Beware of making other single people your intimates.'

'Sorry?'

'Sometimes it sounds to me as if you're substituting your friends for a partner.'

'Like I'm *what*?'

'I see this a lot. A group of close friends can very often fill the emotional space that's meant for a husband or life partner. Keep your goal to the forefront of your mind, Amelia. Your friends are important but you still want to be married. Otherwise, what happens to you if your friends all get hitched and you're left standing pretty in your bridesmaid's dress holding the bouquet and going home alone?'

She moves on to the woman beside me, which is just as well.

I have an instant flashback . . .

THE TIME: *3 January 1996.*
THE PLACE: *Barberstown Castle, Straffan, Co. Kildare.*
THE OCCASION: *Caroline and Mike's wedding day. You can imagine the state we're all in. It's right at the very end of the night and she's just about to throw the bouquet . . .*

Rachel and I are standing outside, freezing cold in our bridesmaids' dresses as Jamie puts the finishing touches to the graffiti he's spraying in silly string all round the sides of the wedding car: 'Officially off the shelf and have the papers to prove it'.

It's been a very long and emotionally draining day. I've been struggling hard to fight the tears back, but now that Caroline and Mike are almost off on their way to the airport to begin a six-week-long honeymoon, it's all getting too much. The sobs start.

'I'm so happy for them both,' I blubber. 'I'm just so . . . *haaaaaaappy.*'

'I know,' says Rachel, lighting up a fag. 'Thank Christ it's over though. Not my idea of a wedding.'

'No?' I don't have a tissue and have to resort to wiping my eyes on the ribbon of my bouquet.

'Too tense, too formal, too many guests. That's Mrs Egan showing off and inviting all her golf-club buddies, but at one stage I looked around me at the dinner and apart from you guys and Christian, I knew no one. Ughhhhh.'

She shudders a bit and I know what she means. It was a huge, impersonal wedding; there must have been well over three hundred guests, none of whom any of us even vaguely recognized. It was as if Caroline's mum was trying to stage a royal wedding. No expense spared.

'Mrs Egan will go bananas when she sees what you've done to the car,' Rachel says to Jamie. 'So that'll be a laugh. Be sure and get a photo of the old she-devil's face, won't you?'

'Here they come!' says Jamie as Caroline and Mike emerge from the main entrance of the castle, surrounded by hordes of well-wishers all showering them with confetti. This starts me off again.

'I'm so happy for her!' I bawl. 'So happy . . . !'

'OK, now you're starting to look like the runner-up in a

beauty pageant that Caroline just won,' says Jamie. 'Brave face. We're almost home and dry. Then I'll buy you a nice hot whiskey at the free bar, deal?'

'Thanks, honey,' I say, squeezing his arm. Then Rachel links my other arm as Caroline makes her way through the throng and comes over to us. You've never seen a bride like her. I know all brides look beautiful on their wedding day, but Caroline's something more. She's glowing, radiating sheer, unadulterated happiness.

The four of us hug.

'I love you,' she says simply. 'Don't forget me now I'm married.'

'We love you too,' we all chorus.

It's too much for me, I start howling again. 'Ignore me,' I wail, 'these are happy tears.'

'Don't mind Amelia, she's been tippling away at the sherry all day,' says Jamie. 'You know, the way spinsters do. Ever the cliché.'

'You take her back inside and find her a lovely man, do you hear?' Caroline says, hugging us all again. Then she doesn't so much throw her bouquet as hand it to me. 'Here, sweetheart, this is for you,' she says. 'You're next.'

Next thing, Mike is over to drag her away from us into the graffiti-covered car and off to India. 'Come on, Mrs Holmes, time we were going.'

'She isn't Mrs Holmes,' says her mother, hatchet-faced as ever. 'She is Caroline Egan-Holmes. A double-barrelled surname is so much more elegant, I always think.'

And they're gone.

I don't think I ever felt as desolate in my life as when the car drove down the long driveway, clanking tin cans behind it.

Rachel, Jamie and I head back inside to the warmth, still

linking arms. I think we're all feeling a bit vulnerable and we certainly could do with a drink.

'What would we do without each other?' I ask, teary-eyed.

'Oh, come on, there's nothing wrong with you that a good fling won't put right,' says Rachel. 'I've got Christian, Jamie's got what's-his-name—'

'It's Kurt, actually,' says Jamie. 'I'd be very grateful if you could put yourself to the bother of memorizing his name. I have been seeing him for almost a week now, I'll have you know. Quite serious, for me.'

'Before this night is out, you are going to get drunk and get laid, in that order,' says Rachel. 'We're all feeling the loss of our best friend and believe me, this is the only thing that'll fill the void.'

Which brings me neatly to ex-boyfriend number nine on the list: Gary O'Neill.

There he was, standing at the bar when we went back inside, looking dark, swarthy, tanned and right up my alley.

'Target identified,' I say to Rachel, instantly cheering up as we head in his general direction.

'Yummy, yummy,' she agrees. 'How come we didn't spot him earlier?'

He saw us coming, literally. Well, how could he miss us? Our bridesmaids' dresses are Little-Bo-Peep style.

'You should have a staff and a stuffed sheep to complete the outfit,' he says to me, giving me a not-very-subtle once-over as Rachel gives me a discreet wink and moves off to find Christian.

'Nice suntan,' I say, standing right beside him and pretending that this is the only available spot where I can stand to order a drink.

'Thanks,' he says, looking right at me with devilment in his dancing black eyes. 'I'm just back from a skiing trip. Annual thing. I rent the same chalet in Klosters at this time every year. The après-ski there is just amazing.'

Already I'm impressed. I don't know anyone who skis regularly, let alone rents the same chalet every year. Jamie and I are always talking about going, but we're both novices and secretly ashamed of being overtaken by five-year-olds on the nursery slopes.

'So, are you on Mike's side or Caroline's?' I ask, coyly. *Definitely not Caroline's*, I'm thinking. *She'd have told me if she had any distant relations who were complete and utter rides like this one.*

He's very fit-looking, tall and lean . . . incredibly sexy. He's smouldering at me and all I can do is wonder what he looks like naked. Utterly divine, I silently bet myself, like a Greek God . . .

'Mike's my first cousin,' he says.

'And what do you work at?' I ask, now in full flirtation mode.

'Actually it's very exciting. I'm a financier, and I'm putting together a fantastic investment package at the moment.'

'Oh really? What do you invest in?' *If he has a few quid as well as looking like this,* I'm busily thinking, *he'd be the perfect guy for me . . . It's so true, that old saying: 'Going to one wedding is the makings of another.'*

'I don't really like to talk about it.' He's grinning at me now, and I know he's almost egging me on, dying for me to ask more.

No problem. My big mouth will always win out. 'Oh, come on,' I say, swishing my hair in what I hope is a come-to-bed, Bardotesque, sex-kitten way. I lean in and whisper in his ear: 'I can keep a secret.'

'OK then, you asked for it,' he whispers back, grinning. He smells gorgeous and the physical attraction I'm feeling for him is so overwhelming that all I can do is stare at his lips and wish I could be snogging the face off him. In front of Mrs Egan; in front of them all.

I don't care who he is or what he does. If he sweeps the streets or is a bin man's assistant, I don't care. All I want to say to this guy is, 'Get your coat, you've pulled.'

'OK,' he says teasingly, 'you asked for it. I'm setting up my own airline.'

Score . . .

Now, I've always said that I have a guardian angel and boy did they put in overtime on Gary O'Neill. Exactly six weeks later, just as Caroline and Mike were coming back from their honeymoon, I was on the verge of investing in Gary's airline project. Not a huge amount of money, but pretty much all my savings from my first few years working my ass off as a journalist and doing bits of freelance work on TV.

'I would conservatively estimate that you will quadruple your money in a year,' Gary had said and I believed him. It was hard not to: he was so utterly convincing. He even presented me with a business plan, basing the airline on a low-cost model, a bit like Ryanair. You know, the ones where the flights go out either at ridiculously early or ridiculously late times, land you a minimum of eighty kilometres from your destination city and have loss-leader-style pricing. Flights for ninety-nine pence, that type of thing. It sounds gullible, it sounds naïve, but had Gary asked me for anything I'd have gladly given it to him.

Besides, you should have seen the list he showed me of all his other investors. It read like a who's who of Irish multi-millionaire businessmen, with even a few government ministers thrown in for good measure.

I'm going to be a shareholder in an airline, I told myself at the time. Free flights for life and a yummy boyfriend to boot . . . As far as I was concerned, I was the luckiest gal on the planet.

Until Caroline and Mike got back from honeymoon, that is.

First up, Mike pointed out that he had never heard of anyone called Gary O'Neill.

'But he said you're cousins!' I said.

'Amelia, I only had two very distant cousins at the wedding. One was my mother's eighty-seven-year-old second cousin Muriel, who you'll have noticed because she's in a wheelchair, and the other was her daughter and carer, Gloria.'

Caroline had never heard of anyone called Gary O'Neill either and nor had Mrs Egan, who checked and rechecked her carefully thought-out guest list, at Caroline's insistence.

'Then what was he doing there?' I almost wailed, my dreams of being a multi-millionaire going up in smoke. Not to mention my sex god boyfriend . . .

'Sweetie, we think he might have gatecrashed the party,' said Caroline gently.

'*What?*'

Now I'm feeling a sharp stab of almost physical pain.

'Sounds crazy, but people do, you know,' said Mike. 'Look at the facts. There were hundreds of people at Barberstown Castle; he could easily have slipped into the wedding once the dinner bit was over. A free bar is a free bar. No one would ever have guessed that we didn't know him.'

He was looking at me so sadly, as if I was some idiot spinster about to hand over her life savings to a confidence trickster. Which, in a way, I was . . .

'We know absolutely nothing about him,' said Mike firmly. Which, again, was true . . .

Ever since the honeymoon couple had got back I'd been

suggesting meeting up with them as a foursome, but Gary always had a cast-iron excuse. He was tied up in meetings out at the airport; he had to go to New York unexpectedly; or, on one occasion, he was meeting up with the Minister for Development who was giving him a huge grant. He always looked the part in his Savile Row suits and was always utterly convincing, but basically, whenever I would mention either Caroline's name or Mike's, he'd do a complete disappearing trick.

Oh dear. Of all the lovely, eligible men at that wedding, there was one idiot wide-boy chancer and I had to go and fall for him . . .

If I ever needed final proof that Gary was some kind of fly-by-night, it was this. After Caroline and Mike voiced their concerns to me, I faithfully promised (*a*) to confront him about not being invited to the wedding and (*b*) not even to think about shelling out one penny of my savings until this mess was cleared up.

I called him and left a message, saying I needed to talk.

Not only did he never return the call, but when my next credit-card statement arrived, there was a total of about a thousand pounds outstanding, all stuff which I never bought, all purchased over the phone using my credit card number: airline tickets, a few cases of Veuve Clicquot and, worst of all, expensive costume jewellery, purchased online and certainly never given to me . . .

I wish I could say that I never saw Gary again, but the tale does have a twist, of sorts.

About eighteen months later, August 1997 to be exact, Princess Diana was tragically killed in a car crash at the Pont d'Alma in Paris. The following week led to the most extraordinary scenes in London, with oceans of flowers being left outside Kensington Palace and Buckingham Palace, candlelit vigils and a rising tide of anger against the royal family, perceived as being distant and remote, holed up in Balmoral. I was a rookie producer on current affairs then and was dispatched over to London with a reporter and a cameraman to cover these astonishing displays of raw grief, live from the capital.

It was a late-evening flight and I've never been a very good flier, so I was sitting nervously by the aisle, waiting for the drinks cart to trundle down, absolutely gagging for a good stiff gin and tonic.

'Can I get you anything, madam?' the steward asked.

There was just something familiar in his voice that made me look up. 'I'd love a gin—' I broke off. There he was, Gary O'Neill, wearing the British Airways uniform and a neat navy apron tied around his waist.

I couldn't resist. 'So, how's the airline business going, Gary?'

He played it like the pro he was. What an actor he'd have made; he actually looked like he was thrilled to bump into me. 'Fantastic, Amelia. Great to see you. I'm just doing this for charity. You know, one of those days where all the head honchos come down to the coalface and learn about the operation from the ground up.'

'Are you for real?' I said in a low voice so none of the other passengers can overhear. 'Has the cabin suddenly depressurized? Is that why you're coming out with all this *utter shite* . . . lack of oxygen to your brain?'

'It's the absolute truth,' he says, smiling at me with that sincerity he can fake to a T.

'My friend Richard does it all the time. That's Richard Branson, by the way. Lets the staff know I'm really just one of them.'

'Move on, could you please?' his supervisor said crisply

343

from behind. 'You're blocking the aisle and this passenger needs to use the bathroom.'

He wheeled the trolley onwards and it was just as well. He was so convincing, I'd almost have believed him. In another minute he'd have been telling he was a majority shareholder in British Airways.

Please understand I'm completely cool and calm as I'm remembering all of this sorry episode. All I can think is: talk about your lucky escapes . . .

Back to class and Ira is busy giving out instructions for next week's homework. There's loads of it: we all have to do a 'program evaluation audit' where you reassess the progress you've made (or lack of it in my case) over the past few weeks. Is your appearance up to scratch; is your attitude remaining positive; are you really casting your net as wide as possible to include dating men who aren't your type?

Yes, actually, I think, mentally ticking that one off. Well, I did ask Philip Burke out, didn't I?

As class wraps up and Ira cheerily tells us to 'Go, get results!' Mags comes over to me and gives me a hug.

'Hey! I heard you got nominated for a big TV award and I just wanted to congratulate you.'

'Thanks. I'm kind of nervous, but I'm really looking forward to it. Should be a great night.'

'Yeah.' She laughs. 'That's just what Philip said.'

'He told you I asked him to be my date, then?' I try not to look embarrassed. After all, isn't that what this class is all about?

'Yes, he told me. Give him a chance, Amelia, that's all I'm saying.'

'Yeah, of course I will.' I try to sound upbeat and positive about the prospect of a scary night out with him, but I'm really thinking, *I'm only putting myself through this because Ira says you should date what's not your type.*

'I think he likes you.'

'Really?' I'm about to say. 'How do you tell?' but opt for smiling politely instead.

'Yes, I do. Look, I know he can be a bit, well, aloof, but just remember that if you sand him down, there's a good heart under all that . . . well, all those clangers he sometimes comes out with. Think of him like a rough diamond. OK, he needs a bit of polishing and working on, but it would be so worth it. Then you and he could come out on foursomes with Damien and me. Wouldn't that be so much fun?'

Chapter Thirty-Two

Get Down off Your Crucifix, We Need the Wood

There's a deeply unpleasant surprise waiting for me when I get home. I go into my building, pick up the post and step into the lift, dying for (in no particular order) a good, long soak in the tub and a lovely chilled glass of Sancerre.

The lift doors glide apart and there he is, waiting for me. *He-whose-name-shall-forever-remain-unspoken.* He's slumped up against the door of my apartment with the biggest bouquet of stargazer lilies you ever saw lying on the ground beside him.

Oh help . . .

He hops to his feet the minute he sees me and I brace myself for what's coming. Keep cool, I tell myself. Just stay calm and get it over with.

'Hi Amelia,' he says, thrusting the flowers at me. 'Congratulations. I just got you these to say well done on being nominated in the TV awards.'

I look at him, deliberately not taking the flowers. 'You have to stop this.'

'Stop what?'

'Trying to be all pally with me. Being here. Lurking

outside my apartment. The flowers, everything. It's not going to happen, ever. I'm sorry if this sounds harsh, but I'm not your friend, I didn't ask to be, I don't want to be and I never will be.'

'Well, actually, I was kind of hoping we could have a chat.'

'About what? Wedding plans? Seating arrangements? Next thing you'll be inviting me out on your stag night.'

'No, nothing like that. I just thought I could talk to you about something.'

I don't answer, just fish around in my handbag for my door keys.

'Poppy wants us to take a break,' he blurts out.

'What?' *Am I hearing things?* Half of me wants to go inside to the safety of my flat and slam the door in his face, but the other half is dying to find out what's going on.

Naturally enough, the nosey half wins out. I look at him quizzically and he takes this as his cue to continue.

'She says she needs time, that the whole wedding thing has been too rushed. Then there's the age-gap issue. Half the time I don't even know what she and her friends are talking about and they all look at me like I'm some sleazy, lecherous old granddad. Her best friend keeps ringing me up from nightclubs at five in the morning wanting lifts home, as if I'm some sort of twenty-four-hour on-call taxi . . .'

I was right. It's almost like there's a generation gap between them and now the cracks are beginning to show.

Too bloody bad . . .

'Amelia, I can tell you this, because you'll understand. You know me so well, better than anyone, I think.' Then he looks around, a bit embarrassed. 'Look, can I come inside, just for a few minutes? I really don't want to discuss this out on the corridor.'

'There's nothing wrong with the corridor. Say what you

have to say and let me go. I'm tired, I'm narky and I'm starting to think I've heard enough.'

He looks at me, realizes the lady is not for turning, then goes for it. 'This isn't easy for me to say, but over the last few weeks, I've realized what a terrible mistake I made in letting you go. You wanted a commitment and at the time I couldn't do it, but this whole experience with Poppy has been such a major eye-opener for me.' He takes a long pause for effect. 'Amelia, I think I'm with the wrong woman and I let the right one slip through my fingers.'

For once in my life, I can't even think of a smart comment to throw back at him. The pain and the agony and the hurt that this man put me through and now he's saying: Ooooops, sorry about that, made a bad move, can we just forget about the past and by the way, please take me back?

Suddenly the last few months flash before my eyes . . . every one of my exes that I painstakingly tracked down, full of hope that I'd learn something that would all stand me in good stead when I met *the one.*

I can handle that none of my previous relationships worked out. I can handle the sad fact that you could summarize my entire twenty-year dating history in three words: crash and burn. I accept that I made bad choices in the past.

What I can't handle is that it's still ongoing. Whatever I'm doing wrong, I'm still doing it: viz, this arsehole on my doorstep fully expecting me to take him back with open arms. If I'm really honest, yes, there was a time after we first broke up when I probably would have taken him back, in spite of everything, but not now. Not after everything he's put me through. Maybe I'm a million miles wrong, but I can't help feeling I deserve a bit better. And *anything's* better than this . . .

'Amelia?'

'What?'

'You're doing your drifting-off-into-space thing again. Did you hear what I just said?'

'Yes, I was just doing my best to tune it out.'

'I was apologizing for the huge mistake I made. I didn't know what I had with you until I lost it. I guess you're an acquired taste.'

'Like Guinness,' I mutter, taking out my keys and opening the hall door. I've had enough. Quite enough.

He looks at me, crestfallen as I turn to close the door. 'So I'm not welcome inside then? Are you sure we couldn't talk about this over a nice bottle of Sancerre, your favourite? Poppy's out with her friends again tonight and I really don't want to be alone. Come on, Amelia, let me in, for old times' sake. I've missed you and if you're honest you'll admit that you've missed me too.' Then he grabs my arm and moves in close. 'Don't be like this, honey, let me inside. You know you want to.'

Now he's done it.

I turn to him, boiling with fury at the sheer *brass neck* of him. 'I'm really glad I'm not crying because I'd hate for what I'm saying to be clouded by emotion. It is not OK for you to camp out on my doorstep just because your fiancée is having second thoughts about you. I am no one's second choice nor am I your consolation prize. Do you understand?'

He gives me the puppy-dog eyes but sensibly says nothing.

'Oh and FYI?' I add, unable to resist this.

'Yeah?' He looks at me half hopefully, half expectantly.

'When a woman says she wants to take a break, allow me to translate. It means she wants a break from *you*.'

I go inside, collapse on the sofa and burst into angry, bitter tears.

⋆ ⋆ ⋆

As ever, it takes Jamie to put a smile back on my face. I call him from work the next day, desperate to talk.

'Hey, hon!' he growls, sounding hungover as a dog and dying for a good long gossip, 'So what's the word from planet crackpot?'

I fill him in on last night's developments, in glorious Technicolor, no detail, however tiny, omitted.

'Oh, Jamie, I honestly can't remember the last time I cried that much. My head is splitting today and I'm supposed to be working and I just can't bring myself to do anything. This is awful. It's just so bloody awful.'

'Jeez,' he says, concerned, 'you really sound like you're stuck in a slough of despond. Not like yourself at all.'

'If you'd only seen him; he was just so *sure* of himself. In his warped head he thought all it would take would be a bunch of flowers for him to be on a one-way ticket to pantyland.'

'OK, are you ready for my take on this?' says Jamie, sounding like the Exorcist after smoking fifty fags. 'Although you don't have to be Sherlock Holmes to figure out what's going on there.'

'Please.'

'Elementary, my dear. Poppy's finally got bored with him and now wants to hang out with her twenty-something friends. So if I were in your shoes, I would now be dancing on rooftops going "he, he, hee". What a kick in the teeth for him. I'm sorry, but isn't some evil part of you just haemorrhaging bittersweet laughter, my favourite kind?'

'No, that's the thing. It turns my stomach to think that I'm his also-ran woman and, now that he's a dumpee, he thinks all he has to do is doorstep me and I'll fall back into his arms. After what he put me through.'

'Come on, babe, you have to stay strong. You have a big awards do coming up and the last thing you need are stress lines breaking out on your face. Refocus. Regroup. So what's the plan for today?'

I'm so shell-shocked by the last twelve hours, I can't even think straight . . . Then it comes back to me. 'Oh, you'll love this. I have to contact Gary O'Neill.'

Jamie snorts. 'The original dirty rotten scoundrel? The Nick Leeson of the skies? Take great care, angel, in fact take a tip from me. Do it over the phone. You don't want him getting his thieving paws on your credit card. Again.'

He's dead right, I'm thinking, *God knows what Gary's up to now. He could even be in prison for all I know . . . In fact, if he's a free man, I'll be very surprised . . .*

'Ooooh, this is just *way* too much drama for me this early in the day,' says Jamie. 'Keep safe and keep me posted, won't you, hon? Oh, here, I have to go, the dead have arisen.' In the background, I can hear a loo flushing and heavy footsteps thumping around Jamie's flat.

'I'm not finished with you yet,' I say. 'Have you got someone there? Did you score last night?'

'At it like students after lights out all night long, baby,' he says, dropping his voice to a whisper. 'I'll call you back, darling. I was very drunk and now I have to try and remember which lies I told him. I definitely remember saying that I was a black belt in karate and that I was fluent in Greek and Arabic and that I was acting part-time while I did a Ph.D. in genetic research.'

'Jamie!'

'In fact the only thing I didn't lie about was being single. Cheerie-bye, dearest, chat later. Love you, mean it!'

I seize the moment. I have about half an hour before my next meeting, with the advertising department, so I make sure the conference-room door is shut tight and I go for it. After all, time is running out and here I am, still single and now dealing with an ex-boyfriend who thinks I'm fair game.

Right, here goes.

One deep, soothing breath later and I'm on the phone to the British Airways personnel department.

Then I do something I'm not very proud of.

In my defence, when I was in current affairs, we used to do this all the time. If we needed to talk to someone and get specific information, we'd say, 'Hi, I'm calling from the *News Time* TV show, can you tell me . . . ?' It was like uttering a magic formula. People would tell you all kinds of stuff which they probably shouldn't have. But it worked then and it works now.

The lady in personnel I speak to sounds crisp and efficient. Definitely not a rule-breaker, so I chance my arm. 'I know you're not supposed to give out personal information,' I say tentatively, 'but, you see, I'm a producer calling from TV One and I'm trying to track down an employee of yours.'

OK, it sounds like I'm about to make a documentary about the airline industry but, so far, it's only a half-lie.

'Any information you can give me would of course be treated in the strictest confidence,' I add, doing my best to sugar it up.

It works like a charm. 'Who did you wish to contact?' she asks.

'One Gary O'Neill,' I answer, feeling a bit more confident.

'Gary O'Neill?' she asks, repeating the name slowly.

'That's right. He was employed as cabin crew for you, oh, about eight years ago. He may easily have left the company by now, I realize that, but if you had any contact details, you'd be doing me a very big favour.'

There's a long, long silence and I can hear her tap-tap-tapping away at the keys of her computer. 'O'Neill, Gary. Yes, here we go. He took a voluntary redundancy package from the company in two thousand. I have an address and a mobile phone number I can give you, if that's of any use.'

'Thank you so much,' I say, delighted, 'I really am so grateful.'

'No problem,' she says brusquely. 'Just one more thing. If you do manage to get hold of him, could you tell him I'm still waiting on him to repay the cash he borrowed from me? Thanks ever so much.'

It's like phoning the Pot Noodle of ex-boyfriends. I don't particularly want to do it; I know it's bad for me; but I just can't help myself . . .

It takes about four goes of his phone just ringing and ringing out again before I eventually do get him.

'Hello?' he answers, sounding groggy and half-asleep, even though it's two in the afternoon.

'Gary?'

'Ehh . . . depends. Who's this?'

'It's a blast from the past. Amelia Lockwood. You'll be surprised to hear from me after so long—'

'No, are you kidding?' he whistles. 'Amelia Lockwood, I don't believe it. It's great to hear from you. I was just reading in the paper that you're up for a big TV award. Best producer, isn't it? Well done, good on you.'

I can hear him lighting up a cigarette as he's talking. *OK,* says my inner voice sternly, *just get to the point quickly and then get off the phone. You don't want Gary O'Neill of all people getting the wrong idea about why you're getting in touch after all this time . . .*

'Gary I just wanted to ask you something.' I pause for a minute, wondering what would be a polite way of saying:

'Why did you lie to me/use me/run off without saying a word? Oh, and let's not forget the clincher. I don't actually have proof, but I do have a fair idea that you used my credit card to run up a huge bill . . .'

I don't get the chance to finish my sentence, though. He barrels right over me.

'It's fantastic that you rang, Amelia.'

'Yeah?'

'Yeah. This could be your lucky day. I have a proposition for you which I think you'll be very interested in.'

Do not let the charm get to you and under no circumstances are you to part with money . . . 'Oh, really? What kind of proposition?'

There's just the tiniest pause. 'I'm doing a lot of charity work at the moment to help build an orphanage for the homeless kids in Belarus. I think this could be a fantastic opportunity for you to make a no-holds-barred documentary about the great work we're doing out there.'

'What work is that exactly?'

'We're only in the very early stages, really. Fundraising mostly. But TV exposure could really give us a boost. Basically, what we're asking people to do is to pledge two thousand euro a head to sponsor a child. We'll raise the money in advance and then the building work proper can go ahead. My financial advisers are telling me we need to raise one point two million and then we're home and dry. It's for a fantastic cause. You could do worse than consider investing yourself, Amelia. Think of the children.'

He chats on and I let him, but my thoughts have long since drifted. At this stage, it's not a relationship coach I need. It's Lourdes.

Chapter Thirty-Three
And Then There Were None

Rachel, as ever, is completely fantastic. Friday comes and we're all on our way over to Caroline's for one of her yummy big mammy dinners, as I call them.

'I love feeding you guys at least once a week,' Caroline said with Joshua screeching in her arms. 'It's getting to be my raison d'être. At least then I know you're all eating one square meal in a seven-day period. Honestly, Rachel's practically gone skeletal. Her idea of dinner is to uncork a bottle of wine and light up a cigarette. And someone should really tell her that mints are not a food group.'

But, before we head out there, Rachel suggests I pop into Urban Chic to have a look at a particular outfit she's put by for me, for the awards do.

'Oh my Gowwwd!' I squeal when I see what she's earmarked. 'I'm not worthy!'

'As your stylist, I've made an executive call. I neither know nor care what the glamourometer usually is for these TV awards, but you, my darling, are going for all-out Hollywood-on-Oscar-night look. I've even made an appointment for you to have your hair done at Marshall's.'

'Wow! I'm well impressed. The wait to have your hair done there is about three months. The too-posh-to-push brigade all plan their Caesarean sections around getting their hair done in there.'

Rachel steers me over to the mirror, comes behind me and pulls my hair up. 'You see?' she says. 'A classic chignon with absolutely no jewellery whatsoever would be fantastic. Very chic, very French. Come on, try the Peter O'Brien on, I have a good feeling about this frock.'

The dress is more like a 1940s ball gown, a real show-stopper in every way. It's very, very tight fitting with a flamenco-style ruffle skirt in the most elegant silvery colour you ever saw. The fabric is bias-cut and it has what look like hundreds and thousands of minuscule bugle beads sewn knee deep across the hem line. I'm almost afraid getting into it, it's probably worth more than I am.

As I'm shoehorning myself into it inside the fitting room, I fill Rachel in on the Gary O'Neill saga.

'You know what that worthless bastard is?' she calls back to me. 'Puff Daddy without the gun charge. But that's probably right around the corner for him. More to the point, what happened with *He-whose-name-shall-forever-remain-unspoken*? Jamie said you had an unwanted late-night visit the other night.'

'Put it this way: poppy-seed bagels are officially now back on the menu. Either she's getting sense or he's physically boring her and her friends to death. His basic tack was: "My engagement doesn't seem to be working out, so here I am, please disregard everything I ever said about not wanting to make a commitment to you and take me back."'

'Do you want me to sort him out for you? Believe you me, by the time I'm finished with him, the rabid dogs on the streets will refuse to feast on his rotting carcass.'

'Bless you for that lovely sentiment, but I think even he must have got the message by now. I practically slammed the door in his face. OK, I'm coming out now, ready or not.'

I step out of the fitting room and Rachel physically gasps.

'Bloody hell,' I say when I see my own reflection in the mirror. 'It's *stunning*. The dress, I mean, not me.'

'You're breathtaking,' she says, which makes me feel doubly good because Rachel's not given to using superlatives, ever. 'Just don't let Philip Whatever-his-name-is get drool marks all over it when he's ogling you. It's only borrowed.'

'Oh, Rachel,' I say, 'I solemnly swear I will give you my first-born child if I get as much as a stain on it. I'll even send it to that posh dry-cleaner's in Paris where Rania of Jordan gets her clothes dry-cleaned. I have never felt this good in anything in my entire life.'

She winks at me just as a last-minute customer comes in who she has to go and deal with. I loiter in front of the mirror, feeling utterly sensational in the dress and doing a quick creative visualization on me standing on the podium, receiving the award.

'Ahem, ahem. I'd like to thank my best friends for putting up with me over the last few weeks, when I've been such a complete nightmare to be around. Not only because of the long hours I've put in on *Celtic Tigers*, but because, you see, I've been doing a night course where you have to track down all your ex-boyfriends, with hilarious and sometimes quite crushing consequences. I'd like to take this opportunity to apologize unreservedly to my nearest and dearest for being such a pain in the face while I gamely endured humiliation after humiliation in my quest to find a husband. Oh, and by the way, if there are any kind-hearted, single male viewers watching who would be at all interested in taking me out on a date, my mobile number is now being flashed across the bottom of your screens. Or you could always text your number, along with a brief biography, to DESPERADO 1850 321321 and I'll be in touch. Ladies and gentlemen, thank you.'

Don't worry; I didn't say any of this out loud.

Rachel is a good while dealing with her customer, so I carefully step out of the dress and put it safely back into its plastic covering.

Nine ex-boyfriends done and one to go, I start thinking as I patiently wait for her by the cash register. I start humming that Frank Sinatra song, 'My Way', you know, the line about the end being near and having to face the final curtain.

And then, what do you know, I'm off again . . .

THE TIME: *December 1999.*
THE PLACE: *The* News Time *TV studio.*
THE OCCASION: *The end of a very heated debate between the Minister for Health, the editor of the* Irish Press *and a young, up-and-coming county councillor by the name of Bill Yeats . . .*

'And we're out,' I say into the headset as the programme wraps. 'Well done, everyone, what a fantastic show!'

The debate made for electrifying television. If the Minister thought he was in for a very easy ride on tonight's show, boy did he have another thing coming. Bill Yeats went for him like a dreadnought. You name it, he tackled it: every issue you could think of from the Y2K bug to the social-housing issue, from immigration to people dying on hospital trolleys, Bill Yeats kept the questions coming like bullets from a sniper. At one point, the camera actually caught droplets of sweat rolling down the Minister's heated, red face.

Needless to say, he didn't linger long after the broadcast.

No sooner were we 'out' than he left the studio and disappeared off into the night in the back of his government Mercedes. I never even got the chance to thank him for agreeing to do the show, which is a shame because it's highly unlikely he'll ever want to come back on again. Not after tonight.

'Looks terrible that he didn't even stay for a drink afterwards,' says Anne, *News Time*'s incredibly hard-working production assistant.

'Yeah, doesn't it?' I agree. 'The incredible sulk.'

'But what about Bill Yeats?' she says. 'Isn't he something?'

I know just what she means. Without being handsome in a conventional way (think less Alec Baldwin and more Billy), he has the 'it' factor in spades. Charisma, energy, fire and passion. That along with a great body and the deepest green eyes you ever saw.

Anne and I both look at each other and ask the question simultaneously. 'Wonder if he's single?'

We make our way downstairs to the hospitality room, or the hostility room as I've nicknamed it. Predictably enough, it's packed with all the crew, dying for a well-earned drink after such a rollercoaster of a show.

There's a group of girls from the make-up department clustered around Bill Yeats, all proffering giddy, hysterical congratulations. Anne and I both head for the bar and I'm just about to order some drinks when there's a gentle tap on my shoulder.

It's him, Bill.

'Hello. Amelia, isn't it?'

'Yes, hi, lovely to meet you. Well done out there tonight. You were so . . .' I want to say sexy but have to remind myself that I'm a fully fledged producer now and producers don't come out with that kind of teenage drivel. '. . . so . . . emm . . . great.'

Well done, Amelia. Big improvement on 'sexy'. Way to go . . .

'I really just wanted to thank you for inviting me on to the show tonight. Sure, I couldn't buy a slot like that. I was dying to have a go at the Minister and you were great to let me loose at him. Plenty of producers would have gone for the safe option and cut to an ad break.'

'Are you kidding me? This will be such a ratings hit. Audiences *love* this kind of thing. I'm really pleased with tonight's show. Wish they were all like this.' *Wish all the guests were like you, is what I really mean to say, you get my first preference in an election any time.*

'It's fierce crowded in here altogether, isn't it?' he says. 'And to be honest with you, I think I've done enough networking for one night. I don't suppose you fancy going back to my local for a quiet jar? Sure, the least you can do is let me buy you a drink. After all the great exposure you're after giving me on the show, like.'

It was as simple as that.

He took me to a pub on Parkgate Street and we spent the whole night chatting. When I look back on it, we had so much in common back then. We were both young, hungry and with that single-minded determination to succeed that you only really get once in your life. It's as if we both knew we were on the right course career-wise and, by God, we were going to make it work.

Before long, he was my proper, official boyfriend.

We made a great team. Every local protest meeting or fundraising do he had to go to, I was at his side. (Well, I always fancied being a politician's wife, except I was thinking more in the Jackie Kennedy/Eva Peron mode.) I must have canvassed the length and breadth of his constituency with him and he in turn would come to each and every one of my *News Time* broadcasts and coach me in how best to sharpen my questions and tighten up the show's format.

Jamie even had a nickname for us: Bamelia. You know, like Billary for Bill and Hillary Clinton. I loved it. Bill and Amelia . . . Bamelia . . .

'Amelia?'

'Oh, sorry.'

'You'd drifted off there,' says Rachel. 'Come on, I'm all locked up. Let's GTFOOH.'

(That's her codeword for 'get the f★★k out of here'. Very handy in nightclubs when we both want to make a speedy getaway without attracting attention to ourselves. Her other great one is MEGO, meaning 'my eyes glaze over'. Equally handy for indicating when someone's boring the arse off you.)

Leaving the shop is a bit like one of those World War One movies where the infantry 'go over the top', as Rachel has to check and double check that poor Gormless Gordon isn't looking out the window of the bistro he runs across the street, in the hope he can catch her. Rumour has it that he has binoculars trained on the door of Urban Chic at all times.

'Coast clear,' she says. 'On my count, run for it. One, two, three, GO!'

We make it safely to my car without being accosted.

'I was just thinking about my last and final ex-boyfriend,' I say, starting up the engine.

'Oh yeah, the politician guy. Bill, wasn't it? I love politics. It's kind of show business for ugly people. Remind me why you broke up with him?'

Rachel was still in Paris when I was seeing Bill and so was kind of out of the loop, gossip-wise.

'It was a classic case of relationship fizzle,' I say thoughtfully. 'There was no falling out or argument, nothing like that. Our careers just took each of us in very different directions. At the time, we were both flat-out workaholics. He's done very well for himself since though, so not being with me clearly agreed with him. He's a backbencher now but, mark my words, he'll have a ministry one day.'

'Isn't he married to that awful woman? What's her real name again?'

'Ugh, Claire. Yup, they're still married. Do you think she'd let a guy like that out of her sight?'

If ever there was a straw poll taken of Ireland's least popular public figures, Claire Yeats would be right up there along with the two fellas who put VAT on children's shoes and banned smoking in the workplace respectively.

She came from a political family, her father was Minister for Finance and her grandfather had been one of the founders of the fledgling State. Nothing would do for her though but to become a household name in her own right, so, a few years back, she invited a documentary team into her home to film a fly-on-the-wall documentary. Bill came out of it smelling of roses but, unfortunately, Claire's attempt at styling herself as a 'people's politician's wife' was a public-relations disaster. I remember seeing the programme at the time and a few choice quotes of hers still linger in the memory.

'We paid five hundred thousand for this house and now it's worth three million, I'll have you know,' she'd said to camera, 'so ye needn't all hate me just because I bought at the right time. The cost of keeping it up is ridiculous. Sure, I have to employ a full-time housekeeper, an ironing lady *and* a gardener. The villa in Marbella costs a fortune to run too and we're expected to entertain when we're down there so it all adds up. And that's all coming out of a politician's salary, you know. Sure, by the time all the bills are paid, I barely have enough left over to run the Mercedes and the BMW. You needn't talk to me about the poverty line.'

The papers had a field day as you can imagine. They crowned the programme with the nickname 'The Claire Witch Project' and the name stuck. Now every time you see a picture of her and Bill in the tabloids, the tag-line always reads: 'Mr Bill Yeats and his wife, the Claire Witch'.

'Last on your list, I can't believe it,' says Rachel, rolling down the car window so she can have a fag. Then she looks at me astutely. 'So, now. Tell me honestly. As one who was violently opposed to you doing the whole bloody course in the first place, here's the million-dollar question. Was it worth it?'

Just as I'm about to answer, a not-at-all-bad-looking guy smoking outside a pub spots Rachel and shouts at her, as we're sitting stuck in traffic, 'Heya! Gorgeous! Are you coming in? I'll let you buy me a pint.'

'Piss off,' snaps Rachel without a second glance.

All perfectly normal, just the lethal Rachel pheromone in action on a Friday night. I turn to face her. 'I'll tell you what I've learned,' I say, slowly. 'Romance is very much alive and well. It's just not returning my calls.'

I've come this far, I think the following morning as I pull my car up outside Bill's constituency office in Phibsboro. I've nothing to lose.

I had rung his office that morning, fully expecting an answering machine, but to my surprise, his secretary answered and said he was having a clinic from ten till four. Brilliant. It's a good sign.

I go inside the office, which is dark, a bit dingy and unwelcoming, like a doctor's surgery. There're three other people sitting on very uncomfortable-looking plastic chairs and I join them.

I notice I'm the only one under the age of about seventy, but then I'm not here on constituency business. Not by a long shot.

There's a lot of coughing and shuffling and the wait is so long that I'm seriously thinking I might just chicken out and leave a message with his secretary instead, but then my recurrent image comes back to haunt me. The headless groom, the Vera Wang . . . Except in this head rush, I'm almost on the verge of turning into Miss Havisham, with rotting teeth and cobwebs all over my decaying dress and rats eating the wedding cake . . .

The door opens and out comes Bill, shaking hands with an elderly pensioner. 'Don't be worrying now, Mrs Murphy, we'll sort out that medical card for you in no time. Go on home now, love, and remember the council elections are coming up soon and you know what we always say to the party faithful. Vote early and vote often!'

He spots me (well, I must look like a foetus compared with the rest of them) and is over to me like a shot. 'Amelia Lockwood! Well, look at you! It's only great to see so, so it is! Come in, come in, till I chat to you properly,' he says, steering me into his office.

'But, Bill, there're people who were ahead of me, I'm skipping the queue.'

'Ah, don't be bothering your head about that,' he says. Then he turns to the room. 'Excuse me, I'm sure none of you mind if I see Amelia first, do you? She's a television producer.'

You'd think I was a cardinal working for the Pope in Rome, the way Bill talked me up, but no one seems to object, so in I go.

'Jeez, Amelia, am I glad to see you, pet. You couldn't have called to see me at a better time. Did you see the polls in last week's *Times*? Forty-five per cent dissatisfaction with me personally, hard to believe, I know. And 07's an election year, you know! It's all down to that useless documentary they did on poor aul' Claire, stitched her up good so they did. Sure, she never came out with half the stuff they said she did, they just made her look desperate in the edit. That's the power of telly for you.'

OK, I'm thinking, *does he realize he's speaking to me like I'm his press secretary?*

'I did see it, Bill, but that's not actually why I came to see you—'

'She was done for speeding in her new sports car the other day, fifty she was doing in a forty-mile zone but the *garda* recognized her and breathalysed her. Like there was any need for that, you know? Victimization, that's what it is, pure and simple. They had a headline in the paper the next morning calling her "Lady Macbreath".'

'That's awful for your wife, Bill, but you see, the reason I—'

'Election year not far off, do you understand me, Amelia? We need to do a full one eighty on her public image. If people knew the real Claire they'd stop calling her the Claire Witch behind her back and slagging her off for shelling out cash all the time. Very hurtful, you know. She rang me bawling from Louis Vuitton the other day because someone in the shop let it slip, behind her back. Give a dog a bad name, do you see? Now, you with all your media contacts could be worth your weight in gold to us. My idea is that we adopt one of them Chernobyl kids, get great photo opportunities, maybe you could set that up for us? Come on, Amelia, you and I always worked well together. My back is to the wall here. I'll make it worth your while. The head of television is a personal friend of mine, you know. Fella by the name of Philip Burke. You just think about it. Maybe I'll do the same for you one day.'

Chapter Thirty-Four
Cometh the Hour, Cometh the Man . . .

It's a ladyshave assault course. I don't think I've gone to so much bother to get ready for anything since my debs, all of twenty years ago.

Rachel and Jamie are going to Caroline's to watch the awards, which are being broadcast live, but first, the pair of them have called over to me for a calming, relaxing glass of champagne.

Calming and relaxing for them, that is. I could do with one laced with valium.

'Wow! Goddess alert!' says Jamie as I come into the living room in my borrowed Peter O'Brien dress, hot to trot.

'Isn't it fab?' I say, twirling in front of the two of them.

'Sen-bloody-sational, sweetie.' Jamie wolf-whistles. 'Jeez, I so hope you win just so everyone will see the dress!'

'I hope I don't! You know me and my fear of public speaking. I'm very happy to sit there and applaud the winner and get drunk and not have to speechify.'

'One alcoholic shot of bubbly now, sweetie,' says Rachel, pouring me a very large glass, 'then none till after your award's been announced. I don't want you tripping up on your six-inch Dolce and Gabbanas on the way up to the podium.'

'Deal,' I say, gratefully taking a gulp. Anything to steady my nerves.

'What time's Philip collecting you at?' says Jamie.

'Should be here any minute. Look at me, I'm shaking. I'd be tetchy enough if I just had the awards to worry about, but a date with him on top of it . . .'

'Oh, listen to you, fear of success, that's your trouble,' says Jamie. 'You look like a million dollars, that's the important thing. Remember: smile, wave, kick.'

'Kick?'

'Yup. Smile at every camera pointing in your face, wave like the Queen as often as you can and kick the train of your dress back every time you're walking around, so it doesn't end up wrapped round your legs like an elastoplast.'

'As if I didn't have enough to worry about.'

'Ignore him,' says Rachel. 'The only thing he was ever nominated for was Rear of the Year in the Dragon bar. You really look wonderful, darling, the hair turned out great.'

I've spent the whole afternoon like a preening princess, slaving away under a hot hairdryer in Marshall's salon, while having my nails manicured. The stylist curled my hair from here to France, then shaped it into an elegant chignon, so for once it looks really thick and full of body.

'Thanks hon,' I say, taking another gulp of champagne and pacing up and down.

'Will you sit still? You're making me nervous.'

'I'm practising walking in the Dolce and Gabbanas, like you told me to. They should be called limo shoes; I don't think I'll make it any further than from the car to the hotel, that's it. If there's dancing, they can forget about it.'

'Hold out your arms till I check them one last time,' says Rachel.

I obediently do as I'm told.

'Good, much better. Streaky fake tan disaster narrowly avoided. Yet again, good old-fashioned body make-up saves the day.'

'That happened to me once with the St Tropez stuff,' says Jamie. 'Honestly, they write all these instructions on the bottle about how you're supposed to exfoliate and moisturize before you lash it on, but they leave out the most important one. Stay sober.'

Just then, a car horn blows loudly from below my balcony window. 'Oh Jesus, it's him,' I say, peeping out.

The horn toots again.

'Let him come up and ring the door like a normal person,' snaps Rachel. 'Where does he think he is, a drive-in?'

Another few toots later and Philip eventually realizes that he's actually going to have to leave his car and come upstairs.

Our three heads duck in unison, so he doesn't see us.

'I have to say, the bit I saw of him, he looked very cute in a dress suit,' says Jamie.

'He's *straight*,' says Rachel.

'Oh yeah, because by saying cute, I'm virtually shagging him.'

I take another gulp of champagne and he buzzes on the door.

'Show time,' says Jamie, theatrically.

'Go easy on him,' I say, panicking now. 'Remember his social skills sometimes aren't all they should be.'

'I'll get it,' says Rachel. 'You just leave him to me.'

Two minutes later, she's leading him into the living room to where I'm standing by the fireplace, trying to look all

369

relaxed and casual, yet terrified to sit down in case the dress crumples.

'Philip, how are you?' I say as he gives me a chaste peck on the cheek. 'You remember Jamie, and, well, you met my friend Rachel at the door.'

'Yeah. Hi, Jamie,' he says as Rachel eyes him up. I swear I can physically *see* her trying to decide whether she likes him or not. He's barely looking at her at all, which in itself is odd. Certainly makes him the first man in a long, long time who's been oblivious to the lethal Rachel pheromone . . .

Then there's an awkward silence.

'Would you like a drink?' I ask.

'I'm driving.'

'Oh yeah, sorry.'

Another long pause, which Philip makes no attempt to fill.

'Do you like Amelia's dress?' asks Jamie eventually.

'Ehh . . . very nice,' he says. 'My mother used to have something like that.'

'What?' says Rachel disbelievingly.

'Well, of course, she wouldn't wear it *now*. She's eighty-two.'

Rachel throws me a puzzled look, as would anyone who wasn't used to the Philip Burkeisms.

Another silence.

'Did you have any difficulty getting the tickets?' Jamie asks.

I laugh nervously. 'I doubt it, given that Philip's the head of television.'

'Only trying to make conversation,' says Jamie.

'No, you're all right,' says Philip indifferently. 'Actually I won them in *Bella* magazine.'

We all just look at him.

'That was a joke,' he adds.

'Oh, right,' we chorus, all doing our best to look amused.

Yet another silence.

Oh God, this is going to be the most excruciating night of my life. What have I let myself in for?

'I suppose we'd better get going then,' I eventually say to Philip.

'OK then, my love,' says Jamie, air-kissing me so as not to ruin the make-up. 'Just remember my golden rule, whether you win or lose: don't take the highs too high and don't take the lows too low.'

'It's the TV awards, not the shallow awards,' says Rachel, hugging me. 'Good luck, sweetie.' She squeezes my arm significantly as if to say, 'And good luck with this guy, who quite honestly is as odd as a bucket of shite.'

I know just what she means.

Jamie and Rachel wave us off, promising to lock up the apartment and to keep up constant mobile-phone contact throughout the night. I slip into the passenger seat beside Philip and we drive off in silence.

We haven't been gone two minutes before I notice something I'd rather not have. *He-whose-name-shall-forever-remain-unspoken* is outside his house, polishing his jeep. He sees us and we see him and it's pure *awful*.

'Isn't that the South African guy who gatecrashed your singles party?' asks Philip, who misses nothing.

'Emm, yeah,' I reply, trying to sound nonchalant – as if men crashing singles parties in my flat is the kind of thing that happens to me every day of the week.

'Ex-boyfriend, isn't he?'

'Yes.'

'I'd say that's quite an interesting story.'

Is he fishing for information? Or is this his Philip-Burkeish way of drawing me into conversation?

Hard to tell . . .

One thing's for sure, though. This is not a subject I want to be drawn on. Not tonight. I turn to Philip and smile brightly. 'Not so much interesting, as long.'

He glances over at me.

'That was my idea of a joke,' I trail off.

But he doesn't laugh.

Dear God, I'm thinking, *this night is going to replace the horse's head at the bottom of the bed in my nightmares . . .*

Nor do things improve when we get to the Four Seasons. Philip refuses to park in the hotel car park on the grounds that they charge ten euro to valet park, so he leaves the car way down the street outside. This, from a man who earns an annual six-figure salary. Smile and get through this with a good grace, I tell myself as we walk up to the hotel, each step nearly crippling me in the heels.

The foyer is buzzing when we do eventually get there and I'm delighted to see Dave Bruton and his wife, along with Janet, our designer, who's brought Suzy from the production office with her. We all hug and squeal at each other, exclaiming over each other's dresses/hairstyles/or in my case drastic new look.

Things are looking up. At least there's a good gang from work here, normal people that I can have a laugh with.

Well, mostly normal people.

Unfortunately Good Grief O'Keefe is here too, with a much younger-looking guy who she introduces to us all as Garth. For a few minutes, it drives me nuts trying to remember where I know him from, and then it hits me. He's lead singer in a boy band called Boyz On Fire. Then the lovely Sadie Smyth joins us, looking resplendent in a gold lamé dress and there's more hugs and air-kisses and shrieking and complimenting each other's outfits.

OK, the night mightn't be too bad after all . . .

'So what's the story with you and Philip Burke?' Janet whispers to me. 'Are you going out with him? Cos that's what I call hot gossip.'

On second thoughts . . .

Because it's a live broadcast, everything is punctual to the second, so bang on the dot of eight p.m. we're all being shepherded into our seats. The organizers have spared no expense; there's a gorgeous meal, after which we're live for the actual awards. Philip and I are at the same table as the rest of the *Celtic Tigers* gang, which is great. Well, except that he spends most of the meal talking shop with Dave Bruton, who's looking more and more bored and keeps throwing for-the-love-of-God-please-rescue-me looks across the table to his wife.

The awards are to begin at nine-thirty, so at twenty-five past, there's a stampede to the ladies, for last-minute hair and make-up retouches. The great thing about having my hair in a 'do' is that it's hardly budged since I left the hairdresser's. In fact, I have a vision in my head of me with a hammer, chisel and blowtorch just trying to get it back to normal when I get home.

'Looking good, Miss Nominee,' says Suzy, who's a bit pissed by now.

'Come eleven-thirty, when it's all over, then I'll relax,' I say. 'How are you doing?'

'Locked. Veeeeeery squiffy. That's the thing about having the awards after the dinner, just means you've been drinking for hours before we go live. Are my teeth gone black?'

'Ehh . . . no. Definitely not. You're all right.'

'Red wine does that to me. So what's the story with you and Philip Burke? Doesn't he scare you?'

'Yes and no. Yes, he scares me a bit and no, there's no story.'

'I used to work with him on the *Late Night Talk* show, oh, years ago, before he got promoted, and I swear we all used to run in fear. I once hid in a toilet to avoid a meeting with him. "Ming the Merciless" we used to call him. Do you know what he said to me tonight?' She giggles.

'What?'

'You know the way he's so abrupt? He barked at me, "What have you done to your hair? It's a completely different colour from the last time I saw you." So I said, "Yes, Philip, it's highlighted. Lots of women do it, all very normal, you know." And he said, "You show me a natural blonde and I'll show you a dirty big liar." Can you *believe* him?'

'Philip Burkeisms, I call them.'

'Whatever. He's very lucky to be with you tonight, otherwise we'd all be too terrified to talk to him.' Then she gives me a tight hug. 'Good luck, Amelia. We're all rooting for you!'

I make it back to our table just in time, as they're rolling out the opening credits, with a fanfare of drum rolls. The lights dim and it's all very exciting, like being at the Oscars or the Baftas, I imagine.

'Another two minutes and you'd have been late,' says Philip.

OK, now I'm starting to think asking him to be my date has been a horrible mistake. *Just wait till I get my hands on Mags when I see her in class next week . . .*

I smile at him and grit my teeth. *I will get through this night. Attitude is everything and I have a very positive attitude – once I don't have to go up to the podium and make a speech, that is . . . At least I gave Philip a whirl, so that's something, isn't it?*

Our host for the evening is a well-known stand-up comedian called Jay Jones who comes bouncing out and immediately gets the party rolling with a hilarious opening set, basically slagging the knickers off everyone. He even does an impression of Good Grief O'Keefe trying to cry and I have to stuff a napkin in my mouth, I'm laughing so hard, while she just sits at the table looking stonily ahead. My mobile phone is on silent, but it lights up with a text message.

Jamie: U R ON TV! TAKE THAT F**KING NAPKIN OUT OF YOUR GOB RIGHT NOW!!!

Oh shit. I look around me for the camera. There it is, right behind me, a hand-held one, circulating the tables. I shove the napkin back on the table and clasp my hands in front of me, trying my best to look demure.

The first few awards are all in the technical categories: best lighting, sound, editing and effects. This basically means that everyone not directly involved can go up to the bar to get as many rounds in before the major gongs are handed out.

'Would somebody else mind getting this round?' says Philip. 'I don't want to break a fifty.'

Yet another Philip Burkeism in a whole sea of them; at one point he called Dave's wife Martini. Her actual name is Olive.

Then the best actress award, which goes to an actress who played a leading role in a hospital drama series. She's a popular winner and it's the first standing ovation of the night.

'This time next year, it'll be you,' I hiss over to Sadie and she beams and blushes.

Then best actor, which goes to a well-known theatre actor for a film where he played a gangland crime lord. I haven't seen the movie but from the clip they showed of it, the award was well deserved; he was so impressive: terrifying, chilling, scary.

Jamie texts: OH PLEASE, THEY SHOWED THE ONLY DECENT BIT IN THAT WHOLE MOVIE AND NOW YOU ALL THINK THAT GUY'S FAB. REST OF THE FILM WAS TOTAL CRAP.

Then a text from Rachel: NEXT AWARD IS BEST PRODUCER. PUT LIP GLOSS ON NOW BUT CHECK NO CAMERA POINTING AT YOU FIRST.

Then one from Caroline. I CAN'T LOOK!!! AM HIDING BEHIND SOFA!!! GOOD LUCK DARLING. AM PRAYING FOR YOU!!!

'She and her friends can't go to the loo without texting each other twenty times,' I hear Philip saying to Dave.

I take a deep, soothing breath.

There's a hand-held camera pointing right at me, which I do my best to ignore, looking straight ahead to where Jay Jones is about to read out the nominees' names. It's as if everything is happening in slow motion.

'Best producer time,' says Jay, from the podium. 'Don't worry; all the nominees here will have plenty of time to buttonhole them and harass them for work later. We're even showing close-ups so you all know what they look like.'

Big roll of laughter.

I look up at a TV monitor behind the stage and see myself, in glorious Technicolor. I smile and concentrate on breathing.

It'll all be over in a few minutes.

'The first nominee for best producer is Kevin O'Dea for *Expensive Ireland*.'

Thunderous applause. I know Kevin well – we trained as producers together – and I almost blister my hands I'm clapping so hard for him.

I'd so love it if he won. Then I wouldn't have to talk in public.

A clip of his show follows, which was an exposé on how consumers are being ripped off in overpriced Ireland and was a huge ratings winner.

'Hang on to your seats, folks, our next nominee is none other than Frederick Jordan-Murphy for *Undersea Odyssey*.'

Massive applause. Frederick Jordan-Murphy is probably the best known of all the nominees, as he scripts, presents and produces the series, which is a widely popular nature documentary with the most stunning camerawork you've ever seen. Sharks mating in shallow water, that type of thing.

'Fifty euro says he wins,' says Philip.

'Our third nominee is Patrick Griffin for *The Ward*,' says Jay to even louder applause. 'Just about the only medical drama that can make *ER* look like a bunch of under-fives dressing up as doctors and nurses.'

I look around to where Patrick Griffin is sitting at the table directly behind us, looking like he's had one or two brandies too many. He's a big, florid man, sitting well back in his chair with his arms draped around two very pretty blonde girls, who look like they're having great crack altogether. And then I see.

It's one of those weird things, almost like an out-of-body experience, where you find yourself thinking: *Is this really happening? Now? Tonight? To Me?*

Striding through the ballroom door, looking like he owns the place, comes *He-whose-name-shall-forever-remain-unspoken.*

Oh dear God, please let me be hallucinating . . .

No, it's him. Being pursued at a discreet distance by a hotel security guard.

I want to either (*a*) pass out, (*b*) throw up or (*c*) break into a run and, as Rachel would say, GTFOOH as fast as I can in six-inch heels. But I can't, because my award is about to be announced.

He spots me.

Before I even have time to wipe the beads of worry sweat from my face, he's over to where I'm sitting.

It's as if it's all unfolding in sickening slow motion. First of all I hear Jay Jones calling out my name. I'm dimly aware that there's deafening applause and a lot of foot-stomping from everyone at our table. Next thing, *He-whose-name-shall-forever-remain-unspoken* is down on bended knee right beside where I'm sitting.

They cut to a clip of the show. Thank God, at least I'm not on live TV.

For the moment.

'Amelia, will you look at me?' he's saying although the whooshing body-rush sensation I'm feeling is blocking a lot of it out.

Everyone at the table is staring at me and I just want to die.

'What's *he* doing here?' asks Philip.

Someone must ask him who it is that's kneeling on the floor like an eejit beside me, because then I clearly hear Philip saying, 'Her ex-boyfriend.'

It's like Chinese whispers all round the table; all I can pick up is: 'Ex-boyfriend'; 'What does he want?'; 'Will someone get rid of him before the winner's name is called out?'

Then Jay makes a huge show of opening the envelope.

By now, *He-whose-name-shall-forever-remain-unspoken* has grabbed my hand and won't let go.

'Get off!' I manage to hiss at him, but he just grips on tighter.

'And the winner is . . . oh, I'm so happy!'

'Amelia, I want to marry you.'

'What did you say?' I turn to him, mortified at the scene we're causing.

'I said I want to marry you.'

I look at him, stunned. So does everyone else within hearing distance and then . . .

'Best producer is . . . Amelia Lockwood for *Celtic Tigers!*'

A roar of applause and now I think I'll faint.

There's a camera practically up my nostril and everyone is

staring at me and my phone keeps beep-beeping as a load of texts from the Lovely Girls come through and all the time *He-whose-name-shall-forever-remain-unspoken* won't release this iron grip he has on my hand.

I stand up and try to shake him off, but I can't.

I'm in deep, total shock but somewhere at the back of my mind, I know I now have to get up to the podium where Jay is standing with a big trophy, looking at me.

They're all looking at me.

The applause gradually dies down.

The silence will haunt me to my grave.

'I asked you to marry me,' repeats *He-whose-name-shall-forever-remain-unspoken*, slowly, calmly. You'd swear he had this planned. 'I made the biggest mistake in my life when I let you go and now I'm asking. On bended knee. In front of all these people. Will you marry me?'

It's a nightmare. On the huge screen behind the stage all I can see is a giant close-up of my face, scarlet with sheer mortification and what's worse is that *He-whose-name-shall-forever-remain-unspoken* seems to be getting a kick out of the fact that there are probably a million people watching this at home.

'Come on, Amelia. Don't all women love big, romantic gestures?'

I don't know how, but somehow I manage to break free from him and stumble up to the stage. Jay reaches down for my hand and helps me up the steps.

I'm the only winner in history who has to walk up to collect their award in absolute, stony silence.

Jay hands me the trophy. 'Quite a side show you had going there,' he quips. 'I'm the draw here, you know. There'll be no upstaging.'

There's a tiny ripple of laughter and I realize that I'll have to speak. There's no way out of it. *Make a joke,* says my inner voice. *Just do it quick. Anything, absolutely anything's better than the silence.* 'Thank . . . thank you all so much,' I say into the microphone, in a tiny voice that you'd swear was coming from a continent away.

Three hundred faces are looking up at me. *He-whose-name-shall-forever-remain-unspoken* is still at my table, just standing there.

'Well,' I say, 'as you'll all have noticed, I was very unprepared for this.'

A ripple of laughter.

'If you saw that as a plot on *Celtic Tigers* you probably wouldn't believe it.'

More laughs.

Then someone at the very front table shouts up at me, 'So will you marry him? Poor eejit is standing there waiting on an answer.'

Murmurings and mutterings, which in my shocked state I can somehow still take in.

'No, I won't,' I hear myself saying.

There's an audible gasp.

'I'm sorry, but if you all knew the full story, you wouldn't either.'

More shocked ripples and murmurings.

'Are you with this guy? Is that what the problem is?' says *He-whose-name-shall-forever-remain-unspoken,* pointing at Philip.

'No,' Philip and I both say in unison.

Then, for even further public humiliation on live TV, Philip adds, 'I'm not her boyfriend.'

'Ahhh, go on, marry him,' someone shouts from the back row. 'That's very romantic what he's doing. You can't dump the poor guy in public like this.'

A sort of chant starts up. 'SAY YES! SAY YES! SAY YES!'

'You don't understand, none of you understands,' I almost wail. 'He dumped *me* in the worst way possible and if it weren't for my best friends I'd never have got through it.'

'Why did he do that?' asks Jay, who's standing right beside me.

'You know yourself, wouldn't make the commitment. He said it wasn't me, he didn't want to be with anyone,' I answer, almost forgetting that there's a microphone in front of me. 'And by the way, if there's anyone watching who's with a guy who says he doesn't want to make a commitment, let me translate. It just means he doesn't want to make a commitment to *you*.'

A few tsks–tsks from the audience.

'Then, only a few months later he got engaged to a twenty-three-year-old.'

There's a tiny bit of booing from the back of the ballroom now.

'Then they moved in right across the road from me.'

Now the booing's growing and beginning to get scary.

'Then his fiancée got second thoughts about him and he tried to come back to me. He thought it was just going to be that easy.'

'Don't do it, Amelia!' I can hear a woman's voice shout. 'Say no!'

'I am saying no. No, all the way. He doesn't love me. If he did, he'd have asked me to marry him when we were together. He'd plenty of opportunity. We were together years. He just wants someone to pick up the pieces for him. No. Not me. It's not good enough.'

Tears are streaming down my face now and the audience start cheering. Now there's a new chant. 'SAY NO! SAY NO! SAY NO!'

My voice sounds stronger now. I can see *He-whose-name-shall-forever-remain-unspoken* being forcefully escorted towards the exit by security, and I smile, relieved.

Mortified, but relieved.

They're still all looking at me and I decide to go out on a gag. 'Ladies and gentlemen,' I say firmly. 'I'm so sorry you had to witness that. I'm used to humiliation, but not quite on this scale or in front of so large a crowd. Believe you me, I will be recounting the last few minutes of my life on therapists' couches for years to come. I will now use this award to bash my ex over the head with for putting all of you through the last few, excruciating minutes. Thank you all again!'

The applause almost raises the roof and Jay takes the microphone from me as I make my way back to the table. 'Well, thanks for the cabaret, Amelia,' he says, a bit stunned. 'I think we'd better go to a commercial break after that!'

And we're out.

They're still cheering and clapping as I get back to the table. With all the dignity I can muster, I pick up my handbag and make to go.

Suzy hugs me, squealing. 'I can't believe what I just saw with my own two eyes!' she screeches. 'Way to go!'

'That was some spectacle,' says Dave. 'This is the only gong show I've ever been to where the lifetime-achievement award is going to be an anticlimax.'

'You'll all forgive me if I call it a night?' I say, trembling. 'I . . . I just . . . I need to be where other people are not.'

There's a chorus of: 'No! Not at all! Congratulations!' from the gang and it's just brilliant. I so badly need to be out of there.

Shit. One thing I forgot. Philip.

I turn to him, aware that everyone's still looking at me.

'I really am very sorry,' I say.

'Not your fault your ex is a headcase.'

'I meant about leaving now. You understand I can't stay.'

'Shortest date in history, then.'

I can't even say: Yes, I'm sorry, let's do it again sometime. Mainly because I don't want to. 'Goodnight, Philip,' I say. 'I'll see you in work.'

I smile and am about to go when I hear him say, 'And to think we gave women the vote.' It's a Philip Burkeism, but they're not my problem any more.

I get a huge round of applause as I leave the ballroom and I wave as gracefully as I can. It's only when I get outside that, with a trembling hand, I think to check my mobile phone.

Fifteen text messages.

Jamie: SO PROUD OF U MY DARLING! U R LIKE THE WINNER WITH FEET OF CLAY!!

Rachel: IT WAS EMPOWERING WATCHING U GIVE THAT BASTARD WHAT FOR ON LIVE TV! SO PROUD TO BE YR FRIEND! WHO DO U THINK WILL PLAY U WHEN THE EVENTS OF TONITE R MADE INTO A MOVIE?

I've made it outside the Four Seasons and the doorman, seeing the state I'm in, hails me a taxi. 'Are you all right, madam?' he asks, concerned. 'Can I get you anything? Some water, maybe?'

'I'm . . . I'll be fine, thanks,' I half whisper, taking in deep, soothing gulps of air.

He backs off, tactfully realizing that I need to be alone, and my mind races. *Did that really happen? Did* He-whose-name-shall-forever-remain-unspoken *really propose to me, live to the nation? And I turned him down . . .*

And you know what the really funny thing is?

Now that the initial shock is wearing off and I'm starting to think straight, I'm absolutely rock-solid one hundred per cent certain that I did the right thing. It would have been so simple just to say yes and forget the past and hope he'd have a personality change and that I'd have some chance of a happy married life with him. I could have gone back into Ira's class next week and gloated. I could have finally got a foot into the Vera Wang. But it wouldn't have made me happy. The easy thing would have been to say yes; the hard thing is to hold out and believe that there has to be something better out there for me.

Then a text from Caroline: SWEETHEART U DID THE RIGHT THING. ONLY THING U COULD HAVE DONE. SUGGEST U LEAVE THERE RIGHT NOW AND COME OVER HERE. WE R WAITING FOR U WITH A BOTTLE OF CHAMPAGNE TO TOAST OUR WINNER. A WINNER IN EVERY WAY.

My eyes start to well.

Bless them. Where would I be without my friends?

The taxi pulls up and I hop in, give the driver Caroline's address and ask if he can get me there as fast as he can.

OK, I think as the car pulls off.

So . . . I've just turned down a proposal of marriage.

So . . . I walked out on a date with a guy I wasn't really interested in and who sure as hell didn't seem to have the slightest interest in me.

So . . . I spent the last few weeks chasing ex-boyfriends in the hope it would help me find a husband, all with zero-per-cent success.

So . . . I've been chasing rainbows.

There's nothing to be ashamed of. There's nothing wrong with me. I just haven't met the right one.

Not yet.

But you know something? Watch this space . . .

THE END . . . ?